# NEBULA AWARDS 26

# NEBULA AWARDS 26

## SFWA's Choices for the Best Science Fiction and Fantasy of the Year

EDITED BY JAMES MORROW

Harcourt Brace Jovanovich, Publishers
*New York   San Diego   London*

Requests for permission to make copies of any part of the work should be mailed to:
Permissions Department,
Harcourt Brace Jovanovich, Publishers, 8th Floor,
Orlando, Florida 32887.

The Library of Congress has cataloged this serial as follows:

The Nebula awards.—No. 18—New York [N.Y.]: Arbor House, c1983–
v.; 22 cm.
Annual.
Published: San Diego, Calif.: Harcourt Brace Jovanovich, 1984–
Published for: Science Fiction Writers of America, 1983–
Continues: Nebula award stories (New York, N.Y.: 1982)
ISSN 0741-5567 = The Nebula awards
1. Science fiction, American—Periodicals. I. Science Fiction Writers of America.
PS648.S3N38    83-647399
813'.0876'08—dc19
AACR 2 MARC-S
Library of Congress    [8709r84]rev
ISBN 0-15-164934-0
ISBN 0-15-665472-5 (Harvest/HBJ: pbk)

Designed by G. B. D. Smith
Printed in the United States of America

First edition
A B C D E

Permissions acknowledgments appear on page 333,
which constitutes a continuation of the copyright page.

In Memory of
Donald A. Wollheim
1914–1990

# Contents

. . .

vii

# Introduction

**· · ·**

*James Morrow*

Language is the blood of the mind. As George Orwell never tired of reminding us, vocabulary and grammar determine not only the shape of a particular thought, but also whether that thought exists in the first place. There is no freedom without "freedom," no truth without a word for it.

In recent years, the Science Fiction Writers of America has invested much energy wondering what to call its art. Members seek to distinguish complex and mature work from the juvenilia that clogs the marketplace. The problem is genuine. Enter the average bookstore, and you'll instantly find yourself among ready-to-run dungeons and off-the-shelf dragons. Glance at the ads in *Locus*: stupefying swords, stultifying sorcerers, soulless space operas. Thomas Disch once sarcastically remarked that science fiction "can best be understood as a branch of children's literature," and in my darker moods it occurs to me that the term "children's literature" is actually inadequate to the indictment, for the great children's books commonly depict pain, joy, death, loneliness, and a kind of encoded eroticism with an honesty that leaves the average SF trilogy in the shadows. Shall we stop mincing words and say "best be understood as a branch of second-rate children's literature"?

One solution—a strategy on which I believe Orwell would have smiled—consists in arguing that the stuff that teleports Disch, myself, and others to the Slough of Despond is not science fiction at all. It is sci-fi. Genuine science fiction partakes of a different sensibility entirely, the sort of witty and subversive vision found in the works of such writers as H. G. Wells, Philip K. Dick, Stanislaw Lem, Kurt Vonnegut, Italo Calvino, Ursula K. Le Guin, Harlan Ellison, and Disch himself, and in the pages of such periodicals as *Isaac Asimov's Science Fiction Magazine* and *The Magazine of Fantasy and Science Fiction*.

Surely this sensibility permeates the following four lists: the novels, novellas, novelettes, and short stories nominated by SFWA for the 1990 Nebula Awards. From the titles alone—headings like the deliberately oxymoronic "Mr. Boy," the deliciously wry "Love and Sex Among the Invertebrates," the insidiously whimsical "The Coon Rolled Down and Ruptured His Larinks, A Squeezed Novel by Mr. Skunk"—we can infer the fact that, whatever their quirks and foibles, however cavalier their attitudes toward quotidian reality, these works deal forthrightly with what William Styron calls "the appalling enigma of human existence." They are not sci-fi. They are science fiction.

### For Novel

\* *Tehanu: The Last Book of Earthsea* by Ursula K. Le Guin (Atheneum)
*Mary Reilly* by Valerie Martin (Doubleday)
*Only Begotten Daughter* by James Morrow (William Morrow)
*The Fall of Hyperion* by Dan Simmons (Doubleday Foundation)
*Redshift Rendezvous* by John Stith (Ace)
*White Jenna* by Jane Yolen (Tor)

### For Novella

\* "Weatherman" by Lois McMaster Bujold (*Analog*, February 1990)
"Fool to Believe" by Pat Cadigan (*Isaac Asimov's Science Fiction Magazine*, February 1990)
\* "The Hemingway Hoax" by Joe Haldeman (*Isaac Asimov's Science Fiction Magazine*, April 1990)
"Mr. Boy" by James Patrick Kelly (*Isaac Asimov's Science Fiction Magazine*, June 1990)
"Bones" by Pat Murphy (*Isaac Asimov's Science Fiction Magazine*, May 1990)

### For Novelette

"The Coon Rolled Down and Ruptured His Larinks, A Squeezed Novel by Mr. Skunk" by Dafydd ab Hugh (*Isaac Asimov's Science Fiction Magazine*, August 1990)
\* "Tower of Babylon" by Ted Chiang (*Omni*, November 1990)

\* Indicates winner

"The Shobies' Story" by Ursula K. Le Guin (*Universe 1*, Doubleday Foundation)

"1/72nd Scale" by Ian MacLeod (*Weird Tales*, Fall 1990)

"The Manamouki" by Mike Resnick (*Isaac Asimov's Science Fiction Magazine*, July 1990)

"A Time for Every Purpose" by Kristine Kathryn Rusch (*Amazing Stories*, May 1990)

"Loose Cannon" by Susan Shwartz (*What Might Have Been, Volume 2*, Bantam Spectra)

"Over the Long Haul" by Martha Soukup (*Amazing Stories*, March 1990)

## For Short Story

* "Bears Discover Fire" by Terry Bisson (*Isaac Asimov's Science Fiction Magazine*, July 1990)

"The Power and the Passion" by Pat Cadigan (*Omni*, March 1990)

"Lieserl" by Karen Joy Fowler (*Isaac Asimov's Science Fiction Magazine*, July 1990)

"Love and Sex Among the Invertebrates" by Pat Murphy (*Alien Sex*, Dutton)

"Before I Wake" by Kim Stanley Robinson (*Isaac Asimov's Science Fiction Magazine*, April 1990)

"Story Child" by Kristine Kathryn Rusch (*Aboriginal Science Fiction*, September/October 1990)

For some writers and critics, the term "science fiction" cannot, in fact, be redeemed. In this view, the cream of a final Nebula ballot is really "slipstream fiction" or "magic realism" or "fabulation" or something.

While I can understand the impulse behind this maneuver, I'm not yet ready to cede the field to the enemy. I'm not yet ready to hand "science fiction" over to the hacks and dragon biographers. Just as the great film director John Ford never hesitated to call himself a maker of "westerns," I hope that SFWA's most talented practitioners will continue to profess that they write "science fiction." For to deny the SF label, I feel, is to endorse the bigotry with which the Academy greets any text so designated—the sort of gentlemen's agreement whereby *The New Yorker* will not cover science fiction novels *qua* science fiction or whereby creative writing professors routinely forbid students to employ SF trappings. Quality, I feel, is where we find it, not where the *literati* tell us to look. If, after a quarter of a century of Nebula anthologies, the Academy remains incurious about science fiction, then that is the Academy's loss.

As Kathryn Cramer points out in the essay that follows, the Nebula system is eminently democratic. Any active SFWA member can participate, mailing in the recommendations and ballots that determine contenders, finalists, and winners. Under the present rules, SFWA impanels both a novel jury and a short fiction jury to oversee the voting process and, in cases where a worthy title was neglected by the membership at large, to supplement the five nominees with a sixth choice. Thus, the appearance of extra finalists in any category bespeaks two distinct processes: jury discretion and ties.

The centerpiece of *Nebula Awards 26* is Joe Haldeman's winning novella, "The Hemingway Hoax," surely one of the best riffs on the physicists' "many-worlds hypothesis" ever to surface in this particular universe. Among its immediate rivals, Pat Murphy's "Bones" offered a gripping account of the real-life Irish giant Charlie Brynne and the equally real-life surgeon who wanted his skeleton, Pat Cadigan's "Fool to Believe" took us on a harrowing odyssey in quest of an actor's stolen mind, and Lois McMaster Bujold's "Weatherman" made us feel the plight of a physically handicapped cadet assigned to a brutal Arctic outpost. My personal favorite among the novella runners-up was James Patrick Kelly's "Mr. Boy," a coming-of-age tale in which genetic engineering, virtual reality, and a half dozen other SF conceits fused into a drama at once poignant and surreal. (Interested readers can locate "Mr. Boy" in Gardner Dozois's estimable *The Year's Best Science Fiction: Eighth Annual Collection*.)

SFWA's choice for best novel, Ursula K. Le Guin's *Tehanu: The Last Book of Earthsea*—the capstone to one of SF's most endearing series—appears in *Nebula Awards 26* by proxy: the author's nominated novelette, "The Shobies' Story," leads off this volume. *Tehanu* claimed its prize from an extraordinarily diverse group of contenders. Dan Simmons's *The Fall of Hyperion* picked up where the previous year's *Hyperion* left off, bringing this literate epic to a satisfying conclusion. John E. Stith's *Redshift Rendezvous*, which deftly explored the implications of relativity theory, proved a paragon of the "hard SF" approach. Jane Yolen's mosaic novel *White Jenna* comprised, in the author's words, "stories, ballads, legends, historical conundrums, adages, and an overarching narrative told by a storyteller who is probably as untrustworthy as the historian, ballad-maker, legend-speaker, and the rest." The canny conceit behind Valerie Martin's *Mary Reilly*—what if Dr. Jekyll's maidservant kept a journal?—drew enthusiastic notices both within the science fiction community and without. My own candidate, *Only Begotten Daughter*, was similarly postmodern: a sequel to the New Testament set in Atlantic City.

Rounding out the roster of winners are Ted Chiang's "Tower of Babylon" and Terry Bisson's "Bears Discover Fire." When it came to selecting additional fiction for *Nebula Awards 26*, I included as many nominated novelettes and short stories as geometry and finances allowed. To a degree, then, this anthology permits its readers to second-guess SFWA. Perusing these remarkable works, you can decide for yourself just how formidable was the competition faced by Chiang's breathtaking allegory and Bisson's affecting fable. I assume there will be discussion. Quite possibly there will be dissent. But that's what makes alternate-universe, virtual-reality, recombinant-DNA horse racing.

Before signing off, I want to acknowledge the people who made my job easier. My predecessors at this post, George Zebrowski and Michael Bishop, were always willing to share their expertise. John Radziewicz of Harcourt Brace Jovanovich edited my editing with intelligence and panache. Jean Morrow, to whom I have the good fortune to be married, advised me on the introductions, handled the correspondence, and pasted up the tearsheets, thereby inhaling more glue than is breathed by the hero of "1/72nd Scale."

—*State College, Pennsylvania*
May 25, 1991

# NEBULA AWARDS
## 26

# "Democrazy," the Marketplace, and the American Way: Remarks on the Year 1990 in Science Fiction

### • • •

*Kathryn Cramer*

The pilgrim in the science fiction world is quickly confronted by a curious fact. Most of the key critical voices—Norman Spinrad, Ian Watson, Ursula K. Le Guin, Orson Scott Card, Bruce Sterling— are themselves prominent producers of fiction. The genre boasts a dozen John Updike equivalents, but virtually no Leslie Fiedlers, Frank Kermodes, or Brendan Gills. (John Clute is the exception that comes immediately to mind.) This is not to suggest that the perceptions of the critic/practitioner are necessarily corrupt, merely that they are inevitably constrained. What the field needs, I think, is a different sort of a critical sensibility, sympathetic but also detached, enthusiastic but unencumbered.

As the features editor of *The New York Review of Science Fiction*, Kathryn Cramer has for the last three years been providing the genre with some fresh perspectives on itself. In Cramer's capable hands, SF criticism becomes far more surprising, cosmopolitan, and—to use an unpopular word in a positive context— theoretical than what we've been conditioned to expect.

Beyond her controversial *NYRSF* pieces, Cramer is known in the field primarily as an editor. In 1988, the World Fantasy Award for best anthology went to *The Architecture of Fear*, the treasury of original haunted-house stories she commissioned in collaboration with Peter D. Pautz. *Walls of Fear*, a follow-up volume assembled in 1990 by Cramer alone, was also a World Fantasy nominee. With David Hartwell she has edited *Christmas Ghosts*, *Spirits of Christmas*, and a forthcoming omnibus of "hard science fiction." Proficient in German, she translated Johannes Bobrowski's "The Mouse Festival" for Hartwell's 1989 anthology *Masterpieces of Fantasy and Wonder*.

Cramer's scholarly papers include "Logic, Fantasy, and Criticism," presented at the Tenth Annual International Conference on the Fantastic, and "Our Pious Hope: Marketing, Countermarketing, and Transcendence," presented at the 1990 Eaton Conference. Readers wishing to track down the specific novels and stories discussed in the piece that follows should consult the appendix called "Selected Titles from the 1990 Preliminary Nebula Ballot."

Cramer dedicates this essay to the memories of Ioan Couliano and Sharon Baker, both of whom died suddenly during its preparation.

My most memorable images of 1990 all come from the late summer. We were stuck in a traffic jam, inching past hop fields and little *Dorfs* up the Autobahn from Munich to Berlin, toward what was still the East German border. All around us were "Trabis," little green-and-beige cars that sounded like motorcycles, jammed to their roofs with Western consumer goods, plastered with DDR stickers, and towing trailers loaded with wrecked VWs and broken mopeds. Over the radio, the Süddeutsche Rundfunk played "I'd Like to Teach the World to Sing."

Crossing the border, we all slowed down, as if no one really believed the cubicles of the East German customs inspectors were empty. But they were. The only official presence consisted in a convoy of bulldozers scooping up concrete rubble. The Cold War was over.

The 1990 World Science Fiction Convention in Holland was the first Worldcon that Eastern Bloc fans and professionals attended in force. Many were experiencing their first trip to an industrialized democracy, and their excitement was contagious. One Rumanian reader, dropping by a panel in honor of Joe Haldeman, informed Haldeman that he was his favorite author; the Rumanian revealed that Haldeman's books had been translated underground and were circulating in the form of typed manuscripts, passed hand to hand. A Soviet science fiction editor told of publishing an anthology, *The Green Book of Science Fiction*, filled with stories containing the word "green" in the title. It seems that the publisher had unearthed a large stock of green paper—Soviet publishing has been continually plagued by paper shortages—and so the editors fashioned an anthology to match. The creators of the Polish SF magazine *Nowa Fantastyka* explained that Party membership was no longer a requirement for serving on the editorial board; the whole enterprise had just gone private. Toward the end of the convention, there were many invitations. If you're ever in Leningrad . . . in Warsaw . . . in Leipzig . . .

Beyond the new friends we made, the Hague Worldcon served to remind those of us in American publishing that science fiction is, and always has been, a world literature. And yet, to my knowledge, no work in translation has ever been nominated for a Nebula Award, though the rules specify nothing about a candidate's country of origin. The Nebula process has traditionally celebrated an exclusively domestic notion of what the genre is all about, bypassing the Continent and treating England mainly as a particularly promising colony. When SFWA members say, for example, that British SF exhibits an unnatural fascination with disaster, the implicit comparison is always with the cheerful and unaffected American norm. David Brin, who during his stay in the UK is said to have impressed the natives with his Americanness, embodies this attitude in the preface to his 1990 novel, *Earth*:

> As writers go, I suppose I'm known as a bit of an optimist, so it seems only natural that this novel projects a future where there's a little more wisdom than folly . . . maybe a bit more hope than despair.
>
> In fact, it's about the most encouraging tomorrow I can imagine right now.
>
> What a sobering thought.

Like the hero of James Patrick Kelly's fine Nebula-nominated novella, "Mr. Boy," in which for those who can afford it all manner of physical and genetic alterations are available, American science fiction is a boy who's always twelve no matter how old he gets.

And yet, despite its native optimism, our enterprise has grown somewhat gloomy of late. Brin isn't the only author to entertain a "sobering thought" or two. Most American SF writers don't expect ever to go to the moon, nor do they imagine their grandchildren living there, nor do they necessarily feel it's a good idea for human beings to move into space. These days, travel to other planets is seen as a retreat from the crises unfolding here on Earth. And while nobody hesitates to concoct even the most implausible nightmare scenarios, the average writer would be embarrassed to extrapolate anything resembling a healthy and functional future. As one of Kim Stanley Robinson's characters observes in *Pacific Edge*, "utopia is increasingly difficult to imagine." American SF, it seems, is losing its callowness, a change I've noticed not only in the novels and stories, but also in the current mood of SFWA itself: an introspective and essentially downbeat assessment of what popular taste and marketplace democracy portend for the professional writer.

■ ■ ■

Although our Bicentennial seems to have occurred eons ago, the founding of the American republic is still only about two hundred years old. On May 29, 1790, Rhode Island, the last of the thirteen states, ratified the Constitution. Once political independence was won, Americans also sought intellectual independence. Thus, Article I, Section 8 of the Constitution empowers Congress to "promote the Progress of Science and useful Arts, by securing for limited Times to Authors and Inventors the exclusive Right to their respective Writings and Discoveries."

This is a passage to gladden the heart of any SFWA member. Indeed, as practitioners of an art that aims to "promote the Progress of Science," might not science fiction writers be the very folks the Founding Fathers had in mind when they wrote Article I, Section 8? So it is perhaps no coincidence that in 1990, on the two-hundredth anniversary of the final ratification of the Constitution, SFWA, with considerable help from the enthusiastic young staff at Pulphouse Publishing, put out a reincarnation of the legendary *Science Fiction Writers of America Handbook: The Professional Writer's Guide to Writing Professionally*.

As both John Clute and Brian Stableford have pointed out, the new *SFWA Handbook* vibrates with anxiety. "The writer who only does the things he does well is dead," Frederik Pohl explains in his essay. And after all the unindexed chitchat about contracts, copyrights, payment, editing, promotion, reselling your work, agents, packagers, "how to make a short story long," and "writing a series," the reader may very well envy the dead. Is this really what it means to be a "professional writer writing professionally"? Has the situation always been this depressing?

The name of Charles Brockden Brown looms large in that post-revolutionary era from which we glean so many of our heroes. Brockden Brown is often credited with being America's first professional fiction writer, although this is not, strictly speaking, true. (The first American novelist to really support himself by writing was James Fenimore Cooper, who reaped his profits by having his books privately printed and selling them himself.) But despite its falsity, the legend of Charles Brockden Brown, First Professional Writer in America, cultural patriot and patron saint of commercial authors, has special relevance for SFWA members.

As it turns out, Brockden Brown hated the idea of writing for a living, and he would have been appalled by his posthumous reputation as the father of professionalism. But he did see the problem clearly. Without sponsorship, Brown realized, or sinecures from the Academy, a writer must survive from the sales of his books, a prospect even more terrifying in postrevolutionary America than it is today. In an 1803 essay entitled "Authorship," published in *The Literary Magazine and American Register*, he meditated upon the distinction between the "poor author," who writes to support himself (a trade that is "the refuge of idleness and poverty," definitely to be avoided if one can get work as, say, a carpenter or a blacksmith), and the "author," a literary aristocrat who writes for the sheer pleasure of it. Brown explains, "[As] there is nothing I should more fully deprecate than to be enrolled in the former class, so there is nothing to which I more ardently aspire, than to be numbered among the latter. To write, because the employment is delightful, or because I have a passion for fame or usefulness, is the summit of terrestrial joys."

Thus, when we experience discomfort at the *SFWA Handbook*'s grim enumeration of the professional author's burdens—and at the absence of any comment on the joys (terrestrial or otherwise) of writing—we feel echoes of Brown's own quandary. How, he wondered, could one become an "author" rather than a "poor author" in a country lacking the requisite infrastructure? While today we have the Guggenheim Foundation, the National Endowment for the Arts, state arts councils, and faculty positions in university creative writing departments, notably lacking from the *SFWA Handbook* is a chapter on how to get a grant or any advice on securing a tenure-track teaching job. The science fiction writer, clearly, is the descendant of Brown's "poor author," and must therefore coax pennies from the pockets of the Philistines.

And whom did the Philistines want in 1990? As the voices of the masses, the Waldenbooks and B. Dalton best-seller lists tell us they wanted Piers Anthony, David Eddings, Margaret Weis & Tracy Hickman, Robert Jordan, Anne McCaffrey, and Terry Brooks. *What* did they want? Magic Kingdoms, Forgotten Realms, almost anything with "dragon" in the title, books based on games, and sequels that authors too weary to write themselves were able to provide with a little help from their friends, the talented younger authors coming through for their elders much as little Therru pulls Ged and Tenar's bacon out of the fire at the end of Ursula K. Le Guin's Nebula-winning novel, *Tehanu: The Last Book of Earthsea*. Plus, of course, *Star Trek*. Kirk and Spock continued to enjoy huge sales, and even Thomas Pynchon, in his 1990 novel *Vineland*, threw in a touch of *Trek* for added pop-culture sixties flavor: ". . . the baby with both eyes open now looking right at him with a vast, an unmistakable recognition . . . This look . . . would be there for Zoyd more than once in the years to come, to help him through those times when the Klingons are closing, and the helm won't answer, and the warp engine's out of control."

And when we stand way back and look at the *Publishers Weekly* lists, in 1990 the masses wanted Stephen King, Stephen King again, V. C. Andrews (even though she's one of those fortunate dead authors I mentioned earlier), and Jean Auel. This pantheon won the award that editor Judy-Lynn del Rey once referred to as the only one that matters: the ringing of the cash register. Meanwhile, the rest of SFWA tormented itself with the question posed by the hero of Michael Blumlein's fascinating yet repellent story "Bestseller": "What the hell do I have to do to write a book that sells?"

Blumlein's hero barters away his own body parts to make ends meet. In Rudy Rucker's delightful novel *The Hollow Earth*, an alternate-universe Edgar Allan Poe whose manuscripts keep getting rejected comes up with a plan even bolder than self-cannibalization: "I was dazzled by the sheer effrontery of Eddie's scheme! Counterfeiting the money of a nonexistent bank!" Joe Haldeman's Nebula-winning novella, "The Hemingway Hoax," turns on an equally audacious plan: forging a new work by one of the icons of American letters. In the SF world, it seems, the "poor author" will try almost anything.

At one point, Haldeman's hero, a college English professor and minor writer, jokes, "If you recognized my name from the *Iowa Review* you'd be the first person who ever had." But while most authors crave more attention, the successful ones sometimes wish it were lonelier at the top. In an essay entitled "Xenogenesis" (*Asimov's*, August 1990), Harlan Ellison chronicles the atrocities perpetrated by readers against established writers. While I don't doubt that the bulk of the horror stories he recounts are true—rude and possibly deranged people selecting authors as the targets for practical jokes, unsolicited familiarities, and worse—it's interesting that Ellison stops well short of Brockden Brown's elitism. He never implies that authors should avoid the public, secluding themselves in the palaces of the literary aristocracy. Significantly, Ellison addresses his long complaint not to his fellow writers but to the very fandom from whence the abuses spring: "And those of you in the sane, courteous ninety-five percent . . . well, perhaps this concentrated jolt of nastiness will alert you to the other five percent who roam and foam among us."

■ ■ ■

Perhaps the most sordid event to darken the literary scene in 1990 was Simon and Schuster's cancellation of Bret Easton Ellis's novel *American Psycho*. The National Organization for Women campaigned against the book, claiming it was, in effect, an instruction manual for torturing and murdering women. (Some of those who concurred sent Ellis pictures of himself with his eyes gouged out.) Having read *American Psycho*, I can say that the more graphic scenes, with their enthusiastic, cooking-show prose, really *do* seem to invite imitation. However, NOW's attempt at what might be called class-action censorship, and Simon and Schuster's capitulation, are even more disturbing than Ellis's sensationalism. What does it mean when powerful institutions are unwilling to play by the rules of free expression and marketplace democracy? Doesn't anybody believe in the reader these days?

When Random House's trade paperback line brought *American Psycho* out at the end of March 1991, it immediately made the best-seller lists, thus sparking a rash of articles in *Newsweek* and elsewhere on America's supposed affection for gore. But does the consumption of depravity necessarily imply a depraved consumer? Journalists these days reflexively regard the marketplace as *ipso facto* corrupt. When this country was founded, however, popular taste was regarded much more positively. As Joseph J. Ellis explains in *After the Revolution: Profiles in Early American Culture*, "There was no presumed tension between artistic values on the one hand and . . . the values of the marketplace on the other. The market, in fact, was regarded as a benign environment in which the unrestricted movement of men and ideas would create exciting new cultural possibilities." Pure art, mean-while—art detached from commerce—made people nervous, redo-lent as it was of the decadent aristocracy against which America had just rebelled. Today, of course, the hierarchy is reversed. We trust the arts and regard the marketplace with mixed emotions at best.

Literary awards, the Nebulas among them, are intended to correct the errors of marketplace democracy. Like the magic drug in Lisa Goldstein's fantasy story "The Blue Love Potion," awards incline us to consider that which might otherwise escape our notice. Article XI of the SFWA bylaws states: "The Corporation shall present annual achievement awards to honor outstanding creative performance in the science fiction field. The award winners . . . are to be chosen by a vote of the active members under procedures established by the Nebula Rules." *A vote of the active members*: a quasi-elite remedying the deficiencies of mass taste.

This compensatory function is not one with which SFWA feels wholly at peace. In its heart, the organization is torn between being an academy and being a democracy. More specifically, SFWA wants to be respected like an academy but to function like a democracy. An academy defines aesthetics, handing down rules from on high; any discussion of the relation between the two is tautological: $A = A$; the academic is the aesthetic. But SFWA also contains a bedrock of populism. As anyone who's ever tried it knows, the single most ef-fective way to incur the organization's wrath is to suggest some new scheme for limiting active membership.

Like the major science fiction conventions, SFWA has expanded considerably in the last ten years. It's gotten big, really big. And like the major conventions, SFWA now contains diverse constituencies.

Is it any wonder that so many of the 1990 Nebula nominees can be understood as appeasing particular factions? Should we be surprised to hear people talk of Jane Yolen's *White Jenna* as "representing" young-adult fiction on the final ballot, or John Stith's nuts-and-bolts novel *Red Shift Rendezvous* as filling the hard-SF slot? And as the ranks of fantasy writers swell SFWA, should we wonder that a majority of the novels nominated for the Nebula in 1990 were not, in fact, science fiction?

When members vote a work onto the final ballot, they are ostensibly honoring "outstanding creative performance in the field." But behind these choices lurk political blocs and implied party platforms. (This effect is especially evident when members don't bother to read the works they vote for.) And what are the contents of these platforms? Essentially, each bloc is saying how it thinks the audience at large should behave. They're saying that readers ought to prefer social comment over military adventure, or rigorous extrapolation over social comment, or medieval world-building over quantum-mechanical speculation, or satire over sorcery, or a "good read" over just about anything else. Implicit in this process is the assumption that the ideal audience for science fiction is SFWA itself—a notion that Pulphouse has been pursuing with great success.

We used to regard our best-selling SF authors—the Heinleins, the Herberts, the Bradburys—with awe. No more. Weis & Hickman occupy a very different niche; they keep the insatiable masses at bay while we calmly analyze and endorse the serious trends in the field. Through its direct mail campaigns to SFWA members and its publication of professional self-help books, Pulphouse appears to be making a healthy profit by exploiting the organization's new preoccupation with itself. To paraphrase Pogo, "We have met the audience and he is us." Indeed, if SFWA could get just a little larger, and hardcover print runs just a little cheaper, no one in the outside world need ever actually purchase a book. Things haven't gone quite that far, of course, but at the moment we seem to be experiencing a quiet crisis of faith in the marketplace.

Kelly's "Mr. Boy" offers the year's most explicit platform. The hero's mom is very rich and uses her money to transform herself into the Statue of Liberty while keeping her son perpetually twelve years old. At the end of the novella, the hero sees that staying twelve forever isn't such a hot idea and maybe it's time to grow up. Read allegorically, the story suggests that science fiction's golden age is showing a little tarnish and perhaps some outright corrosion—it's time to grow up and write for adult readers like ourselves.

As the fiction editor for *Omni*, Ellen Datlow cannot buy material that would bewilder the magazine's large audience. Lately, she's turned to exercising her editorial creativity by compiling anthologies. Like Kelly, she seems to want to help SF grow up a bit, in this case by increasing the range of its sexual expression. She begins the introduction to her anthology, *Alien Sex*—source of Pat Murphy's Nebula-nominated "Love and Sex Among the Invertebrates"—by observing, "Sexuality, human or otherwise, has not traditionally been a major concern in science fiction—possibly because the genre was originally conceived for young adults."

There is a climate of frustration in SFWA these days, a discontent over the gap between the ideals of art and the requirements for financial success. But is the customer always wrong? The best-seller syndrome may be an impetus to conservative publishing and hack writing, but perhaps the real fault lies in our techniques for comprehending the mass audience, rather than in the mass audience itself.

■ ■ ■

Interestingly enough, several of 1990's more sophisticated SF offerings invite us to reconsider our contempt for popular taste. If we heed the tacit messages of Ursula K. Le Guin's Nebula-nominated novelette "The Shobies' Story," Gene Wolfe's novel *Castleview*, and several other works, we shall begin exhibiting more curiosity about the readership for Piers Anthony, David Eddings, and Weis & Hickman. Eschewing elitism, we'll ask ourselves what the majority of the SF-and-fantasy audience is reading, why they're reading it, and what they're getting out of it.

"The Shobies' Story" presents a community in which consensus matters more than individual viewpoints. As the narrator puts it:

> A chain of command is easy to describe, a network of response isn't. To those who live by mutual empowerment, "thick" description, complex and open-ended, is normal and comprehensible, but to those whose only model is hierarchical control, such description seems a muddle, a mess, along with what it describes. Who is in charge here? Get rid of all these petty details.

How many cooks spoil a soup? Let's get this perfectly clear now. Take me to your leader!

The term "thick description" was coined by the anthropologist Clifford Geertz, whose 1973 book *The Interpretation of Culture* ends with a long, rich, riveting account of Balinese cockfighting. (Because that example is so well written, some detractors have suggested that the only true practitioner of thick description is Geertz himself.) In a nutshell, Geertz proposes that meaning emerges from the total social context; thus, many of the details heretofore discarded by scientists as irrelevant should be included in ethnographic observations. To illustrate his claim, Geertz catalogs the possible meanings of a person closing and opening one eye. (He could have an involuntary twitch; he could be winking; he could be parodying someone winking.) Le Guin uses the example of not breathing:

"I can't breathe," one said.
"I am not breathing," one said.
"There is nothing to breathe," one said.
"You are, you are breathing, please breathe!" said another.

"The Shobies' Story" posits a reality that emerges as the sum of what all the participants say: a meta-narrative, a democratically constructed myth. Le Guin tells us that the Einsteinian observer, the *Beobachter* of *Gedankenexperiments*, is part of the reality he's trying to describe. Every observer sees things differently, and the melding of these interpretations becomes the world.

*Castleview*, a postmodern antinovel that is also an Arthurian fantasy epic, has similar implications. The beginning is simple and concrete: Illinois, real estate, cookbooks. But to make sense of *Castleview*, we must discard the idea that our identification with the *Beobachter*, Mr. Shields, will make what's going on explicit. The solution to the puzzle lies not in a single viewpoint but in an aggregate of many viewpoints. *Castleview* challenges its readers to absorb all its Wolfean thick description so thoroughly that the narrative becomes coherent. Some reviewers threw up their hands, implicitly saying, "It's Greek to me!" If what Le Guin gives us in "The Shobies' Story" is a single Greek lesson, Wolfe provides a complete course.

In his visionary novel *Pacific Edge*, Kim Stanley Robinson addresses the issue of hierarchy more directly than either Le Guin or

Wolfe. Robinson's hero, Kevin Clairborne, is a town council member in an environmentally blessed community. Even in ecotopia, life goes on: boy meets girl, boy gets girl, boy loses girl. (There's also a techno-thriller plot.) Because Robinson has created a society that works by consensus, however, he cannot give us a satisfying, "novelistic" conclusion. We want the hero to force his will upon the majority—a logical impossibility here. But despite our frustration at the hero's ineffectiveness, this *is* a better world: Robinson's lovely descriptions of the California settings add up to a persuasive paradise.

Not all of 1990's offerings equate consensus with wisdom. Nancy Kress's powerful novel *Brain Rose* posits a new surgical procedure that allows patients to remember their past lives. As in the various "factual" accounts of past-life channeling, it turns out that many of Kress's characters knew each other in a previous existence. While Kress offers up a cosmic answer to the riddle, the novel emerges as something of a critique of New Age theology. For if the reports of all these time trippers are accurate, and they really did interact with earlier incarnations of each other, then the universe makes no sense. Far from bringing us to some higher anthropological truth, the Geertzian collective narrative here leads us into absurdity.

Thomas Ligotti's novelette "The Last Feast of Harlequin," dedicated to the memory of H. P. Lovecraft, at times reads like a parody of Geertz, with a perverse Lovecraftian twist:

> He was a fieldworker par excellence, and his ability to insinuate himself into exotic cultures and situations, thereby gaining insight where other anthropologists merely gathered data, was renowned. . . . There were hints, which were not always responsible or cheaply glamorized, that he was involved in projects of a freakish sort, many of which focused on New England. It is a fact that he spent six months posing as a mental patient at an institution in western Massachusetts, gathering information on the "culture" of the psychically disturbed. . . .

Unlike Le Guin, who values "thick description" for its political idealism, Ligotti loves the technique because, as practiced by him, it thoroughly dislocates the reader. He sends up both Geertz and Lovecraft to marvelous effect, giving us a whole series of unreliable narrators, a process that culminates in one lunatic reporting upon the bizarre scientific paper of another. The winter solstice ritual recounted by Ligotti's mad anthropologist echoes Geertz's Balinese cockfight, but in the end Lovecraft's horror of the masses wins out over Geertz's cultural pluralism.

Geertz and Lovecraft offer two different paradigms by which to interpret the SF audience. While Geertz would challenge us to suspend our judgment, insinuate ourselves into the society of paperback consumers, and learn the secrets behind their buying habits, Lovecraft would have us avoid such contact. The mass audience is profane, and excessive interaction with it will almost certainly cause degeneration, a slide down the evolutionary scale, reversion to type, and so on; before you know it, you'll find yourself squirming on the floor, a spineless worm or worse, reading Harlequin romances. No doubt a middle ground exists—some way to celebrate popular taste without murdering aesthetics—but evidently neither Geertz nor Lovecraft has glimpsed it.

In a similar vein, Dafydd ab Hugh's liberal-libertarian fable "The Coon Rolled Down and Ruptured His Larinks, A Squeezed Novel by Mr. Skunk" explores the tension between the ideals of democracy and the achievements of elites, or, more pessimistically, the Hobson's choice between democracy's leveling effect and elitism's oppressiveness. The style evokes Joel Chandler Harris's Uncle Remus stories. In ab Hugh's future, "Democrazy" is a disease that makes animals smarter and people stupider, until a kind of parity is achieved. The story centers upon a talking skunk and his friends, who want to spread the plague around. At the end, Mr. Skunk glances backwards, as the gifted animals undergo a Lovecraftian devolution and become more like pigeons and less like people: "I confess that sometimes I wonder: have we lost something urgent? But I do not think wondering should be a crime against Democrazy."

Lucius Shepard's compelling *noir* adventure novella "Skull City" implicitly expresses a fear I've heard voiced by other writers: we're on the verge of a "post-literate culture." Shepard's hero, a young heroin addict, is enticed by a sophisticated older man into becoming a guinea pig in experiments worthy of Lovecraft himself. The addict's seeming benefactor is the author of CDs providing virtual-reality experiences complete with the same wish fulfillments and circumscribed choices one finds in Dungeons & Dragons and its spin-offs. Our hero assassinates the "author" of his fantasy world and finds himself under the thumb of a Mafia heavy not unlike certain publishing magnates.

Metaphorically, the assassination of the author is already in progress: fantasy role-playing games, hypertext, and virtual reality all usurp the writer's traditional control over structure, chronology, and plot. The "reader" is now assembling the narrative. One criticism of these new forms is that the resulting "artworks" are meaningless. Traditional narrative forms derive their significance from the choices made by characters, not from those made by consumers. In Tom Godwin's 1954 story "The Cold Equations," for example, the hero decides to shove the girl stowaway out the airlock after the cold equations of the title reveal that otherwise many deaths will result; were he to cut off his legs and put them out the airlock instead, the story would not mean the same thing. But if we grant the possibility of significance to the new flexible-narrative forms, then this virtue will inhere not in decisions, as in the past, but in decision trees—the full spectrum of choices that consumers can make through the course of the "story." It remains to be seen what standards will emerge to guide us in awarding a Nebula for best virtual reality.

Perhaps the author, like God in James Morrow's Nebula-nominated novel *Only Begotten Daughter*, will merely wait offstage for a while. Morrow's plot combines the speculative-fiction premise of a right-wing religious dictatorship (even more brutal than the one in Margaret Atwood's *The Handmaid's Tale*) with the Christian-fantasy premise of a Second Coming. God sends down her female dimension, though this particular incarnation fares no better than Jesus. Morrow pits a vicious fundamentalist preacher who thinks he knows exactly what's on God's mind against a true Messiah who preaches a doctrine of doubt. Although God finally does intervene to set things right, Morrow seems to side with sacred uncertainty.

But if God is out of the picture, then the future is what we make of it. Like the wealthy old woman in Bruce McAllister's "Angels," who uses her riches to make a supernatural being, we shape even the immaterial with our own hands. Is it naïve to embrace the flexible-narrative media as the harbingers of a new and radical form of democracy? Though the options offered by these forms often seem as trivial as the choice between Coke and Pepsi, perhaps the selection process itself educates people for a freedom we cannot yet comprehend. And when, later, authorship returns, it may be more meaningful than ever.

With a bit of tongue-in-cheek extrapolation, John Kessel offers a defense of post-literacy in his novelette "Invaders." When the highly advanced aliens land, they turn out to be neo-McLuhanites:

> Sepulveda swallowed. "Okay. You need to read and sign these papers."
> "We don't read."
> "You don't read Spanish? How about English?"
> "We don't read at all. We used to, but we gave it up. Once you start reading, it gets out of control. You tell yourself you're just going to stick to nonfiction—but pretty soon you graduate to fiction. After that you can't kick the habit. And then there's the oppression."
> "Oppression?"
> "Sure . . . Literature is a tool used by ruling elites to ensure their hegemony. . . ."

We, the SF insiders, make a pretty shabby ruling elite, but we still face a nagging question: to what extent are our aesthetics really just a screen for our politics? When we vote for "art," are we really voting for some unarticulated notion of justice? And what's the point of clinging to any ideals, aesthetic or political, if the market is moving in the opposite direction? Would the future of *Analog* look brighter if its editor, physicist-writer Stan Schmidt, were replaced by marketing wizard and book packager Byron Preiss? Isn't it worth a try? Come walk with me, Young Goodman Brown!

"Invaders," a marvelous deconstruction of the tropes of SF, does not stop with allegory. Kessel addresses his audience directly: "Like any drug addict, the SF reader finds desperate justifications for his habit. SF teaches him science. SF helps him avoid 'future shock.' SF changes the world for the better. Right. So does cocaine." Kessel aspires to lift his addicted readers to a condition of enlightened introspection, a state in which they'll have no illusions about their vice, science fiction.

In "Walking the Moons," a story reminiscent of Philip K. Dick, Jonathan Lethem takes a different but equally bleak look at the dilemma of today's science fiction writer. Like Shepard in "Skull City," he explores the symbolic connotations of "virtual reality." Space travel is no longer affordable, so people use computer simulations to conquer the moons of Jupiter. The space adventurer is really just a guy in his underwear in a garage; in his mind he may be out there, but he's actually marooned in some seedy suburb. Lethem's hero, whom we're inclined to interpret as an SF writer, is at once cheerful and pathetic. Virtual reality, *Lieblingstechnik* to the technologically hip, is in the end as ridiculous and self-deluding as the personal planetarium from *Science Made Stupid* that you cut out and wear on your head. By extension, SF is made to seem equally silly.

• • •

Did any positive, upbeat views of the field appear in 1990? If we read Ted Chiang's hard-fantasy novelette, the Nebula-winning "Tower of Babylon," as an allegory on science fiction, it tells us that when SF goes way out there, exploring the very fringes of the cosmos, we cut through to inner space, to the collective unconscious, to truth.

Geoffrey A. Landis's story "Projects" features a couple of guys sitting around an institute very like MIT, just inventing stuff. And although they're underfunded and despair of ever being listened to, they turn out to be wonderfully right. Landis captures the spirit of hard SF and effectively revives one of its archetypes: the basement inventor. But the optimism in Landis's story is hard won. One of the basic tenets of SF, that technology is power, seems to be undergoing a revision. In its place stands a different totem—money. Technology is simply one form of power at money's disposal; fantastic amounts of money beget the fantastic. Landis's basement inventors haven't the resources to do their own R&D. They must steal.

The power of money emerges again in Ian MacLeod's "Past Magic," in which a rich woman resurrects her drowned daughter and, realizing the child needs a daddy, proceeds to clone her estranged husband. McAllister's "Angels," Blumlein's "Bestseller," Kress's *Brain Rose*, and Kelly's "Mr. Boy" all involve people using their wealth to modify the human body. Arthur C. Clarke's maxim that any sufficiently advanced technology is indistinguishable from magic seems to have been replaced with a new one: any sufficiently large amount of money is indistinguishable from magic.

For some members of the science fiction community, the transforming power of money is much more than a literary theme. After the 1990 Worldcon, Thomas Braatz, president-elect of the Leipzig Science Fiction Society, was kind enough to be our tour guide, taking us to the sites that figured in his country's quiet revolution. In talking with Braatz and other East Germans, we sensed a deep anxiety about the emerging post-Cold War economy. "They want to sell us things, but they don't want to give us jobs," he said of Western corporations. The free market, traditionally the linchpin of democracy, is now regarded by the SF community as the tool by which a capitalist elite controls the rest of us. One of the running gags of Terry Bisson's novel *Voyage to the Red Planet* is that companies keep buying each other. At the beginning of the book, Disney-Gerber is out to thwart the Mars expedition; by the end, it's the corporate sponsor. And while all these mega-corporate-acquisitions are hilarious to read about, they are part of daily life in publishing, where for many years Bisson made his living as a free-lance copy chief.

An even more ominous side effect of the convulsions in Eastern Europe has been the increase in political murders. While preparing this essay, I went to Chimera II, a small, very pleasant fantasy convention outside of Chicago. One of the guests of honor was the Rumanian exile Ioan Couliano, author of two science fiction novels and an expert on Renaissance magic. For the past year or so, Couliano had been receiving death threats connected with the political tracts he'd been writing for publication in Rumania.

On May 21, 1991, Couliano was found in the men's room of the University of Chicago Divinity School, where he was a faculty member, shot in the back of the head. While the crime will very likely go unsolved, it was almost certainly an assassination.

Some of us who attended Chimera were going to get together with Couliano for a cookout in Massachusetts during the summer of 1991. He was a warm, wonderful person, and a good writer. At his memorial service, the University of Chicago's Wendy Doninger said of her dead colleague, "When Ioan Couliano and Rajiv Gandhi are murdered on the same day, you don't have to be an astrologer to know that one of the planets was in the wrong place. *This* planet."

The killing of Ioan Couliano is an injustice of a different order from those cataloged by Ellison in "Xenogenesis." But whenever a writer is silenced, whether through physical violence or mere harassment, an outrage has occurred. No voice is replaceable. While contemporary SF says that anything can be bought and sold, in reality the resurrection of an author is beyond the reach of money. As ab

Hugh reminds us in "The Coon Rolled Down and Ruptured His Larinks," there is no freedom, no justice, no "Democrazy," without the power of speech.

It's probably never been harder for the American science fiction community to envision a positive future. And yet, as the end of the millennium looms, does it not behoove us to put aside our obsession with the marketplace and engage in some good old-fashioned utopian dreaming?

With luck, we'll even get paid for it.

# The Shobies' Story
· · ·
*Ursula K. Le Guin*

In my crustier moments I've been known to assert that, while science
fiction boasts any number of enthralling yarn spinners, brilliant
visionaries, and witty satirists, it has produced only one wholly literary voice. That's not true, of course. It's certainly not fair to
Samuel R. Delany, Thomas Disch, Lucius Shepard, Karen Joy
Fowler, Judith Moffet, Michael Bishop, and perhaps a dozen others.
And yet if SFWA ever got itself into a literary jousting tournament
with some rival guild, the prize being a government grant or a small
planet or a subscription to *The New Yorker* or something, there's
no question whom I'd want to send onto the field.

Ursula K. Le Guin received the National Book Award for *The
Farthest Shore*, the third novel in the Earthsea cycle, as well as a
Hugo and a Nebula for *The Left Hand of Darkness* and the same
pair of trophies for *The Dispossessed*. This volume celebrates her
most recent literary honor—a Nebula for *Tehanu: The Last Book
of Earthsea*—by offering up another Le Guin work from the final
ballot, a complex and audacious novelette called "The Shobies'
Story."

Even if *Tehanu* had not taken the top prize, I would have
accorded "The Shobies' Story" a prime spot in this volume, for I
believe that—through its marvelous conceit of "churten" travel—
it raises crucial questions about social hierarchies, interspecies bond-
ing, and the consensus model of reality. Le Guin aficionados will
quickly notice that it belongs to the "Hainish League" saga, her
ongoing narrative of galactic exploration.

"This story grew out of an idea I have been chewing on for
years about the importance of story, of narrative," Le Guin reports.
"Speaking not metaphorically but fairly literally, it seems that people
who can see their life as a story, with a 'plot' or at least narrative
continuity (possibly even a happy ending), get along okay, while
people who lose that narrative sense are in a lot of trouble, maybe
to the point of psychopathy. I'm not talking about personal control,
being the 'author of your fate,' because in cultures where individuals
don't control their lives much at all, people can be totally content
with the *cultural* narrative, and live it beautifully. Even if the story
itself is stupid or psychopathic, like the war story or the white-

supremacy story, if we believe in it and it makes some sense to us we get along, we stay alive, we even think we know what we're doing.

"Well, then, the idea of using narrative as a means of travel is really just an extension of this basic idea of narrative as means of existence. So the Shobies showed up and started telling their story. Their stories. Of course they were science fiction stories, what else?"

They met at Ve Port more than a month before their first flight together, and there, calling themselves after their ship as most crews did, became the Shobies. Their first consensual decision was to spend their isyeye in the coastal village of Liden, on Hain, where the negative ions could do their thing.

Liden was a fishing port with an eighty-thousand-year history and a population of four hundred. Its fisherfolk farmed the rich shoal waters of their bay, shipped the catch inland to the cities, and managed the Liden Resort for vacationers and tourists and new space crews on isyeye (the word is Hainish and means "making a beginning together," or "beginning to be together," or, used technically, "the period of time and area of space in which a group forms if it is going to form." A honeymoon is an isyeye of two). The fisherwomen and fishermen of Liden were as weathered as driftwood and about as talkative. Six-year-old Asten, who had misunderstood slightly, asked one of them if they were all eighty thousand years old. "Nope," she said.

Like most crews, the Shobies used Hainish as their common language. So the name of the one Hainish crew member, Sweet Today, carried its meaning as words as well as name, and at first seemed a silly thing to call a big, tall, heavy woman in her late fifties, imposing of carriage and almost as taciturn as the villagers. But her reserve proved to be a deep well of congeniality and tact, to be called upon as needed, and her name soon began to sound quite right. She had family—all Hainish have family—kinfolk of all denominations, grandchildren and cross-cousins, affines and cosines, scattered all over the Ekumen, but no relatives in this crew. She asked to be Grandmother to Rig, Asten, and Betton, and was accepted.

The only Shoby older than Sweet Today was the Terran Lidi, who was seventy-two EYs and not interested in grandmothering. Lidi had been navigating for fifty years, and there was nothing she didn't know about NAFAL ships, although occasionally she forgot that their ship was the *Shoby* and called it the *Soso* or the *Alterra*. And there were things she didn't know, none of them knew, about the *Shoby*.

They talked, as human beings do, about what they didn't know.

Churten theory was the main topic of conversation, evenings at the driftwood fire on the beach after dinner. The adults had read whatever there was to read about it, of course, before they ever volunteered for the test mission. Gveter had more recent information and presumably a better understanding of it than the others, but it had to be pried out of him. Only twenty-five, the only Cetian in the crew, much hairier than the others, and not gifted in language, he spent a lot of time on the defensive. Assuming that as an Anarresti he was more proficient at mutual aid and more adept at cooperation than the others, he lectured them about their propertarian habits; but he held tight to his knowledge, because he needed the advantage it gave him. For a while he would speak only in negatives: don't call it the churten "drive," it isn't a drive, don't call it the churten "effect," it isn't an effect. What is it, then? A long lecture ensued, beginning with the rebirth of Cetian physics since the revision of Shevekian temporalism by the Intervallists, and ending with the general conceptual framework of the churten. Everyone listened very carefully, and finally Sweet Today spoke, carefully. "So the ship will be moved," she said, "by ideas?"

"No, no, no, no," said Gveter. But he hesitated for the next word so long that Karth asked a question: "Well, you haven't actually talked about any physical, material events or effects at all." The question was characteristically indirect. Karth and Oreth, the Gethenians who with their two children were the affective focus of the crew, the "hearth" of it, in their terms, came from a not very theoretically minded subculture, and knew it. Gveter could run rings round them with his Cetian physico-philosophico-techno-natter. He did so at once. His accent did not make his explanations any clearer. He went on about coherence and meta-intervals, and at last demanded, with gestures of despair, "Khow can I say it in Khainish? No! It is not physical, it is not not-physical, these are the categories our minds must discard entirely, this is the khole point!"

"Buth-buth-buth-buth-buth-buth," went Asten, softly, passing behind the half circle of adults at the driftwood fire on the wide, twilit beach. Rig followed, also going, "Buth-buth-buth-buth," but louder. They were being spaceships, to judge from their maneuvers around a dune and their communications—"Locked in orbit, Navigator!"— but the noise they were imitating was the noise of the little fishing boats of Liden putt-putting out to sea.

"I crashed!" Rig shouted, flailing in the sand. "Help! Help! I crashed!"

"Hold on, Ship Two!" Asten cried. "I'll rescue you! Don't breathe! Oh, oh, trouble with the Churten Drive! Buth-buth-ack! Ack! Brrrrmmm-ack-ack-ack-rrrrrmmmmm, buth-buth-buth-buth . . ."

They were six and four EYs old. Tai's son Betton, who was eleven, sat at the driftwood fire with the adults, though at the moment he was watching Rig and Asten as if he wouldn't mind taking off to help rescue Ship Two. The little Getherians had spent more time on ships than on planet, and Asten liked to boast about being "actually fifty-eight," but this was Betton's first crew, and his only NAFAL flight had been from Terra to Hain. He and his biomother, Tai, had lived in a reclamation commune on Terra. When she had drawn the lot for Ekumenical service and requested training for ship duty, he had asked her to bring him as family. She had agreed; but after training, when she volunteered for this test flight, she had tried to get Betton to withdraw, to stay in training or go home. He had refused. Shan, who had trained with them, told the others this, because the tension between the mother and son had to be understood to be used effectively in group formation. Betton had requested to come, and Tai had given in, but plainly not with an undivided will. Her relationship to the boy was cool and mannered. Shan offered him fatherly-brotherly warmth, but Betton accepted it sparingly, coolly, and sought no formal crew relation with him or anyone.

Ship Two was being rescued, and attention returned to the discussion. "All right," said Lidi. "We know that anything that goes faster than light, any *thing* that goes faster than light, by so doing transcends the material/immaterial category—that's how we got the ansible, by distinguishing the message from the medium. But if we, the crew, are going to travel as messages, I want to understand *how*."

Gveter tore his hair. There was plenty to tear. It grew fine and thick, a mane on his head, a pelt on his limbs and body, a silvery nimbus on his hands and face. The fuzz on his feet was, at the moment, full of sand. "Khow!" he cried. "I'm trying to tell you khow! Message, information, no no no, that's old, that's ansible technology. This is transilience! Because the field is to be conceived as the virtual field, in which the unreal interval becomes virtually effective through the mediary coherence—don't you see?"

"No," Lidi said. "What do you mean by mediary?"

After several more bonfires on the beach, the consensus opinion was that churten theory was accessible only to minds very highly trained in Cetian temporal physics. There was a less freely voiced conviction that the engineers who had built the *Shoby*'s churten apparatus did not entirely understand how it worked. Or more precisely, what it did when it worked. That it worked was certain. The *Shoby* was the fourth ship it had been tested with, using robot crew; so far sixty-two instantaneous trips, or transiliences, had been effected between points from four hundred kilometers to twenty-seven light-years apart, with stopovers of varying lengths. Gveter and Lidi steadfastly maintained that this proved that the engineers knew perfectly well what they were doing, and that for the rest of them the seeming difficulty of the theory was only the difficulty human minds had in grasping a genuinely new concept.

"Like the circulation of the blood," said Tai. "People went around with their hearts beating for a long time before they understood why." She did not look satisfied with her own analogy, and when Shan said, "The heart has its reasons, which reason does not know," she looked offended. "Mysticism," she said, in the tone of voice of one warning a companion about dog shit on the path.

"Surely there's nothing *beyond* understanding in this process," Oreth said, somewhat tentatively. "Nothing that can't be understood, and reproduced."

"And quantified," Gveter said stoutly.

"But even if people understand the process, nobody knows the human response to it—the *experience* of it. Right? So we are to report on that."

"Why shouldn't it be just like NAFAL flight, only even faster?" Betton asked.

"Because it is totally different," said Gveter.

"What could happen to us?"

Some of the adults had discussed possibilities, all of them had considered them; Karth and Oreth had talked it over in appropriate terms with their children; but evidently Betton had not been included in such discussions.

"We don't know," Tai said sharply. "I told you that at the start, Betton."

"Most likely it will be like NAFAL flight," said Shan, "but the first people who flew NAFAL didn't know what it would be like, and had to find out the physical and psychic effects—"

"The worst thing," said Sweet Today in her slow, comfortable voice, "would be that we would die. Other lives have been on some of the test flights. Crickets. And intelligent ritual animals on the last two *Shoby* tests. They were all all right." It was a very long statement for Sweet Today, and carried proportional weight.

"We know," said Gveter, "that no temporal rearrangement is involved in churten, as it is in NAFAL. And mass is involved only in terms of needing a certain core mass, just as for ansible transmission, but not in itself. So maybe even a pregnant person could be a transilient."

"They can't go on ships," Asten said. "The unborn dies if they do."

Asten was half lying across Oreth's lap; Rig, thumb in mouth, was asleep on Karth's lap.

"When we were Oneblins," Asten went on, sitting up, "there were ritual animals with our crew. Some fish and some Terran cats and a whole lot of Hainish gholes. We got to play with them. And we helped thank the ghole that they tested for lithovirus. But it didn't die. It bit Shapi. The cats slept with us. But one of them went into kemmer and got pregnant, and then the *Oneblin* had to go to Hain, and she had to have an abortion, or all her unborns would have died inside her and killed her too. Nobody knew a ritual for her, to explain to her. But I fed her some extra food. And Rig cried."

"Other people I know cried too," Karth said, stroking the child's hair.

"You tell good stories, Asten," Sweet Today observed.

"So we're sort of ritual humans," said Betton.

"Volunteers," Tai said.

"Experimenters," said Lidi.

"Experiencers," said Shan.

"Explorers," Oreth said.

"Gamblers," said Karth.

The boy looked from one face to the next.

"You know," Shan said, "back in the time of the League, early in NAFAL flight, they were sending out ships to really distant systems—trying to explore everything—crews that wouldn't come back for centuries. Maybe some of them are still out there. But some of them came back after four, five, six hundred years, and they were all mad. Crazy!" He paused dramatically. "But they were all crazy when they started. Unstable people. They had to be crazy to volunteer for a time dilation like that. What a way to pick a crew, eh?" He laughed.

"Are we stable?" said Oreth. "I like instability. I like this job. I like the risk, taking the risk together. High stakes! That's the edge of it, the sweetness of it."

Karth looked down at their children, and smiled.

"Yes. Together," Gveter said. "You aren't crazy. You are good. I love you. We are ammari."

"Ammar," the others said to him, confirming this unexpected declaration. The young man scowled with pleasure, jumped up, and pulled off his shirt. "I want to swim. Come on, Betton. Come on swimming!" he said, and ran off toward the dark, vast waters that moved softly beyond the ruddy haze of their fire. The boy hesitated, then shed his shirt and sandals and followed. Shan pulled up Tai, and they followed; and finally the two old women went off into the night and the breakers, rolling up their pant legs, laughing at themselves.

To Gethenians, even on a warm summer night on a warm summer world, the sea is no friend. The fire is where you stay. Oreth and Asten moved closer to Karth and watched the flames, listening to the faint voices out in the glimmering surf, now and then talking quietly in their own tongue, while the little sisterbrother slept on.

■ ■ ■

After thirty lazy days at Liden the Shobies caught the fish train inland to the city, where a Fleet lander picked them up at the train station and took them to the spaceport on Ve, the next planet out from Hain. They were rested, tanned, bonded, and ready to go.

One of Sweet Today's hemi-affiliate cousins once removed was on duty in Ve Port. She urged the Shobies to ask the inventors of the churten on Urras and Anarres any questions they had about churten operation. "The purpose of the experimental flight is understanding," she insisted, "and your full intellectual participation is essential. They've been very anxious about that."

Lidi snorted.

"Now for the ritual," said Shan, as they went to the ansible room in the sunward bubble. "They'll explain to the animals what they're going to do and why, and ask them to help."

"The animals don't understand that," Betton said in his cold, angelic treble. "It's just to make the humans feel better."

"The humans understand?" Sweet Today asked.

"We all use each other," Oreth said. "The ritual says: we have no right to do so; therefore, we accept the responsibility for the suffering we cause."

Betton listened and brooded.

Gveter addressed the ansible first, and talked to it for half an hour, mostly in Pravic and mathematics. Finally, apologizing, and looking a little unnerved, he invited the others to use the instrument. There was a pause. Lidi activated it, introduced herself, and said, "We have agreed that none of us, except Gveter, has the theoretical background to grasp the principles of the churten."

A scientist twenty-two light-years away responded in Hainish via the rather flat auto-translator voice, but with unmistakable hopefulness, "The churten, in lay terms, may be seen as displacing the virtual field in order to realize relational coherence in terms of the transiliential experientiality."

"Quite," said Lidi.

"As you know, the material effects have been nil, and negative effect on low-intelligence sentients also nil; but there is considered to be a possibility that the participation of high intelligence in the process might affect the displacement in one way or another. And that such displacement would reciprocally affect the participant."

"What has the level of our intelligence got to do with how the churten functions?" Tai asked.

A pause. Their interlocutor was trying to find the words, to accept the responsibility.

"We have been using 'intelligence' as shorthand for the psychic complexity and cultural dependence of our species," said the translator voice at last. "The presence of the transilient as conscious mind nonduring transilience is the untested factor."

"But if the process is instantaneous, how can we be conscious of it?" Oreth asked.

"Precisely," said the ansible, and after another pause continued, "As the experimenter is an element of the experiment, so we assume that the transilient may be an element or agent of transilience. This is why we asked for a crew to test the process, rather than one or two volunteers. The psychic interbalance of a bonded social group is a margin of strength against disintegrative or incomprehensible experience, if any such occurs. Also, the separate observations of the group members will mutually interverify."

"Who programs this translator?" Shan snarled in a whisper. "Interverify! Shit!"

Lidi looked around at the others, inviting questions.

"How long will the trip actually take?" Betton asked.

"No long," the translator voice said, then self-corrected: "No time."

Another pause.

"Thank you," said Sweet Today, and the scientist on a planet twenty-two years of time-dilated travel from Ve Port answered, "We are grateful for your generous courage, and our hope is with you."

They went directly from the ansible room to the *Shoby*.

■ ■ ■

The churten equipment, which was not very space-consuming and the controls of which consisted essentially of an on-off switch, had been installed alongside the Nearly as Fast as Light motivators and controls of an ordinary interstellar ship of the Ekumenical Fleet. The *Shoby* had been built on Hain about four hundred years ago, and was thirty-two years old. Most of its early runs had been exploratory, with a Hainish-Chiffewarian crew. Since in such runs a ship might spend years in orbit in a planetary system, the Hainish and Chiffewarians, feeling that it might as well be lived in rather than endured, had arranged and furnished it like a very large, very comfortable house. Three of its residential modules had been disconnected and left in the hangars on Ve, and still there was more than enough room for a crew of only ten. Tai, Betton, and Shan, new from Terra, and Gveter from Anarres, accustomed to the barracks and the communal austerities of their marginally habitable worlds, stalked about the *Shoby*, disapproving it. "Excremental," Gveter growled. "Luxury!" Tai sneered. Sweet Today, Lidi, and the Gethenians, more used to the amenities of shipboard life, settled right in and made themselves at home. And Gveter and the younger Terrans found it hard to maintain ethical discomfort in the spacious, high-ceilinged, well-furnished, slightly shabby living rooms and bedrooms, studies, high- and low-G gyms, the dining room, library, kitchen, and bridge of the *Shoby*. The carpet in the bridge was a genuine Henyekaulil, soft deep blues and purples woven in the patterns of the constellations of the Hainish sky. There was a large, healthy plantation of Terran bamboo in the meditation gym, part of the ship's self-contained vegetal/respiratory system. The windows of any room could be programmed by the homesick to a view of Abbenay or New Cairo or the beach at Liden, or cleared to look out on the suns nearer and farther and the darkness between the suns.

Rig and Asten discovered that as well as the elevators there was a stately staircase with a curving banister, leading from the reception hall up to the library. They slid down the banister shrieking wildly, until Shan threatened to apply a local gravity field and force them to slide up it, which they besought him to do. Betton watched the little ones with a superior gaze, and took the elevator; but the next day he slid down the banister, going a good deal faster than Rig and Asten because he could push off harder and had greater mass, and nearly broke his tailbone. It was Betton who organized the tray-sliding races, but Rig generally won them, being small enough to stay on the tray all the way down the stairs. None of the children had had any lessons at the beach, except in swimming and being Shobies; but while they waited through an unexpected five-day delay at Ve Port, Gveter did physics with Betton and math with all three daily in the library, and they did some history with Shan and Oreth, and danced with Tai in the low-G gym.

When she danced, Tai became light, free, laughing. Rig and Asten loved her then, and her son danced with her like a colt, like a kid, awkward and blissful. Shan often joined them; he was a dark and elegant dancer, and she would dance with him, but even then was shy, would not touch. She had been celibate since Betton's birth. She did not want Shan's patient, urgent desire, did not want to cope with it, with him. She would turn from him to Betton, and son and mother would dance wholly absorbed in the steps, the airy pattern they made together. Watching them, the afternoon before the test flight, Sweet Today began to wipe tears from her eyes, smiling, never saying a word.

"Life is good," said Gveter very seriously to Lidi.

"It'll do," she said.

Oreth, who was just coming out of female kemmer, having thus triggered Karth's male kemmer, all of which, by coming on unexpectedly early, had delayed the test flight for these past five days, enjoyable days for all—Oreth watched Rig, whom she had fathered, dance with Asten, whom she had borne, and watched Karth watch them, and said in Karhidish, "Tomorrow . . ." The edge was very sweet.

■ ■ ■

Anthropologists solemnly agree that we must not attribute "cultural constants" to the human population of any planet; but certain cultural traits or expectations do seem to run deep. Before dinner that last night in port, Shan and Tai appeared in black-and-silver uniforms of the Terran Ekumen, which had cost them—Terra also still had a money economy—a half year's allowance.

Asten and Rig clamored at once for equal grandeur. Karth and Oreth suggested their party clothes, and Sweet Today brought out silver-lace scarves, but Asten sulked, and Rig imitated. The idea of a *uniform*, Asten told them, was that it was the *same*.

"Why?" Oreth inquired.

Old Lidi answered sharply: "So that no one is responsible."

She then went off and changed into a black velvet evening suit that wasn't a uniform but that didn't leave Tai and Shan sticking out like sore thumbs. She had left Terra at age eighteen and never been back nor wanted to, but Tai and Shan were shipmates.

Karth and Oreth got the idea, and put on their finest fur-trimmed hiebs, and the children were appeased with their own party clothes plus all of Karth's hereditary and massive gold jewelry. Sweet Today appeared in a pure white robe which she claimed was in fact ultra-violet. Gveter braided his mane. Betton had no uniform, but needed none, sitting beside his mother at table in a visible glory of pride.

Meals, sent up from the Port kitchens, were very good, and this one was superb: a delicate Hainish iyanwi with all seven sauces, followed by a pudding flavored with Terran chocolate. A lively evening ended quietly at the big fireplace in the library. The logs were fake, of course, but good fakes; no use having a fireplace on a ship and then burning plastic in it. The neo-cellulose logs and kindling smelled right, resisted catching, caught with spits and sparks and smoke bil-lows, flared up bright. Oreth had laid the fire, Karth lit it. Everybody gathered round.

"Tell bedtime stories," Rig said.

Oreth told about the Ice Caves of Kerm Land, how a ship sailed into the great blue sea-cave and disappeared, and was never found by the boats that entered the caves in search; but seventy years later that ship was found drifting—not a living soul aboard nor any sign of what had become of them—off the coast of Osemyet, a thousand miles overland from Kerm . . .

Another story?

Lidi told about the little desert wolf who lost his wife and went to the land of the dead for her, and found her there dancing with the dead, and nearly brought her back to the land of the living, but spoiled it by trying to touch her before they got all the way back to life, and she vanished, and he could never find the way back to the place where the dead danced, no matter how he looked, and howled, and cried . . .

Another story!

Shan told about the boy who sprouted a feather every time he told a lie, until his commune had to use him for a duster.

Another!

Gveter told about the winged people called gluns, who were so stupid that they died out, because they kept hitting each other head-on in midair. "They weren't real," he added conscientiously. "Only a story."

Another— No. Bedtime now.

Rig and Asten went round as usual for a good-night hug, and this time Betton followed them. When he came to Tai he did not stop, for she did not like to be touched; but she put out her hand, drew the child to her, and kissed his cheek. He fled in joy.

"Stories," said Sweet Today. "Ours begins tomorrow, eh?"

■ ■ ■

A chain of command is easy to describe, a network of response isn't. To those who live by mutual empowerment, "thick" description, complex and open-ended, is normal and comprehensible, but to those whose only model is hierarchic control, such description seems a muddle, a mess, along with what it describes. Who's in charge here? Get rid of all these petty details. How many cooks spoil a soup? Let's get this perfectly clear now. Take me to your leader!

The old navigator was at the NAFAL console, of course, and Gveter at the paltry churten console; Oreth was wired into the AI; Tai, Shan, and Karth were their respective Support, and what Sweet Today did might be called supervising or overseeing if that didn't suggest a hierarchic function. Interseeing, maybe, or subvising. Rig and Asten always naffled (to use Rig's word) in the ship's library, where, during the boring and disorienting experience of travel at near light-speed, Asten could look at pictures or listen to a story tape, and Rig could curl up on and under a certain furry blanket and go to sleep. Betton's crew function during flight was Elder Sib; he stayed with the little ones, provided himself with a barf bag since he was one of those whom NAFAL flight made queasy, and focused the intervid on Lidi and Gveter so he could watch what they did.

So they all knew what they were doing, as regards NAFAL flight. As regards the churten process, they knew that it was supposed to effectuate their transilience to a solar system seventeen light-years from Ve Port without temporal interval; but nobody, anywhere, knew what they were doing.

So Lidi looked around, like the violinist who raises her bow to poise the chamber group for the first chord, a flicker of eye contact, and sent the *Shoby* into NAFAL mode, as Gveter, like the cellist whose bow comes down in that same instant to ground the chord, sent the *Shoby* into churten mode. They entered unduration. They churtened. No long, as the ansible had said.

"What's wrong?" Shan whispered.

"By damn!" said Gveter.

"What?" said Lidi, blinking and shaking her head.

"That's it," Tai said, flicking readouts.

"That's not A-sixty-whatsit," Lidi said, still blinking.

Sweet Today was gestalting them, all ten at once, the seven on the bridge and by intervid the three in the library. Betton had cleared a window, and the children were looking out at the murky, brownish convexity that filled half of it. Rig was holding a dirty, furry blanket. Karth was taking the electrodes off Oreth's temples, disengaging the AI link-up. "There was no interval," Oreth said.

"We aren't anywhere," Lidi said.

"There was no interval," Gveter repeated, scowling at the console. "That's right."

"Nothing happened," Karth said, skimming through the AI flight report.

Oreth got up, went to the window, and stood motionless looking out.

"That's it. M-60-340-nolo," Tai said.

All their words fell dead, had a false sound.

"Well! We did it, Shobies!" said Shan.

Nobody answered.

"Buzz Ve Port on the ansible," Shan said with determined jollity. "Tell 'em we're all here in one piece."

"All where?" Oreth asked.

"Yes, of course," Sweet Today said, but did nothing.

"Right," said Tai, going to the ship's ansible. She opened the field, centered to Ve, and sent a signal. Ships' ansibles worked only in the visual mode; she waited, watching the screen. She resignaled. They were all watching the screen.

"Nothing going through," she said.

Nobody told her to check the centering coordinates; in a network system nobody gets to dump their anxieties that easily. She checked the coordinates. She signaled; rechecked, reset, resignaled; opened the field and centered to Abbenay on Anarres and signaled. The ansible screen was blank.

"Check the—" Shan said, and stopped himself.

"The ansible is not functioning," Tai reported formally to her crew.

"Do you find malfunction?" Sweet Today asked.

"No. Nonfunction."

"We're going back now," said Lidi, still seated at the NAFAL console.

Her words, her tone, shook them apart.

"No, we're not!" Betton said on the intervid while Oreth said, "Back where?"

Tai, Lidi's Support, moved toward her as if to prevent her from activating the NAFAL drive, but then hastily moved back to the ansible to prevent Gveter from getting access to it. He stopped, taken aback, and said, "Perhaps the churten affected ansible function?"

"*I'm* checking it out," Tai said. "Why should it? Robot-operated ansible transmission functioned in all the test flights."

"Where are the AI reports?" Shan demanded.

"I told you, there are none," Karth answered sharply.

"Oreth was plugged in."

Oreth, still at the window, spoke without turning. "Nothing happened."

Sweet Today came over beside the Gethenian. Oreth looked at her and said, slowly, "Yes. Sweet Today. We cannot . . . do this. I think. I can't think."

Shan had cleared a second window, and stood looking out it. "Ugly," he said.

"What is?" said Lidi.

Gveter said, as if reading from the Ekumenical Atlas, "Thick, stable atmosphere, near the bottom of the temperature window for life. Microorganisms. Bacterial clouds, bacterial reefs."

"Germ stew," Shan said. "Lovely place to send us."

"So that if we arrived as a neutron bomb or a black-hole event we'd only take bacteria with us," Tai said. "But we didn't."

"Didn't what?" said Lidi.

"Didn't arrive?" Karth asked.

"Hey," Betton said, "is everybody going to stay on the bridge?"

"I want to come there," said Rig's little pipe, and then Asten's voice, clear but shaky, "Maba, I'd like to go back to Liden now."

"Come on," Karth said, and went to meet the children. Oreth did not turn from the window, even when Asten came close and took Oreth's hand.

"What are you looking at, maba?"

"The planet, Asten."

"What planet?"

Oreth looked at the child then.

"There isn't anything," Asten said.

"That brown color—that's the surface, the atmosphere of a planet."

"There isn't any brown color. There isn't *anything*. I want to go back to Liden. You said we could when we were done with the test."

Oreth looked around, at last, at the others.

"Perception variation," Gveter said.

"I think," Tai said, "that we must establish that we are—that we got here—and then get here."

"You mean, go back," Betton said.

"The readings are perfectly clear," Lidi said, holding on to the rim of her seat with both hands and speaking very distinctly. "Every coordinate in order. That's M-60-Etcetera down there. What more do you want? Bacteria samples?"

"Yes," Tai said. "Instrument function's been affected, so we can't rely on instrumental records."

"Oh, shitsake!" said Lidi. "What a farce! All right. Suit up, go down, get some goo, and then let's get out. Go home. By NAFAL."

"By NAFAL?" Shan and Tai echoed, and Gveter said, "But we would spend seventeen years, Ve time, and no ansible to explain why."

"Why, Lidi?" Sweet Today asked.

Lidi stared at the Hainishwoman. "You want to churten again?" she demanded, raucous. She looked round at them all. "Are you people made of stone?" Her face was ashy, crumpled, shrunken. "It doesn't bother you, seeing through the walls?"

No one spoke, until Shan said cautiously, "How do you mean?"

"I can see the stars through the walls!" She stared round at them again, pointing at the carpet with its woven constellations. "You can't?" When no one answered, her jaw trembled in a little spasm, and she said, "All right. All right. I'm off duty. Sorry. Be in my room." She stood up. "Maybe you should lock me in," she said.

"Nonsense," said Sweet Today.

"If I fall through," Lidi began, and did not finish. She walked to the door, stiffly and cautiously, as if through a thick fog. She said something they did not understand, "Cause," or perhaps, "Gauze."

Sweet Today followed her.

"I can see the stars too!" Rig announced.

"Hush," Karth said, putting an arm around the child.

"I can! I can see all the stars everywhere. And I can see Ve Port. And I can see anything I want!"

"Yes, of course, but hush now," the mother murmured, at which the child pulled free, stamped, and shrilled, "I can! I can too! I can see *everything*! And Asten can't! And there *is* a planet, there is too! No, don't hold me! Don't! Let me go!"

Grim, Karth carried the screaming child off to their quarters. Asten turned around to yell after Rig, "There is *not* any planet! You're just making it up!"

Grim, Oreth said, "Go to our room, please, Asten."

Asten burst into tears and obeyed. Oreth, with a glance of apology to the others, followed the short, weeping figure across the bridge and out into the corridor.

The four remaining on the bridge stood silent.

"Canaries," Shan said.

"Khallucinations?" Gveter proposed, subdued. "An effect of the churten on extrasensitive organisms—maybe?"

Tai nodded.

"Then is the ansible not functioning or are we hallucinating non-function?" Shan asked after a pause.

Gveter went to the ansible; this time Tai walked away from it, leaving it to him. "I want to go down," she said.

"No reason not to, I suppose," Shan said unenthusiastically.

"Khwat reason to?" Gveter asked over his shoulder.

"It's what we're here for, isn't it? It's what we volunteered to do, isn't it? To test instantaneous—transilience—prove that it worked, that we are here! With the ansible out, it'll be seventeen years before Ve gets our radio signal!"

"We can just churten back to Ve and *tell* them," Shan said. "If we did that now, we'd have been . . . here . . . about eight minutes."

"Tell them—tell them what? What kind of evidence is that?"

"Anecdotal," said Sweet Today, who had come back quietly to the bridge; she moved like a big sailing ship, imposingly silent.

"Is Lidi all right?" Shan asked.

"No," Sweet Today answered. She sat down where Lidi had sat, at the NAFAL console.

"I ask a consensus about going down onplanet," Tai said.

"I'll ask the others," Gveter said, and went out, returning presently with Karth. "Go down, if you want," the Gethenian said. "Oreth's staying with the children for a bit. They are—we are extremely disoriented."

"I will come down," Gveter said.

"Can I come?" Betton asked, almost in a whisper, not raising his eyes to any adult face.

"No," Tai said, as Gveter said, "Yes."

Betton looked at his mother, one quick glance.

"Khwy not?" Gveter asked her.

"We don't know the risks."

"The planet was surveyed."

"By robot ships—"

"We'll wear suits." Gveter was honestly puzzled.

"I don't want the responsibility," Tai said through her teeth.

"Khwy is it yours?" Gveter asked, more puzzled still. "We all share it; Betton is crew. I don't understand."

"I know you don't understand," Tai said, turned her back on them both, and went out. The man and the boy stood staring, Gveter after Tai, Betton at the carpet.

"I'm sorry," Betton said.

"Not to be," Gveter told him.

"What is . . . what is going on?" Shan asked in an over-controlled voice. "Why are we—we keep crossing, we keep—coming and going—"

"Confusion due to the churten experience," Gveter said.

Sweet Today turned from the console. "I have sent a distress signal," she said. "I am unable to operate the NAFAL system. The radio—" She cleared her throat. "Radio function seems erratic."

There was a pause.

"This is not happening," Shan said, or Oreth said, but Oreth had stayed with the children in another part of the ship, so it could not have been Oreth who said, "This is not happening," it must have been Shan.

■ ■ ■

A chain of cause and effect is an easy thing to describe; a cessation of cause and effect is not. To those who live in time, sequence is the

norm, the only model, and simultaneity seems a muddle, a mess, a
hopeless confusion, and the description of that confusion hopelessly
confusing. As the members of the crew network no longer perceived
the network steadily, and were unable to communicate their perceptions, an individual perception is the only clue to follow through the
labyrinth of their dislocation. Gveter perceived himself as being on
the bridge with Shan, Sweet Today, Betton, Karth, and Tai. He perceived himself as methodically checking out the ship's systems. The
NAFAL he found dead, the radio functioning in erratic bursts, the
internal electrical and mechanical systems of the ship all in order.
He sent out a lander unmanned and brought it back, and perceived
it as functioning normally. He perceived himself discussing with Tai
her determination to go down onplanet. Since he admitted his un-
willingness to trust any instrumental reading on the ship, he had to
admit her point that only material evidence would show that they had
actually arrived at their destination, M-60-340-nolo. If they were going
to have to spend the next seventeen years traveling back to Ve in real
time, it would be nice to have something to show for it, even if only
a handful of slime.

He perceived this discussion as perfectly rational.

It was, however, interrupted by outbursts of egoizing not char-
acteristic of the crew.

"If you're going, go!" Shan said.

"Don't give me orders," Tai said.

"Somebody's got to stay in control here," Shan said.

"Not the men!" Tai said.

"Not the Terrans," Karth said. "Have you people no self-respect?"

"Stress," Gveter said. "Come on, Tai, Betton, all right, let's go,
all right?"

In the lander, everything was clear to Gveter. One thing happened
after another just as it should. Lander operation is very simple, and
he asked Betton to take them down. The boy did so. Tai sat, tense
and compact as always, her strong fists clenched on her knees. Betton
managed the little ship with aplomb, and sat back, tense also, but
dignified: "We're down," he said.

"No, we're not," Tai said.

"It—it says 'contact,' " Betton said, losing his assurance.

"An excellent landing," Gveter said. "Never even felt it." He was running the usual tests. Everything was in order. Outside the lander ports pressed a brownish darkness, a gloom. When Betton put on the outside lights the atmosphere, like a dark fog, diffused the light into a useless glare.

"Tests all tally with survey reports," Gveter said. "Will you go out, Tai, or use the servos?"

"Out," she said.

"Out," Betton echoed.

Gveter, assuming the formal crew role of Support, which one of them would have assumed if he had been going out, assisted them to lock their helmets and decontaminate their suits; he opened the hatch series for them, and watched them on the vid and from the port as they climbed down from the outer hatch. Betton went first. His slight figure, elongated by the whitish suit, was luminous in the weak glare of the lights. He walked a few steps from the ship, turned, and waited. Tai was stepping off the ladder. She seemed to grow very short—did she kneel down? Gveter looked from the port to the vid screen and back. She was shrinking? Sinking—she must be sinking into the surface—which could not be solid, then, but bog, or some suspension, like quicksand—but Betton had walked on it and was walking back to her, two steps, three steps, on the ground which Gveter could not see clearly but which must be solid, and which must be holding Betton up because he was lighter—but no, Tai must have stepped into a hole, a trench of some kind, for he could see her only from the waist up now, her legs hidden in the dark bog or fog, but she was moving, moving quickly, going right away from the lander and from Betton.

"Bring them back," Shan said, and Gveter said on the suit intercom, "Please return to the lander, Betton and Tai." Betton at once started up the ladder, then turned to look for his mother. A dim blotch that might be her helmet showed in the brown gloom, almost beyond the suffusion of light from the lander.

"Please come in, Betton. Please return, Tai."

The whitish suit flickered up the ladder, while Betton's voice in the intercom pleaded, "Tai—Tai, come back—Gveter, should I go after her?"

"No. Tai, please return at once to lander."

The boy's crew integrity held; he came up into the lander and watched from the outer hatch, as Gveter watched from the port. The vid had lost her. The pallid blotch sank into the formless murk.

Gveter perceived that the instruments recorded that the lander had sunk 3.2 meters since contact with planet surface and was continuing to sink at an increasing rate.

"What is the surface, Betton?"

"Like muddy ground—where is she?"

"Please return at once, Tai!"

"Please return to *Shoby*, Lander One and all crew," said the ship intercom; it was Tai's voice. "This is Tai," it said. "Please return at once to ship, lander and all crew."

"Stay in suit, in decon, please, Betton," Gveter said. "I'm sealing the hatch."

"But—all right," said the boy's voice.

Gveter took the lander up, decontaminating it and Betton's suit on the way. He perceived that Betton and Shan came with him through the hatch series into the *Shoby* and along the halls to the bridge, and that Karth, Sweet Today, Shan, and Tai were on the bridge.

Betton ran to his mother and stopped; he did not put out his hands to her. His face was immobile, as if made of wax or wood.

"Were you frightened?" she asked. "What happened down there?" And she looked to Gveter for an explanation.

Gveter perceived nothing. Unduring a nonperiod of no long, he perceived nothing was had happening happened that had not happened. Lost, he groped, lost, he found the word, the word that saved—"You—" he said, his tongue thick, dumb—"You called us."

It seemed that she denied, but it did not matter. What mattered? Shan was talking. Shan could tell. "Nobody called, Gveter," he said. "You and Betton went out, I was Support; when I realized I couldn't get the lander stable, that there's something funny about that surface, I called you back into the lander, and we came up."

All Gveter could say was, "Insubstantial . . ."

"But Tai came—" Betton began, and stopped. Gveter perceived that the boy moved away from his mother's denying touch. What mattered?

"Nobody went down," Sweet Today said. After a silence and before it, she said, "There is no down to go to."

Gveter tried to find another word, but there was none. He perceived outside the main port a brownish, murky convexity, through which, as he looked intently, he saw small stars shining.

He found a word then, the wrong word. "Lost," he said, and, speaking, perceived how the ship's lights dimmed slowly into a brownish murk, faded, darkened, were gone, while all the soft hum and busyness of the ship's systems died away into the real silence that was always there. But there was nothing there. Nothing had happened. We are at Ve Port! he tried with all his will to say; but there was no saying.

The suns burns through my flesh, Lidi said.

I am the suns, said Sweet Today. Not I, all is.

Don't breathe! cried Oreth.

It is death, Shan said. What I feared, is: nothing.

Nothing, they said.

Unbreathing, the ghosts flitted, shifted, in the ghost shell of a cold, dark hull floating near a world of brown fog, an unreal planet. They spoke, but there were no voices. There is no sound in vacuum, nor in nontime.

In her cabined solitude, Lidi felt the gravity lighten to the half-G of the ship's core mass; she saw them, the nearer and the farther suns, burn through the dark gauze of the walls and hulls and the bedding and her body. The brightest, the sun of this system, floated directly under her navel. She did not know its name.

I am the darkness between the suns, one said.

I am nothing, one said.

I am you, one said.

You— one said—You—

And breathed, and reached out, and spoke: "Listen!" Crying out to the other, to the others, "Listen!"

"We have always known this. This is where we have always been, will always be, at the hearth, at the center. There is nothing to be afraid of, after all."

"I can't breathe," one said.

"I am not breathing," one said.

"There is nothing to breathe," one said.

"You are, you are breathing, please breathe!" said another.

"We're here, at the hearth," said another.

Oreth had laid the fire, Karth lit it. As it caught they both said softly, in Karhidish, "Praise also the light, and creation unfinished."

The fire caught with spark spits, crackles, sudden flares. It did not go out. It burned. The others grouped round.

They were nowhere, but they were nowhere together; the ship was dead, but they were in the ship. A dead ship cools off fairly quickly, but not immediately. Close the doors, come in by the fire; keep the cold night out, before we go to bed.

Karth went with Rig to persuade Lidi from her starry vault. The navigator would not get up. "It's my fault," she said.

"Don't egoize," Karth said mildly. "How could it be?"

"I don't know. I want to stay here," Lidi muttered. Then Karth begged her: "Oh, Lidi, not alone!"

"How else?" the old woman asked coldly.

But she was ashamed of herself, then, and ashamed of her guilt trip, and growled, "Oh, all right." She heaved herself up and wrapped a blanket around her body and followed Karth and Rig. The child carried a little biolume; it glowed in the black corridors, just as the plants of the aerobic tanks lived on, metabolizing, making an air to breathe, for a while. The light moved before her like a star among the stars through darkness to the room full of books, where the fire burned in the stone hearth. "Hello, children," Lidi said. "What are we doing here?"

"Telling stories," Sweet Today replied.

Shan had a little voice-recorder notebook in his hand.

"Does it work?" Lidi inquired.

"Seems to. We thought we'd tell . . . what happened," Shan said, squinting the narrow black eyes in his narrow black face at the firelight. "Each of us. What we—what it seemed like, seems like, to us. So that . . ."

"As a record, yes. In case . . . How funny that it works, though, your notebook. When nothing else does."

"It's voice-activated," Shan said absently. "So. Go on, Gveter."

Gveter finished telling his version of the expedition to the planet's surface. "We didn't even bring back samples," he ended. "I never thought of them."

"Shan went with you, not me," Tai said.

"You did go, and I did," the boy said with a certainty that stopped her. "And we did go outside. And Shan and Gveter were Support, in the lander. And I took samples. They're in the Stasis closet."

"I don't know if Shan was in the lander or not," Gveter said, rubbing his forehead painfully.

"Where would the lander have gone?" Shan said. "Nothing is out there—we're nowhere—outside time, is all I can think— But when one of you tells how they saw it, it seems as if it was that way, but then the next one changes the story, and I . . ."

Oreth shivered, drawing closer to the fire.

"I never believed this damn thing would work," said Lidi, bearlike in the dark cave of her blanket.

"Not understanding it was the trouble," Karth said. "None of us understood how it would work, not even Gveter. Isn't that true?"

"Yes," Gveter said.

"So that if our psychic interaction with it affected the process—"

"Or *is* the process," said Sweet Today, "so far as we're concerned."

"Do you mean," Lidi said in a tone of deep existential disgust, "that we have to *believe* in it to make it work?"

"You have to believe in yourself in order to act, don't you?" Tai said.

"No," the navigator said. "Absolutely not. I don't believe in myself. I *know* some things. Enough to go on."

"An analogy," Gveter offered. "The effective action of a crew depends on the members perceiving themselves as a crew—you could call it believing in the crew, or just *being* it— Right? So, maybe, to churten, we—we conscious ones—maybe it depends on our consciously perceiving ourselves as . . . as transilient—as being in the other place—the destination?"

"We lost our crewness, certainly, for a—are there whiles?" Karth said. "We fell apart."

"We lost the thread," Shan said.

"Lost," Oreth said meditatively, laying another massive, half-weightless log on the fire, volleying sparks up into the chimney, slow stars.

"We lost—what?" Sweet Today asked.

No one answered for a while.

"When I can see the sun through the carpet . . ." Lidi said.

"So can I," Betton said, very low.

"I can see Ve Port," said Rig. "And everything. I can tell you what I can see. I can see Liden if I look. And my room on the *Oneblin*. And—"

"First, Rig," said Sweet Today, "tell us what happened."

"All right," Rig said agreeably. "Hold on to me harder, maba, I start floating. Well, we went to the liberry, me and Asten and Betton, and Betton was Elder Sib, and the adults were on the bridge, and I was going to go to sleep like I do when we naffle-fly, but before I even lay down there was the brown planet and Ve Port and both the suns and everywhere else, and you could see through everything, but Asten couldn't. But I can."

"We never went *anywhere*," Asten said. "Rig tells stories all the time."

"We all tell stories all the time, Asten," Karth said.

"Not dumb ones like Rig's!"

"Even dumber," said Oreth. "What we need . . . What we need is . . ."

"We need to know," Shan said, "what transilience is, and we don't, because we never did it before, nobody ever did it before."

"Not in the flesh," said Lidi.

"We need to know what's—real—what happened, *whether* anything happened—" Tai gestured at the cave of firelight around them and the dark beyond it. "Where are we? Are we here? Where is here? What's the story?"

"We have to tell it," Sweet Today said. "Recount it. Relate it. . . . Like Rig. Asten, how does a story begin?"

"A thousand winters ago, a thousand miles away," the child said; and Shan murmured, "Once upon a time . . ."

"There was a ship called the *Shoby*," said Sweet Today, "on a test flight, trying out the churten, with a crew of ten.

"Their names were Rig, Asten, Betton, Karth, Oreth, Lidi, Tai, Shan, Gveter, and Sweet Today. And they related their story, each one and together . . ."

There was silence, the silence that was always there, except for the stir and crackle of the fire and the small sounds of their breathing, their movements, until one of them spoke at last, telling the story.

"The boy and his mother," said the light, pure voice, "were the first human beings ever to set foot on that world."

Again the silence; and again a voice.

"Although she wished . . . she realized that she really hoped the thing wouldn't work, because it would make her skills, her whole life, obsolete . . . all the same she really wanted to learn how to use it, too, if she could, if she wasn't too old to learn . . ."

A long, softly throbbing pause, and another voice.

"They went from world to world, and each time they lost the world they left, lost it in time dilation, their friends getting old and dying while they were in NAFAL flight. If there were a way to live in one's own time, and yet move among the worlds, they wanted to try it . . ."

"Staking everything on it," the next voice took up the story, "because nothing works except what we give our souls to, nothing's safe except what we put at risk."

A while, a little while; and a voice.

"It was like a game. It was like we were still in the *Shoby* at Ve Port just waiting before we went into NAFAL flight. But it was like we were at the brown planet too. At the same time. And one of them was just pretend, and the other one wasn't, but I didn't know which. So it was like when you pretend in a game. But I didn't want to play. I didn't know how."

Another voice.

"If the churten principle were proved to be applicable to actual transilience of living, conscious beings, it would be a great event in the mind of his people—for all people. A new understanding. A new partnership. A new way of being in the universe. A wider freedom. . . . He wanted that very much. He wanted to be one of the crew that first formed that partnership, the first people to be able to think this thought, and to . . . to relate it. But also he was afraid of it. Maybe it wasn't a true relation, maybe false, maybe only a dream. He didn't know."

It was not so cold, so dark, at their backs, as they sat round the fire. Was it the waves of Liden, hushing on the sand?

Another voice.

"She thought a lot about her people, too. About guilt, and expiation, and sacrifice. She wanted a lot to be on this flight that might give people—more freedom. But it was different from what she thought it would be. What happened—what *happened* wasn't what mattered. What mattered was that she came to be with people who gave *her* freedom. Without guilt. She wanted to stay with them, to be crew with them . . . And with her son. Who was the first human being to set foot on an unknown world."

A long silence; but not deep, only as deep as the soft drum of the ship's systems, steady and unconscious as the circulation of the blood.

Another voice.

"They were thoughts in the mind; what else had they ever been? So they could be in Ve and at the brown planet, and desiring flesh and entire spirit, and illusion and reality, all at once, as they'd always been. When he remembered this, his confusion and fear ceased, for he knew that they couldn't be lost."

"They got lost. But they found the way," said another voice, soft above the hum and hushing of the ship's systems, in the warm fresh air and light inside the solid walls and hulls.

Only nine voices had spoken, and they looked for the tenth; but the tenth had gone to sleep, thumb in mouth.

"That story was told and is yet to be told," the mother said. "Go on. I'll churten here with Rig."

They left those two by the fire, and went to the bridge, and then to the hatches to invite on board a crowd of anxious scientists, engineers, and officials of Ve Port and the Ekumen, whose instruments had been assuring them that the *Shoby* had vanished, forty-four minutes ago, into nonexistence, into silence. "What happened?" they asked. "What happened?" And the Shobies looked at one another and said, "Well, it's quite a story . . ."

# Bears Discover Fire

. . .

## *Terry Bisson*

Attending science fiction conventions over the past several years, I've learned that the ideal way to experience a Terry Bisson story is to hear him read it aloud. He is futuristic fiction's oral tradition. As you're about to discover, Bisson's prose works wonderfully on the printed page, and yet there's something magical in the way that natives of Owensboro, Kentucky, enact the English language, something that does singular justice to the fabulous, the funny, the earnestly weird. (If you can't arrange to hear Bisson reading Bisson, you should at least try to hear him reading his spiritual mentor, R. A. Lafferty: he knows how to make that particular eccentric sing, too.)

Novels by Terry Bisson include *Talking Man*, a World Fantasy Award nominee that tells of the first auto trip to the North Pole; *Fire on the Mountain*, which dramatizes what might have happened if John Brown's raid on Harper's Ferry had succeeded; and *Voyage to the Red Planet*, an idiosyncratic space adventure. His short stories have appeared in *Omni*, *Isaac Asimov's Science Fiction Magazine*, and *The Magazine of Fantasy and Science Fiction*. Bisson's nonfiction efforts include *Hauling Up the Morning*, the book of writings and art by U.S. political prisoners he edited for Red Sea Press; *Nat Turner, Slave Revolt Leader*, a young-adult biography; and *Car Talk with Click and Clack, The Tappet Brothers*, coauthored with National Public Radio's popular call-in mechanics, Tom and Ray Magliozzi.

" 'Bears Discover Fire' is one of those stories you think of while you're driving," Bisson says of his Nebula-winning tale. "It turned out (to my surprise) to be my fictional way of dealing with a series of deaths in my family back in Kentucky, particularly of my mother, who inclined me toward literature, and also of my uncle, J. Sam, who filled my head with cars. J. Sam had the dream about the doctors, and I sat up with my mother while she died. Neither chewed tobacco. The bear stuff is all made up."

I was driving with my brother, the preacher, and my nephew, the preacher's son, on I-65 just north of Bowling Green when we got a flat. It was Sunday night and we had been to visit Mother at the

Home. We were in my car. The flat caused what you might call knowing groans since, as the old-fashioned one in my family (so they tell me), I fix my own tires, and my brother is always telling me to get radials and quit buying old tires.

But if you know how to mount and fix tires yourself, you can pick them up for almost nothing.

Since it was a left rear tire, I pulled over to the left, onto the median grass. The way my Caddy stumbled to a stop, I figured the tire was ruined. "I guess there's no need asking if you have any of that FlatFix in the trunk," said Wallace.

"Here, son, hold the light," I said to Wallace Jr. He's old enough to want to help and not old enough (yet) to think he knows it all. If I'd married and had kids, he's the kind I'd have wanted.

An old Caddy has a big trunk that tends to fill up like a shed. Mine's a '56. Wallace was wearing his Sunday shirt, so he didn't offer to help while I pulled magazines, fishing tackle, a wooden toolbox, some old clothes, a comealong wrapped in a grass sack, and a tobacco sprayer out of the way, looking for my jack. The spare looked a little soft.

The light went out. "Shake it, son," I said.

It went back on. The bumper jack was long gone, but I carry a little quarter-ton hydraulic. I found it under Mother's old *Southern Livings*, 1978–1986. I had been meaning to drop them at the dump. If Wallace hadn't been along, I'd have let Wallace Jr. position the jack under the axle, but I got on my knees and did it myself. There's nothing wrong with a boy learning to change a tire. Even if you're not going to fix and mount them, you're still going to have to change a few in this life. The light went off again before I had the wheel off the ground. I was surprised at how dark the night was already. It was late October and beginning to be cool. "Shake it again, son," I said.

It went back on but it was weak. Flickery.

"With radials you just don't *have* flats," Wallace explained in that voice he uses when he's talking to a number of people at once; in this case, Wallace Jr. and myself. "And even when you *do*, you just squirt them with this stuff called FlatFix and you just drive on. $3.95 the can."

"Uncle Bobby can fix a tire hisself," said Wallace Jr., out of loyalty I presume.

"*Himself*," I said from halfway under the car. If it was up to Wallace, the boy would talk like what Mother used to call "a helock from the gorges of the mountains." But drive on radials.

"Shake that light again," I said. It was about gone. I spun the lugs off into the hubcap and pulled the wheel. The tire had blown out along the sidewall. "Won't be fixing this one," I said. Not that I cared. I have a pile as tall as a man out by the barn.

The light went out again, then came back better than ever as I was fitting the spare over the lugs. "Much better," I said. There was a flood of dim orange flickery light. But when I turned to find the lug nuts, I was surprised to see that the flashlight the boy was holding was dead. The light was coming from two bears at the edge of the trees, holding torches. They were big, three-hundred-pounders, standing about five feet tall. Wallace Jr. and his father had seen them and were standing perfectly still. It's best not to alarm bears.

I fished the lugs out of the hubcap and spun them on. I usually like to put a little oil on them, but this time I let it go. I reached under the car and let the jack down and pulled it out. I was relieved to see that the spare was high enough to drive on. I put the jack and the lug wrench and the flat into the trunk. Instead of replacing the hubcap, I put it in there too. All this time, the bears never made a move. They just held the torches, whether out of curiosity or helpfulness, there was no way of knowing. It looked like there may have been more bears behind them, in the trees.

Opening three doors at once, we got into the car and drove off. Wallace was the first to speak. "Looks like bears have discovered fire," he said.

■ ■ ■

When we first took Mother to the Home almost four years (forty-seven months) ago, she told Wallace and me she was ready to die. "Don't worry about me, boys," she whispered, pulling us both down so the nurse wouldn't hear. "I've drove a million miles and I'm ready to pass over to the other shore. I won't have long to linger here." She drove a consolidated school bus for thirty-nine years. Later, after Wallace left, she told me about her dream. A bunch of doctors were sitting around in a circle discussing her case. One said, "We've done all we can for her, boys, let's let her go." They all turned their hands up and smiled. When she didn't die that fall she seemed disappointed, though as spring came she forgot about it, as old people will.

In addition to taking Wallace and Wallace Jr. to see Mother on Sunday nights, I go myself on Tuesdays and Thursdays. I usually find her sitting in front of the TV, even though she doesn't watch it. The nurses keep it on all the time. They say the old folks like the flickering. It soothes them down.

"What's this I hear about bears discovering fire?" she said on Tuesday. "It's true," I told her as I combed her long white hair with the shell comb Wallace had brought her from Florida. Monday there had been a story in the *Louisville Courier-Journal*, and Tuesday one on NBC or CBS Nightly News. People were seeing bears all over the state, and in Virginia as well. They had quit hibernating and were apparently planning to spend the winter in the medians of the interstates. There have always been bears in the mountains of Virginia, but not here in western Kentucky, not for almost a hundred years. The last one was killed when Mother was a girl. The theory in the *Courier-Journal* was that they were following I-65 down from the forests of Michigan and Canada, but one old man from Allen County (interviewed on nationwide TV) said that there had always been a few bears left back in the hills, and they had come out to join the others now that they had discovered fire.

"They don't hibernate anymore," I said. "They make a fire and keep it going all winter."

"I declare," Mother said. "What'll they think of next!" The nurse came to take her tobacco away, which is the signal for bedtime.

■ ■ ■

Every October, Wallace Jr. stays with me while his parents go to camp. I realize how backward that sounds, but there it is. My brother is a Minister (House of the Righteous Way, Reformed) but he makes two thirds of his living in real estate. He and Elizabeth go to a Christian Success Retreat in South Carolina, where people from all over the country practice selling things to one another. I know what it's like not because they've ever bothered to tell me, but because I've seen the Revolving Equity Success Plan ads late at night on TV.

The schoolbus let Wallace Jr. off at my house on Wednesday, the day they left. The boy doesn't have to pack much of a bag when he stays with me. He has his own room here. As the eldest of our family, I hung on to the old home place near Smiths Grove. It's getting run-down, but Wallace Jr. and I don't mind. He has his own room in Bowling Green, too, but since Wallace and Elizabeth move to a different house every three months (part of the Plan), he keeps his .22 and his comics, the stuff that's important to a boy his age, in his room here at the home place. It's the room his dad and I used to share.

Wallace Jr. is twelve. I found him sitting on the back porch that overlooks the interstate when I got home from work. I sell crop insurance.

After I changed clothes I showed him how to break the bead on a tire two ways, with a hammer and by backing a car over it. Like making sorghum, fixing tires by hand is a dying art. The boy caught on fast, though. "Tomorrow I'll show you how to mount your tire with the hammer and a tire iron," I said.

"What I wish is I could see the bears," he said. He was looking across the field to I-65, where the northbound lanes cut off the corner of our property. From the house at night, sometimes the traffic sounds like a waterfall.

"Can't see their fire in the daytime," I said. "But wait till tonight." That night CBS or NBC (I forget which is which) did a special on the bears, which were becoming a story of nationwide interest. They were seen in Kentucky, West Virginia, Missouri, Illinois (southern), and, of course, Virginia. There have always been bears in Virginia. Some characters there were even talking about hunting them. A scientist said they were heading into the states where there is some snow but not too much, and where there is enough timber in the medians for firewood. He had gone in with a video camera, but his shots were just blurry figures sitting around a fire. Another scientist said the bears were attracted by the berries on a new bush that grew only in the medians of the interstates. He claimed this berry was the first new species in recent history, brought about by the mixing of seeds along the highway. He ate one on TV, making a face, and called it a "newberry." A climatic ecologist said that the warm winters (there was no snow last winter in Nashville, and only one flurry in Louisville) had changed the bears' hibernation cycle, and now they were able to remember things from year to year. "Bears may have discovered fire centuries ago," he said, "but forgot it." Another theory was that they had discovered (or remembered) fire when Yellowstone burned, several years ago.

The TV showed more guys talking about bears than it showed bears, and Wallace Jr. and I lost interest. After the supper dishes were done I took the boy out behind the house and down to our fence. Across the interstate and through the trees, we could see the light of the bears' fire. Wallace Jr. wanted to go back to the house and get his .22 and go shoot one, and I explained why that would be wrong. "Besides," I said, "a .22 wouldn't do much more to a bear than make it mad.

"Besides," I added, "it's illegal to hunt in the medians."

■ ■ ■

The only trick to mounting a tire by hand, once you have beaten or pried it onto the rim, is setting the bead. You do this by setting the tire upright, sitting on it, and bouncing it up and down between your legs while the air goes in. When the bead sets on the rim, it makes a satisfying "pop." On Thursday, I kept Wallace Jr. home from school and showed him how to do this until he got it right. Then we climbed our fence and crossed the field to get a look at the bears.

In northern Virginia, according to "Good Morning America," the bears were keeping their fires going all day long. Here in western Kentucky, though, it was still warm for late October and they only stayed around the fires at night. Where they went and what they did in the daytime, I don't know. Maybe they were watching from the newberry bushes as Wallace Jr. and I climbed the government fence and crossed the northbound lanes. I carried an ax, and Wallace Jr. brought his .22, not because he wanted to kill a bear but because a boy likes to carry some kind of a gun. The median was all tangled with brush and vines under the maples, oaks, and sycamores. Even though we were only a hundred yards from the house, I had never been there, and neither had anyone else that I knew of. It was like a created country. We found a path in the center and followed it down across a slow, short stream that flowed out of one grate and into another. The tracks in the gray mud were the first bear signs we saw. There was a musty but not really unpleasant smell. In a clearing under a big hollow beech, where the fire had been, we found nothing but ashes. Logs were drawn up in a rough circle and the smell was stronger. I stirred the ashes and found enough coals to start a new flame, so I banked them back the way they had been left.

I cut a little firewood and stacked it to one side, just to be neighborly.

Maybe the bears were watching us from the bushes even then. There's no way to know. I tasted one of the newberries and spit it out. It was so sweet it was sour, just the sort of thing you would imagine a bear would like.

■ ■ ■

That evening after supper I asked Wallace Jr. if he might want to go with me to visit Mother. I wasn't surprised when he said yes. Kids have more consideration than folks give them credit for. We found her sitting on the concrete front porch of the Home, watching the cars go by on I-65. The nurse said she had been agitated all day. I wasn't surprised by that, either. Every fall as the leaves change, she gets restless, maybe the word is hopeful, again. I brought her into the dayroom and combed her long white hair. "Nothing but bears on TV anymore," the nurse complained, flipping the channels. Wallace Jr. picked up the remote after the nurse left, and we watched a CBS or NBC Special Report about some hunters in Virginia who had gotten their houses torched. The TV interviewed a hunter and his wife whose $117,500 Shenandoah Valley home had burned. She blamed the bears. He didn't blame the bears, but he was suing for compensation from the state since he had a valid hunting license. The state hunting commissioner came on and said the possession of a hunting license didn't prohibit (enjoin, I think, was the word he used) *the hunted* from striking back. I thought that was a pretty liberal view for a state commissioner. Of course, he had a vested interest in not paying off. I'm not a hunter myself.

"Don't bother coming on Sunday," Mother told Wallace Jr. with a wink. "I've drove a million miles and I've got one hand on the gate." I'm used to her saying stuff like that, especially in the fall, but I was afraid it would upset the boy. In fact, he looked worried after we left and I asked him what was wrong.

"How could she have drove a million miles?" he asked. She had told him 48 miles a day for 39 years, and he had worked it out on his calculator to be 336,960 miles.

"Have *driven*," I said. "And it's 48 in the morning and 48 in the afternoon. Plus there were the football trips. Plus, old folks exaggerate a little." Mother was the first woman school bus driver in the state. She did it every day and raised a family, too. Dad just farmed.

■ ■ ■

I usually get off the interstate at Smiths Grove, but that night I drove north all the way to Horse Cave and doubled back so Wallace Jr. and I could see the bears' fires. There were not as many as you would think from the TV—one every six or seven miles, hidden back in a clump of trees or under a rocky ledge. Probably they look for water as well as wood. Wallace Jr. wanted to stop, but it's against the law to stop on the interstate and I was afraid the state police would run us off.

There was a card from Wallace in the mailbox. He and Elizabeth were doing fine and having a wonderful time. Not a word about Wallace Jr., but the boy didn't seem to mind. Like most kids his age, he doesn't really enjoy going places with his parents.

On Saturday afternoon the Home called my office (Burley Belt Drought & Hail) and left word that Mother was gone. I was on the road. I work Saturdays. It's the only day a lot of part-time farmers are home. My heart literally missed a beat when I called in and got the message, but only a beat. I had long been prepared. "It's a blessing," I said when I got the nurse on the phone.

"You don't understand," the nurse said. "Not *passed* away, gone. *Ran* away, gone. Your mother has escaped." Mother had gone through the door at the end of the corridor when no one was looking, wedging the door with her comb and taking a bedspread that belonged to the Home. What about her tobacco? I asked. It was gone. That was a sure sign she was planning to stay away. I was in Franklin, and it took me less than an hour to get to the Home on I-65. The nurse told me that Mother had been acting more and more confused lately. Of course they are going to say that. We looked around the grounds, which are only a half acre with no trees between the interstate and a soybean field. Then they had me leave a message at the Sheriff's office. I would have to keep paying for her care until she was officially listed as Missing, which would be Monday.

It was dark by the time I got back to the house, and Wallace Jr.

was fixing supper. This just involves opening a few cans, already selected and grouped together with a rubber band. I told him his grandmother had gone, and he nodded, saying, "She told us she would be." I called South Carolina and left a message. There was nothing more to be done. I sat down and tried to watch TV, but there was nothing on. Then, I looked out the back door, and saw the firelight twinkling through the trees across the northbound lane of I-65, and realized I just might know where to find her.

■ ■ ■

It was definitely getting colder, so I got my jacket. I told the boy to wait by the phone in case the Sheriff called, but when I looked back, halfway across the field, there he was behind me. He didn't have a jacket. I let him catch up. He was carrying his .22 and I made him leave it leaning against our fence. It was harder climbing the government fence in the dark, at my age, than it had been in the daylight. I am sixty-one. The highway was busy with cars heading south and trucks heading north.

Crossing the shoulder, I got my pants cuff wet on the long grass, already wet with dew. It is actually bluegrass.

The first few feet into the trees it was pitch black and the boy grabbed my hand. Then it got lighter. At first I thought it was the moon, but it was the high beams shining like moonlight into the treetops, allowing Wallace Jr. and me to pick our way through the brush. We soon found the path and its familiar bear smell.

I was wary of approaching the bears at night. If we stayed on the path we might run into one in the dark, but if we went through the bushes we might be seen as intruders. I wondered if maybe we shouldn't have brought the gun.

We stayed on the path. The light seemed to drip down from the canopy of the woods like rain. The going was easy, especially if we didn't try to look at the path but let our feet find their own way.

Then through the trees I saw their fire.

■ ■ ■

The fire was mostly of sycamore and beech branches, the kind of fire that puts out very little heat or light and lots of smoke. The bears hadn't learned the ins and outs of wood yet. They did okay at tending it, though. A large cinnamon brown northern-looking bear was poking the fire with a stick, adding a branch now and then from a pile at his side. The others sat around in a loose circle on the logs. Most were smaller black or honey bears; one was a mother with cubs. Some were eating berries from a hubcap. Not eating, but just watching the fire, my mother sat among them with the bedspread from the Home around her shoulders.

If the bears noticed us, they didn't let on. Mother patted a spot right next to her on the log and I sat down. A bear moved over to let Wallace Jr. sit on her other side.

The bear smell is rank but not unpleasant, once you get used to it. It's not like a barn smell, but wilder. I leaned over to whisper something to Mother and she shook her head. *It would be rude to whisper around these creatures that don't possess the power of speech,* she let me know without speaking. Wallace Jr. was silent too. Mother shared the bedspread with us and we sat for what seemed hours, looking into the fire.

The big bear tended the fire, breaking up the dry branches by holding one end and stepping on them, like people do. He was good at keeping it going at the same level. Another bear poked the fire from time to time but the others left it alone. It looked like only a few of the bears knew how to use fire, and were carrying the others along. But isn't that how it is with everything? Every once in a while, a smaller bear walked into the circle of firelight with an armload of wood and dropped it onto the pile. Median wood has a silvery cast, like driftwood.

Wallace Jr. isn't fidgety like a lot of kids. I found it pleasant to sit and stare into the fire. I took a little piece of Mother's Red Man, though I don't generally chew. It was no different from visiting her at the Home, only more interesting, because of the bears. There were about eight or ten of them. Inside the fire itself, things weren't so dull, either: little dramas were being played out as fiery chambers were created and then destroyed in a crashing of sparks. My imagination ran wild. I looked around the circle at the bears and wondered what *they* saw. Some had their eyes closed. Though they were gathered together, their spirits still seemed solitary, as if each bear was sitting alone in front of its own fire.

The hubcap came around and we all took some newberries. I

don't know about Mother, but I just pretended to eat mine. Wallace Jr. made a face and spit his out. When he went to sleep, I wrapped the bedspread around all three of us. It was getting colder and we were not provided, like the bears, with fur. I was ready to go home, but not Mother. She pointed up toward the canopy of trees, where a light was spreading, and then pointed to herself. Did she think it was angels approaching from on high? It was only the high beams of some southbound truck, but she seemed mighty pleased. Holding her hand, I felt it grow colder and colder in mine.

■ ■ ■

Wallace Jr. woke me up by tapping on my knee. It was past dawn, and his grandmother had died sitting on the log between us. The fire was banked up and the bears were gone and someone was crashing straight through the woods, ignoring the path. It was Wallace. The state troopers were right behind him. He was wearing a white shirt, and I realized it was Sunday morning. Underneath his sadness on learning of Mother's death, he looked peeved.

The troopers were sniffing the air and nodding. The bear smell was still strong. Wallace and I wrapped Mother in the bedspread and started with her body back out to the highway. The troopers stayed behind and scattered the bears' fire ashes and flung their firewood away into the bushes. It seemed a petty thing to do. They were like bears themselves, each one solitary in his own uniform.

There was Wallace's Olds 98 on the median, with its radial tires looking squashed on the grass. In front of it there was a police car with a trooper standing beside it, and behind it a funeral home hearse, also an Olds 98.

"First report we've had of them bothering old folks," the trooper said to Wallace. "That's not hardly what happened at all," I said, but nobody asked me to explain. They have their own procedures. Two men in suits got out of the hearse and opened the rear door. That to me was the point at which Mother departed this life. After we put her in, I put my arms around the boy. He was shivering even though it wasn't that cold. Sometimes death will do that, especially at dawn, with the police around and the grass wet, even when it comes as a friend.

We stood for a minute watching the cars and trucks pass. "It's a blessing," Wallace said. It's surprising how much traffic there is at 6:22 AM.

■ ■ ■

That afternoon, I went back to the median and cut a little firewood to replace what the troopers had flung away. I could see the fire through the trees that night.

It went back two nights later, after the funeral. The fire was going and it was the same bunch of bears, as far as I could tell. I sat around with them a while but it seemed to make them nervous, so I went home. I had taken a handful of newberries from the hubcap, and on Sunday I went with the boy and arranged them on Mother's grave. I tried again, but it's no use, you can't eat them.

Unless you're a bear.

# Tower of Babylon

### • • •

## *Ted Chiang*

Ted Chiang, I am told, is a modest and self-effacing young man, but this trait evidently does not incline him toward modest and self-effacing subjects. The last story of his I read, "Division by Zero," roundly announces the death of what we're accustomed to calling mathematics. In the Nebula-winning novelette you're about to experience, some postdiluvian miners break into heaven's anteroom. What will Chiang do for an encore? A transcript of God's first press conference, complete with equations?

Born and raised in Port Jefferson, New York, Chiang holds a degree in computer science from Brown University. In 1989 he attended the Clarion Science Fiction Writers Workshop, a program that has incubated and hatched more of today's functioning SFWA members than all its rivals combined. Since gracing the pages of *Omni* with "Tower of Babylon," Chiang has enjoyed sales to *Asimov's* and *Full Spectrum 3* (source of "Division by Zero").

"The inspiration for this story came during a conversation with a friend," Chiang tells us, "when he mentioned the version of the Tower of Babel myth he'd been taught in Hebrew school. I knew only the Old Testament account, and it had never made a big impression on me. But in the full-length version, the tower is so tall that it takes a year to climb; when a man falls to his death, no one mourns, but when a brick is dropped, the workers at the top weep because it will take a year to replace it.

"I suppose the original storyteller was questioning the morality of the project. For me, however, the tale conjured up images of a fantastic city in the sky, reminiscent of Magritte's *Castle in the Pyrenees*. I was astonished at the audacity, the chutzpah of the person who had imagined such a thing.

"Readers have commented on the science-fictional way this story extrapolates from a primitive world view. I must admit I didn't notice that aspect of the story while writing it. (Perhaps because I was acutely aware of how many scientific laws I was breaking; the Babylonians themselves knew enough physics and astronomy to recognize this story as utter fantasy.) What I *did* think was science-fictional about the story was the rationalistic position it takes on the existence of God. If you believe God exists, you can easily interpret 'the universe in a way that supports your belief. But if you believe the universe is purely mechanistic, you can find abundant evidence for that view too."

Were the tower to be laid down across the plain of Shinar, it would be two days' journey to walk from one end to the other. While the tower stands, it takes a full month and a half to climb from its base to its summit, if a man walks unburdened. But few men climb the tower with empty hands; the pace of most men is much slowed by the cart of bricks that they pull behind them. Four months pass between the day a brick is loaded onto a cart and the day it is taken off to form a part of the tower.

■ ■ ■

Hillalum had spent all his life in Elam, and knew Babylon only as a buyer of Elam's copper. The copper ingots were carried on boats that traveled down the Karun to the Lower Sea, headed for the Euphrates. Hillalum and the other miners traveled overland, alongside a merchant's caravan of loaded onagers. They walked along a dusty path leading down from the plateau, across the plains, to the green fields sectioned by canals and dikes.

None of them had seen the tower before. It became visible when they were still leagues away: a line as thin as a strand of flax, wavering in the shimmering air, rising up from the crust of mud that was Babylon itself. As they drew closer, the crust grew into the mighty city walls, but all they saw was the tower. When they did lower their gazes to the level of the river plain, they saw the marks the tower had made outside the city: the Euphrates itself now flowed at the bottom of a wide, sunken bed, dug to provide clay for bricks. To the south of the city could be seen rows upon rows of kilns, no longer burning.

As they approached the city gates, the tower appeared more massive than anything Hillalum had ever imagined: a single column that must have been as large around as an entire temple, yet it rose so high that it shrank into invisibility. All of them walked with their heads tilted back, squinting in the sun.

Hillalum's friend Nanni prodded him with an elbow, awestruck. "We're to climb that? To the top?"

"Going *up* to dig. It seems . . . unnatural."

The miners reached the central gate in the western wall, where another caravan was leaving. While they crowded forward into the narrow strip of shade provided by the wall, their foreman Beli shouted to the gatekeepers who stood atop the gate towers. "We are the miners summoned from the land of Elam."

The gatekeepers were delighted. One called back, "You are the ones who are to dig through the vault of heaven?"

"We are."

■ ■ ■

The entire city was celebrating. The festival had begun eight days ago, when the last of the bricks were sent on their way, and would last two more. Every day and night, the city rejoiced, danced, feasted.

Along with the brickmakers were the cart pullers, men whose legs were roped with muscle from climbing the tower. Each morning a crew began its ascent; they climbed for four days, transferred their loads to the next crew of pullers, and returned to the city with empty carts on the fifth. A chain of such crews led all the way to the top of the tower, but only the bottommost celebrated with the city. For those who lived upon the tower, enough wine and meat had been sent up earlier to allow a feast to extend up the entire pillar.

In the evening, Hillalum and the other Elamite miners sat upon clay stools before a long table laden with food, one table among many laid out in the city square. The miners spoke with the pullers, asking about the tower.

Nanni said, "Someone told me that the bricklayers who work at the top of the tower wail and tear their hair when a brick is dropped, because it will take four months to replace, but no one takes notice when a man falls to his death. Is that true?"

One of the more talkative pullers, Lugatum, shook his head. "Oh no, that is only a story. There is a continuous caravan of bricks going up the tower; thousands of bricks reach the top each day. The loss of a single brick means nothing to the bricklayers." He leaned over to them. "However, there is something they value more than a man's life: a trowel."

"Why a trowel?"

"If a bricklayer drops his trowel, he can do no work until a new one is brought up. For months he cannot earn the food that he eats, so he must go into debt. The loss of a trowel is cause for much wailing. But if a man falls, and his trowel remains, men are secretly relieved. The next one to drop his trowel can pick up the extra one and continue working without incurring debt."

Hillalum was appalled, and for a frantic moment he tried to count how many picks the miners had brought. Then he realized. "That cannot be true. Why not have spare trowels brought up? Their weight would be nothing against all the bricks that go up there. And surely the loss of a man means a serious delay, unless they have an extra man at the top who is skilled at bricklaying. Without such a man, they must wait for another one to climb from the bottom."

All of the pullers roared with laughter. "We cannot fool this one," Lugatum said with much amusement. He turned to Hillalum. "So you'll begin your climb once the festival is over?"

Hillalum drank from a bowl of beer. "Yes. I've heard that we'll be joined by miners from a western land, but I haven't seen them. Do you know of them?"

"Yes, they come from a land called Egypt, but they do not mine ore as you do. They quarry stone."

"We dig stone in Elam, too," said Nanni, his mouth full of pork.

"Not as they do. They cut granite."

"Granite?" Limestone and alabaster were quarried in Elam, but not granite. "Are you certain?"

"Merchants who have traveled to Egypt say that they have stone ziggurats and temples, built with limestone and granite, huge blocks of it. And they carve giant statues from granite."

"But granite is so difficult to work."

Lugatum shrugged. "Not for them. The royal architects believe such stoneworkers may be useful when you reach the vault of heaven."

Hillalum nodded. That could be true. Who knew for certain what they would need? "Have you seen them?"

"No, they are not here yet, but they are expected in a few days' time. They may not arrive before the festival ends, though; then you Elamites will ascend alone."

"You will accompany us, won't you?"

"Yes, but only for the first four days. Then we must turn back, while you lucky ones go on."

"Why do you think us lucky?"

"I long to make the climb to the top. I once pulled with the higher crews, and reached a height of twelve days' climb, but that is as high as I have ever gone. You will go far higher." Lugatum smiled ruefully. "I envy you, that you will touch the vault of heaven."

To touch the vault of heaven. To break it open with picks. Hillalum felt uneasy at the idea. "There is no cause for envy—" he began.

"Right," said Nanni. "When we are done, all men will touch the vault of heaven."

■ ■ ■

The next morning, Hillalum went to see the tower. He stood in the giant courtyard surrounding it. There was an temple off to one side that would have been impressive if seen by itself, but it stood unnoticed beside the tower.

He could sense the utter solidity of it. According to all the tales, the tower was constructed to have a mighty strength that no ziggurat possessed; it was made of baked brick all the way through, while ordinary ziggurats were mere sun-dried mud brick, having baked brick only for the facing. The bricks were set in a bitumen mortar, which soaked into the fired clay and hardened to form a bond as strong as the bricks themselves.

The tower's base resembled the first two platforms of an ordinary ziggurat. There stood a giant square platform some two hundred cubits on a side and forty cubits high, with a triple staircase against its south face. Stacked upon that first platform was another level, a smaller platform reached only by the central stair. It was atop the second platform that the tower itself began.

It was sixty cubits on a side and rose like a square pillar that bore the weight of heaven. Around it wound a gently inclined ramp, cut into the side, that banded the tower like the leather strip wrapped around the handle of a whip. No; upon looking again, Hillalum saw that there were two ramps, and they were intertwined. The outer edge of each ramp was studded with pillars, not thick but broad, to provide some shade behind them. In running his gaze up the tower, he saw alternating bands, ramp, brick, ramp, brick, until they could no longer be distinguished. And still the tower rose up and up; farther than the eye could see; Hillalum blinked, and squinted, and grew dizzy. He stumbled backwards a couple steps, and turned away with a shudder.

Hillalum thought of the story told to him in childhood, the tale following that of the Deluge. It told of how men had once again populated all the corners of the earth, inhabiting more lands than they ever had before. How men had sailed to the edges of the world, and seen the ocean falling away into the mist to join the black waters of the Abyss far below. How men had thus realized the extent of the earth, and felt it to be small, and desired to see what lay beyond its borders, all the rest of Yahweh's Creation. How they looked skyward, and wondered about Yahweh's dwelling place, above the reservoirs that contained the waters of heaven. And how, many centuries ago, there began the construction of the tower, a pillar to heaven, a stair that men might ascend to see the works of Yahweh, and that Yahweh might descend to see the works of men.

It had always seemed inspiring to Hillalum, a tale of thousands of men toiling ceaselessly, but with joy, for they worked to know Yahweh better. He had been excited when the Babylonians came to Elam looking for miners. Yet now that he stood at the base of the tower, his senses rebelled, insisting that nothing should stand so high. He didn't feel as if he were on the earth when he looked up along the tower.

Should he climb such a thing?

■ ■ ■

On the morning of the climb, the second platform was covered edge to edge with stout two-wheeled carts arranged in rows. Many were loaded with nothing but food of all sorts: sacks filled with barley, wheat, lentils, onions, dates, cucumbers, loaves of bread, dried fish. There were countless giant clay jars of water, date wine, beer, goat's milk, palm oil. Other carts were loaded with such goods as might be sold at a bazaar: bronze vessels, reed baskets, bolts of linen, wooden stools and tables. There was also a fattened ox and a goat that some priests were fitting with hoods so that they could not see to either side and would not be afraid on the climb. They would be sacrificed when they reached the top.

Then there were the carts loaded with the miners' picks and

hammers, and the makings for a small forge. Their foreman had also ordered a number of carts be loaded with wood and sheaves of reeds.

Lugatum stood next to a cart, securing the ropes that held the wood. Hillalum walked up to him. "From where did this wood come? I saw no forests after we left Elam."

"There is a forest of trees to the north, which was planted when the tower was begun. The cut timber is floated down the Euphrates."

"You planted a entire *forest*?"

"When they began the tower, the architects knew that far more wood would be needed to fuel the kilns than could be found on the plain, so they had a forest planted. There are crews whose job is to provide water, and plant one new tree for each that is cut."

Hillalum was astonished. "And that provides all the wood needed?"

"Most of it. Many other forests in the north have been cut as well, and their wood brought down the river." He inspected the wheels of the cart, uncorked a leather bottle he carried, and poured a little oil between the wheel and axle.

Nanni walked over to them, staring at the streets of Babylon laid out before them. "I've never before been even this high, that I can look down upon a city."

"Nor have I," said Hillalum, but Lugatum simply laughed.

"Come along. All of the carts are ready."

Soon all the men were paired up and matched with a cart. The men stood between the cart's two pull rods, which had rope loops for pulling. The carts pulled by the miners were mixed in with those of the regular pullers, to ensure that they would keep the proper pace. Lugatum and another puller had the cart right behind that of Hillalum and Nanni.

"Remember," said Lugatum, "stay about ten cubits behind the cart in front of you. The man on the right does all the pulling when you turn corners, and you'll switch every hour."

Pullers were beginning to lead their carts up the ramp. Hillalum and Nanni bent down and slung the ropes of their cart over their opposite shoulders. They stood up together, raising the front end of the cart off the pavement.

"Now PULL," called Lugatum.

They leaned forward against the ropes, and the cart began rolling. Once it was moving, pulling seemed to be easy enough, and they wound their way around the platform. Then they reached the ramp, and they again had to lean deeply.

"This is a light wagon?" muttered Hillalum.

The ramp was wide enough for a single man to walk beside a cart if he had to pass. The surface was paved with brick, with two grooves worn deep by centuries of wheels. Above their heads, the ceiling rose in a corbelled vault, with the wide, square bricks arranged in overlapping layers until they met in the middle. The pillars on the right were broad enough to make the ramp seem a bit like a tunnel. If one didn't look off to the side, there was little sense of being on a tower.

"Do you sing when you mine?" asked Lugatum.

"When the stone is soft," said Nanni.

"Sing one of your mining songs, then."

The call went down to the other miners, and before long the entire crew was singing.

■ ■ ■

As the shadows shortened, they ascended higher and higher. With only clear air surrounding them, and much shade from the sun, it was much cooler than in the narrow alleys of a city at ground level, where the heat at midday could kill lizards as they scurried across the street. Looking out to the side, the miners could see the dark Euphrates, and the green fields stretching out for leagues, crossed by canals that glinted in the sunlight. The city of Babylon was an intricate pattern of closely set streets and buildings, dazzling with gypsum whitewash; less and less of it was visible, as it seemingly drew nearer the base of the tower.

Hillalum was again pulling on the right-hand rope, nearer the edge, when he heard some shouting from the upward ramp one level below. He thought of stopping and looking down the side, but he didn't wish to interrupt their pace, and he wouldn't be able to see the lower ramp clearly anyway. "What's happening down there?" he called to Lugatum behind him.

"One of your fellow miners fears the height. There is occasionally such a man among those who climb for the first time. Such a man embraces the floor, and cannot ascend further. Few feel it so soon, though."

Hillalum understood. "We know of a similar fear, among those who would be miners. Some men cannot bear to enter the mines, for fear that they will be buried."

"Really?" called Lugatum. "I had not heard of that. How do you feel yourself about the height?"

"I feel nothing." But he glanced at Nanni, and they both knew the truth.

"You feel nervousness in your palms, don't you?" whispered Nanni.

Hillalum rubbed his hands on the coarse fibers of the rope, and nodded.

"I felt it too, earlier, when I was closer to the edge."

"Perhaps we should go hooded, like the ox and the goat," muttered Hillalum jokingly.

"Do you think we too will fear the height, when we climb farther?"

Hillalum considered. That one of their comrades should feel the fear so soon did not bode well. He shook it off; thousands climbed with no fear, and it would be foolish to let one miner's fear infect them all. "We are merely unaccustomed. We will have months to grow used to the height. By the time we reach the top of the tower, we will wish it were taller."

"No," said Nanni. "I don't think I'll wish to pull this any farther." They both laughed.

■ ■ ■

In the evening they ate a meal of barley and onions and lentils, and slept inside narrow corridors that penetrated into the body of the tower. When they woke the next morning, the miners were scarcely able to walk, so sore were their legs. The pullers laughed, and gave them salve to rub into their muscles, and redistributed the load on the carts to reduce the miners' burden.

By now, looking down the side turned Hillalum's knees to water. A wind blew steadily at this height, and he anticipated that it would grow stronger as they climbed. He wondered if anyone had ever been blown off the tower in a moment of carelessness. And the fall; a man would have time to say a prayer before he hit the ground. Hillalum shuddered at the thought.

Aside from the soreness in the miners' legs, the second day was similar to the first. They were able to see much farther now, and the breadth of land visible was stunning; the deserts beyond the fields were visible, and caravans appeared to be little more than lines of insects. No other miner feared the height so greatly that he couldn't continue, and their ascent proceeded all day without incident.

On the third day, the miners' legs had not improved, and Hillalum felt like a crippled old man. Only on the fourth day did their legs feel better, and they were pulling their original loads again. Their climb continued until the evening, when they met the second crew of pullers leading empty carts rapidly along the downward ramp. The upward and downward ramps wound around each other without touching, but they were joined by the corridors through the tower's body. When the crews had intertwined thoroughly on the two ramps, they crossed over to exchange carts.

The miners were introduced to the pullers of the second crew, and they all talked and ate together that night. The next morning, the first crew readied the empty carts for their return to Babylon, and Lugatum bade farewell to Hillalum and Nanni.

"Take care of your cart. It has climbed the entire height of the tower, more times than any man."

"Do you envy the cart, too?" asked Nanni.

"No, because every time it reaches the top, it must come all the way back down. I could not bear to do that."

■ ■ ■

When the second crew stopped at the end of the day, the puller of the cart behind Hillalum and Nanni came over to show them something. His name was Kudda.

"You have never seen the sun at this height. Come, look." The puller went to the edge and sat down, his legs hanging over the side. He saw that they hesitated. "Come. You can lie down and peer over the edge, if you like." Hillalum did not wish to seem like a fearful child, but he could not bring himself to sit at a cliff face that stretched for thousands of cubits below his feet. He lay down on his belly, with only his head at the edge. Nanni joined him.

"When the sun is about to set, look down the side of the tower."

Hillalum glanced downward, and then quickly looked to the horizon. "What is different about the way the sun sets here?"

"Consider, when the sun sinks behind the peaks of the mountains to the west, it grows dark down on the plain of Shinar. Yet here, we are higher than the mountaintops, so we can still see the sun. The sun must descend farther for us to see night."

Hillalum's jaw dropped as he understood. "The shadows of the mountains mark the beginning of night. Night falls on the earth before it does here."

Kudda nodded. "You can see night travel up the tower, from the ground up to the sky. It moves quickly, but you should be able to see it."

He watched the red globe of the sun for a minute, and then looked down and pointed. "Now!"

Hillalum and Nanni looked down. At the base of the immense pillar, tiny Babylon was in shadow. Then the darkness climbed the tower, like a canopy unfurling upward. It moved slowly enough that Hillalum felt he could count the moments passing, but then it grew faster as it approached, until it raced past them faster than he could blink, and they were in twilight.

Hillalum rolled over and looked up, in time to see darkness rapidly ascend the rest of the tower. Gradually, the sky grew dimmer, as the sun sank beneath the edge of the world, far away.

"Quite a sight, is it not?" said Kudda.

Hillalum said nothing. For the first time, he knew night for what it was: the shadow of the earth itself, cast against the sky.

■ ■ ■

After climbing for two more days, Hillalum had grown more accustomed to the height. Though they were the better part of a league straight up, he could bear to stand at the edge of the ramp and look down the tower. He held onto one of the pillars at the edge and cautiously leaned out to look upward. He noticed that the tower no longer looked like a smooth pillar.

He asked Kudda. "The tower seems to widen farther up. How can that be?"

"Look more closely. There are wooden balconies reaching out from the sides. They are made of cypress, and suspended by ropes of flax."

Hillalum squinted. "Balconies? What are they for?"

"They have soil spread on them, so people may grow vegetables.

At this height water is scarce, so onions are most commonly grown. Higher up, where there is more rain, you'll see beans."

Nanni asked, "How can there be rain above that does not just fall here?"

Kudda was surprised at him. "It dries in the air as it falls, of course."

"Oh, of course." Nanni shrugged.

By the end of the next day they reached the level of the balconies. They were flat platforms, dense with onions, supported by heavy ropes from the tower wall above, just below the next tier of balconies. On each level the interior of the tower held several narrow rooms, in which the families of the pullers lived. Women could be seen sitting in the doorways sewing tunics, or out in the gardens digging up bulbs. Children chased each other up and down the ramps, weaving amidst the pullers' carts and running along the edge of the balconies without fear. The tower dwellers could easily pick out the miners, and they all smiled and waved.

When it came time for the evening meal, all the carts were set down and much food and other goods were taken off to be used by the people here. The pullers greeted their families, and invited the miners to join them for the evening meal. Hillalum and Nanni ate with the family of Kudda, and they enjoyed a fine meal of dried fish, bread, date wine, and fruit.

Hillalum saw that this section of the tower formed a tiny kind of town, laid out in a line between two streets, the upward and downward ramps. There was a temple, in which the rituals for the festivals were performed; there were magistrates, who settled disputes; there were shops, which were stocked by the caravan. Of course, the town was inseparable from the caravan: neither could exist without the other. And yet any caravan was essentially a journey, a thing that began at one place and ended at another. This town was never intended as a permanent place, it was merely part of a centuries-long journey.

After dinner, he asked Kudda and his family, "Have any of you ever visited Babylon?"

Kudda's wife, Alitum, answered. "No, why would we? It's a long climb, and we have all we need here."

"You have no desire to actually walk on the earth?"

Kudda shrugged. "We live on the road to heaven; all the work that we do is to extend it further. When we leave the tower, we will take the upward ramp, not the downward."

■ ■ ■

As the miners ascended, in the course of time there came the day when the tower appeared to be the same when one looked upward or downward from the ramp's edge. Below, the tower's shaft shrank to nothing long before it seemed to reach the plain below. Likewise, the miners were still far from being able to see the top. All that was visible was a length of the tower. To look up or down was frightening, for the reassurance of continuity was not provided; they were no longer part of the ground. The tower might have been a thread suspended in the air, unattached to either earth or heaven.

There were moments during this section of the climb when Hillalum despaired, feeling displaced and estranged from the world; it was as if the earth had rejected him for his faithlessness, while heaven disdained to accept him. He wished Yahweh would give a sign, to let men know that their venture was approved; otherwise how could they stay in a place that offered so little welcome to the spirit?

The tower dwellers at this altitude felt no unease with their station; they always greeted the miners warmly and wished them luck with their task at the vault. They lived inside the damp mists of clouds, they saw storms from below and from above, they harvested crops from the air, and they never feared that this was an improper place for men to be. There were no divine assurances or encouragements to be had, but the people never knew a moment's doubt.

With the passage of the weeks, the sun and moon peaked lower and lower in their daily journeys. The moon flooded the south side of the tower with its silver radiance, glowing like the eye of Yahweh peering at them. Before long, they were at precisely the same level as the moon when it passed; they had reached the height of the first of the celestial bodies. They squinted at the moon's pitted face, marveled at its stately motion that scorned any support.

Then they approached the sun. It was the summer season, when the sun appears nearly overhead from Babylon, making it pass close by the tower at this height. No families lived in this section of the tower, nor were there any balconies, since the heat was enough to roast barley. The mortar between the tower's bricks was no longer bitumen, which would have softened and flowed, but clay, which had been virtually baked by the heat. As protection against the day temperatures, the pillars had been widened until they formed a nearly continuous wall, enclosing the ramp into a tunnel with only narrow slots admitting the whistling wind and blades of golden light.

The crews of pullers had been spaced very regularly up to this point, but here an adjustment was necessary. They started out earlier and earlier each morning, to gain more darkness for when they pulled. When they were at the level of the sun, they traveled entirely at night. During the day, they tried to sleep, naked and sweating in the hot breeze. The miners worried that if they did manage to sleep, they would be baked to death before they awoke. But the pullers had made the journey many times, and never lost a man, and eventually they passed above the sun's level, where things were as they had been below.

Now the light of day shone *upward*, which seemed unnatural to the utmost. The balconies had planks removed from them so that the sunlight could shine through, with soil on the walkways that remained; the plants grew sideways and downward, bending down to catch the sun's rays.

Then they drew near the level of the stars, small fiery spheres spread on all sides. Hillalum had expected them to be spread more thickly, but even with the tiny stars invisible from the ground, they seemed to be thinly scattered. They were not all set at the same height, but instead occupied the next few leagues above. It was difficult to tell how far away they were, since there was no indication of their size, but occasionally one would make a close approach, evidencing its astonishing speed. Hillalum realized that all the objects in the sky hurtled by with similar speed, in order to travel the world from edge to edge in a day's time.

During the day, the sky was a much paler blue than it appeared from the earth, a sign they were nearing the vault. When studying the sky, Hillalum was startled to see that there were stars visible during the day. They couldn't be seen from the earth amidst the glare of the sun, but from this altitude they were quite distinct.

One day Nanni came to him hurriedly and said, "A star has hit the tower!"

"What!" Hillalum looked around, panicked, feeling like he had been struck by a blow.

"No, not now. It was long ago, more than a century. One of the tower dwellers is telling the story; his grandfather was there."

They went inside the corridors, and saw several miners seated around a wizened old man.

". . . Lodged itself in the bricks about half a league above here. You can still see the scar it left; it's like a giant pockmark."

"What happened to the star?"

"It burned and sizzled, and was too bright to look upon. Men considered prying it out, so that it might resume its course, but it was too hot to approach closely, and they dared not quench it. After weeks it cooled into a knotted mass of black heaven-metal, as large as a man could wrap his arms around."

"So large?" said Nanni, his voice full of awe. When stars fell to the earth of their own accord, small lumps of heaven-metal were sometimes found, tougher than the finest bronze. The metal could not be melted for casting, so it was worked by hammering when heated red; amulets were made from it.

"Indeed, no one had ever heard of a mass of this size found on the earth. Can you imagine the tools that could be made from it!"

"You did not try to hammer it into tools, did you?" asked Hillalum, horrified.

"Oh no. Men were frightened to touch it. Everyone descended from the tower, waiting for retribution from Yahweh for disturbing the workings of Creation. They waited for months, but no sign came. Eventually they returned, and pried out the star. It sits in a temple in the city below."

There was silence. Then one of the miners said, "I have never heard of this in the stories of the tower."

"It was a transgression, something not spoken of."

■ ■ ■

As they climbed higher up the tower, the sky grew lighter in color, until one morning Hillalum awoke and stood at the edge and yelled from shock: what had before seemed a pale sky now appeared to be a white ceiling stretched far above their heads. They were close enough now to perceive the vault of heaven, to see it as a solid carapace enclosing all the sky. All of the miners spoke in hushed tones, staring up like idiots, while the tower dwellers laughed at them.

As they continued to climb, they were startled at how *near* they actually were. The blankness of the vault's face had deceived them, making it undetectable until it appeared, abruptly, seeming just above their heads. Now instead of climbing into the sky, they climbed up to a featureless plain that stretched endlessly in all directions.

All of Hillalum's senses were disoriented by the sight of it. Sometimes when he looked at the vault, he felt as if the world had flipped around somehow, and if he lost his footing he would fall upward to meet it. When the vault did appear to rest above his head, it had an oppressive *weight*. The vault was a stratum as heavy as all the world, yet utterly without support, and he feared what he never had in the mines: that the ceiling would collapse upon him.

Too, there were moments when it appeared as if the vault was a vertical cliff face of unimaginable height rising before him, and the dim earth behind him was another like it, and the tower was a cable stretched taut between the two. Or worst of all, for an instant it seemed that there was no up and no down, and his body did not know which way it was drawn. It was like fearing the height, but much worse. Often he would wake from an unrestful sleep, to find himself sweating and his fingers cramped, trying to clutch the brick floor.

Nanni and many of the other miners were bleary-eyed too, though no one spoke of what disturbed their sleep. Their ascent grew slower, instead of faster as their foreman Beli had expected; the sight of the vault inspired unease rather than eagerness. The regular pullers became impatient with them. Hillalum wondered what sort of people were forged by living under such conditions; did they escape madness? Did they grow accustomed to this? Would the children born under a solid sky scream if they saw the ground beneath their feet?

Perhaps men were not meant to live in such a place. If their own natures restrained them from approaching heaven too closely, then men should remain on the earth.

When they reached the summit of the tower, the disorientation faded, or perhaps they had grown immune. Here, standing upon the square platform of the top, the miners gazed upon the most awesome scene ever glimpsed by men: far below them lay a tapestry of soil and sea, veiled by mist, rolling out in all directions to the limit of the eye. Just above them hung the roof of the world itself, the absolute upper demarcation of the sky, guaranteeing their vantage point as the highest possible. Here was as much of Creation as could be apprehended at once.

The priests led a prayer to Yahweh; they gave thanks that they were permitted to see so much, and begged forgiveness for their desire to see more.

■ ■ ■

And at the top, the bricks were laid. One could catch the rich, raw smell of tar, rising out of the heated caldrons in which the lumps of bitumen were melted. It was the most earthy odor the miners had smelled in four months, and their nostrils were desperate to catch a whiff before it was whipped away by the wind. Here at the summit, where the ooze that had once seeped from the earth's cracks now grew solid to hold bricks in place, the earth was growing a limb into the sky.

Here worked the bricklayers, the men smeared with bitumen who mixed the mortar and deftly set the heavy bricks with absolute precision. More than anyone else, these men could not permit themselves to experience dizziness when they saw the vault, for the tower could not vary a finger's width from the vertical. They were nearing the end of their task, finally, and after four months of climbing, the miners were ready to begin theirs.

The Egyptians arrived shortly afterwards. They were dark of skin and slight of build, and had sparsely bearded chins. They had pulled carts filled with dolerite hammers, and bronze tools, and wooden wedges. Their foreman was named Senmut, and he conferred with Beli, the Elamites' foreman, on how they would penetrate the vault. The Egyptians built a forge with what they had brought, as did the Elamites, for recasting the bronze tools that would be blunted during the mining.

The vault itself remained just above a man's outstretched fingertips; it felt smooth and cool when one leapt up to touch it. It seemed to be made of fine-grained white granite, unmarred and utterly featureless. And therein lay the problem.

Long ago, Yahweh had released the Deluge, unleashing waters from both below and above; the waters of the Abyss had burst forth from the springs of the earth, and the waters of heaven had poured through the sluice gates in the vault. Now men saw the vault closely, but there were no sluice gates discernible. They squinted at the surface in all directions, but no openings, no windows, no seams interrupted the granite plain.

It seemed that their tower met the vault at a point between any reservoirs, which was fortunate indeed. If a sluice gate had been visible, they would have had to risk breaking it open and emptying the reservoir. That would mean rain for Shinar, out of season and heavier than the winter rains; it would cause flooding along the Euphrates. The rain would most likely end when the reservoir was emptied, but there was always the possibility that Yahweh would punish them and continue the rain until the tower fell and Babylon was dissolved into mud.

Even though there were no visible gates, a risk still existed. Perhaps the gates had no seams perceptible to mortal eyes, and a reservoir lay directly above them. Or perhaps the reservoirs were huge, so that even if the nearest sluice gates were many leagues away, a reservoir still lay above them.

There was much debate over how best to proceed.

"Surely Yahweh will not wash away the tower," argued Qurdusa, one of the bricklayers. "If the tower were sacrilege, Yahweh would have destroyed it earlier. Yet in all the centuries we've been working, we have never seen the slightest sign of Yahweh's displeasure. Yahweh will drain any reservoir before we penetrate it."

"If Yahweh looked upon this venture with such favor, there would already be a stairway prepared for us in the vault," countered Eluti, an Elamite. "Yahweh will neither help nor hinder us; if we penetrate a reservoir, we will face the onrush of its waters."

Hillalum could not keep his doubts silent at such a time. "And if the waters are endless?" he asked. "Yahweh may not punish us, but Yahweh may allow us to bring our judgment upon ourselves."

"Elamite," said Qurdusa, "even as a newcomer to the tower, you should know better than that. We labor for our love of Yahweh, we have done so for all our lives, and so have our fathers for generations back. Men as righteous as we could not be judged harshly."

"It is true that we work with the purest of aims, but that doesn't mean we have worked wisely. Did men truly choose the correct path when they opted to live their lives away from the soil from which they were shaped? Never has Yahweh said that the choice was proper. Now we stand ready to break open heaven, even when we know that water lies above us. If we are misguided, how can we be sure Yahweh will protect us from our own errors?"

"Hillalum advises caution, and I agree," said Beli. "We must ensure that we do not bring a second Deluge upon the world, nor even dangerous rains upon Shinar. I have conferred with Senmut of the Egyptians, and he has shown me designs that they have employed to seal the tombs of their kings. I believe their methods can provide us with safety when we begin digging."

■ ■ ■

The priests sacrificed the ox and the goat in a ceremony in which many sacred words were spoken and much incense was burned, and the miners began work.

Even before the miners reached the vault it had been obvious that simple digging with hammers and picks would be impractical: even if they were tunneling horizontally, they could make no more than two fingers-widths of progress a day through granite, and tunneling *upward* would be far, far slower. Instead, they employed fire setting.

With the wood they had brought, a bonfire was built below the chosen point of the vault, and fed steadily for a day. Before the heat of the flame, the stone cracked and spalled. After letting the fire burn out, the miners splashed water onto the stone to further the cracking. They could then break the stone into large pieces, which fell heavily onto the tower. In this manner they could progress the better part of a cubit for each day the fire burned.

The tunnel did not rise straight up, but at the angle a staircase takes, so that they could build a ramp of steps up from the tower to meet it. The fire setting left the walls and floor smooth; the men built a frame of wooden steps underfoot, so that they would not slide back down. They used a platform of baked bricks to support the bonfire at the tunnel's end.

After the tunnel rose ten cubits into the vault, they leveled it out and widened it to form a room. Then, once the miners had removed all the stone that had been weakened by the fire, the Egyptians began work. They used no fire in their quarrying. With only their dolerite balls and hammers, they began to build a sliding door of granite.

They first chipped away stone to cut an immense block of granite out of one wall. Hillalum and the other miners tried to help, but found it very difficult: one did not wear away the stone by grinding, but instead pounded chips off, using hammer blows of one strength alone, and lighter or heavier ones would not do.

After some weeks, the block was ready. It stood taller than a man, and was even wider than that. To free it from the floor, they cut slots around the base of the stone, and pounded in dry wooden wedges. Then they pounded thinner wedges into the first wedges to split them, and poured water in the cracks so that the wood would swell. In a few hours, a crack traveled into the stone, and the block was freed.

At the rear of the room, on the right-hand side, the miners burnt out a narrow upward-sloping corridor, and in the floor in front of the chamber entrance they dug a downward-sloping channel into the floor for a cubit. Thus there was a smooth, continuous ramp that cut across the floor immediately in front of the entrance, and ended just to its left. On this ramp the Egyptians loaded the block of granite. They dragged and pushed the block up into the side corridor, where it just barely fit, and propped it in place with a stack of flat mud bricks braced against the bottom of the left wall, like a pillar lying on the ramp.

With the sliding stone to hold back the waters, it was safe for the miners to continue tunneling. If they broke into a reservoir and the waters of heaven began pouring down into the tunnel, they would break the bricks one by one, and the stone would slide down until it rested in the recess in the floor, utterly blocking the doorway. If the waters flooded in with such force that they washed men out of the tunnels, the mud bricks would gradually dissolve, and again the stone would slide down. The waters would be retained, and the miners could then begin a new tunnel in another direction, to avoid the reservoir.

The miners again used fire setting to continue the tunnel, beginning at the far end of the room. To aid the circulation of air within the vault, ox hides were stretched on tall frames of wood, and placed obliquely on either side of the tunnel entrance at the top of the tower. Thus the steady wind that blew underneath the vault of heaven was guided upward into the tunnel; it kept the fire blazing and cleared the air after the fire was extinguished, so that the miners could dig without breathing smoke.

The Egyptians did not stop working once the sliding stone was in place. While the miners swung their picks at the tunnel's end, the Egyptians labored at the task of cutting a stair into the solid stone, to replace the wooden steps. This they did with the wooden wedges, and the blocks they removed from the sloping floor left steps in their place.

■ ■ ■

Thus the miners worked, extending the tunnel on and on. The tunnel always ascended, though it reversed direction regularly like a thread in a giant stitch, so that its general path was straight up. They built other sliding-door rooms, so that only the uppermost segment of the tunnel would be flooded if they penetrated a reservoir. They cut channels in the vault's surface from which they hung walkways and platforms; starting from these platforms, well away from the tower, they dug side tunnels, which joined the main tunnel deep inside. The wind was guided through these to provide ventilation, clearing the smoke from deep inside the tunnel.

For years the labor continued. The pulling crews no longer hauled bricks, but wood and water for the fire setting. People came to inhabit those tunnels just inside the vault's surface, and on hanging platforms they grew downward-bending vegetables. The miners lived there at the border of heaven; some married, and raised children. Few ever set foot on the earth again.

■ ■ ■

With a wet cloth wrapped around his face, Hillalum climbed down from wooden steps onto stone, having just fed some more wood to the bonfire at the tunnel's end. The fire would continue for many hours, and he would wait in the lower tunnels, where the wind was not thick with smoke.

Then there was a distant sound of shattering, the sound of a mountain of stone being split through, and then a steadily growing roar. And then a torrent of water came rushing down the tunnel.

For a moment, Hillalum was frozen in horror. The water, shockingly cold, slammed into his legs, knocking him down. He rose to his feet, gasping for breath, leaning against the current, clutching at the steps.

They had hit a reservoir.

He had to descend below the highest sliding door, before it was closed. His legs wished to leap down the steps, but he knew he couldn't remain on his feet if he did, and being swept down by the raging current would likely batter him to death. Going as fast as he dared, he took the steps one by one.

He slipped several times, sliding down as many as a dozen steps each time; the stone steps scraped against his back, but he felt no pain. All the while he was certain the tunnel would collapse and crush him, or else the entire vault would split open, and the sky would gape beneath his feet, and he would fall down to earth amidst the heavenly rain. Yahweh's punishment had come, a second Deluge.

How much farther until he reached the sliding stone? The tunnel seemed to stretch on and on, and the waters were pouring down even faster now. He was virtually running down the steps.

Suddenly he stumbled and splashed into shallow water. He had run down past the end of the stairs, and fallen into the room of the sliding stone, and there was water higher than his knees.

He stood up, and saw Damqiya and Ahuni, two fellow miners, just noticing him. They stood in front of the stone that already blocked the exit.

"No!" he cried.

"They closed it!" screamed Damqiya. "They did not wait!"

"Are there others coming?" shouted Ahuni, without hope. "We may be able to move the block."

"There are no others," answered Hillalum. "Can they push it from the other side?"

"They cannot hear us." Ahuni pounded the granite with a hammer, making not a sound against the din of the rushing water.

Hillalum looked around the tiny room, only now noticing that an Egyptian floated face down in the water.

"He died falling down the stairs," yelled Damqiya.

"Is there nothing we can do?"

Ahuni looked upward. "Yahweh, spare us."

The three of them stood in the rising water, praying desperately, but Hillalum knew it was in vain: Yahweh had not asked men to build the tower or to pierce the vault; the decision to build it belonged to men alone, and they would die in this endeavor just as they did in any of their earthbound tasks. Their righteousness could not save them from the consequences of their deeds.

The water reached their chests. "Let us ascend," shouted Hillalum.

They climbed the tunnel laboriously, against the onrush, as the water rose behind their heels. The few torches illuminating the tunnel had been extinguished, so they ascended in the dark, murmuring prayers that they couldn't hear. The wooden steps at the top of the tunnel had dislodged from their place, and were jammed farther down in the tunnel. They climbed past them, until they reached the smooth stone slope, and there they waited for the water to carry them higher.

They waited without words, their prayers exhausted. Hillalum imagined that he stood in the black gullet of Yahweh, as the mighty one drank deep of the waters of heaven, ready to swallow the sinners.

The water rose, and bore them up, until Hillalum could reach up with his hands and touch the ceiling. The giant fissure from which the waters gushed forth was right next to him. Only a tiny pocket of air remained. Hillalum shouted, "When this chamber is filled, we can swim heavenward."

He could not tell if they heard him. He gulped his last breath as the water reached the ceiling, and swam up into the fissure. He would die closer to heaven than any man ever had before.

The fissure extended for many cubits. As soon as Hillalum passed through, the stone stratum slipped from his fingers, and his flailing limbs touched nothing. For a moment he felt a current carrying him, but then he was no longer sure. With only blackness around him, he once again felt that horrible vertigo that he had experienced when first approaching the vault: he could not distinguish any directions, not even up or down. He pushed and kicked against the water, but did not know if he moved.

Helpless, he was perhaps floating in still water, perhaps swept furiously by a current; all he felt was numbing cold. Never did he see any light. Was there no surface to this reservoir that he might rise to?

Then he was slammed into stone again. His hands felt a fissure in the surface. Was he back where he had begun? He was being forced into it, and he had no strength to resist. He was drawn into the tunnel, and was rattled against its sides. It was incredibly deep, like the longest mine shaft: he felt as if his lungs would burst, but there was still no end to the passage. Finally his breath would not be held any longer, and it escaped from his lips. He was drowning, and the blackness around him entered his lungs.

But suddenly the walls opened out away from him. He was being carried along by a rushing stream of water; he felt air above the water! And then he felt no more.

■ ■ ■

Hillalum awoke with his face pressed against wet stone. He could see nothing, but he could feel water near his hands. He rolled over and groaned; his every limb ached, he was naked, and much of his skin was scraped raw or wrinkled from wetness, but he breathed air.

Time passed, and finally he could stand. Water flowed rapidly about his ankles. Stepping in one direction, he found the water deepened. In the other, there was dry stone—shale, by the feel of it.

It was utterly dark, like a mine without torches. With torn fingertips he felt his way along the floor, until it rose up and became a wall. Slowly, like some blind creature, he crawled back and forth. He found the water's source, a large opening in the floor. He remembered! He had been spewed up from the reservoir through this hole. He continued crawling for what seemed to be hours; if he was in a cavern, it was immense.

He found a place where the floor rose in a slope. Was there a passage leading upward? Perhaps it could still take him to heaven.

Hillalum crawled, having no idea of how much time passed, not caring that he would never to able to retrace his steps, for he could not return whence he had come. He followed upward tunnels when he found them, downward ones when he had to. Though earlier he had swallowed more water than he would have thought possible, he began to feel thirst, and hunger.

And eventually he saw light, and raced to the outside.

The light made his eyes squeeze closed, and he fell to his knees, his fists clenched before his face. Was it the radiance of Yahweh? Could his eyes bear to see it? Minutes later he could open them, and he saw desert. He had emerged from a cave in the foothills of some mountains, and rocks and sand stretched to the horizon.

Was heaven just like the earth? Did Yahweh dwell in a place such as this? Or was this merely another realm within Yahweh's Creation, another earth above his own, while Yahweh dwelled still higher?

A sun lay near the mountaintops behind his back. Was it rising or falling? Were there days and night here?

Hillalum squinted at the sandy landscape. A line moved along the horizon. Was it a caravan?

He ran to it, shouting with his parched throat until his need for breath stopped him. A figure at the end of the caravan saw him, and brought the entire line to a stop. Hillalum kept running.

The one who had seen him seemed to be man, not spirit, and was dressed like a desert crosser. He had a waterskin ready. Hillalum drank as best he could, panting for breath.

Finally he returned it to the man, and gasped, "Where is this place?"

"Were you attacked by bandits? We are headed to Erech."

Hillalum stared. "You would deceive me!" he shouted. The man drew back, and watched him as if he were mad from the sun. Hillalum saw another man in the caravan walking over to investigate. "Erech is in Shinar!"

"Yes it is. Were you not traveling to Shinar?" The other man stood ready with his staff.

"I came from—I was in—" Hillalum stopped. "Do you know Babylon?"

"Oh, is that your destination? That is north of Erech. It is an easy journey between them."

"The tower. Have you heard of it?"

"Certainly, the pillar to heaven. It is said men at the top are tunneling through the vault of heaven."

Hillalum fell to the sand.

"Are you unwell?" The two caravan drivers mumbled to each other, and went off to confer with the others. Hillalum was not watching them.

He was in Shinar. He had returned to the earth. He had climbed above the reservoirs of heaven, and arrived back at the earth. Had Yahweh brought him to this place to keep him from reaching farther above? Yet Hillalum still hadn't seen any signs, any indication that Yahweh had noticed him. He had not experienced any miracle that Yahweh had performed to place him here. As far as he could see, he had merely swum up from the vault and entered the cavern below.

Somehow, the vault of heaven lay beneath the earth. It was as if they lay against each other, though they were separated by many leagues. How could that be? How could such distant places touch? Hillalum's head hurt trying to think about it.

And then it came to him: *a seal cylinder*. When rolled upon a tablet of soft clay, the carved cylinder left an imprint that formed a picture. Two figures might appear at opposite ends of the tablet, though they stood side by side on the surface of the cylinder. All the world was as such a cylinder. Men imagined heaven and earth as being at the ends of a tablet, with sky and stars stretched between; yet the world was wrapped around in some fantastic way so that heaven and earth touched.

It was clear now why Yahweh had not struck down the tower, had not punished men for wishing to reach beyond the bounds set for them: for the longest journey would merely return them to the place whence they'd come. Centuries of their labor would not reveal to them any more of Creation than they already knew. Yet through their endeavor, men would glimpse the unimaginable artistry of Yahweh's work, in seeing how ingeniously the world had been constructed. By this construction, Yahweh's work was indicated, and Yahweh's work was concealed.

Thus would men know their place.

Hillalum rose to his feet, his legs unsteady from awe, and sought out the caravan drivers. He would go back to Babylon. Perhaps he would see Lugatum again. He would send word to those on the tower. He would tell them about the shape of the world.

# In Memoriam:
# Donald A. Wollheim

...

*George Zebrowski*

The death of Donald A. Wollheim on November 2, 1990, inclined me less to wonder how old this remarkable editor was—though the answer is seventy-six—than to marvel at how young our common enterprise is. To the degree that one regards contemporary American SF as the offshoot of *Astounding*, *Amazing Stories*, and other classic pulps, here was a man who grew up with science fiction itself. Indeed, it was none other than Hugo Gernsback who gave Donald A. Wollheim his first break, publishing "The Man from Ariel" in a 1934 issue of *Wonder Stories*. SF and DAW: the two are in many ways each other's progenitors.

When casting about for a proper eulogy, I was drawn to the short but heartfelt memoir George Zebrowski had written for *The Bulletin of the Science Fiction Writers of America*, the journal he edited throughout most of the 1980s. I asked him to expand the piece, and the results appear below.

In *The New Encyclopedia of Science Fiction*, scholar Jeffrey M. Elliot notes that Zebrowski's work is distinguished by his "willingness to tackle difficult themes . . . and his ability to write about them in his distinctive, carefully wrought, and often poetic prose style." Zebrowski's twenty-six books include novels, anthologies, collections, and critical works. His short fiction has been nominated for the Nebula Award and the Theodore Sturgeon Memorial Award, while his symphonic space saga *Macrolife* was recently accorded two honors: a place on *Library Journal*'s list of the hundred best SF novels of all time, and a special leatherbound edition from Easton Press as part of its Masterpieces of Science Fiction collection. Zebrowski's most recent novel, *Stranger Suns*, initially appeared in Easton's signed First Edition series and then, as a Bantam mass-market release, went on to become a *New York Times* Notable Book for 1991.

My memories of Donald A. Wollheim begin in the early 1960s. I look back and see a shy, skinny high school kid talking to a tall, wiry man in his middle years who had already accomplished much of what I was hoping to do. Don was a frequent customer at Stephen's Book Service on the lower East Side of Manhattan, then the only SF shop in New York City. This was a dusty store with a big glass window, one flight up from the street. Inside, old pulps rested on a big table in the center of the bare wood floor. The shelves were packed with expensive old hardcovers, but new hardcover books and paperbacks were also for sale. We met by chance, either on the street or in the store, usually on Saturdays, which was my book-hounding day.

I already knew him as the author of several SF novels in the Avalon and Winston series, and as the editor of many SF anthologies. I was aware that he was also David Grinnell, author of "The Rag Thing," a striking, much reprinted horror story about a bloody rag that comes to life behind an old steam radiator, and of *Across Time* and *Edge of Time*, two vivid, crisply written novels filled with inge-nuity. As with many of the great writer-editors who shaped SF, Woll-heim wrote more fiction than many a full-time writer. I was less aware that he was the editor-in-chief at Ace Books.

Don quickly learned from me that I wanted to be a writer. When I told him about the big novel I was planning, he was encouraging. "Try it on Campbell for serialization in *Astounding*," he told me one day. "And keep that title." John W. Campbell died before I had a chance to show him *Macrolife*. The novel eventually appeared as a hardcover in 1979, and I sent Don a copy.

We met casually at SF gatherings throughout the sixties. When my first novel, *The Omega Point*, was ready in 1971, he accepted it at Ace. He gave me all the contract terms I asked for, praised the story for its pace and ideas, assured me that the title would not be changed, put me in touch with Bob Pepper, the artist who painted the wraparound cover that I credit with making the book a success, and still had time to make sure my advance was paid (the job of editing my novel and getting me to make revisions fell to Frederik Pohl, who replaced Don) before he left to start DAW Books (after his initials), the company he had always dreamed of founding. I might have followed him to this new publishing venture if I had not started selling novels and anthologies to Harper & Row.

I always thought well of Don, not only because he accepted my first novel, but also because of his commitment to science fiction, and because Terry Carr, who worked with him for a long time, also had a high opinion of him. Don belonged to that group of writer-editors who nurtured science fiction out of love and in whose caretakership SF properly belongs. They are even more necessary today, when SF has big money behind it, and when even good editors are ignorant of the field's history and herd authors into print with scant awareness of their previous work or much sensitivity toward them as human beings.

Don was highly opinionated and sometimes wrong, working under the constraints placed by commerce on creative work; he did not always overcome them, but his unswerving love for SF gave him the editorial "voice" that makes many of his books from Ace and DAW so collectible today. In 1943 he edited *The Pocket Book of Science Fiction*, the field's first paperbook anthology. In 1945 he edited *The Portable Novels of Science* for Viking, the first hardcover omnibus of full-length SF novels. I still own the deluxe, boxed special edition I bought at Stephen's Book Service, issued as *The Indispensible Novels of Science* by The Book Society in 1951. These two successful collections were very important in advancing the acceptance of SF in American publishing and became highly desirable collector's items. In the fifties he created Ace Double Novels, a paperback series that helped start a number of important SF careers by presenting a lesser known writer bound back to back with a better known one. These books became very popular with readers and collectors; Samuel R. Delany, Roger Zelazny, and Ursula K. Le Guin were three writers who first appeared in Ace Doubles. When Terry Carr joined Ace in 1964, the two editors launched a best-of-the-year series and the justly famous Ace Specials.

At DAW, the first mass-market house devoted exclusively to new science fiction and fantasy in paperback (and later in hardcover), Wollheim helped establish C. J. Cherryh, Tanith Lee, Ian Watson, and John Brunner, among others. Less noticed is the fact that he published many SF works in translation from French, German, and Russian, among them novels by Gerard Klein, Herbert W. Franke, and the Strugatsky brothers. As an editor he received the Hugo Award, the World Fantasy Award, and the British Fantasy Award. As a publisher Don always had a sharp eye for the pictorial possibilities of SF publishing, and his choice of artists at Ace and DAW was often inspired. (Frank Frazetta, Frank Kelly Freas, Bob Pepper, Ed Emsh, and Leo and Diane Dillon contributed outstanding work; in my mind I can still see the covers for Philip K. Dick's *The Man Who Japed* and *The World Jones Made*.) But in addition to his good commercial sense, Don always maintained a certain visionary involvement with serious issues, a commitment that kept him sensitive to genuinely artistic works. He was a concerned man, "a disillusioned idealist," in his own words, who never stopped caring about the future of humankind. His short study of SF, *The Universe Makers* (1971), is an excellent statement of what was most important to him. "I have a very critical attitude toward reality," he wrote in the introduction to his short story collection *Two Dozen Dragon Eggs* (1969). "I am not sure anyone really knows what it is." He followed the development of space travel with keen interest and worried about the arms race and what we were doing to the environment. His place of honor in the history of the writing, editing, and publishing of SF is assured.

# A Tribute to Lester del Rey

### ...

## *Terry Brooks*

According to the bylaws of the Science Fiction Writers of America, the Grand Master Nebula Award may be given no more than six times in a decade. It is a rare and hard-won honor, recognizing a lifetime of achievement in the field.

In 1990, Grand Master status was accorded to Lester del Rey. At the Nebula Awards banquet, Terry Brooks provided a piquant homage to this legendary writer and editor, and I deemed it appropriate to reprint his words in *Nebula Awards 26*.

Ever since he entered the field, in 1936, Lester del Rey's involvement with SF has followed a classic curve: fan to short story writer to novelist to magazine editor to book editor. His career reached an apex when he and his wife, Judy-Lynn Benjamin del Rey, founded Del Rey Books, under which aegis he discovered and nurtured some of the most significant new names in fantasy, including Stephen R. Donaldson and Terry Brooks. Until her death in 1986, Judy-Lynn del Rey handled the science fiction side of the line.

In his acceptance speech, Lester del Rey noted that he was never ashamed to be part of the lowly "pulp fiction" trade. He pointed out that such prominent writers as Joseph Conrad and H. G. Wells had appeared in periodicals of dubious repute.

As for del Rey's protégé, it's safe to say that, over the past fifteen years, Terry Brooks has parceled out as much pleasure as anyone currently working in the domain of popular fiction. Equipped with degrees in both English literature and law, Brooks was until recently a practicing attorney but now spends all his time writing. His fabulously successful Shannara cycle comprises *The Sword of Shannara*, *The Elfstones of Shannara*, and *The Wishsong of Shannara*. A new series, "The Heritage of Shannara," thus far includes *The Scions of Shannara* and *The Druid of Shannara*. He has also constructed the Magic Kingdom of Landover, locus of *Magic Kingdom for Sale—Sold!*, *Black Unicorn*, and *Wizard at Large*.

For a very long time I have believed, as I believe now, that no one deserves the Grand Master Nebula Award more than this year's recipient, Lester del Rey. I cannot begin to measure what he has given to me, both as a colleague and as a friend.

Writer, critic, and editor, Lester del Rey boasts a career in the field of science fiction/fantasy spanning more than half a century. It's not commonly known that Lester got into the field on a dare. He made a bet with a girlfriend that he could write a science fiction story as good as one he had just finished reading and that, when he sent it off, he would get back a personal letter from the editor in the bargain. He did both, and got the story published to boot. The title of the story was "The Faithful," the editor's name was John W. Campbell, and the year was 1937.

Lester has written lots of stories since then, as well as a number of novels, solid nail-biting thrillers like *The Eleventh Commandment* and *Nerves*, and he continues to write in his seventh decade.

But I believe that Lester's most important contributions have been as an editor, particularly during the last fifteen years at Ballantine Books, where science fiction/fantasy is published under the imprint that bears his name. During this time he has virtually revolutionized the field, doing what many have failed to do and what many more have called impossible. He established that science fiction/fantasy can sell competitively with any kind of book, that it can appear on the best-seller lists regularly, and that it can find a readership beyond fandom. In the process he discovered many of our most talented and successful writers, he revived the careers of several others, and he brought back into print the books of still others. He took science fiction/fantasy out of the backwater where it had languished as "category fiction," presumably destined to sell in limited numbers to a limited few, and placed it squarely in the competitive and creative forefront of mainstream commercial fiction.

I'd like you to consider for just a moment what this means for all of us at this Nebula banquet. Walk into almost any bookstore, and you'll find at least one cardboard "dump" displaying a work of science fiction/fantasy sitting near the front entrance in a prime location. Check out the new hardcover releases in that store, and you'll find half a dozen of our books. Study the store's best-seller lists, and you'll find one or more of our names. To a very large extent, Lester del Rey made that possible. As writers, editors, publishers, and men and women who have a commitment to and a love for speculative fiction, we owe him a tremendous debt.

Not only are there a large number of stories by Lester del Rey, there are also hundreds of stories about him. The most memorable anecdotes, I think, are the ones where Lester starts a discussion on one side of an argument and ends it on the other. This can be a pretty disconcerting experience, especially if you're a young writer meeting Lester for the first time. But I'm not going to describe any such encounters here. What I'd like to do instead is offer one small example of what he has given to me—an example that, I believe, illustrates what he has given to so many writers.

I wrote a novel called *The Sword of Shannara*, published in 1977, a book that was fortunate enough to be on the *New York Times* best-seller list for twenty-six weeks straight. I celebrated that by submitting a second effort to Lester, who promptly rejected it—four hundred-plus pages of manuscript that I had been working on for nearly two years. And he didn't just reject it, he rejected it categorically. He told me in essence that I should take the novel out and burn it, that I should start over completely. Then, after allowing the impact of his decision to sink in, he did something quite extraordinary.

He told me that I could publish this book elsewhere if I chose, that I wouldn't really have any trouble doing so, that on the strength of the success of *The Sword of Shannara* I could get a lot of money for it. And to convince me that I should *not* do this, he returned the manuscript to me with yellow sheets inserted throughout, one every third page or so, often more frequently, and on those yellow sheets he had written down in detail his thoughts about why the book didn't work: a chapter-by-chapter, page-by-page, paragraph-by-paragraph analysis of what had gone wrong.

It was a writer's clinic for a young author, and I can't imagine to this day the kind of time this must have taken. It was the sort of thing that good friends do for each other, the sort of thing that my father did for me now and again when I was growing up, and it was without question the best thing that anyone has ever done for me as a writer.

I expect there are a lot of stories like this about Lester del Rey, and I think that these stories are at the heart of why this honor is so well deserved.

# Love and Sex Among
# the Invertebrates

## ...

## *Pat Murphy*

Four times a year, the peculiar and pellucid mind of Pat Murphy reaches my home in the form of *Exploratorium Quarterly*, the magazine she edits with an eye to investigating, as the masthead puts it, "interconnections between apparently unrelated phenomena, revealing the essential unity of nature." *Exploratorium Quarterly* is the official organ of San Francisco's famous museum of science, art, and human perception, and as a nonscientist I greatly value its vernacular accounts of technical matters. One recent issue of *EQ* taught me how to make a battery from a pickle.

Murphy's trenchant anthropological fantasy, *The Falling Woman*, garnered her the 1987 Nebula Award for best novel, while in that same year her poignant account of interspecies romance, "Rachel in Love," emerged as SFWA's choice for best novelette. (Check out the latter in *Nebula Awards 23.*) Not content to rest on her Lucite, this hypnotic and humane writer went on to publish the critically acclaimed novel *The City, Not Long After*, as well as a collection, *Points of Departure*, winner of the 1990 Philip K. Dick Award.

"Love and Sex Among the Invertebrates" initially appeared in *Alien Sex*, a compendium of stories dealing with the eternally vexing question of gender. "I rarely write for theme anthologies," Murphy explains. "Generally, when an editor mentions a particular anthology concept to me, all ideas I might ever have had that related to the subject immediately evaporate.

"*Alien Sex* is the exception. When Ellen Datlow asked me to write a story for her collection, I started to give her my standard excuses. Then I realized that half the stories I write have to do with alien sex in one way or another. I had been considering writing 'Love and Sex Among the Invertebrates,' and Ellen's request provided the final push. The inspiration for the story came from the essays of Loren Eiseley, who made me aware that the forces that brought about the opposable thumb and the upright stance are with us still. We are not the endpoint of evolution, just an oddity along the way."

This is not science. This has nothing to do with science. Yesterday, when the bombs fell and the world ended, I gave up scientific thinking. At this distance from the blast site of the bomb that took out San Jose, I figure I received a medium-size dose of radiation. Not enough for instant death, but too much for survival. I have only a few days left, and I've decided to spend this time constructing the future. Someone must do it.

It's what I was trained for, really. My undergraduate studies were in biology—structural anatomy, the construction of body and bone. My graduate studies were in engineering. For the past five years, I have been designing and constructing robots for use in industrial processing. The need for such industrial creations is over now. But it seems a pity to waste the equipment and materials that remain in the lab that my colleagues have abandoned.

I will put robots together and make them work. But I will not try to understand them. I will not take them apart and consider their inner workings and poke and pry and analyze. The time for science is over.

■ ■ ■

*The pseudoscorpion,* Lasiochernes pilosus, *is a secretive scorpionlike insect that makes its home in the nests of moles. Before pseudoscorpions mate, they dance—a private underground minuet—observed only by moles and voyeuristic entomologists. When a male finds a receptive female, he grasps her claws in his and pulls her toward him. If she resists, he circles, clinging to her claws and pulling her after him, refusing to take no for an answer. He tries again, stepping forward and pulling the female toward him with trembling claws. If she continues to resist, he steps back and continues the dance: circling, pausing to tug on his reluctant partner, then circling again.*

*After an hour or more of dancing, the female inevitably succumbs, convinced by the dance steps that her companion's species matches her own. The male deposits a packet of sperm on the ground that has been cleared of debris by their dancing feet. His claws quiver as he draws her forward, positioning her over the package of sperm. Willing at last, she presses her genital pore to the ground and takes the sperm into her body.*

*Biology texts note that the male scorpion's claws tremble as he* dances, but they do not say why. They do not speculate on his emotions, his motives, his desires. That would not be scientific.

I theorize that the male pseudoscorpion is eager. Among the everyday aromas of mole shit and rotting vegetation, he smells the female, and the perfume of her fills him with lust. But he is fearful and confused: a solitary insect, unaccustomed to socializing, he is disturbed by the presence of another of his kind. He is caught by conflicting emotions: his all-encompassing need, his fear, and the strangeness of the social situation.

I have given up the pretense of science. I speculate about the motives of the pseudoscorpion, the conflict and desire embodied in his dance.

■ ■ ■

I put the penis on my first robot as a kind of joke, a private joke, a joke about evolution. I suppose I don't really need to say it was a private joke—all my jokes are private now. I am the last one left, near as I can tell. My colleagues fled—to find their families, to seek refuge in the hills, to spend their last days running around, here and there. I don't expect to see anyone else around anytime soon. And if I do, they probably won't be interested in my jokes. I'm sure that most people think the time for joking is past. They don't see that the bomb and the war are the biggest jokes of all. Death is the biggest joke. Evolution is the biggest joke.

I remember learning about Darwin's theory of evolution in high school biology. Even back then, I thought it was kind of strange, the way people talked about it. The teacher presented evolution as a *fait accompli*, over and done with. She muddled her way through the complex speculations regarding human evolution, talking about *Ramapithecus*, *Australopithecus*, *Homo erectus*, *Homo sapiens*, and *Homo sapiens neanderthalensis*. At *Homo sapiens* she stopped, and that was it. The way the teacher looked at the situation, we were the last word, the top of the heap, the end of the line.

I'm sure the dinosaurs thought the same, if they thought at all. How could anything get better than armor plating and a spiked tail? Who could ask for more?

Thinking about the dinosaurs, I build my first creation on a reptilian model, a lizardlike creature constructed from bits and pieces that I scavenge from the industrial prototypes that fill the lab and the storeroom. I give my creature a stocky body, as long as I am tall; four legs, extending to the side of the body then bending at the knee to reach the ground; a tail as long as the body, spiked with decorative metal studs; a crocodilian mouth with great curving teeth.

The mouth is only for decoration and protection; this creature will not eat. I equip him with an array of solar panels, fixed to a sail-like crest on his back. The warmth of sunlight will cause the creature to extend his sail and gather electrical energy to recharge his batteries. In the cool of the night, he will fold his sail close to his back, becoming sleek and streamlined.

I decorate my creature with stuff from around the lab. From the trash beside the soda machine, I salvage aluminum cans. I cut them into a colorful fringe that I attach beneath the creature's chin, like the dewlap of an iguana. When I am done, the words on the soda cans have been sliced to nonsense: Coke, Fanta, Sprite, and Dr. Pepper mingle in a collision of bright colors. At the very end, when the rest of the creature is complete and functional, I make a cock of copper tubing and pipe fittings. It dangles beneath his belly, copper bright and obscene looking. Around the bright copper, I weave a rat's nest of my own hair, which is falling out by the handful. I like the look of that: bright copper peeking from a clump of wiry black curls.

Sometimes, the sickness overwhelms me. I spend part of one day in the ladies' room off the lab, lying on the cool tile floor and rousing myself only to vomit into the toilet. The sickness is nothing that I didn't expect. I'm dying, after all. I lie on the floor and think about the peculiarities of biology.

■ ■ ■

*For the male spider, mating is a dangerous process. This is especially true in the spider species that weave intricate orb-shaped webs, the kind that catch the morning dew and sparkle so nicely for nature photographers. In these species, the female is larger than the male. She is, I must confess, rather a bitch; she'll attack anything that touches her web.*

*At mating time, the male proceeds cautiously. He lingers at the edge of the web, gently tugging on a thread of spider silk to get her attention. He plucks in a very specific rhythm, signaling to his would-*

*be lover, whispering softly with his tugs: "I love you. I love you."*

*After a time, he believes that she has received his message. He feels confident that he has been understood. Still proceeding with caution, he attaches a mating line to the female's web. He plucks the mating line to encourage the female to move onto it. "Only you, baby," he signals. "You are the only one."*

*She climbs onto the mating line—fierce and passionate, but temporarily soothed by his promises. In that moment, he rushes to her, delivers his sperm, then quickly, before she can change her mind, takes a hike. A dangerous business, making love.*

■ ■ ■

Before the world went away, I was a cautious person. I took great care in my choice of friends. I fled at the first sign of a misunderstanding. At the time, it seemed the right course.

I was a smart woman, a dangerous mate. (Odd—I find myself writing and thinking of myself in the past tense. So close to death that I consider myself already dead.) Men would approach with caution, delicately signaling from a distance: "I'm interested. Are you?" I didn't respond. I didn't really know how.

An only child, I was always wary of others. My mother and I lived together. When I was just a child, my father had left to pick up a pack of cigarettes and never returned. My mother, protective and cautious by nature, warned me that men could not be trusted. People could not be trusted. She could trust me and I could trust her, and that was all.

When I was in college, my mother died of cancer. She had known of the tumor for more than a year; she had endured surgery and chemotherapy, while writing me cheery letters about her gardening. Her minister told me that my mother was a saint—she hadn't told me because she hadn't wanted to disturb my studies. I realized then that she had been wrong. I couldn't really trust her after all.

I think perhaps I missed some narrow window of opportunity. If, at some point along the way, I had had a friend or a lover who had made the effort to coax me from hiding, I could have been a different person. But it never happened. In high school, I sought the safety of my books. In college, I studied alone on Friday nights. By the time

I reached graduate school, I was, like the pseudoscorpion, accustomed to a solitary life.

I work alone in the laboratory, building the female. She is larger than the male. Her teeth are longer and more numerous. I am welding the hip joints into place when my mother comes to visit me in the laboratory.

"Katie," she says, "why didn't you ever fall in love? Why didn't you ever have children?"

I keep on welding, despite the trembling of my hands. I know she isn't there. Delirium is one symptom of radiation poisoning. But she keeps watching me as I work.

"You're not really here," I tell her, and realize immediately that talking to her is a mistake. I have acknowledged her presence and given her more power.

"Answer my questions, Katie," she says. "Why didn't you?"

I do not answer. I am busy and it will take too long to tell her about betrayal, to explain the confusion of a solitary insect confronted with a social situation, to describe the balance between fear and love. I ignore her just as I ignore the trembling of my hands and the pain in my belly, and I keep on working. Eventually, she goes away.

I use the rest of the soda cans to give the female brightly colored scales: Coca-Cola red, Sprite green, Fanta orange. From soda cans, I make an oviduct, lined with metal. It is just large enough to accommodate the male's cock.

■ ■ ■

*The male bowerbird attracts a mate by constructing a sort of art piece. From sticks and grasses, he builds two close-set parallel walls that join together to make an arch. He decorates this structure and the area around it with gaudy trinkets: bits of bone, green leaves, flowers, bright stones, and feathers cast off by gaudier birds. In areas where people have left their trash, he uses bottle caps and coins and fragments of broken glass.*

*He sits in his bower and sings, proclaiming his love for any and all females in the vicinity. At last, a female admires his bower, accepts his invitation, and they mate.*

*The bowerbird uses discrimination in decorating his bower. He chooses his trinkets with care—selecting a bit of glass for its glitter, a shiny leaf for its natural elegance, a cobalt-blue feather for a touch of color. What does he think about as he builds and decorates? What passes through his mind as he sits and sings, advertising his availability to the world?*

■ ■ ■

I have released the male and I am working on the female when I hear rattling and crashing outside the building. Something is happening in the alley between the laboratory and the nearby office building. I go down to investigate. From the mouth of the alley, I peer inside, and the male creature runs at me, startling me so that I step back. He shakes his head and rattles his teeth threateningly.

I retreat to the far side of the street and watch him from there. He ventures from the alley, scuttling along the street, then pauses by a BMW that is parked at the curb. I hear his claws rattling against metal. A hubcap clangs as it hits the pavement. The creature carries the shiny piece of metal to the mouth of the alley and then returns for the other three, removing them one by one. When I move, he rushes toward the alley, blocking any attempt to invade his territory. When I stand still, he returns to his work, collecting the hubcaps, carrying them to the alley, and arranging them so that they catch the light of the sun.

As I watch, he scavenges in the gutter and collects things he finds appealing: a beer bottle, some colorful plastic wrappers from candy bars, a length of bright yellow plastic rope. He takes each find and disappears into the alley with it.

I wait, watching. When he has exhausted the gutter near the mouth of the alley, he ventures around the corner and I make my move, running to the alley entrance and looking inside. The alley floor is covered with colored bits of paper and plastic; I can see wrappers from candy bars and paper bags from Burger King and McDonald's. The yellow plastic rope is tied to a pipe running up one wall and a protruding hook on the other. Dangling from it, like clean clothes on the clothesline, are colorful pieces of fabric: a burgundy-colored bath towel, a paisley print bedspread, a blue satin bedsheet.

I see all this in a glance. Before I can examine the bower further, I hear the rattle of claws on pavement. The creature is running at me, furious at my intrusion. I turn and flee into the laboratory, slamming the door behind me. But once I am away from the alley, the creature does not pursue me.

From the second-story window, I watch him return to the alley and I suspect that he is checking to see if I have tampered with anything. After a time, he reappears in the alley mouth and crouches there, the sunlight glittering on his metal carapace.

In the laboratory, I build the future. Oh, maybe not, but there's no one here to contradict me, so I will say that it is so. I complete the female and release her.

The sickness takes over then. While I still have the strength, I drag a cot from a back room and position it by the window, where I can look out and watch my creations.

What is it that I want from them? I don't know exactly.

I want to know that I have left something behind. I want to be sure that the world does not end with me. I want the feeling, the understanding, the certainty that the world will go on.

I wonder if the dying dinosaurs were glad to see the mammals, tiny ratlike creatures that rustled secretively in the underbrush.

■ ■ ■

When I was in seventh grade, all the girls had to watch a special presentation during gym class one spring afternoon. We dressed in our gym clothes, then sat in the auditorium and watched a film called *Becoming a Woman*. The film talked about puberty and menstruation. The accompanying pictures showed the outline of a young girl. As the film progressed, she changed into a woman, developing breasts. The animation showed her uterus as it grew a lining, then shed it, then grew another. I remember watching with awe as the pictures showed the ovaries releasing an egg that united with a sperm, and then lodged in the uterus and grew into a baby.

The film must have delicately skirted any discussion of the source of the sperm, because I remember asking my mother where the sperm came from and how it got inside the woman. The question made her very uncomfortable. She muttered something about a man and a woman being in love—as if love were somehow all that was needed for the sperm to find its way into the woman's body.

After that discussion, it seems to me that I was always a little confused about love and sex—even after I learned about the mechanics of sex and what goes where. The penis slips neatly into the vagina—but where does the love come in? Where does biology leave off and the higher emotions begin?

Does the female pseudoscorpion love the male when their dance is done? Does the male spider love his mate as he scurries away, running for his life? Is there love among the bowerbirds as they copulate in their bower? The textbooks fail to say. I speculate, but I have no way to get the answers.

■ ■ ■

My creatures engage in a long, slow courtship. I am getting sicker. Sometimes, my mother comes to ask me questions that I will not answer. Sometimes, men sit by my bed—but they are less real than my mother. These are men I cared about—men I thought I might love, though I never got beyond the thought. Through their translucent bodies, I can see the laboratory walls. They never were real, I think now.

Sometimes, in my delirium, I remember things. A dance back at college; I was slow-dancing, with someone's body pressed close to mine. The room was hot and stuffy and we went outside for some air. I remember he kissed me, while one hand stroked my breast and the other fumbled with the buttons of my blouse. I kept wondering if this was love—this fumbling in the shadows.

In my delirium, things change. I remember dancing in a circle with someone's hands clasping mine. My feet ache, and I try to stop, but my partner pulls me along, refusing to release me. My feet move instinctively in time with my partner's, though there is no music to help us keep the beat. The air smells of dampness and mold; I have lived my life underground and I am accustomed to these smells.

Is this love?

I spend my days lying by the window, watching through the dirty glass. From the mouth of the alley, he calls to her. I did not give him a voice, but he calls in his own way, rubbing his two front legs together so that metal rasps against metal, creaking like a cricket the size of a Buick.

She strolls past the alley mouth, ignoring him as he charges toward her, rattling his teeth. He backs away, as if inviting her to follow. She walks by. But then, a moment later, she strolls past again and the scene repeats itself. I understand that she is not really oblivious to his attention. She is simply taking her time, considering her situation. The male intensifies his efforts, tossing his head as he backs away, doing his best to call attention to the fine home he has created.

I listen to them at night. I cannot see them—the electricity failed two days ago and the streetlights are out. So I listen in the darkness, imagining. Metal legs rub together to make a high creaking noise. The sail on the male's back rattles as he unfolds it, then folds it, then unfolds it again, in what must be a sexual display. I hear a spiked tail rasping over a spiny back in a kind of caress. Teeth chatter against metal—love bites, perhaps. (The lion bites the lioness on the neck when they mate, an act of aggression that she accepts as affection.) Claws scrape against metal hide, clatter over metal scales. This, I think, is love. My creatures understand love.

I imagine a cock made of copper tubing and pipe fittings sliding into a canal lined with sheet metal from a soda can. I hear metal sliding over metal. And then my imagination fails. My construction made no provision for the stuff of reproduction: the sperm, the egg. Science failed me there. That part is up to the creatures themselves.

■ ■ ■

My body is giving out on me. I do not sleep at night; pain keeps me awake. I hurt everywhere, in my belly, in my breasts, in my bones. I have given up food. When I eat, the pains increase for a while, and then I vomit. I cannot keep anything down, and so I have stopped trying.

When the morning light comes, it is gray, filtering through the haze that covers the sky. I stare out the window, but I can't see the male. He has abandoned his post at the mouth of the alley. I watch for an hour or so, but the female does not stroll by. Have they finished with each other?

I watch from my bed for a few hours, the blanket wrapped around my shoulders. Sometimes, fever comes and I soak the blanket with my sweat. Sometimes, chills come, and I shiver under the blankets. Still, there is no movement in the alley.

It takes me more than an hour to make my way down the stairs. I can't trust my legs to support me, so I crawl on my knees, making my way across the room like a baby too young to stand upright. I carry the blanket with me, wrapped around my shoulders like a cape.

At the top of the stairs, I rest, then I go down slowly, one step at a time.

The alley is deserted. The array of hubcaps glitters in the dim sunlight. The litter of bright papers looks forlorn and abandoned. I step cautiously into the entrance. If the male were to rush me now, I would not be able to run away. I have used all my reserves to travel this far.

The alley is quiet. I manage to get to my feet and shuffle forward through the papers. My eyes are clouded, and I can just make out the dangling bedspread halfway down the alley. I make my way to it. I don't know why I've come here. I suppose I want to see. I want to know what has happened. That's all.

I duck beneath the dangling bedspread. In the dim light, I can see a doorway in the brick wall. Something is hanging from the lintel of the door.

I approach cautiously. The object is gray, like the door behind it. It has a peculiar, spiraling shape. When I touch it, I can feel a faint vibration inside, like the humming of distant equipment. I lay my cheek against it and I can hear a low-pitched song, steady and even.

When I was a child, my family visited the beach and I spent hours exploring the tidepools. Among the clumps of blue-black mussels and the black turban snails, I found the egg casing of a horn shark in a tidepool. It was spiral-shaped, like this egg, and when I held it to the light, I could see a tiny embryo inside. As I watched, the embryo twitched, moving even though it was not yet truly alive.

■ ■ ■

I crouch at the back of the alley with my blanket wrapped around me. I see no reason to move—I can die here as well as I can die anywhere. I am watching over the egg, keeping it safe.

Sometimes, I dream of my past life. Perhaps I should have handled it differently. Perhaps I should have been less cautious, hurried out on the mating line, answered the song when a male called from his bower. But it doesn't matter now. All that is gone, behind us now.

My time is over. The dinosaurs and the humans—our time is over. New times are coming. New types of love. I dream of the future, and my dreams are filled with the rattle of metal claws.

# 1/72nd Scale

...

## *Ian MacLeod*

As the decade turned, an astonishing new talent appeared on the scene, favoring the pages of the major SF magazines—*Asimov's, Interzone, Fantasy and Science Fiction, Amazing*—with the kind of stories that remind us why God invented science fiction. I am delighted to offer up Ian MacLeod's first professional sale, a resonant psychological fantasy called, provocatively, "1/72nd Scale."

Born thirty-six years ago in Solihull, West Midlands, England, MacLeod took a degree in law from Birmingham Polytechnic and subsequently spent ten years in the civil service. In 1990, galvanized by a rash of sales and the support of his solicitor wife, he quit his job to pursue a full-time writing career. When not changing nappies and pushing prams on behalf of his daughter, Emily, MacLeod produces stories, novelettes, novel chapters, and—as you might infer from "1/72nd Scale"—an occasional plastic model.

"What I wanted to achieve was a focus that gave some everyday object an unremitting life of its own," MacLeod explains. "Hardly a new idea, but it felt fresh at the time I was writing the piece." Whether the premise is fresh or not, the author has realized it with uncommon grace. Moving but never sentimental, MacLeod's novelette makes for a compelling comparison with this volume's other tale of loss and transfiguration, Terry Bisson's "Bears Discover Fire."

David moved into Simon's room. Mum and Dad said they were determined not to let it become a shrine: Dad even promised to redecorate it anyhow David wanted. New paint, new curtains, Superman wallpaper, the lot. You have to try to forget the past, Dad said, enveloping him in his arms and the smell of his sweat, things that have been and gone. You're what counts now, Junior, our living son.

On a wet Sunday afternoon (the windows steamed, the air still thick with the fleshy smell of pork, an afternoon for headaches, boredom, and family arguments if ever there was one) David took the small stepladder from the garage and lugged it up the stairs to Simon's room. One by one, he peeled Simon's posters from the walls, careful not to tear the corners as he separated them from yellowed Sellotape and blobs of Blutac. He rolled them into neat tubes, each held in place by an elastic band, humming along to Dire Straits on Simon's Sony portable as he did so. He was halfway through taking the dog-fighting aircraft down from the ceiling when Mum came in. The dusty prickly feel of the fragile models set his teeth on edge. They were like big insects.

"And what do you think you're doing?" Mum asked.

David left a Spitfire swinging on its thread and looked down. It was odd seeing her from above, the dark half moons beneath her eyes.

"I'm . . . just . . ."

Dire Straits were playing "Industrial Disease." Mum fussed an-grily with the Sony, trying to turn it off. The volume soared. She jerked the plug out and turned to face him through the silence. "What makes you think this thing is yours, David? We can hear it blaring all through the bloody house. Just what do you think you're doing?"

"I'm sorry," he said. A worm of absurd laughter squirmed in his stomach. Here he was perched up on a stepladder, looking down at Mum as though he was seven feet tall. But he didn't climb down: he thought she probably wouldn't get angry with someone perched up on a ladder.

But Mum raged at him. Shouted and shouted and shouted. Her face went white as bone. Dad came up to see what the noise was, his shirt unbuttoned and creased from sleep, the sports pages crumpled in his right hand. He lifted David down from the ladder and said it was all right. This was what they'd agreed, okay?

Mum began to cry. She gave David a salty hug, saying she was sorry. Sorry. My darling. He felt stiff and awkward. His eyes, which had been flooding with tears a moment before, were suddenly as dry as the Sahara. So dry it hurt to blink.

Mum and Dad helped him finish clearing up Simon's models and posters. They smiled a lot and talked in loud, shaky voices. Little sis Victoria came and stood at the door to watch. It was like packing away the decorations after Christmas. Mum wrapped the planes up in tissues and put them carefully in a box. She gave a loud sob that sounded like a burp when she broke one of the propellers.

When they'd finished (just the bare furniture, the bare walls. Growing dark, but no one wanting to put the light on), Dad promised that he'd redecorate the room next weekend, or the weekend after at the latest. He'd have the place better than new. He ruffled David's hair in a big, bearlike gesture and slipped his other arm around Mum's waist. Better than new.

• • •

That was a year ago.

The outlines of Simon's posters still shadowed the ivy wallpaper. The ceiling was pinholed where his models had hung. Hard little patches of Humbrol enamel and polystyrene cement cratered the carpet around the desk in the bay window. There was even a faint greasy patch above the bed where Simon used to sit up reading his big boy's books. They, like the model aircraft, now slumbered in the attic. *The Association Football Yearbook, Aircraft of the Desert Campaign, Classic Cars 1945–1960, Tanks and Armored Vehicles of the World, The Modeler's Handbook* . . . all gathering dust, darkness, and spiders.

David still thought of it as Simon's room. He'd even called it that once or twice by accident. No one noticed. David's proper room, the room he'd had before Simon died, the room he still looked into on his way past it to the toilet, had been taken over by Victoria. What had once been his territory, landmarked by the laughing-face crack on the ceiling, the dip in the floorboards where the fireplace had once been, the corner where the sun pasted a bright orange triangle on summer evenings, was engulfed in frilly curtains, Snoopy lampshades, and My Little Ponys. Not that Victoria seemed particularly happy with her new, smart bedroom. She would have been more than content to sleep in Simon's old room with his posters curling and yellowing like dry skin and his models gathering dust around her. Little Victoria had idolized Simon; laughed like a mad thing when he dandled her on his knee and tickled her, gazed in wonderment when he told her those clever stories he made up right out of his head.

David started Senior School in the autumn. Archbishop Lacy; the one Simon used to go to. It wasn't as bad as he'd feared, and for a while he even told himself that things were getting better at home as well. Then on a Thursday afternoon as he changed after Games (shower stream and sweat. Cowering in a corner of the changing rooms. Almost ripping his Y-fronts in his hurry to pull them up and

hide his winkle) Mr. Lewis, the gamesmaster, came over and handed
him a brown window envelope addressed to his parents. David popped
it into his blazer pocket and worried all the way home. No one else
had got one and he couldn't think of anything he'd done sufficiently
well to deserve special mention, although he could think of lots of
things he'd done badly. He handed it straight to Mum when he came
in, anxious to find out the worst. He waited by her as she stood reading
it in the kitchen. The Blue Peter signature tune drifted in from the
lounge. She finished the letter, and folded it in half, sharpening the
crease with her nails. Then in half again. And again, until it was a
fat, neat square. David gazed at it in admiration as Mum told him in
a matter-of-fact voice that School wanted back the hundred-meters
swimming trophy that Simon had won the year before. For a moment,
David felt a warm wave of relief break over him. Then he looked up
and saw Mum's face.

There was a bitter argument between Mum and Dad and the
School. In the end—after the local paper had run an article in its
middle pages headlined "Heartless Request"—Archbishop Lacy
agreed to buy a new trophy and let them keep the old one. It stayed
on the fireplace in the lounge, regularly tarnishing and growing bright
again as Mum attacked it with Duraglit. The headmaster gave several
assembly talks about becoming too attached to possessions and Mr.
Lewis, the gamesmaster, made Thursday afternoons Hell for David
in the special ways that only a gamesmaster can.

Senior School also meant Homework. As the nights lengthened
and the first bangers echoed down the suburban streets, David sat
working at Simon's desk in the bay window. He always did his best,
and although he never came much above the middle of the class in
any subject, his handwriting was often remarked on for its neatness
and readability. He usually left the curtains open and had just the
desk light (blue-and-white wicker shade. Stand of turned mahogany
on a wrought-iron base. Good enough to have come from British
Home Stores and all Simon's work. All of it) on so that he could see
out. The streetlamp flashed through the hairy boughs of the monkey
puzzle tree in the front garden. Dot, dot, dash. Dash, dash, dot. He
often wondered if it was a message.

Sometimes, way past the time when she should have been asleep,
Victoria's door would squeak open and her slippered feet would patter

along the landing and halfway down the stairs. There she would sit, hugging her knees and watching the TV light flicker through the frosted glass door of the lounge. Cracking open his door quietly and peering down through the top banisters, David had seen her there. If the lounge door opened she would scamper back up and out of sight into her bedroom faster than a rabbit. Mum and Dad never knew. It was Victoria's secret, and in the little he said to her, David had no desire to prick that bubble. He guessed that she was probably waiting for Simon to return.

Dad came up one evening when David had just finished algebra and was turning to the agricultural revolution. He stood in the doorway, the light from the landing haloing what was left of his hair. A dark figure with one arm hidden, holding something big behind its back. For a wild moment, David felt his scalp prickle with incredible, irrational fear.

"How's Junior?" Dad said.

He ambled through the shadows of the room into the pool of yellow light where David sat.

"All right, thank you," David said. He didn't like being called Junior. No one had ever called him Junior when Simon was alive and he was now the eldest in any case.

"I've got a present for you. Guess what?"

"I don't know." David had discovered long ago that it was dangerous to guess presents. You said the thing you wanted it to be and upset people when you were wrong.

"Close your eyes."

There was a rustle of paper and a thin, scratchy rattle that he couldn't place. But it was eerily familiar.

"Now open them."

David composed his face into a suitable expression of happy surprise and opened his eyes.

It was a big, long box wrapped in squeaky folds of shrink-wrap plastic. An Airfix 1/72nd-scale Flying Fortress.

David didn't have to pretend. He was genuinely astonished. Overawed. It was a big model, the biggest in the Airfix 1/72nd series. Simon (who always talked about these things; the steady pattern of triumphs that peppered his life. Each new obstacle mastered and overcome) had been planning to buy one when he'd finished the

Lancaster he was working on and had saved up enough money from his paper round. Instead, the Lancaster remained an untidy jumble of plastic, and in one of those vicious conjunctions that are never supposed to happen to people like Simon, he and his bike chanced to share the same patch of tarmac on the High Street at the same moment as a Pickfords lorry turning right out of a service road. The bike had twisted into a half circle around the big wheels. Useless scrap.

"I'd never expected . . . I'd . . ." David opened and closed his mouth in the hope that more words would come out.

Dad put a large hand on his shoulder. "I knew you'd be pleased. I've got you all the paints it lists on the side of the box, the glue." Little tins pattered out onto the desk, each with a colored lid. There were three silvers. David could see from the picture on the side of the box that he was going to need a lot of silver. "And look at this." Dad flashed a craft knife close to his face. "Isn't that dinky? You'll have to promise to be careful, though."

"I promise."

"Take your time with it, Junior. I can't wait to see it finished." The big hand squeezed his shoulder, then let go. "Don't allow it to get in the way of your homework."

"Thanks, Dad. I won't."

"Don't I get a kiss?"

David gave him a kiss.

"Well, I'll leave you to it. I'll give you any help you want. Don't you think you should have the big light on? You'll strain your eyes."

"I'm fine."

Dad hovered by him for a moment, his lips moving and a vague look in his eyes as though he was searching for the words of a song. Then he grunted and left the bedroom.

David stared at the box. He didn't know much about models, but he knew that the Flying Fortress was The Big One. Even Simon had been working up to it in stages. The Everest of models in every sense. Size. Cost. Difficulty. The guns swiveled. The bomb bay doors opened. The vast and complex undercarriage went up and down. From the heights of such an achievement one could gaze serenely down at the whole landscape of childhood. David slid the box back into its large paper bag along with the paints and the glue and the knife. He put it down on the carpet and tried to concentrate on the agricultural revolution. The crumpled paper at the top of the bag made creepy crackling noises. He got up, put it in the bottom of his wardrobe, and closed the door.

"How are you getting on with the model?" Dad asked him at tea two days later.

David nearly choked on a fish finger. He forced it down, the dry bread crumbs sandpapering his throat. "I, I, er—" He hadn't given the model any thought at all (just dreams and a chill of unease. A dark mountain to climb) since he'd put it away in the wardrobe. "I'm taking it slowly," he said. "I want to make sure I get it right."

Mum and Dad and Victoria returned to munching their food, satisfied for the time being.

After tea, David clicked his bedroom door shut and took the model out from the wardrobe. The paper bag crackled excitedly in his hands. He turned on Simon's light and sat down at the desk. Then he emptied the bag and bunched it into a tight ball, stuffing it firmly down into the wastepaper bin beside the chair. He lined the paints up next to the window. Duck-egg green. Matt black. Silver. Silver. Silver . . . a neat row of squat little soldiers.

David took the craft knife and slit open the shining shrink-wrap covering. It rippled and squealed as he skinned it from the box. Then he worked the cardboard lid off. A clean, sweet smell wafted into his face. Like a new car (a hospital waiting room. The sudden taste of metal in your mouth as Mum's heirloom Spode tumbles toward the fireplace tiles) or the inside of a camera case. A clear plastic bag filled the box beneath a heavy wad of instructions. To open it he had to ease out the whole gray chittering weight of the model and cut open the seal, then carefully tease the innards out, terrified that he might lose a piece in doing so. When he'd finished, the unassembled Flying Fortress jutted out from the box like a huge pile of jack-straws. It took him another thirty minutes to get them to lie flat enough to close the lid. Somehow, it was very important that he closed the lid.

So far, so good. David unfolded the instructions. They got bigger and bigger, opening out into a vast sheet covered with dense type and arrows and numbers and line drawings. But he was determined not to be put off. Absolutely determined. He could see himself in just a few weeks' time, walking slowly down the stairs with the great silver bird cradled carefully in his arms. Every detail correct. The paintwork perfect. Mum and Dad and Victoria will look up as he enters the bright warm lounge. And soon there is joy on their faces. The Flying Fortress is marvelous, a miracle (even Simon couldn't have done better), a work of art. There is laughter and wonder like Christmas firelight as David demonstrates how the guns swivel, how the undercarriage goes up and down. And although there is no need to say it, everyone understands that this is the turning point. The sun will shine again, the rain will be warm and sweet, clear white snow will powder the winter, and Simon will be just a sad memory, a glint of tears in their happy, smiling eyes.

The preface to the instructions helpfully suggested that it was best to paint the small parts before they were assembled. Never one to ignore sensible advice, David reopened the box and lifted out the gray clusters of plastic. Like coat hangers, they had an implacable tendency to hook themselves onto each other. Every part was attached to one of the trees of thin plastic around which the model was molded. The big pieces such as the sides of the aircraft and the wings were easy to recognize, but there was also a vast number of odd shapes that had no obvious purpose. Then, as his eyes searched along rows of thin bits, fat bits, star-shaped bits, and bits that might be parts of bombs, he saw a row of little gray men hanging from the plastic tree by their heads.

The first of the men was crouching in an oddly fetal position. When David pulled him off the plastic tree, his neck snapped instead of the join at the top of his head.

David spent the evenings and most of the weekends of the next month at work on the Flying Fortress.

"Junior," Dad said one day as he met him coming up the stairs, "you're getting so absorbed in that model of yours. I saw your light on last night when I went to bed. Just you be careful it doesn't get in the way of your homework."

"I won't let that happen," David answered, putting on his good-boy smile. "I won't get too absorbed."

But David was absorbed in the model, and the model was absorbed into him. It absorbed him to the exclusion of everything else. He could feel it working its way into his system. Lumps of glue and plastic, sticky sweet-smelling silver enamel worming into his flesh.

Crusts of it were under his nails, sticking in his hair and to his teeth, his thoughts. Homework—which had been a worry to him—no longer mattered. He simply didn't do it. At the end-of-lesson bells he packed the exercise books into his satchel, and a week later he would take them out again for the next session, pristine and unchanged. Nobody actually took much notice. There was, he discovered, a group of boys and girls in his class who never did their homework—they just didn't do it. More amazing still, they weren't bothered about it and neither were the teachers. He began to sit at the back of the class with the cluster of paper-pellet flickers, boys who said "fuck," and lunchtime smokers. They made reluctant room for him, wrinkling their noses in suspicion at their new, paint-smelling, hollow-eyed colleague. As far as David was concerned, the arrangement was purely temporary. Once the model was finished, he'd work his way back up the class, no problem.

The model absorbed David. David absorbed the model. He made mistakes. He learned from his mistakes and made other mistakes instead. In his hurry to learn from those mistakes he repeated the original ones. It took him aching hours of frustration and eyestrain to paint the detailed small parts of the model. The Humbrol enamel would never quite go where he wanted it to, but unfailingly ended up all over his hands. His fingerprints began to mark the model, the desk, and the surrounding area like the evidence of a crime. And everything was so tiny. As he squinted down into the yellow pool of light cast by Simon's neat lamp, the paintbrush trembling in one hand and a tiny piece of motor sticking to the fingers of the other, he could feel the minute, tickly itchiness of it drilling through the breathless silence into his brain. But he persevered. The pieces came and went, turning from gray to blotched and runny combinations of enamel. He arranged them on sheets of the *Daily Mirror* on the right-hand corner of his desk, peeling them off his fingers like half-sucked Murraymints. A week later the paint was still tacky: he hadn't stirred the pots properly.

The nights grew colder and longer. The monkey puzzle tree whispered in the wind. David found it difficult to keep warm in Simon's bed. After shivering wakefully into the gray small hours, he would often have to scramble out from the clinging cold sheets to go for a pee. Once, weary and fumbling with the cord of his pajamas, he glanced down from the landing and saw Victoria sitting on the stairs. He tiptoed down to her, careful not to make the stairs creak and wake Mum and Dad.

"What's the matter?" he whispered.

Little Victoria turned to him, her face as expressionless as a doll's. "You're not Simon," she hissed. Then she pushed past him as she scampered back up to bed.

On Bonfire Night, David stood beneath a dripping umbrella as Dad struggled to light a Roman candle in a makeshift shelter of paving stones. Tomorrow, he decided, I will start to glue some bits together. Painting the rest of the details can wait. The firework flared briefly through the wet darkness, spraying silver fire and soot across the paving slab. Victoria squealed with fear and chewed her mitten. The after-image stayed in David's eyes. Silver, almost airplane-shaped.

The first thing David discovered about polystyrene cement was that it came out very quickly when the nozzle was pricked with a pin. The second was that it had a remarkable ability to melt plastic. He was almost in tears by the end of his first evening of attempted construction. There was a mushy crater in the middle of the left tailplane and gray smears of plastic all along the side of the motor housing he'd been trying to join. It was disgusting. Gray runners of plastic were dripping from his hands, and he could feel the reek of the glue bringing a crushing headache down on him.

"Getting on all right?" Dad asked, poking his head around the door.

David nearly jumped out of his skin. He desperately clawed un-made bits of the model over to cover up the mess as Dad crossed the room to peer over his shoulder and mutter approvingly for a few seconds. When he'd gone, David discovered that the new pieces were now also sticky with glue and melting plastic.

David struggled on. He didn't like the Flying Fortress and would have happily thrown it away, but the thought of Mum and Dad's disappointment—even little Victoria screwing her face up in contempt—was now as vivid as his imagined triumph had been before. Simon never gave up on things. Simon always (David would show them) did everything right. But by now the very touch of the model, the tiny bumps of the rivets, the rough little edges where the molding had seeped out, made his flesh crawl. And for no particular reason (a dream too bad to remember) the thought came to him that maybe even real Flying Fortresses (crammed into the rear gunner's turret like a corpse in a coffin. Kamikaze Zero Zens streaming out of the sky. Flames everywhere and the thick stink of burning. Boiling gray plastic pouring like treacle over his hands, his arms, his shoulders, his face. His mouth. Choking, screaming. Choking) weren't such wonderful things after all.

Compared with constructing the model, the painting—although a disaster—had been easy. Night after night, he struggled with meaningless bits of tiny plastic. And a gray voice whispered in his ear that Simon would have finished it now. Yes siree. And it would have been perfect. David was under no illusions now as to how difficult the model was to construct (those glib instructions to fit this part to that part that actually entailed hours of messy struggle. The suspicious fact that Airfix had chosen to use a painting of a real Flying Fortress on the box rather than a photograph of the finished model), but he knew that if anyone could finish it, Simon could. Simon could always do anything. Even dead, he amounted to more than David.

In mid-November, David had a particularly difficult Thursday at Games. Mr. Lewis wasn't like the other teachers. He didn't ignore little boys who kept quiet and didn't do much. As he was always telling them, he *Cared*. Because David hadn't paid much attention the week before, he'd brought along his rugger kit instead of his gym kit. He was the only boy dressed in green amid all the whites. Mr. Lewis spotted him easily. While the rest of the class watched, laughing and hooting, David had to climb the ropes. Mr. Lewis gave him a bruising push to get started. His muscles burning, his chest heaving with tears and exertion, David managed to climb a foot. Then he slid back. With an affable, aching clout, Mr. Lewis shoved him up again. More quickly this time, David slid back, scouring his hands, arms, and the insides of his legs red raw. Mr. Lewis spun the rope; the climbing bars, the mat-covered parquet floor, the horse, and the tall windows looking out on the wet playground all swirled dizzily. He spun the rope the other way. Just as David was starting to wonder whether he could keep his dinner of liver, soggy chips, and apple snow down for much longer, Mr. Lewis stopped the rope again, embracing David in a sweaty hug. His face was close enough for David to count the big black pores on his nose—if he'd had a few hours to spare.

"A real softy, you are," Mr. Lewis whispered. "Not like your brother at all. Now he was a proper lad." And then he let go.

David dropped to the floor, badly bruising his knees.

As he limped up the stairs that evening, the smell of glue, paint, and plastic—which had been a permanent fixture in the bedroom for some time—poured down from the landing to greet him. It curled around his face like a caressing hand, fingering down his throat and into his nose. And there was nothing remotely like a Flying Fortress on Simon's old desk. But David had had enough. Tonight, he was determined to sort things out. Okay, he'd made a few mistakes, but they could be covered up, repaired, filled in. No one else would notice, and the Flying Fortress would look (David, we knew you'd do a good job but we'd never imagined anything this splendid. We must ring Granny, tell the local press) just as a 1/72nd-scale top-of-the-range Airfix model should.

David sat down at the desk. The branches of the monkey puzzle tree outside slithered and shivered in the rain. He stared at his yellow-lit reflection in the glass. The image of the rest of the room was dim, like something from the past. Simon's room. David had put up one or two things of his own now: a silver seagull mobile, a big Airlines of the World poster that he'd got by sending off ten Ski yogurt foils; but, like cats in a new home, they'd never settled in.

David drew the curtains shut. He clicked the Play button on Simon's Sony portable and Dire Straits came out. He didn't think much of the music one way or another but it was nice to have a safe, predictable noise going on in the background. Simon's Sony was a special one that played one side of a cassette and then the other as often as you liked without having to turn it over. David remembered the trouble Simon had gone to in getting the right machine at the right price, the pride with which he'd demonstrated the features to Mum and Dad, as though he'd invented them all himself. David had never felt that way about anything.

David clenched his eyes shut, praying that Simon's clever fingers and calm confidence would briefly touch him, that Simon would peek over his shoulder and offer some help. But the thought went astray. He sensed Simon standing at his shoulder all right, but it was Simon as he would be now after a year under the soil, his body still twisted like the frame of his bike, mossy black flesh sliding from his bones.

David shuddered and opened his eyes to the gray plastic mess that was supposed to be a Flying Fortress. He forced himself to look over his shoulder. The room was smugly quiet.

Although there was still much to do, David had finished with planning and detail. He grabbed the obvious big parts of the plane that the interminable instructions (slot parts A, B, and C of the rear side bulkhead together, ensuring that the *upper* inside brace of the support joint fits into dovetail *iv* as illustrated) never got around to mentioning and began to push them together, squeezing out gouts of glue. Dire Straits droned on, "Love Over Gold," "It Never Rains," then back to the start of the tape. The faint hum of the TV came up through the floorboards. Key bits of plastic snapped and melted in his hands. David ignored them. At his back, the shadows of Simon's room fluttered in disapproval.

At last, David had something that bore some similarity to a plane. He turned its sticky weight in his hands and a great bird shadow flew across the ceiling behind him. One of the wings drooped down, there was a wide split down the middle of the body, smears of glue and paint were everywhere. It was, he knew, a sorry mess. He covered it over with an old sheet in case Mum and Dad should see it in the morning, then went to bed.

Darkness. Dad snoring faintly next door. The outline of Simon's body still there on the mattress beneath his back. David's heart pounded loudly enough to make the springs creak. The room and the Airfix-laden air pulsed in sympathy. It muttered and whispered (no sleep for you my boy. Nice and restless for you all night when everyone's tucked up warm and you're the only wide-awake person in the whole gray universe) but grew silent whenever he lay especially still and dared it to make a noise. The street light filtered through the monkey puzzle tree and the curtains on to Simon's desk. The sheet covering the model looked like a face. Simon's face. As it would be now.

David slept. He dreamed. The dreams were worse than waking.

When he opened his eyes to Friday morning, clawing up out of a nightmare into the plastic-scented room, Simon's decayed face still yawned lopsidedly at him, clear and unashamed in the gray wash of the winter dawn. He couldn't bear touching the sheet, let alone taking it off and looking at the mess underneath. Shivering in his pajamas, he found a biro in a drawer and used it to poke the yellowed cotton folds until they formed an innocuous shape.

It didn't feel like a Friday at school. The usual sense of sunny relief, the thought of two whole days of freedom, had drained away. His eyes sore from lack of sleep and the skin on his hands flaky with glue, David drifted through Maths and Art, followed by French in the afternoon. At the start of Social Studies, the final lesson of the week, he sat down on a drawing pin that had been placed on his chair: now that Mr. Lewis had singled him out, the naughty boys he shared the back of the class with were beginning to think of him as fair game. Amid the sniggers and guffaws, David pulled the pin out of his bottom uncomplainingly. He had other things on his mind. He was, in fact, a little less miserable about the Flying Fortress than he had been that morning. It probably wasn't as bad as he remembered (could anything really be that bad?), and if he continued tonight, working slowly, using silver paint freely to cover up the bad bits, there might still be a possibility that it would look reasonable. Maybe he could even hang it from the ceiling before anyone got a chance to take a close look. As he walked home through the wet mist, he kept telling himself that it would (please, please, oh, please, God) be all right.

He peeled back the sheet, tugging it off the sticky bits. It was like taking a bandage from a scabby wound. The model looked dreadful. He whimpered and stepped back. He was sure it hadn't been that bad the night before. The wings and the body had sagged and the plastic had a bubbly, pimply look in places as though something was trying to erupt from underneath. Hurriedly, he snatched the sheet up again and threw it over, then ran downstairs into the lounge.

Mum glanced up from *The Price Is Right*. "You're a stranger down here," she said absently. "I thought you were still busy with that thing of yours."

"It's almost finished," David said to his own amazement as he flopped down, breathless, on the sofa.

Mum nodded slowly and turned back to the TV. She watched TV a lot these days. David had occasionally wandered in and found her staring at pages from Ceefax.

David sat in a daze, letting program after program go (as Simon used to say) in one eye and out of the other. He had no desire to go back upstairs to his (Simon's) bedroom, but when the credits rolled on *News at Ten* and Dad smiled at the screen and suggested it was time that Juniors were up in bed, he got up without argument. There was something less than affable about Dad's affable suggestions recently. As though if you didn't hop to it he might (slam your head against the wall until your bones stuck out through your face) grow angry.

After he'd found the courage to turn off the bedside light, David lay with his arms stiffly at his sides, his eyes wide open. Even in the darkness, he could see the pin marks on the ceiling where Simon had hung his planes. They were like tiny black stars. He heard Mum go up to bed, her nervous breathing as she climbed the stairs. He heard the whine of the TV as the channel closed, Dad clearing his throat before he turned it off, the sound of the toilet, the bedroom door closing. Then silence.

Silence. Like the taut skin of a drum. Dark pinprick stars on the grainy white ceiling like a negative of the real sky, as though the whole world had twisted itself inside out around David and he was now in a place where up was down, black was white, and people slithered in the cracks beneath the pavement. Silence. He really missed last night's whispering voices. Expectant silence. Silence that screamed Something Is Going To Happen.

Something did. Quite matter-of-factly, as though it was as ordinary as the kettle in the kitchen switching itself off when it came to the boil or the traffic lights changing to red on the High Street, the sheet began to slide off the Flying Fortress. Simon's face briefly stretched into the folds, then vanished as the whole sheet flopped to the floor. The Fortress sat still for a moment, outlined in the light of the street lamp through the curtains. Then it began to crawl across the desk, dragging itself on its wings like a wounded beetle.

David didn't really believe that this could be happening. But as it moved it even made the sort of scratchy squeaky noises that a living model of a Flying Fortress might be expected to make. It paused at the edge of the desk, facing the window; it seemed to be wondering what to do next. As though, David thought with giggly hilarity, it hasn't done quite enough already. But the Fortress was far from finished. With a jerky, insect movement, it launched itself toward the window. The curtain sagged and the glass went bump. Fluttering its wings like a huge moth, it clung on and started to climb up toward the curtain rail. Halfway up, it paused again. It made a chittering sound and a ripple of movement passed along its back, a little shiver of pleasure: alive at last. And David knew it sensed something else alive in the room. Him. The Fortress launched itself from the curtains, setting the street light shivering across the empty desk and, more like a huge moth than ever, began to flutter around the room, bumping blindly into the ceiling and walls. Involuntarily, he covered his face with his hands. Through the cracks between his fingers he saw the gray flitter of its movement. He heard the shriek of soft, fleshy plastic. He felt the panicky breath of its wings. Just as he was starting to think it couldn't get any worse, the Fortress settled on his face. He felt the wings embracing him, the tail curling into his neck, thin gray claws scrabbling between his fingers, hungry to get at the liquid of his eyes and the soft flesh inside his cheeks.

David began to scream. The fingers grew more persistent, pulling at his hands with a strength he couldn't resist.

"David! What's the matter with you!"

The big light was on. Dad's face hovered above him. Mum stood at the bottom of the bed, her thin white hands tying and untying in knots.

". . ." He was lost for words, shaking with embarrassment and relief.

Mum and Dad stayed with him for a few minutes, their faces drawn and puzzled. Simon never pulled this sort of trick. Mum's hands knotted. Dad's made fists. Victoria's white face peered around the door when they weren't looking, then vanished again, quick as a ghost. All David could say was that he'd had a bad dream. He glanced across the desk through the bland yellow light. The Fortress was covered by its sheet again. Simon's rotting face grinned at him from the folds. You can't catch me out that easily, the grin said.

Mum and Dad switched off the big light when they left the room. They shuffled back down the landing. As soon as he heard their bedroom door clunk shut, David shot out of bed and clicked his light on again. He left it blazing all night as he sat on the side of the bed, staring at the cloth-covered model. It didn't move. The thin scratches on the backs of his hands were the only sign that anything had happened at all.

As David stared into his bowl of Rice Krispies at breakfast, their snap and crackle and pop fast fading into the sugary milk, Mum announced that she and Dad and Victoria were going to see Gran that afternoon for tea; did he want to come along? David said no. An idea had been growing in his mind, nurtured through the long hours of the night: with the afternoon free to himself, the idea became a fully fledged plan.

Saying he was off to the library, David went down to the Post Office on the High Street before it closed at lunchtime. The clouds were dark and low and the streets were damp. After waiting an age behind a shopkeeper with bags of ten-pence bits to change, he presented the fat lady behind the glass screen with his savings book and asked to withdraw everything but the one pound needed to keep the account open.

"That's a whole eleven pounds, fifty-two pence," she said to him. "Have we been saving up for something special?"

"Oh, yes," David said, dragging his good-boy smile out from the wardrobe and giving it a dust-down for the occasion.

"A nice new toy? I know what you lads are like, all guns and armor."

"It's, um, a surprise."

The lady humphed, disappointed that he wouldn't tell her what it was. She took out a handful of dry-roasted nuts from a drawer beneath the counter and popped them into her mouth, licking the salt off her fingers before counting out his money.

Back at home, David returned the savings book to the desk (his hands shaking in his hurry to get back out of the room, his eyes desperately focused away from the cloth-covered model on the top) but kept the two five-pound notes and the change crinkling against his leg in the front pocket of his jeans. He just hoped that Dad wouldn't have one of his occasional surges of interest in his finances and ask to see the savings book. He'd thought that he might say something about helping out a poor school friend who needed a loan for a new pair of shoes, but the idea sounded unconvincing even as he rehearsed it in his mind.

Fish fingers again for lunch. David wasn't hungry and slipped a few across the plastic tablecloth to Victoria when Mum and Dad weren't looking. Victoria could eat fish fingers until they came out of her ears. When she was really full up she sometimes even tried to poke a few in there to demonstrate that no more would fit.

Afterwards, David sat in the lounge and pretended to watch *Grandstand* while Mum and Dad and Victoria banged around upstairs and changed into their best clothes. He was tired and tense, feeling rather like the anguished ladies at the start of the headache-tablet adverts, but underneath there was a kind of exhilaration. After all that had happened, he was still determined to put up a fight. Finally, just as the runners and riders for the two o'clock Holsten Pils Handicap at rainswept Wetherby were getting ready for the off, Mum and Dad called bye-bye and slammed the front door.

The doorbell rang a second later.

"Don't forget," Mum said, standing on the doorstep and fiddling with the strap of the black handbag she'd bought for Simon's funeral, "there's some fish fingers left in the freezer for your tea."

"No, I won't," David said.

He stood and watched as the Cortina reversed out of the concrete drive and turned off down the estate road through a gray fog of exhaust.

It was a dark, moist afternoon, but the rain that was making the going heavy at Wetherby was still holding off. For once, the fates seemed to be conspiring in his favor. He took the old galvanized bucket from the garage and, grabbing the stiff-bristled outside broom for good measure, set off up the stairs toward Simon's bedroom. The reek of plastic was incredibly strong now—he wondered why no one else in the house had noticed or complained.

The door to Simon's room was shut. Slippery with sweat, David's hand slid uselessly around the knob. Slowly, deliberately, forcing his muscles to work, he wiped his palms on his jeans and tried again. The knob turned. The door opened. The cloth face grinned at him through the stinking air. It was almost a skull now, as though the last of the flesh had been worried away, and the off-white of the sheet gave added realism. David tried not to think of such things. He walked briskly toward the desk, holding the broom out in front of him like a lance. He gave the cloth a push with it, trying to get rid of the face. The model beneath stirred lazily, like a sleeper awakening in a warm bed. More haste, less speed, he told himself. That was what Dad always said. The words became a meaningless jumble as he held the bucket beneath the lip of the desk and prodded the cloth-covered model toward it. More haste, less speed. Plastic screeched on the surface of the desk, leaving a wet gray trail. More waste, less greed. Little aircraft-shaped bumps came and went beneath the cloth. Hasting waste, wasting haste. The model plopped into the bucket; mercifully, the cloth still covered it. It squirmed and gave a plaintive squeak. David dropped the broom, took the bucket in both hands, and shot down the stairs.

Out through the back door. Across the damp lawn to the black patch where Dad burned the garden refuse. David tipped the bucket over quickly, trapping the model like a spider under a glass. He hared back into the house, snatching up a book of matches, a bottle of meths, firelighters, and newspapers, then sprinted up the garden again before the model had time to think about getting out.

He lifted up the bucket and tossed it to one side. The cloth slid out over the blackened earth like a watery jelly. The model squirmed from the folds, stretching out its wings. David broke the cap from the meths bottle and tipped out a good pint over cloth and plastic and earth. The model hissed in surprise at the cool touch of the alcohol. He tried to light a match from the book. The thin strips of card crumpled. The fourth match caught, but puffed out before he could touch it to the cloth. The model's struggles were becoming increasingly agitated. He struck another match. The head flew off. Another. The model started to crawl away from the cloth. Toward him, stretching and contracting like a slug. Shuddering and sick with disgust, David shoved it back with the toe of his trainer. He tried another match, almost dropping the crumpled book to the ground in his hurry. It flared. He forced himself to crouch down—moving slowly to preserve the precious flame—and touch it to the cloth. It went up with a satisfying *whooph*.

David stepped back from the cheery brightness. The cloth soon charred and vanished. The model mewed and twisted. Thick black smoke curled up from the fire. The gray plastic blistered and ran. Bubbles popped on the aircraft's writhing skin. It arched its tail in the heat like a scorpion. The black smoke grew thicker. The next-door neighbor, Mrs. Bowen, slammed her bedroom window shut with an angry bang. David's eyes streamed as he threw on firelighters and balled-up newspapers for good measure.

The aircraft struggled in the flames, its blackened body rippling in heat and agony. But somehow, its shape remained. Against all the rules of the way things should be, the plastic didn't run into a sticky pool. And, even as the flames began to dwindle around it, the model was clearly still alive. Wounded, shivering with pain. But still alive.

David watched in bitter amazement. As the model had no right to exist in the first place, he supposed he'd been naïve to imagine that an ordinary thing like a fire in the garden would be enough to kill it. The last of the flames puttered on the blackened earth. David breathed the raw, sick smell of burnt plastic. The model—which had lost what little resemblance it had ever had to a Flying Fortress and now reminded David more than anything of the dead seagull he'd once seen rotting on the beach at Blackpool—whimpered faintly and, slowly lifting its blistered and trembling wings, tried to crawl toward him.

He watched for a moment in horror, then jerked into action. The galvanized bucket lay just behind him. He picked it up and plonked it down hard on the model. It squealed: David saw that he'd trapped one of the blackened wings under the rim of the bucket. He lifted it up an inch, kicked the thing under with his trainer, then ran to find something to weigh down the bucket.

With two bricks on top, the model grew silent inside, as though accepting its fate. Maybe it really is dying (why haven't you got the courage to run and get the big spade from the shed like big brave Simon would do in a situation like this? Chop the thing up into tiny bits), he told himself. The very least he hoped for was that it wouldn't dig its way out.

David looked at his watch. Three-thirty. So far, things hadn't gone as well as he'd planned, but there was no time to stand around worrying. He still had a lot to do. He threw the book of matches into the bin, put the meths and the firelighters back where he had found them, hung the broom up in the garage, pulled on his duffle coat, locked up the house, and set off toward the High Street.

The grayness of a dull day was already sliding into the dark of evening. Pacing swiftly along the wet-leafed pavement, David glanced over privet hedges into warmly lit living rooms. Mums and Dads sitting on the sofa together, Big Sis doing her nails in preparation for a night down at the pub with her boyfriend, little Jimmy playing with his He-Man doll in front of the fire. Be careful, David thought, seeing those blandly absorbed faces, things can fall apart so easily. Please, be careful.

He took the shortcut across the park where a few weary players chased a muddy white ball through the gloom and came out onto the High Street by the public toilets. Just across the road, the back tires of the Pickfords lorry had rolled Simon into the next world.

David turned left. Woolworth's seemed the best place to start. The High Street was busy. Cars and lorries grumbled between the numerous traffic lights, and streams of people dallied and bumped and pushed in and out of the fluorescent heat of the shops. David was surprised to see that the plate-glass windows were already brimming with cardboard Santas and tinsel, but he didn't feel the usual thrill of anticipation. Like the Friday-feeling and the Weekend-feeling, the Christmas-feeling seemed to have deserted him. Still, he told himself, there's plenty of time yet. Yes, plenty.

Everything had been switched around in Woolworth's. The shelves where the models used to sit between the stick-on soles and the bicycle repair kits were now filled with displays of wire coolers and silk flowers. He eventually found them on a small shelf beside the compact disks, but he could tell almost at a glance that they didn't have any Flying Fortresses. He lifted out the few dusty boxes—a Dukes of Hazzard car, a skeleton, a Tyrannosaurus rex; kids' stuff, not the sort of thing that Simon would ever have bothered himself with—then set out back along the High Street toward W. H. Smith's. They had a better selection, but still no Flying Fortresses. A sign in black and orange suggested IF YOU CAN'T FIND WHAT YOU WANT ON DISPLAY PLEASE ASK AN ASSISTANT, but David was old and wise enough not to take it seriously. He tried the big news agents across the road, and then Debenhams opposite Safeway, where Santa Claus already had a poky grotto of fairy lights and hardboard, and the speakers gave a muffled rendition of "Merry Christmas (War Is Over)." Still no luck. It was quarter to five now. The car lights, traffic lights, streetlights, and shop windows glimmered along the wet pavement, haloed by the beginnings of a winter fog. People were buttoning up their anoraks, tying their scarves, and pulling up their detachable hoods, but David felt sweaty and tired, dodging between prams and slow old ladies and arm-in-arm girls with green punk hair. He was running out of shops. He was running out of time. Everyone was supposed to know about

Airfix Flying Fortresses. He didn't imagine that the concerns of childhood penetrated very deeply into the adult world, but there were
some things that were universal. You could go into a fish-and-chip
shop and the man in the fat-stained apron would say yes, he knew
exactly what you meant, they just might have one out the back with
the blocks of fat and the potatoes. Or so David had thought. A whole
High Street without one seemed impossible. Once he'd got the model
he would, of course, have to repeat the long and unpleasant task of
assembling the thing, but he was sure that he'd make a better go of
it a second time. In its latter stages the first model had shown ten-
dencies that even Simon with his far greater experience of model
making had probably never experienced. For a moment, he felt panic
rising in his throat like sour vomit. The model, trapped under its
bucket, squirmed in his mind. He forced the thought down. After all,
he'd done his best. Of course, he could always write to Airfix and
complain, but he somehow doubted whether they were to blame.

He had two more shops on his mental list and about twenty
minutes to reach them. The first, an old-fashioned craft shop, had,
he discovered, become the new offices of a building society. The
second, right up at the far end of the High Street, beyond the near-
legendary marital aids shop and outside his normal territory, lay in a
small and less than successful precinct built as a speculation five years
before and still half-empty. David ran past the faded "To Let" signs
into the square. There was no Christmas rush here. Most of the lights
in the fiberglass pseudo-Victorian lamps were broken. In the near
darkness a cluster of youths sat drinking Shandy Bass on the concrete
wall around the dying poplar at the center of the square. The few
shops that were open looked empty and about to close. The one David
was after had a window filled unpromisingly with giant nylon teddies
in various shades of green, pink, and orange.

An old woman in a grubby housecoat was mopping the marleytiled
floor, and the air inside the shop was heavy with the scent of the
same cheap disinfectant they used in the school toilets. David glanced
around, pulling the air into his lungs in thirsty gulps. The shop was
bigger than he'd imagined, but all he could see on display were a few
dusty Sindy outfits, a swivel stand of practical jokes, and a newish
rack of Slime Balls ("You Squeeze 'Em and They Ooze"), the fad of
the previous summer.

The man standing with his beer belly resting on the counter

glanced up from picking the dirt from under his nails. "Looking for something?"

"Um, models, er, please." David gasped. His throat itched, his lungs ached. He wished he could just close his eyes and curl up in a corner somewhere to sleep.

"Upstairs."

David blinked and looked around again. There was indeed a stairway leading up to another floor. He took it, three steps at a time.

A younger man in a leather-tasseled coat sat with his cowboy boots resting up on a glass counter, smoking and reading *Interview With the Vampire*. He looked even less like an assistant than the man downstairs, but David couldn't imagine what else he could be, unless he was one of the nonspeaking baddies who hung around at the back of the gang in spaghetti westerns. A faulty fluorescent tube flickered on and off like lightning in the smoky air, shooting out bursts of unpredictable shadow. David walked quickly along the few aisles. Past a row of Transformer robots, their bubble-plastic wrapping stuck back into the card with strips of yellowing Sellotape, he came to the model section. At first it didn't look promising, but as he crouched down to check along the rows, he saw a long box poking out from beneath a Revelle Catalina on the bottom shelf. There was an all-too-familiar picture on the side: a Flying Fortress. He pulled it out slowly, half expecting it to disappear in a puff of smoke. But no, it stayed firm and real. An Airfix Flying Fortress, a little more dusty and faded than the one Dad had given him, but the same gray weight of plastic, the same painting on the box, £7.75, glue and paints not included, but then he still had plenty of both. David could feel his relief fading even as he slowly drew the long box from the shelf. After all, he still had to make the thing.

The cowboy behind the counter coughed and lit up a fresh Rothmans from the stub of his old one. David glanced along the aisle. What he saw sent a warm jolt through him that destroyed all sense of tiredness and fatigue. There was a display inside the glass cabinet beneath the crossed cowboy boots. Little plastic men struck poses on a greenish sheet of Artexed hardboard that was supposed to look like grass. There were neat little huts, a fuel tender, and a few white dashes and red markers to indicate the start of a runway. In the middle of it all, undercarriage down and bomb bay doors open, was a silver Flying Fortress. His mouth dry, David slid the box back onto the shelf and strolled up to take a closer look, hands casually thrust into the itchy woolen pockets of his duffle coat, placing his feet down carefully to control the sudden trembling in his legs. It was finished, complete; it looked nothing like the deformed monstrosity he had tried to destroy. Even at a distance through the none-too-clean glass of the display case, he could make out the intricate details, the bright transfers (something he'd never been able to think about applying to his Fortress), and he could tell just from the look of the gun turrets that they would swivel up, down, sideways, any way you liked.

The cowboy recrossed his boots and looked up. He raised his eyebrows questioningly.

"I, er . . . just looking."

"We close now," he said, and returned to his book.

David backed away down the stairs, his eyes fixed on the completed Fortress until it vanished from sight behind a stack of Fisher-Price baby toys. He took the rest of the stairs slowly, his head spinning. He could buy as many models as he liked, but he was absolutely sure he would never be able to reach the level of perfection on display in that glass case. Maybe Simon could have done it better, but no one else.

David took another step down. His spine jarred; without noticing, he'd reached the ground floor. The man cleaning his nails at the desk had gone. The woman with the mop was working her way behind a pillar. He saw a door marked PRIVATE behind a jagged pile of unused shelving. He had an idea; the best he'd had all day.

Moving quickly but carefully so that his trainers didn't squeak, he crossed the shining wet floor, praying that his footsteps wouldn't show. The door had no handle. He pushed it gently with the tips of his fingers. It opened.

There was no light inside. As the door slid closed behind him, he glimpsed a stainless-steel sink with a few mugs perched on a draining board, a couple of old chairs, and a girlie calendar on the wall. It was a small room; there didn't seem to be space for anything else. Certainly no room to hide if anyone should open the door. David backed his way carefully into one of the chairs. He sat down. A spring boinged gently. He waited.

As he sat in the almost absolute darkness, his tiredness fought with his fear. The woman with the mop shuffled close by outside. She paused for a heart-stopping moment, but then she went on and David heard the clang of the bucket and the whine of the water pipes through the thin walls from a neighboring room. She came out again, humming a snatch of a familiar but unplaceable tune. Da-de-da de-de-de dum-dum. Stevie Wonder? The Beatles? Wham? David felt his eyelids drooping. His head began to nod.

Footsteps down the stairs. Someone coughing. He wondered if he was back at home. And he wondered why he felt so happy to be there.

He imagined that he was Simon. He could feel the mannish strength inside him, the confident hands that could turn chaotic plastic into perfect machines, the warm, admiring approval of the whole wide world surrounding him like the glowing skin of the boy in the Ready Brek advert.

A man's voice calling good night and the clink of keys drew David back from sleep. He opened his eyes and listened. After what might have been ten minutes but seemed like an hour there was still silence. He stood up and felt for the door. He opened it a crack. The lights were still on at the windows but the shop was locked and empty. Quick and easy as a shadow, he made his way up the stairs. The Fortress was waiting for him, clean lines of silvered plastic, intricate and marvelous as a dream. He slid back the glass door of the case (no lock or bolt—he could hardly believe how careless people could be with such treasure) and took it in his hands. It was beautiful. It was perfect, and it lacked any life of its own. He sniffed back tears. That was the best thing of all. It was dead.

It wasn't easy getting the model home. Fumbling his way through the darkness at the back of the shop, he managed to find the fire escape door, but when he leaned on the lever and shoved it open an alarm bell started to clang close above his head. He stood rigid for a moment, drenched in cold shock, then shot out across the loading yard and along the road behind. People stared at him as he pounded the streets on the long, aching run home. The silver Fortress was far too big to hide. That—and the fact that the man in the shop would be bound to remember that he'd been hanging around before closing time—made David sure that he had committed a less than perfect crime. As with Bonnie and Clyde or Butch Cassidy, David guessed, it was only a matter of time before the Law caught up with him. But first he would have his moment of glory; perhaps a moment glorious enough to turn around everything that had happened so far.

Arriving home with a bad cramp in his ribs and Mum and Dad and Victoria still out at Gran's, he found that the bucket in the garden still sat undisturbed with two bricks on top. Although he didn't have the courage to lift it up to look, there was nothing to suggest that the old Fortress wasn't sitting quietly (perhaps even dead) underneath. Lying on his bed and blowing at the model's propellers to make them spin, he could already feel the power growing within him. Tomorrow, in the daylight, he knew he'd feel strong enough to get the spade and sort things out properly.

All in all, he decided, the day had gone quite well. Things never happen as you expect, he told himself; they're either far better or far worse. This morning he'd never have believed that he'd have a finished Flying Fortress in his hands by the evening, yet here he was, gazing into the cockpit at the incredible detail of the crew and their tiny controls as a lover would gaze into the eyes of his beloved. And the best was yet to come. Even as he smiled to himself, the lights of Dad's Cortina swept across the bedroom curtains. The front door opened. David heard Mum's voice saying shush, then Dad's. He smiled again. This was, after all, what he'd been striving for. He had in his hands the proof that he was as good as Simon. The Fortress was the healing miracle that would soothe away the scars of his death. The family would become one. The gray curse would be lifted from the house.

Dad's heavy tread came up the stairs. He went into Victoria's bedroom. After a moment, he stuck his head around David's door.

"Everything all right, Junior?"

"Yes, Dad."

"Try to be quiet. Victoria fell asleep in the car and I've put her straight to bed."

Dad's head vanished. He pulled the door shut. Opening and closing the bomb bay doors, David gazed up at the model. Dad hadn't noticed the Fortress. Odd, that. Still, it probably showed just how special it was.

The TV boomed downstairs. The start of *3-2-1*; David recognized the tune. He got up slowly from his bed. He paused at the door to glance back into the room. No longer Simon's room, he told himself—*His Room*. He crossed the landing and walked down the stairs. Faintly, he heard the sound of Victoria moaning in her sleep. But that was all right. Everything would be all right. The finished model was cradled in his hands. It was like a dream.

He opened the lounge door. The quiz-show colors on the TV filled his eyes. Red and silver and gold, bright and warm as Christmas. Mum was sitting in her usual chair wearing her usual TV expression. Dad was stretched out on the sofa.

He looked up at David. "All right, Junior?"

David held the silver Fortress out toward his father. The fuselage glittered in the TV light. "Look, I've finished the model."

"Let's see." Dad stretched out his hand. David gave it to him. "Sure . . . that's pretty good, Junior. You'll have to save up and buy something more difficult with that money you've got in the post office. . . . Here." He handed it back to David.

David took the Fortress. One of the bomb bay doors flipped open. He clicked it back into place.

On the TV Steve and Yvette from Rochdale were telling Ted Rogers a story about their honeymoon. Ted finished it off with a punchline that David didn't understand. The audience roared.

Dad scratched his belly, worming his fingers into the gaps between the buttons of his shirt. "I think your mother wanted a word with you," he said, watching as Steve and Yvette agonized over a question. He raised his voice a little. "Isn't that right, pet? Didn't you want a word with him?"

Mum's face turned slowly from the TV screen.

"Look," David said, taking a step toward her, "I've—"

Mum's head continued turning. Away from David, toward Dad. "I thought *you* were going to speak to him," she said.

Dad shrugged. "You found them, pet, you tell him . . . and move, Junior. I can't see the program through you."

David moved.

Mum fumbled in the pocket of her dress. She produced a book of matches. "I found these in the bin," she said, looking straight at him. Through him. David had to suppress a shudder. "What have you been up to?"

"Nothing." David grinned weakly. His good-boy smile wouldn't come.

"You haven't been smoking?"

"No, Mum. I promise."

"Well, as long as you don't." Mum turned back to the TV. Steve and Yvette had failed. Instead of a Mini Metro they had won Dusty Bin. The audience was in raptures. Back after the break, said Ted Rogers.

David stood watching the bright screen. A gray tombstone loomed toward him. This is what happens, a voice said, if you get AIDS.

Dad gave a theatrical groan that turned into a cough. "Those queers make me sick," he said when he'd hawked his throat clear.

Without realizing what he was doing, David left the room and went back upstairs to Simon's bedroom.

He left the lights on and reopened the curtains. The monkey puzzle tree waved at him through the wet darkness; the rain from Wetherby had finally arrived. Each droplet sliding down the glass held a tiny spark of street light.

He sat down and plonked the Fortress on the desk in front of him. A propeller blade snapped; he hadn't bothered to put the undercarriage down. He didn't care. He breathed deeply, the air shuddering in his throat like the sound of running past railings. Through the bitter phlegm he could still smell the reek of plastic. Not the faint, tidy smell of the finished Fortress. No, this was the smell that had been with him for weeks. But now it didn't bring sick expectation in his stomach; he no longer felt afraid. Now, in his own way, he had reached the summit of a finished Flying Fortress, a high place from where he could look back at the remains of his childhood. Everything had been out of scale before, but now he saw, he really saw. 1/72nd scale; David knew what it meant now. The Fortress was big, as heavy and gray as the rest of the world. It was he that was tiny, 1/72nd scale.

He looked at the Fortress: big, ugly, and silver. The sight of it sickened him more than the old model had ever done. At least that had been his. For all its considerable faults, he had made it.

David stood up. Quietly, he left the room and went down the stairs, past the lounge and the booming TV, into the kitchen. He found the waterproof torch and walked out into the rain.

The bucket still hadn't moved. Holding the torch in the crook of his arm, David removed the two bricks and lifted the bucket up. For a moment, he thought that there was nothing underneath, but then, pointing the torch's rain-streamed light straight down, he saw that the model was still there. As he'd half expected, it had tried to burrow its way out from under the bucket. But it was too weak. All it had succeeded in doing was to cover itself in wet earth.

The model mewed gently and tried to raise itself up toward David. This time he didn't step back. "Come on," he said. "We're going back inside."

David led the way, leveling the beam of the torch through the rain like a scaled-down searchlight, its yellow oval glistening on the muddy wet grass just ahead. The rain was getting worse, heavy drops rattling on David's skull and plastering his hair down like a wet swimming cap. The model moved slowly, seeming to weaken with every arch of its rotting fuselage. David clenched his jaw and tried to urge it on, pouring his own strength into the wounded creature. Once, he looked up over the roofs of the houses. Above the chimneys and TV aerials, cloud-heavy sky seemed to boil. Briefly, he thought he saw shapes form, ghosts swirling on the moaning wind. And the ghosts were not people, but simple inanimate things. Clocks and cars, china and jewelry, toys and trophies all tumbling uselessly through the night. But then he blinked and there was nothing to be seen but the rain, washing his face and filling his eyes like tears.

He was wet through by the time they reached the back door. The concrete step proved too much for the model, and David had to stoop and quickly lift it onto the lino inside, trying not to think of the way it felt in his hands.

In the kitchen's fluorescent light, he saw for the first time just how badly injured the creature was. Clumps of earth clung to its sticky, blistered wings, and gray plastic oozed from gaping wounds along its fuselage. And the reek of it immediately filled the kitchen, easily overpowering the usual smell of fish fingers. It stank of glue and paint and plastic; but there was more. It also smelled like something dying.

It moved on, dragging its wings, whimpering in agony, growing weaker with every inch. Plainly, the creature was close to the end of its short existence.

"Come on," David whispered, crouching down close beside it. "There's not far to go now. Please try. Please . . . don't die yet."

Seeming to understand, the model made a final effort. David held the kitchen door open as it crawled into the hall, onwards toward the light and sound of the TV through the frosted lounge door.

"You made *that?*" An awed whisper came from halfway up the stairs.

David looked up and saw little Victoria peering down at the limping model, her hands gripping the banister like a prisoner behind bars. He nodded, feeling an odd sense of pride. It was, after all, his. But he knew you could take pride too far. The model belonged to the whole family as well. To Victoria sitting alone at night on the stairs, to Simon turning to mush and bones in his damp coffin—and to Mum and Dad. And that was why it was important to show them. David was old for a child; he knew that grown-ups were funny like that. If you didn't show them things, they simply didn't believe in them.

"Come on," he said, holding out his hand.

Victoria scampered quickly down the stairs and along the hall, stepping carefully over the model and putting her cold little hand inside his slightly larger one.

The model struggled on, leaving a trail of slimy plastic behind on the carpet. When it reached the lounge door, David turned the handle and the three of them went in together.

# Lieserl

### ...

## *Karen Joy Fowler*

"If I am a contrary writer," Karen Joy Fowler explains in a preface
to "The Faithful Companion at Forty," her wildly imaginative leap
into the troubled mind of Tonto, "I am even worse as a reader. I
never like the character I am supposed to like; the protagonist
generally strikes me as self-important, self-indulgent, and more than
a bit careless with his loved ones.

"But somewhere in the book I can usually find a character I
do like, someone whose heroism is without theatrics, someone genuinely self-sacrificing, someone doing the dishes."

Fowler's affection for the peripheral and the put-upon also
informs the story you're about to read, a relativity-theory extrapolation at once wistful and angry. Lieserl, I suspect, did more than
her share of dishes.

Chuckleheads have succeeded in making many people uncomfortable with the word "feminist" these days, and when I label
Fowler as such, I hope somehow to recapture the visionary connotations of that excellent adjective. Fowler is a feminist. She is
also an artist. Fiction lovers desiring to read more of her art should
consult her two remarkable collections, *Artificial Things* from Bantam and *Peripheral Vision* from Pulphouse Publishing; the fine
novella "Black Glass" showcased in *Full Spectrum 3*; and her marvelous first novel, *Sarah Canary*.

Although Fowler is presently a bit like one of her characters,
lacking the recognition she deserves, her talents have not gone
unnoticed. She has received a fiction-writing grant from the National
Endowment for the Arts, and in 1987 the custodians of the John
W. Campbell Award voted her best new writer.

Asked to comment on the genesis of "Lieserl," Fowler replied:
"Thirty-two years after Einstein's death, Princeton Press published
the first volume of a biography entitled *The Early Years, 1879–
1902*. Included in this book, along with material that was already
well known, were fifty-one unknown and astonishing letters. They
were, for the most part, the correspondence between Einstein and
his first wife, Mileva Maric.

"These letters were full of surprises. Apparently, Einstein once
loved Maric desperately. Apparently, there was once a daughter.
Apparently, Einstein was once a very young man."

Einstein received the first letter in the afternoon post. It had traveled in bags and boxes all the way from Hungary, sailing finally through the brass slit in Einstein's door. *Dear Albert,* it said. *Little Lieserl is here. Mileva says to tell you that your new daughter has tiny fingers and a head as bald as an egg. Mileva says to say that she loves you and will write you herself when she feels better.* The signature was Mileva's father's.

The letter was sent at the end of January, but arrived at the beginning of February, so even if everything in it was true when written, it was entirely possible that none of it was true now. Einstein read the letter several times. He was frightened. Why could Mileva not write him herself? The birth must have been a very difficult one. Was the baby really as bald as all that? He wished for a picture. What kind of little eyes did she have? Did she look like Mileva? Mileva had an aura of thick, dark hair.

Einstein was living in Bern, Switzerland, and Mileva had returned to her parents' home in Titel, Hungary, for the birth. Mileva was hurt because Einstein sent her to Hungary alone, although she had not said so. The year was 1902. Einstein was twenty-two years old. None of this is as simple as it sounds, but one must start somewhere even though such placement inevitably involves the telling of a lie.

Outside Einstein's window, large star-shaped flakes of snow swirled silently in the air like the pretend snow in a glass globe. The sky darkened into evening as Einstein sat on his bed with his papers. The globe had been shaken and Einstein was the still, ceramic figure at its swirling heart, the painted Father Christmas. Lieserl. How I love her already, Einstein thought, dangerously. Before I even know her, how I love her.

■ ■ ■

The second letter arrived the next morning. *Liebes Schatzerl,* Mileva wrote. *Your daughter is so beautiful. But the world does not suit her at all. With such fury she cries! Papa is coming soon, I tell her. Papa will change everything for you, everything you don't like, the whole world if this is what you want. Papa loves Lieserl. I am very tired still. You must hurry to us. Lieserl's hair has come in dark and I think she is getting a tooth.* Einstein stared at the letter.

A friend of Einstein's will tell Einstein one day that he, himself, would never have the courage to marry a woman who was not absolutely sound. He will say this soon after meeting Mileva. Mileva walks with a limp although it is unlikely that a limp is all this friend means. Einstein will respond that Mileva has a lovely voice.

Einstein had not married Mileva yet when he received this letter, although he wanted to very badly. She was his Liebes Dockerl, his little doll. He had not yet found a way to support her. He had just run an advertisement offering his services as a tutor. He wrote Mileva back. *Now you can make observations,* he said. *I would like once to produce a Lieserl myself, it must be so interesting. She certainly can cry already, but to laugh she'll learn later. Therein lies a profound truth.* On the bottom of his letter he sketched his tiny room in Bern. The sketch resembled the drawings he will do later to accompany his Gedanken, or thought experiments, how he would visualize physics in various situations. In this sketch, he labeled the features of his room with letters. Big B for the bed. Little b for the picture. He was trying to figure a way to fit Mileva and Lieserl into his room. He was inviting Mileva to help.

In June he will get a job with the Swiss Civil Service. A year after Lieserl's birth, the following January, he will marry Mileva. Years later, when friends ask him why he married her, his answer will vary. Duty, he will say sometimes. Sometimes he will say that he has never been able to remember why.

■ ■ ■

A third letter arrived the next day. *Mein liebes, boses Schatzerl!* it said. *Lieserl misses her Papa. She is so clever, Albert. You will never believe it. Today she pulled a book from the shelf. She opened it, sucking hard on her fingers. Can Lieserl read? I asked her, joking. But she pointed to the letter E, making such a sweet, sticky fingerprint beside it on the page. E, she said. You will be so proud of her. Already she runs and laughs. I had not realized how quickly they grow up. When are you coming to us? Mileva.*

His room was too small. The dust collected over his books and danced in the light with Brownian-like movements. Einstein went out for a walk. The sun shone, both from above him and also as reflected off the new snowbanks in blinding white sheets. Icicles shrank visibly at the roots until they cracked, falling from the eaves like knives into the soft snow beneath them. Mileva is a book, like you, his mother had told him. What you need is a housekeeper. What you need is a wife.

Einstein met Mileva in Zürich at the Swiss Federal Polytechnical School. Entrance to the school required the passage of a stiff examination. Einstein himself failed the General Knowledge section on the first try. She will ruin your life, Einstein's mother said. No decent family will have her. Don't sleep with her. If she gets a child, you'll be in a pretty mess.

It is not clear what Einstein's mother's objection to Mileva was. She was unhappy that Mileva had scholastic ambitions and then more unhappy when Mileva failed her final examinations twice and could not get her diploma.

■ ■ ■

Five days passed before Einstein heard from Mileva again. *Mein liebes Schatzerl. If she has not climbed onto the kitchen table, then she is sliding down the banisters,* Mileva complained. *I must watch her every minute. I have tried to take her picture for you as you asked, but she will never hold still long enough. Until you come to her, you must be content with my descriptions. Her hair is dark and thick and curly. She has the eyes of a doe. Already she has outgrown all the clothes I had for her and is in proper dresses with aprons. Papa, papa, papa, she says. It is her favorite word. Yes, I tell her. Papa is coming. I teach her to throw kisses. I teach her to clap her hands. Papa is coming, she says, kissing and clapping. Papa loves his Lieserl.*

Einstein loved his Lieserl whom he had not met. He loved Mileva. He loved science. He loved music. He solved scientific puzzles while playing the violin. He thought of Lieserl while solving scientific puzzles. Love is faith. Science is faith. Einstein could see that his faith was being tested.

Science feels like art, Einstein will say later, but it is not. Art involves inspiration and experience, but experience is a hindrance to the scientist. He has only a few years in which to invent, with his innocence, a whole new world that he must live in for the rest of his life. Einstein will not always be such a young man. Einstein will not have all the time in the world.

Einstein waited for the next letter in the tiny cell of his room. The letters were making him unhappy. He did not want to receive another so he would not leave, even for an instant, and risk delaying it. He had not responded to Mileva's last letters. He did not know how. He made himself a cup of tea and stirred it, noticing that the tea leaves gathered in the center of the cup bottom, but not about the circumference. He reached for a fresh piece of paper and filled it with drawings of rivers, not the rivers of a landscape, but the narrow, twisting rivers of a map.

The letter came only a few hours later in the afternoon post, sliding like a tongue through the slit in the door. Einstein caught it as it fell. *Was treibst Du, Schatzerl?* it began. *Your little Lieserl has been asked to a party and looks like a princess tonight. Her dress is long and white like a bride's. I have made her hair curl by wrapping it over my fingers. She wears a violet sash and violet ribbons. She is dancing with my father in the hallway, her feet on my father's feet, her head only slightly higher than his waist. They are waltzing. All the boys will want to dance with you, my father said to her, but she frowned. I am not interested in boys, she answered. Nowhere is there a boy I could love like I love my papa.*

In 1899 Einstein began writing to Mileva about the electro-dynamics of moving bodies, which will become the title of his 1905 paper on relativity. In 1902 Einstein loved Mileva, but in 1916 in a letter to his friend Besso, Einstein will write that he would have become mentally and physically exhausted if he had not been able to keep his wife at a distance, out of sight and out of hearing. You cannot know, he will tell his friends, the tricks a woman such as my wife will play.

Mileva, trained as a physicist herself, though without a diploma, will complain that she has never understood the special theory of relativity. She will blame Einstein, who, she will say, has never taken the time to explain it properly to her.

Einstein wrote a question along the twisting line of one river. Where are you? He chose another river for a second question. How are you moving? He extended the end of the second river around many curves until it finally merged with the first.

■ ■ ■

*Liebes Schatzerl!* the next letter said. It came four posts later. *She is a lovely young lady. If you could only see her, your breath would catch in your throat. Hair like silk. Eyes like stars. She sends her love. Tell my darling papa, she says, that I will always be his little Lieserl, always running out into the snowy garden, caped in red, to draw angels. Suddenly I am frightened for her, Albert. She is as fragile as a snowflake. Have I kept her too sheltered? What does she know of men? If only you had been here to advise me.* Even after its long journey, the letter smelled of roses.

Two friends came for dinner that night to Einstein's little apartment. One was a philosophy student named Maurice Solovine. One was a mathematician named Konrad Habicht. The three together called themselves the Olympia Academy, making fun of the serious bent of their minds.

Einstein made a simple dinner of fried fish and bought wine. They sat about the table, drinking and picking the last pieces of fish out with their fingers until nothing remained on their plates but the spines with the smaller bones attached like the naked branches of winter trees. The friends argued loudly about music. Solovine's favorite composer was Beethoven, whose music, Einstein suddenly began to shout, was emotionally overcharged, especially in C minor. Einstein's favorite composer was Mozart. Beethoven created his beautiful music, but Mozart discovered it, Einstein said. Beethoven wrote the music of the human heart, but Mozart transcribed the music of God. There is a perfection in the humanless world which will draw Einstein all his life. It is an irony that his greatest achievement will be to add the relativity of men to the Newtonian science of angels.

He did not tell his friends about his daughter. The wind outside was a choir without a voice. All his life, Einstein will say later, all his life, he tried to free himself from the chains of the *merely personal.* Einstein rarely spoke of his personal life. Such absolute silence suggests that he escaped from it easily or, alternatively, that its hold was so powerful he was afraid to ever say it aloud. One or both or neither of these things must be true.

■ ■ ■

Let us talk about the merely personal. The information received through the five senses is appallingly approximate. Take sight, the sense on which humans depend most. Man sees only a few of all the colors in the world. It is as if a curtain has been drawn over a large window, but not drawn so that it fully meets in the middle. The small gap at the center represents the visual abilities of man.

A dog hears an upper register of sounds that men must only imagine.

Some insects can identify members of their own species by smell at distances nearing a mile.

A blindfolded man holding his nose cannot distinguish the taste of an apple from an onion.

Of course man fumbles about the world, perceiving nothing, understanding nothing. In a whole universe, man has been shut into one small room. Of course, Einstein could not begin to know what was happening to his daugher or to Mileva deprived of even these blundering senses. The postman was careless with Mileva's next letter. He failed to push it properly through the door slit so that it fell back into the snow, where it lay all night and was ice the next morning. Einstein picked the envelope up on his front step. It was so cold it burned his fingers. He breathed on it until he could open it.

*Another quiet evening with your Lieserl. We read until late and then sat together talking. She asked me many questions tonight about you, hoping, I think, to hear something, anything I had not yet told her. But she settled, sweetly, for the old stories all over again. She got out the little drawing of your room you sent just after her birth; have I told you how she treasures it? When she was a child she used to point to it. Papa sits here, she would say, pointing. Papa sleeps here. I wished that I could gather her into my lap again. It would have been so silly, Albert. You must picture her with her legs longer than mine and new gray in the black of her hair. Was I silly to want it, Schatzerl? Shouldn't someone have warned me that I wouldn't be able to hold her forever?*

Einstein set the letter back down into the snow. He had not yet found it. He had never had such a beautiful daughter. Perhaps he had not even met Mileva yet, Mileva whom he still loved, but who was not sound and liked to play tricks.

Perhaps, he thought, he will find the letter in the spring when the snow melts. If the ink has not run, if he can still read it, then he will decide what to do. Then he will have to decide. It began to snow again. Einstein went back into his room for his umbrella. The snow covered the letter. He could not even see the letter under the snow when he stepped over it on his way to the bakery. The snow filled his footprints behind him. He did not want to go home where no letter was hidden by the door. He was twenty-two years old and he stood outside the bakery, eating his bread with gloved hands, reading a book in the tiny world he had made under his umbrella in the snow.

Several years later, after Einstein has married Mileva and neither ever mentions Lieserl, after they have two sons, a colleague will describe a visit to Einstein's apartment. The door will be open so that the newly washed floor can dry. Mileva will be hanging dripping laundry in the hall. Einstein will rock a baby's bassinet with one hand and hold a book open with the other. The stove will smoke. How does he bear it? the colleague will ask in a letter which still survives, a letter anyone can read. That genius. How can he bear it?

The answer is that he could not. He will try for many years and then Einstein will leave Mileva and his sons, sending back to them the money he wins along with the Nobel Prize.

When the afternoon post came, the postman had found the letter again and included it with the new mail. So there were two letters, only one had been already opened.

■ ■ ■

Einstein put the letter aside. He put it under his papers. He hid it in his bookcase. He retrieved it clumsily because his hands were shaking. He had known this letter was coming, known it perhaps with Lieserl's first tooth, certainly with her first dance. It was exactly what he had expected, worse than he could have imagined. *She is as bald as ice and as mad as a goddess, my Albert,* Mileva wrote. *But she is still my Liebes Dockerl, my little doll. She clings to me, crying if I must leave her for a minute. Mama, mama! Such madness in her eyes and her mouth. She is toothless and soils herself. She is my baby. And yours, Schatzerl. Nowhere is there a boy I could love like my papa, she says, lisping again just the way she did when she was little. She has left a message for you. It is a message from the dead. You will get what you really want, Papa, she said. I have gone to get it for you. Remember that it comes from me. She was weeping and biting her hands until they bled. Her eyes were white with madness. She said something else. The brighter the light, the more shadows, my papa, she said. My darling papa. My poor papa. You will see.*

The room was too small. Einstein went outside where his breath came in a cloud from his mouth, tangible, as if he were breathing on glass. He imagined writing on the surface of a mirror, drawing one of his Gedanken with his finger in his own breath. He imagined a valentine. Lieserl, he wrote across it. He loved Lieserl. He cut the word in half, down the S with the stroke of his nail. The two halves of the heart opened and closed, beating against each other, faster and faster, like wings, until they split apart and vanished from his mind.

# Rhysling Award Winners

• • •

In 1947 Robert A. Heinlein published "The Green Hills of Earth," a story featuring a kind of pangalactic Homer named Rhysling. Years later, when the Science Fiction Poetry Association faced the problem of what to call its annual award, they were naturally attracted to the "blind poet of the spaceways" and forthwith secured Heinlein's permission to use the name.

The Rhysling Award "for excellence in speculative, science-oriented, science fiction, fantasy, horror, and related poetry published during the preceding year" was founded, along with the Science Fiction Poetry Association itself, by Suzette Haden Elgin in 1978. In the absence of an official SFWA poetry competition, a tradition has emerged whereby the winners in both categories— short poem (under fifty lines) and long poem (over fifty lines)— appear in the annual Nebula anthology.

The 1990 Rhysling for best short poem went to G. Sutton Breiding, a West Virginia native who traces his earliest inspirations to the "salamander-haunted streams of the mythic woodlands." But Breiding's sensibility was also shaped by his years in San Francisco, a sojourn extending from the late 1960s through the middle of the 1980s. *Autumn Roses*, a collection of his earliest work, was published by Silver Scarab Press, and his subsequent poems have appeared in such maverick journals as *Nyctalops*, *Grue*, *Moonbroth*, *Foxfire*, and *Grimoire*. His most recent book, *Journal of an Astronaut*, will soon appear from Ocean View Books.

"This piece sums up certain philosophical concerns of my life," Breiding writes of his winning poem, "a life to be always, I hope, enhanced in romantic, erotic, and morbid ways by continuous visions of the utterly strange. The Kings and Queens of Dreams are indeed dead; certain of us still seek the tracery of their existences in the murex dust of a post-Romantic world."

Patrick McKinnon, winner in the long-poem category, is the founder of Poetry Harbor, a Duluth arts organization that, among its many activities, publishes an anthology series called *Poets Who Haven't Moved to Minneapolis*. His poetry, prose, collages, and criticism have appeared in over six hundred periodicals in the U.S. and abroad, and his collections include *Searching for Spiders*, *Straddling the Bony Death*, *Walking Behind My Breath*, and *Cherry Ferris Wheels*, the latter a nominee for the 1991 Minnesota Book Award.

On the origins of "dear spacemen," McKinnon writes, "In America, where our history has been written, published, and distributed by the economic and military winners of the continental struggle to dominate, and has then been sold to the losers in order that they may know their proper place in serfdom, I felt it necessary to write from the vantage of the dropout, the guy who is neither winner nor loser because he isn't playing the game. There is no audience for this sort of unsponsored writing, except, perhaps, some spacemen out there . . . maybe . . ."

## EPITAPH FOR DREAMS
### G. Sutton Breiding

These are the ancient hours
Of silence, dust and autumn sunlight.

These are the blue flowers of the empire,
Of grief and midnights made of endless cups

Of wine, and memory, and your face.
These are my fingers,

Lost in the lace of afternoons
When the aeons passed us by,

As we lolled in the coolest rooms
Of ivory, ice and sapphire.

This is my skull,
Behind the fretwork of flesh,

My fallen eyes gazing from an empty dynasty
Of darkness, still blind with visions

Of your radiant thighs half-wrapped
In silken coverlets,

Your breast sighing in pleasure
And in sorrow for the dying of our race,

We two, King and Queen,
Holding court amidst the shadows of the dead

Who lurk beyond the pillars
Of our guarded spells.

Morning glories hang from my ribs;
Tiny blue violets entwine my finger bones.

I watch the wine pass through me,
Into the silence, the dust, the autumn sunlight.

I wait now, in these ancient hours.

## DEAR SPACEMEN
*Patrick McKinnon*

dear spacemen,

i met you on tevee when i was a boy in the sixties.
back then you wore a lot of chrome-plated mylar
& had the heads of bugs.
have styles changed much for you?

i'm afraid i never should have sent this piece of earth;
there's disease down here
& disease can spread,
even to you, way out there in deep space.
i'm banking on its never arriving.
i know it's mad
but then again, you may have met my mother
somewhere in yr travels
on earth, before she died,
she was 4 foot 9 by 4 foot 9, big smile, drove a plymouth . . .

so, peace to you, spacemen.
we are all animals & rocks, humans, plants & gases down here
& it's always a battle going on
over who's the strongest & smartest & best fucker.
the humans have big brains but don't use them very well.
i'm a human
& i'm worried
& just want you spacemen to know
about this planet we are beating up

same as we used to beat up jeff burdick and mat wenzel
& maurie pearlman in my old neighborhood.

this is a message in a bottle about humans
& may god bless whichever of you spacemen found it.
we have a joke here that goes:
there were three guys stranded on this desert island. one day a
bottle floats to shore & they can't believe it. they uncork the
bottle & out comes this genie, sez *hi boys, i'll grant you each
one wish.* right away the first guy sez all he wants in the world
is to go back to his wife & family & *blink* he's gone. so the
second guy sez he too wants to go home & *blink* he's gone. this
leaves the third guy, overcome w/grief because he did not have
a home or wife or family or friends anywhere on the planet. in
despair at being left so abruptly alone, he blurts out, *damn i
sure wish those other two guys hadn't left me,* & *blink blink* there
they are again, back on the desert island.

this is the sort of misfortune that's funny to us.

we continue building
this outrageous industrial complex
like mrs. winchester,
lone heiress to a brand
of rifles & guns we love so much.
thot if she never stopped
adding on to her house,
she'd live forever.
so for years the crews worked
round the clock
putting up wing after wing
& wall after wall &
staircase & hallways that lead to nowhere
& bathrooms & closets no one ever used
until finally the old girl died.
only five rooms were ever furnished.

but mrs. winchester wasn't the only one to die.
everyone who was alive when she was doing this
is certainly dead by now
& that's probably what makes us

so crazy here—
all the dying.

so spacemen take heed;
this may be ripe as comet juice
from a planet that's getting out of balance.
think of this as a snake
& don't open it.
don't let its fangs pierce yr skin.
don't let its tongue fondle & linger
inside yr pointy silver ears.
we like to kill things here.
it does something to us
like i guess we are always relieved it wasn't us who got killed.
in the end
we killed all of you
didn't we?

really tho, i'm sorry we constantly attacked yr ships
but it was just tevee
& i assume you got paid okay
& i imagine you got a little taste of our sex.
did the girls like yr shiny dicks?
did the boys like yr exotic vaginas?
did you ever have any babies from us?
what are their names?
do you have a name for us?
does it mean anything?
does it rhyme?

i want terribly to know what yr planet looks like. i
want to wander space like you do. i
want to stretch myself way out there
into some next place & stay for a while.
on coming back i'd walk among the trees
& feel the distance,
feel the time it took
& live the rest of my life amazed.

o spacemen, i am groaning
against the limits of my human being,

leaning & breathing heavy as a man
who has grown too large for his only room.
my hands reach out
but i'm too far away for you to see.
please send me the secret
of yr silver suits
& the secret of your fishbowl helmets,
yr neon frisbee ship.
give me the secret of getting yrselves on tevee so much.

i'm a bartender down here
& i'm a writer too
tho not many people know about my writing.
i've been told to believe this is important
& somehow i've believed it.
maybe this letter will make me famous among *you*.
anyway, i pour drinks & people give me money to do it.
they wouldn't need me to pour drinks
if people didn't have to pay for them w/money.
is there money in space?

the way it works here is
they give me the money & i put it in the cash register.
i'd never trust the drinkers
to pour their own drinks
or put their own cash in the register
while i went downstairs to smoke some pot
& read a book for a few hours.

down here, doing something like that
would be called irresponsible
or crazy & they wouldn't give me any food.
they'd make me hitchhike the interstates as my home.
you can't trust anyone
so i pour all the drinks & take all the money
over & over again & sometimes i get drunk
because closing time comes faster that way
& i don't have to listen to the drinkers

telling me the same old crap one more time.
is pot legal in outer space?

if you raise your children well on our planet
they will grow up to be wiser than you are
& if you are afraid of that & raise them poorly
you'll be in the greater percentile.
you could listen to one of our creeks or rivers
for a hundred years & never
hear it all but we don't do much of that anymore.
most of us never get off the playground
chasing mirages of pleasure.
are yr people so incomplete?

i'm sorry to say we are very busy
climbing all over each other
like a mound of maggots in a pile of fresh dung.
we are so busy doing this,
we don't have time to come visit you
tho i realize it's our turn;
but believe me,
things haven't changed much since last you saw us.
we still want to kick yr asses all over space
& be in charge & take yr stuff & never give it back
& blow up a few stars along the way,
maybe even a sun
or some asteroids or a moon
or seal a black hole, collapse the entire universe.
we're so mad & confused & spend our entire lives,
the lives we keep inside ourselves,
trying to get away from our idiot parents
or back to them & like i sed earlier,
my mother's dead;
have you seen her?
do you know anything about where the dead go,
if anywhere? please write.

do you have the mafia in space?
or communists or anarchists or ministers or liberals?

is there any corporate structure up there?
any bills to pay? any winter?
i heat w/electricity
& i see at night w/electricity
& use it to keep my food cold.
in fact, most of what goes on down here
happens somehow thru the use of electricity.
even our brains work on electromagnetic charges
& i've heard that electricity
may be what's causing all this recent cancer we've been having.
wouldn't that present a dilemma? i mean,
electricity is so useful & pretty
& profitable. & it paints over those unnervingly deep stars.
we are afraid of everything.

does our planet pulsate our fear into space
real loud like white noise cacophony?
do we radiate our darkness really far?
are we known about the universe
as that awful black sore
over in the milky way?
do you have any idea what we are supposed to be doing here?

are there cars on yr planet?
do you love them as much as we love ours?
are they more interesting & important to you
than yr children & yr grandchildren
& what sort of filth they are going to have to breathe?
we drive everywhere in our cars.
they make us fast as cheetahs
& stronger than grizzly bears & we don't like our bodies
so we've got the nice metal ones now.
& when we get tired of our particular model,
we can trade it in on something new & exciting.
& these cars are choking us to death
because our planet is just a large garage
w/the door forever closed
& so many of us putting keys into ignitions,
turning them on, relaxing in the bucket seats

w/the radio blaring songs that help us count backwards from
ten.

o spacemen,
please come & get my family & me.
i don't know what we could do for you
except we are good at walking
& could go to yr store
& pick up whatever you might need for dinner.
andrea makes great bread & beautiful origami boxes
& really loves to garden. the children
have sweet music in their throats
& hearts full of trust & tremendous imaginations.
i blow the harmonica & see visions & tell stories.
i'm sure we'd have a good time.
we could take a picnic
to yr lakes & put our feet in yr water.
are yr lakes full of mercury?
do yr fish live or do they only die?
i hope you have eliminated malls on yr planet
& factories & suburbs & airports &
free enterprise. i hope yr topsoil
won't be gone by 2025.

on the other hand,
i'm pretty sure
that by the time you get this letter,
there'll be no need
to reply.

sincerely,
pat mckinnon
planet earth
1989

# Science Fiction Movies of 1990: Spiders, Scissors, and Schwarzenegger
## ● ● ●
### *Bill Warren*

Bill Warren's definitive survey of Hollywood's greatest science fiction era—the period from 1950 to 1962—takes as its title the last words spoken in the original version of *The Thing*: "Keep watching the skies!" In so celebrating a line of dialogue, Warren implicitly reminds us of an important fact. Every year, writers contribute crucially to a handful of memorable science fiction films and television presentations. The annals of SF cinema resonate with pithy and amusing—if not exactly Shakespearean—speeches by the main characters. "An intellectual carrot—the mind boggles!" "Man does not behold the face of the Gorgon and live!" "All the universe or nothingness—which shall it be, Passworthy, which shall it be?" (Answers: *The Thing, Forbidden Planet, Things to Come.*)

In 1973, 1974, and 1975, a Nebula Award for best dramatic presentation went to *Soylent Green, Sleeper,* and *Young Frankenstein* respectively. The flaw in this system is immediately apparent: the year's most endearing dramatic presentation does not necessarily contain anything resembling great science fiction writing. (Indeed, two of these "dramatic presentations" were knockabout comedies more concerned with squeezing laughs from SF's metaphors than with exploring their power.) By 1976, films were no longer listed on the final Nebula ballot. Beyond the so-called Special Award accorded *Star Wars* in 1977, SFWA has made no further attempt to acknowledge cinematic science fiction.

The issue isn't dead. Today, some SFWA members are arguing that voters could simply weigh the verbal and narrative elements in a given year's film crop and award a corresponding Nebula for best screenplay. Another current proposal has SFWA intercepting scripts as they make the rounds in Hollywood, then binding the best work into a small-press anthology that members could peruse with an eye to making Nebula recommendations.

In the absence of a more formal method of honoring the visual media, this series once again turns to Bill Warren for the lowdown on which of the year's genre movies were art, which were trash, and which, art or trash, were actually worth seeing. While the following report identifies many Hollywood writers, it necessarily focuses on the gestalt of each film. As Warren makes abundantly clear, movies are a collaborative medium, deriving their impact from the synergy of script, direction, acting, editing, music, design, and technical effects.

Beyond the hundreds of reviews that constitute *Keep Watching the Skies!*—a two-volume *magnum opus* currently available from McFarland and Company—Warren's cogent film criticism has appeared in *Starlog, Fangoria, Cinefantastique, American Film,* and other periodicals. When not at the movies, he operates the "Show Biz Round Table" for the popular computer network GEnie.

Trends move in great, sweeping masses, covering decades, not years. People who pounce upon a few examples in a given calendar year as signaling a revolutionary new wave are at best premature and at worst idiots. In movies, especially, the inertia of complacency is gargantuan. Not only does a film generally take a couple of years from inception to popcorn, but moviemakers are slow to be convinced of anything, and then once they *are* convinced, it's virtually impossible to change their minds *again*.

A few years ago, the Conventional Wisdom in Hollywood was that the only people who could get away with making profitable science fiction movies were George Lucas and Steven Spielberg. Slowly but inevitably, the great weight of that opinion has shifted, and not without ample evidence. Now executives are convinced that for a big-budget SF movie to be a hit, it must star Arnold Schwarzenegger. (Even Schwarzenegger, a very intelligent man, doesn't quite buy this one—but the money guys do.)

Lucas's last major fantasy outing, *Willow*, in 1988, was not a smash hit. In 1990, Spielberg's *Always* (hanging on from a Christmas 1989 release) did well, but not spectacularly. Those genre films he executive-produced and that displayed his name prominently—*Arachnophobia, Back to the Future Part III,* and *Gremlins 2*—made a lot less money than was expected. But Schwarzenegger's *Predator, The Running Man, The Terminator,* and, now, *Total Recall* were international successes, even when (as with *Predator*) the U.S. grosses weren't sensational. (Sylvester Stallone has seen the handwriting on the wall and will battle a monster in an upcoming film.)

People were expecting *Dick Tracy* to do well. The advertising campaign closely mimicked *Batman*'s, and the picture was hyped madly in virtually every magazine and newspaper. The strategy paid off; reviews were mostly favorable (though rarely enthusiastic), and audience response ranged from bemused to mildly approving—in short, the movie was successful, though profits did not begin to approach *Batman*'s. (A note about *Batman*: it is widely viewed in Hollywood as little more than mediocre, so no one can really understand why it was such a hit. At Warners, many executives are firmly convinced that the profits were due to that ubiquitous bat emblem. No studio chief wants to face the possibility that he is out of step with the audience—who, after all, *loved Batman.*)

*Ghost* and *Teenage Mutant Ninja Turtles*, mammoth hits, blindsided Hollywood. The appeal of *Ghost*, executives assumed, would be Patrick Swayze in a romantic role, but whatever did the trick—and this is a good movie—the magic went way beyond Swayze. Heads are still being scratched, but you can rest assured that 1992 will see any number of romantic fantasies.

Children returned again and again to see *Teenage Mutant Ninja Turtles*. Who can blame them? The movie features decent, honest heroes who fight evil because they believe in good, and who, besides indulging in jokes, harmless action, pizza, and a wild melange of surfer, Valley-dude, and street-gang slang, happen to be *turtles*. What kid could resist?

And of course, there was *Total Recall*, whose long, convoluted production history would make a fascinating book. One reason for *Recall*'s success was that it satisfied the Arnold Schwarzenegger Movie Requirements: action, some jokes, more action, lots of violence, and Arnold. But the film crossed over to non-Arnold fans; despite occasionally confusing twists and scientific outrageousness, the plot played some truly intelligent mind games. It's the first Schwarzenegger science fiction movie that inspired talk about *the story* rather than merely a wow-wasn't-that-great recapitulation of his quips and stunts.

The other SF films of the year were mostly sequels, or movies that *looked* like sequels even when they weren't, such as *Darkman*. Many SF readers pinned high hopes on *The Handmaid's Tale*, but it was didactic and flat. The most sheer fun was to be found in *Tremors*, a perfectly realized updating of a 1950s-type monster movie, but box-office returns were disappointing.

Predicting any future trends based on the SF and fantasy movies of 1990—beyond assuming that *Ghost* will generate more romantic fantasies—would be a mistake. For one thing, SF movies are no longer regarded as something separate from Ordinary Movies; they *are* the ordinary movies of Hollywood these days, part of the standard output. People compared *Total Recall* to *Die Hard 2*, not to, for instance, *Back to the Future Part III*. And well they should. The distinction between SF and not-SF has been largely erased in the minds of moviegoers.

Even for the pedantic, distinctions blur. Into what genre, for example, would you place *Arachnophobia*? "Arachnophobia" means "fear of spiders," and if the movie doesn't *generate* arachnophobia in its audiences, it's not for want of trying. Clever and amusing, *Arachnophobia* emerged as the closest thing to a horror movie from Amblin Entertainment since *Gremlins* and, like that hit, deals with the invasion of a small town by nasty little critters. And, like that movie, *Arachnophobia* is a lot of fun.

Frank Marshall, Steven Spielberg's longtime associate at Amblin, made his directorial debut with *Arachnophobia*. He chose the script, by Don Jakoby and Al Williams, wisely: to a certain degree, the movie is director-proof, since the basic idea—spiders—is so primal. But Marshall acquits himself well, erring primarily in portraying some of the provincial characters as cartoons, while depicting the cosmopolitan hero and his family much more realistically. This condescension is distasteful.

The movie is SF insofar as it deals with the discovery of an unknown species of spider, organized like ants or bees, with neuter workers and a central "queen"—or, in this case, a king. The biggest spider (the size of a dinner plate) is accidentally shipped from South America to a small California town. Against all biological likelihood, it mates with local spiders and produces squillions of venomous little offspring, which spread through the town and begin wiping out the locals.

As in any good monster movie, no one knows at first what is causing the mysterious deaths. The newly arrived doctor (Jeff Daniels), who really does suffer from arachnophobia, is the first to realize what's going on. But of course no one believes him, so things escalate pretty swiftly.

Into the movie's beautiful opening Venezuelan jungle scenes, Marshall builds a sense of dread, after which we're whisked through the movie breathlessly. The cast is fine, especially Daniels; by making the central character an actual arachnophobe, the movie communicates this (really pretty baseless) fear and increases the creepiness of the highly deadly spiders of its story. This time, of course, Daniels is *right* to be afraid.

*Arachnophobia* is overplotted; it doesn't need the locals-versus-the-newcomers subplot, and, delightful as he is, John Goodman seems shoehorned in as the two-gun exterminator. But overall, this was the ideal summer movie, as the countless spiders skittered around tables, benches, lamps, and the landscape. It didn't score as well as anticipated at the box office, but it was a nice try.

*Teenage Mutant Ninja Turtles* is as hard to classify as *Arachnophobia*, but wasn't nearly as good, though it was a lot better than grown-ups were expecting—and it was a colossal hit.

A spunky quartet of radioactively altered shell-backed heroes lives in the sewers of New York. Their favorite food is pizza, and they talk in a bizarre argot that's a blend of 1960s surfer slang and Valspeak. Their first words, in fact, were "pizza" and "radical." Their mentor and guide is a gigantic Japanese-accented rat, who sends them out on nocturnal forays to right wrongs. You tell me—is this science fiction or wild-eyed fantasy or what?

The original comic book was created by Peter Laird and Kevin Eastman as a spoof of two series then being done by maestro Frank Miller, *Daredevil* and *Ronin*, with elements of *The X-Men* thrown in. Laird and Eastman's comic was entertaining enough, but hardly the sort of thing that earmarked the Turtles for their ultimate celebrity. It was adapted as a TV cartoon miniseries by David Wise and Patti Howath; many of the movie's most striking elements come more from the animated version than from the comic book, although Wise and Howath are not credited; the script is signed by Todd W. Langen and Bobby Herbeck.

At its core, *Teenage Mutant Ninja Turtles* is much like a standard Asian "chopsocky" movie, the sort of thing in which the leader of a martial arts school is murdered by his nefarious rival; the leader's star pupil begins training his own students, who will eventually confront the nefarious rival. In *Turtles*, the nefarious rival, the Shredder (James Saito), has, Fagin-like, been turning disaffected teenage boys into thieves. There's other stuff, too, of course. Tough April O'Neil (Judith Hoag), a TV reporter investigating the crime wave plaguing New York, discovers the turtles. All of them are eventually befriended by ex-hockey player Casey Jones (Elias Koteas), who's been trying to clean up crime himself.

It's hardly the plot, therefore, that makes the movie such a kick—it's the outrageous premise, the sassy lines, the performances of the turtles, and the pacing. Early on, one of the turtles dashes past a taxi, startling the passenger, who asks just what the heck that was. The seen-it-all cabbie's response: "Looked like a big turtle in a trench-coat. You goin' to LaGuardia, or what?" Just another night in New York.

Despite a surface similarity—talking animals in a live-action film—*Teenage Mutant Ninja Turtles* is no *Howard the Duck*. This irrepressible action-comedy develops a lot of sympathy for its adolescent reptile heroes. Director Steven Barron seems more comfortable, in fact, with the bizarrely costumed quartet than with real live people; when the turtles aren't around, the movie slams to a halt and suddenly looks grainy and drab.

April and Casey aren't very interesting characters; their romance is strictly by rote—but the movie isn't about them. It's about the Teenage Mutant Ninja Turtles. And in making them funny, appealing heroes, the movie is an unqualified success. Somewhat to my shock, I was looking forward to a continuation of the Teenage Mutant Ninja Turtle saga. However, when the sequel arrived less than a year later, it was, sequel-like, a letdown.

There were other comic-book movies in 1990, but two of those —*The Punisher* and *Captain America*—sat on the shelf. *The Punisher* did play outside the U.S. and finally arrived here on tape in 1991, but *Captain America* is still unseen. *Dick Tracy*, of course, was a major release.

Warren Beatty directed *Dick Tracy* and plays Chester Gould's square-jawed, square-dealing comic-strip police detective, backed by a big cast and a splendid, unique production. Visually and dramatically stylized, the film deftly walks a knife edge between parody and tribute. But there is something ultimately hollow about Beatty's effort, something a bit too polished. We want a movie that looks this great to *be* great, but *Dick Tracy* misses classic status.

The script, credited to Jim Cash and Jack Epps, Jr. (although the final draft was rumored to be by Bo Goldman and Beatty), is broad and flamboyant, at once tongue-in-cheek and straight-faced, the kind of effort that would-be hip people regard as comic-book writing but that really isn't.

The true heroes of the film are cinematographer Vittorio Storaro and production designer Richard Sylbert, as well as Michael Lloyd and Harrison Ellenshaw, in charge of the film's extensive design effects. The visual style is not simply lush, not simply comic strip–like, but a world unto itself, a dazzling depiction of a colossal city full of cops whose only job is to catch bad guys, and bad guys whose only mission in life is to conquer cops. (No one seems to do *anything* else.)

The colors used throughout were limited to the seven available to Gould in the Sunday comic strip, and this restricted pallette somehow makes the film seem to belong to its odd, remote period (the Mythic late 1930s). The creamy lemon yellow of Tracy's coat and hat is the only yellow in the film; cars, walls, suits, poker chips, dresses —everything yellow is the same yellow. Likewise with the other six hues—but the limitation on the *kinds* of color is not a limitation on the *amount* of color. This movie is chromatically dense, layered, saturated. The streets are always wet, gleaming, and lit by one of the seven color choices. Buildings are brightly painted, and the shades blend and match. In its use of color, the film is both unique and daring.

*Dick Tracy* slows down from time to time, mostly in the musical numbers, and occasionally tries too hard, as when Tracy escapes from a locked room by catapulting himself upward through the skylight. But it wins more than it loses, it satisfies more than it disappoints, and most of all, it has the dark, nightmarish look of a pop-art dream.

Although it wasn't adapted from a comic book, *Darkman* played very much like one. Those who were looking for a carefully structured script, with logic firmly in place and all threads sewn tight, came to the wrong movie. It's a flamboyant, richly romantic, and colorful diversion, laced with humor and horror. The baroque excesses alienated some, and there were those who stubbornly insisted that the wit was *accidental*. But I'm pretty aware of "bad laughs"—the kind a moviemaker doesn't want—and *Darkman* got only one when I saw it.

Sam Raimi is unlike any other director working today. His visual style is astounding—complex and dynamic, involving not just moving cameras but *rocketing* cameras, *twirling* cameras, *plunging* cameras (and actors), longshots that zippitybang turn into closeups. It's a broad technique that owes nothing at all to television or the stage—it's entirely M*O*V*I*E, and for those who share Raimi's delirious joy in the possibilities of the film medium, *Darkman* is a delight.

Raimi conceived the story, and successive drafts were written by Chuck Pfarrer, by Sam and his brother Ivan, and by Daniel and Joshua Goldin. It involves scientist Peyton Westlake (Liam Neeson), a researcher into artificial skin, who's severely burned by an explosion in his laboratory and assumed dead. He allows his longtime lover Julie (Frances McDormand) to believe this and sets out to get revenge on his attackers.

Dressed in a long ragged cloak and floppy hat, and swathed in bandages like The Mummy, Westlake constructs a new lab in an abandoned factory and, perfecting his artificial skin formula, tries to restore his own ruined face. To bring off his revenge scheme, he uses the synthetic flesh to impersonate each of the gang members in turn. (The film practically quivers with its resonances of The Phantom of the Opera, The Shadow, Dr. X, and any number of other predecessors.)

Raimi hits a fever pitch early, and he manages to sustain it. *Darkman* is, to say the least, swiftly paced—we're thrown headlong from one event to another, with the sharp editing and wild camerawork (Bill Pope was cinematographer) magnifying Westlake's torment and distracting us from the holes in the plot. Danny Elfman's sonorous music is perhaps too reminiscent of his *Batman* score, but it still fills the bill effectively.

*Darkman* is not a great movie, but it's dynamic and exciting, even poignant. With this promising, entertaining effort, Sam Raimi takes a bold step away from the low-budget arena of his *Evil Dead* films into the world of big budgets and bigger responsibilities.

*RoboCop* was a fierce, funny comic-book movie, with vivid characters, intense action, and a sensibility that was somehow both jaded and optimistic. It's one of the few thrillers of recent years that look better upon repeated viewings; the film's breathtaking cynicism toward big business becomes sharper, the human elements become more touching.

*RoboCop 2* is an altogether more ordinary movie than *RoboCop*, partly because Irvin Kershner, a competent old-line Hollywood director, does his best work in intimate, romantic dramas. Here, he gets the scale right—it's a bigger movie than the first one—but the intensity that Paul Verhoeven brought to *RoboCop* simply isn't there.

The script, by Frank Miller and Walon Green, is so full of themes, subplots, and unresolved issues that it's almost impossible to say just what the main story line of *RoboCop 2* actually *is*. There are two key plot threads: (1) RoboCop (Peter Weller again) vs. some vicious drug dealers, led by the messianic Cain (Tom Noonan), and (2) the attempt by monstrous business firm Omni Consumer Products (OCP) to create a working RoboCop 2, not only to replace Murphy, but to market around the world. The plots awkwardly mingle when Cain's brain is used as that of RoboCop 2, and the two machine-men duke it out in an excellent stop-motion climax directed by Phil Tippet. (Too bad the design of RoboCop 2 is so cumbersome and hard to "read," visually.) There are subplots involving RoboCop's further acceptance of his status as a machine, plus a police strike and other digressions, but they add little to the film.

The many elements of *RoboCop 2* never really connect, although the movie plays as if they do. Frank Miller is best known as a comic-book writer and illustrator; his most famous work is *The Dark Knight Returns*, in which the aging Batman makes one last stand against the armies of the night. It's obvious why producer Jon Davison approached him to write *RoboCop 2*, for a cyborg cop is unquestionably a comic-book concept. However, Miller made his mark on comic books by flouting conventions. *RoboCop* was actually more like the comics that Miller was turning away from than it was like his unusual treatment of the Dark Knight of Gotham.

There's a cumbersome quality to Miller's script, which seems obsessed with keeping each character's motivations consistent, while simultaneously missing their pop-culture richness. *RoboCop 2* fails to provide a single bad guy, even among the major ones, as interesting, amusing, or colorful as any of Kurtwood Smith's *henchmen* in *RoboCop*.

All these defects could have been overcome if Irvin Kershner had allowed the material to, well, shout, as Paul Verhoeven did in the first movie. It's as if Kershner wanted *RoboCop 2* to be realistic rather than flamboyant; he doesn't even let the characters become angry. People not only talk differently in this *RoboCop* adventure, they even move differently. Except for Peter Weller's fine, mimelike portrayal of RoboCop himself, the dynamic performances of *RoboCop* have been replaced with conventional acting.

Though well made, *RoboCop 2* is merely competent; the clash between the demands of satire and those of action-adventure distances audiences, the violence lacks the exuberance of the first movie, and RoboCop's essential humanity is never affirmed, as it was so powerfully in the climax of the original. *RoboCop 2* opened well at the box office, but grosses swiftly fell off; nonetheless, *RoboCop 3*—without Weller—went into production in January 1991.

■ ■ ■

*Predator 2* is much like the skull-hunting alien of the title: an efficient killing machine, brutal, unforgiving, humorless—something perhaps to be admired and respected, but probably not *liked*. Stephen Hopkins directs in a baroque, bravura style, but gets carried away too often: concentrating on techniques, he loses the thread of the narrative, like so many other directors who've come to movies from rock videos. *Predator 2* assaults the audience with an unrelenting barrage of violence, action, and directorial flourishes. It boasts an exceptional cast, but only Danny Glover has much of a chance to make an impression—and that's in a stereotyped role.

It's 1997, and Los Angeles is torn by open street warfare between beleaguered cops and arrogant drug dealers, the latter apparently from every oppressed Third World country in the Western Hemisphere. Into this seething urban hell comes an interplanetary trophy hunter, soon pitted against good cop Danny Glover and his pals. As with *RoboCop 2*, the plot involves the variety of urban villain that movies find it safest to depict these days: drug pushers.

Like the original, *Predator 2* was written by the brothers Jim and John Thomas; this time, they create stronger, slightly less stereotyped characters, but their work is still thick-eared and by-the-book. Whatever interest the characters arouse traces to the exceptional cast that producers Lawrence Gordon, Joel Silver, and John Davis have assembled. Danny Glover, Gary Busey, Ruben Blades, Maria Conchita Alonso, Bill Paxton, and Robert Davi would be virtues in any film— to find them in an action-SF-horror thriller is surprising and pleasing. It's too bad Hopkins and the Thomas brothers found so little for them to do. The late Kevin Peter Hall again plays the Predator.

Despite the film's resolutely grim outlook—there's not a microsecond of joy—Hopkins's intensity nails the audience to the screen. You might want to look away, but you can't. Watching this film may not exactly be a *pleasant* experience, but it's certainly *some* kind of experience. When the Predator rips open a subway car and slaughters the well-armed passengers, the scene occurs almost entirely in brief, stroboscopic flashes. Visually and dramatically, this is a tour de force. The movie doesn't spare its audience anything; Hopkins's abilities are real and admirable, but whatever he made in *Predator 2*, it wasn't really *entertainment*. Audiences agreed; it did not do well.

*Tremors* also didn't do well, but it's the best all-out monster movie since *Alien*: cheeky, fast, and very enjoyable. It consciously and lovingly hearkens back to the heyday of Hollywood SF, the 1950s, not just in content but in setting—the story takes place in the southwestern desert. Director Ron Underwood even includes stray images that seem to echo *It Came from Outer Space*, *Them*, and *Tarantula*.

Fortunately, he has more going for him than impish nostalgia. The script, by S. S. Wilson and Brent Maddock (from a story by them and Underwood—they're all longtime friends), is sharp and funny, with interesting characters and a steady flow of logical happenings. The premise is unlikely, to say the least, but it's carefully developed. The burrowing monsters are intelligent, yes, but they're really just big carnivores; they aren't supernatural. Once their powers and abilities are established, Wilson and Maddock work strictly within those limits, in the best science fiction monster-movie tradition.

Kevin Bacon and Fred Ward are the leads, and the reluctant principal opponents of the monsters, which are enormous (and unexplained) carnivorous worms that burrow through the sandy desert soil like missiles shooting through subway tubes.

For most of its length, *Tremors* rockets along like one of its subterranean monsters, but when everyone takes refuge atop the dusty buildings of Perfection, the story necessarily slows down—just as the characters are trapped by the monsters, Maddock, Wilson, and Underwood are trapped by their own logic. But it picks up speed again as the monsters wise up, and it heads for a satisfying, if guessable, climax.

For a man-eating-monster movie, *Tremors* shows a *lot* of personality. Fluff it may be, but this kind of thing is extremely difficult to do well. The archives of movie history are littered with pathetic proofs that it's very hard to move from laughter to thrills and back, but Underwood, his writers, and his cast manage it again and again. We care about these characters; they're funny—but they are *heroic*, too. *Tremors* is a delight.

Joe Dante's *Gremlins 2: The New Batch* is a great big cartoon. It even opens and closes with animated segments directed by Chuck Jones and featuring (principally) Daffy Duck. The original *Gremlins* was a horror movie with some comedy; this is a comedy with some horror, and not much of that. Even more than in the first film, the Gremlins and the Mogwai are very lifelike, thanks to the special-effects genius of Rick Baker.

The story line is not as strong as in the first film. Three quarters of the way through, the movie merely marks time; not a lot happens, although there's a great deal going on. The only other significant flaw is that four of Gizmo's furry Mogwai offspring are established very strongly as characters, but after they become reptilian Gremlins, we don't see as much of them. We especially miss the googly-eyed, giggling one, who's a riot whenever he's on screen.

Dante and his writer Charlie Haas have structured their film like an extended Robin Williams routine, loopily taking off from the plot and heading into their own cloud-cuckoo land. At the end, as the Gremlins prepare to burst out of the "smart building" where they're currently confined, they engage in their propensity for show-biz take-offs, singing "New York, New York" ("Start spreadin' the news . . .") in a wild potpourri of styles, including not only Busby Berkeley, but also both the Andrew Lloyd Webber *and* the Lon Chaney Phantoms of the Opera. (Even one of their biggest foes, Mr. Futterman, is impressed. "These guys are great!" he exclaims, just before a Gremlin spits in his eye.)

The "smart building" is a gray concrete-and-glass tower in Manhattan, owned by Donald Trump–like developer Daniel Clamp (John Glover, in a quirky and endearing performance), who's out to buy almost everything. This is the kind of computerized building where the elevators talk to you in a creamy voice, where the men's room speaks in a hearty masculine tone, and where, when the fire alarm is pulled, instead of a siren, you hear a calm voice offering advice along the lines of "Yes, it's time to act out the age-old drama of self-preservation. The building is on fire." This is a place that *needs* Gremlins—and as Clamp himself remarks at the end, "You build a place for Things, and Things will come."

Respectful of—in fact, hamstrung by—the rules screenwriter Chris Columbus established for the Gremlins in the original film, the sequel frantically sets everything up in the first half hour. Zach Galligan and Phoebe Cates return as the hero and heroine, now working in New York for Clamp; little Gizmo is back, too, and again unwillingly gives birth to a passel of swiftly multiplying monsters. As usual with a Dante movie, there are inside jokes and a lot of terrific supporting performances, particularly by Robert Picardo as Clamp's majordomo. It's especially fun to see Christopher Lee; despite his long, mournful face (he should play H. P. Lovecraft) and British reserve, he's wonderful at comedy. But perhaps the biggest delight among the cast is John Glover, surely one of the best character actors around these days. His Daniel Clamp is a funny mixture of the innately greedy and the genuinely sweet.

Dante, a top-notch editor, knows how to break up the rhythm and kick in the action. This is a more accomplished film than *Gremlins*, defter, freer, more relaxed. It gives us a great pop-art satirist working at the top of his form: Hollywood studio moviemaking at its slickest sleekest. *Gremlins 2: The New Batch* is a funny, endlessly surprising treat.

Another Amblin Entertainment sequel, *Back to the Future Part III*, is simultaneously satisfying and disappointing. It's satisfying because writer Bob Gale and director Robert Zemeckis answer all questions and settle all issues in entertaining, gratifying ways. But it's disappointing for that very reason—the movie has no tension, it takes no real risks. We know from the first scene that the heroes will triumph, so it's really just a matter of waiting to see *how*.

The first *Back to the Future* was stuffed with amusing, surprising, and swift-paced incidents, a time-travel comedy that played fair with the audience, as well as with the conventions of scientific time travel that have evolved since H. G. Wells. Zemeckis is an awesomely proficient director, with some of the greatest, quickest comedy timing since the silent days; *Back to the Future III* is an elegant entertainment machine.

This time out, Marty McFly (Michael J. Fox), the kid from the present trapped in 1955 at the end of *Back to the Future II*, enlists the aid of *that* year's Doc Brown (Christopher Lloyd) into sending him back to 1885, where the Doc Brown from our present has wound up—and is doomed, apparently, to die. Through mind-twisting but fully time-travel-logical plot turns, Marty himself goes back to the Old West, where, as in the other *BTTF* films, he finds the ancestors of people he knows, and where, true to form, he gets into a lot of trouble. Doc Brown, meanwhile, becomes involved with schoolmarm Clara Clayton (Mary Steenburgen, who already took a time journey in *Time After Time*), despite Doc's conviction that he's probably doomed. I was especially pleased that Doc and Clara begin to fall in love partly because they are both science fiction fans.

Zemeckis and Gale have a lot of fun both celebrating and subverting the conventions of Westerns. They play their scenes for a certain kind of realism; production designer Rex Carter has provided an authentic-looking frontier town, not movielike at all. On the other hand, there is a gunfight, there is a schoolmarm, and there are three wisecracking old coots sitting around the saloon—Dub Taylor, Harry Carey, Jr., and Pat Buttram, longtime Western fixtures, treated here as exactly that. Unfortunately, this balancing act between homage and spoof keeps the film from finding solid ground; the satirizing of 1955 in the first movie rang true because many in the audience could remember that year, while others were familiar with it from sitcoms. But for most of us, the Real West is very remote; even the Movie West is distant for a lot of people, while still seeming more familiar than the real thing. *BTTF III* strands us between those two distinct worlds.

Gale and Zemeckis insist this is the last *BTTF* film. And it should be. Though we're happy to see Marty and Doc get what they want, we're also happy to see the last of them. Let's leave them where they are, enjoying whatever time they've ended up in. Gale and Zemeckis are talented guys, and surely they can find different stories to tell.

*Flatliners* is different, but it's also irritating. Gorgeously produced—in fact, *over*produced—and featuring some appealing young actors, the movie is as irresponsible as the dashing young medical students who are its heroes. Visually, the film is thick with smoke and swathed in plastic sheeting; dramatically, the script is thin and the characters mere one-line-description stereotypes; it is pretentious, pompous, and overstated.

But despite that, we stay with *Flatliners* all the way to its predictable, overly happy ending. This is a High Concept film where, for once, the high concept is compelling enough to keep us engaged.

"Philosophy failed, religion failed," says arrogant, ambitious Nelson (Kiefer Sutherland), "now it's up to the physical sciences." This man wants to explore nothing less than eternity itself. What happens to people after they die? The word "soul" is never heard in the movie, but that's what the story is about.

Nelson has worked out a method, involving cryonics and electrical shocks, to temporarily die and be safely revived. Of course, this really does depend on the *definition* of "death," but for the sake of argument we can accept that the characters in *Flatliners* die and return to life.

He has persuaded four other students to help him with his experiments, which he's doing largely to become famous. Brilliant Rachel (Julia Roberts), driven by childhood memories of her father's suicide, is obsessed with death. Iconoclastic Labraccio (Kevin Bacon) has been suspended from school. Unimaginative Joe (William Baldwin) is a Lothario who secretly videotapes himself having sex with dozens of young women. Steckle (Oliver Platt) sees himself as worthy of an autobiography already and is taking notes to that end.

When Nelson dies, we see what he sees, and at first it seems to be an idyllic scene of children playing in a golden field, but elements from the dream begin to turn up, menacingly, in Nelson's real life. His resurrection excites the group, and one by one, all but Steckle try this "ultimate high." Each experimenter, however, is haunted by strange specters from his or her past. Improbably, they don't *tell* each other about these visitations.

For one character to have this experience is acceptable, but for *each* of them to endure virtually the same trauma, during and after death, makes the film repetitious. Nelson and Labraccio even have similar sins to expiate: they were both childhood bullies. Couldn't screenwriter Peter Filardi have brought as much imagination to his plot as he did to the central idea?

The title refers to that moment when all cardiovascular and neurological activity ceases, when the lines indicating heartbeat and brain functioning go absolutely flat. Filardi's script insists that, in real life, there has been a near-uniformity among those who have been medically resurrected, including that now-famous "tunnel of light." But others have reported quite different experiences, and some researchers say that the "tunnel of light" is simply a symptom of the brain shutting down.

Actually, Filardi's script is staunchly religious; even the atheist in the group, Labraccio, is converted after he's been a flatliner. Filardi assumes that the only possible explanation for such sensations is some kind of survival of the mind beyond death. But what the film *shows* us is unconscious people worrying over childhood traumas. Director Joel Schumacher is visually baroque but a conventional thinker—his best-known earlier films were *St. Elmo's Fire*, *The Lost Boys*, and *Cousins*—which makes his work both very shallow and visually very flashy. When the central idea itself is shallow, as in *The Lost Boys*, Schumacher can turn out a fairly entertaining movie. But when the story deals with Big Issues, as does *Flatliners*, Schumacher's overripe visuals seem corrupt. The film is crammed with insistently symbolic images; frescoes and statuary show up absolutely everywhere, even behind the credits. The school looks more like a museum of discarded Renaissance splendor than an institution of medical training.

The movie wants desperately to *mean* something, to deal in some significant way with guilt, sin, and atonement, but it can't really conjure up any true sins for these people. All of this guilt-sin stuff, and the expiation, is in the characters' heads anyway—so who, exactly, are they atoning to? Themselves? Schumacher reduces the flatlining process to an instant psychiatric session.

Along with *Ghost* and *Jacob's Ladder*, *Flatliners* is one of several nouveau-religious films. If there are more to come, I hope they develop their ideas better than did *Flatliners*.

■ ■ ■

The sweetly lyrical, affectionately satirical *Edward Scissorhands* is director Tim Burton's first movie since *Batman*. It's a charming but bizarre suburban fable, suggestive of Steven Spielberg crossed with John Waters, a bright, comic-book-colored tale not quite like any other movie ever made. The title character, sensitively played by Johnny Depp, is an artificial man with scissors for hands; they cut his face and make it difficult for him to engage in normal behavior, but he uses them to create beautiful sculptures. As with his previous movies (before *Batman* there were *Pee-wee's Big Adventure* and *Beetlejuice*), Tim Burton tells a tale of a misfit loner happiest in his own world.

*Edward Scissorhands* is obviously a metaphor for the artist and his/her relationship with society, but Burton and his screenwriter, Caroline Thompson, can't seem to decide just what that relationship *is*. The first half of the film is funny, light, and delicate as a floating feather, carrying you dreamily along on Danny Elfman's marvelous, dancelike score. The timing of everything is knife-edged but graceful; there's not a wasted moment or frame. It's clear storytelling, surprising us again and again by its simple, cheerful refusal to go along with anything like the expected plot twists.

In the second half, the story becomes more conventional and much less interesting. Finally, at the climax, we're left wanting something more than Burton gives us, and whatever point he has been striving to make goes wafting out Edward's window along with his miraculous snow.

Are Burton and Thompson saying that the artist can never really fit into society? That we can love our artists, but we mustn't expect them to be "one of us"? That the artist is forever alone? A final conclusion cannot really be drawn, but perhaps this is due to the film's almost elegiac approach: suburban and mystical simultaneously.

In an effort to sell her wares, Avon lady Peg Boggs (Dianne Wiest) decides to check out the giant castle looming atop a black, twisted crag at the end of her pastel-colored housing development. There, amid a splendid array of topiary sculptures, deep within the dusty and deserted castle, she finds lonely, pale Edward. A mommy to the core, Peg determinedly takes Edward home with her. It's as if a Cenobite from *Hellraiser* has moved in with Ozzie and Harriet. Edward is full of trepidation, but so lonely that he's willing to go along with almost anything.

He develops a crush on Kim (Winona Ryder), the daughter of

Peg and Bill (Alan Arkin), but she's a teenager, more concerned about status and acceptance than gentle Edward, and scorns him at first. Her lowlife boyfriend, Ken (Anthony Michael Hall), is openly contemptuous of this bizarre outsider, as well as jealous of his acceptance by the community, a situation that leads eventually to the climax.

Edward is an artist, and he must create. Left to his own devices in the Boggs home, he sculpts bushes, his fingers flashing, leaves pouring past him in a steady stream. Everyone is delighted with his skills, and soon all the bushes in the neighborhood are transformed —ballerinas, penguins, horses, even a bust of Elvis. He also becomes a wizard hairdresser.

Though Edward can talk, he's usually silent (and physically resembles his creator, Tim Burton), and Johnny Depp plays him somewhat like a sad-faced silent-movie clown. It's a remarkable, imaginative performance, for Edward is never merely endearing— he is complex: both winsome and sad, naïve and sophisticated.

Vincent Price has only a few scenes in flashback as the eccentric inventor who creates Edward, but even those who adore Price, our last great beloved horror star, will be more than happy with these moments. He has announced that this is his final movie, and it is a beautiful farewell to the screen. Burton's first film was an animated short about a little boy who wanted to *be* Vincent Price, and he understands the actor's oddly complex appeal. Price can be splendidly sinister, but we can always perceive his own lightly sardonic personality, with his winning refusal to take anything, including himself, too seriously. In these few scenes, Burton melds the two sides of Price: the inventor is benign and scary, wonderful and awesome. I wish I could communicate how much it means to me that, if this is indeed Vincent Price's adieu, it occurs in such a remarkable movie, and under the direction of a man who understands him so thoroughly, and who obviously loves him as much as I do myself.

The brilliant, unique qualities of *Edward Scissorhands* will make it a favorite of young people the world over; it could exert the same long-lasting influence as similar oddities, from *The Wizard of Oz* through *Invaders from Mars* and *The 5000 Fingers of Dr. T*, and on to *Phantom of the Paradise*. That it ultimately loses its way is, I suspect, of no lasting importance whatsoever. Tim Burton is just beginning his career; *Edward Scissorhands* is the first of his features to be truly *his* film—and indicates that rare and beautiful wonders lie ahead of us.

Every few years, we get a very literary dystopian best-seller, invariably promoted as *not* being science fiction. *1984* was one such book; so was George R. Stewart's *Earth Abides*, and, more recently, Margaret Atwood's *The Handmaid's Tale*. Often political and satiric, such novels tend to be simply conceived, extending disturbing trends to what seem like logical ends, and emphasize (usually thinly drawn) characters over plot. And they're more likely to be filmed than anything that is marketed as science fiction.

I have not read the novel, so I cannot discuss how faithful director Volker Schlöndorff and writer Harold Pinter have been to Atwood. I can only judge *The Handmaid's Tale* as a film, and as a film it's weak. The story is set in the "recent future," as an opening title announces; the location is the U.S. (now called Gilead), and everything looks pretty much like what you see out your front window. Except for those bodies hanging from lampposts and outside prison walls. We soon learn that women are being rounded up and sorted into the fertile and the infertile, for the cumulative effects of pollution, nuclear accidents, and other tamperings have rendered most females sterile. The new regime is headed by religious fundamentalists—clearly Christian, but the film is too timid to criticize real Bible-thumpers.

Kate (Natasha Richarson) tries to flee to Canada, but her husband is shot down at the border. She's captured and eventually trained to be a Handmaid, servant to the wealthy and bearer of their children. She's sent to the home of the Commander (Robert Duvall), whose wife, Serena Joy (Faye Dunaway), apparently like *all* wives of the elite, is infertile.

Part of the problem with *The Handmaid's Tale* is that this society is not entirely credible. It seems to consist solely of Handmaids, Wives, Commanders, Chauffeurs, and a scant few others. What about those *below* the level of the elite? Who's growing the food? Who's refining the oil? Where does the power come from? What about *anything* that doesn't fit into the structure of the story? Granted, we are seeing things strictly from Kate's point of view, and can know only what she knows, but this society doesn't really seem functional, more like a polemicist's invention.

And, unfortunately, that's the way the film plays, too—it's didactic and artificial. Everyone on Kate's side is essentially good; everyone opposed to her is either banally cruel, like the Commander, or calculatingly malign, like Serena Joy. There's no irony to the vision, no subtlety to the attack. Even the target is unclear. Yes, all this is very bad, but the society isn't textured enough to hold our interest in and of itself; the objects of the satire are so unspecific that the point is diffused. It takes the profeminist slant of *The Stepford Wives* a step further, but that's about all.

Granted, things would hardly go well for many if fundamentalists ran the country, but *The Handmaid's Tale* never suggests why this particular religion led to this particular society, and the key plot device—a ninety percent sterility rate among women—confuses the issue endlessly. Given such a crisis, obviously *some* drastic measures would need to be taken, even under the most humanitarian of regimes. Atwood has not only stacked the deck, she's dealt herself a pat hand. No one, not even zealots, could find balm in this Gilead. But what if the story *had* depicted a future where the fundamentalists were happy? Wouldn't that have been more interesting? A nightmare world that grows out of trends in *our* society, better than ours on some levels but rotten at the core (as in Huxley's *Brave New World*), would seem to offer greater opportunities for disturbing, vital satire. A dystopia always needs to be a utopia for the few, hell for the many.

*The Handmaid's Tale* is a *respectable* movie, but it should have been more rambunctious, with its agenda clearer. Schlöndorff (best known for *The Tin Drum*) was probably the wrong person to film Pinter's script. Pinter's genius is at hiding strong emotions and rich characterization within banal dialogue; he needs a director who can offset the blandness of the speeches with visual richness, but Schlöndorff backs off from being stylish—everything is simply shown to us in a perfunctory manner. Pinter's flat dialogue is further flattened, and despite the occasional compelling details, our interest drains away. And with scenes such as that of the Commander attempting to impregnate poor Kate, with Serena beside him, everyone fully dressed, Schlöndorff allows the film to slip into absurdity.

*Total Recall*, absurd on some levels, zings along at such speed that it makes the fastest movie you ever saw seem like it was unreeling *backward*. It spins your head with the surprise of its ideas and dazzles you with brilliantly conceived special effects.

Director Paul Verhoeven never loses track of the strong, intricate story. The characters are drawn in broad strokes, but that's appropriate for this kind of movie, and for the talents of Arnold Schwarzenegger. He's no actor, but he's a star, and absolutely great at playing himself; do not underestimate that ability. Arnold is comfortable on screen, and has always exhibited a wry sense of humor about his appearance and background. Even in bad movies, Schwarzenegger is more likable than his primary rival, Sylvester Stallone, who's almost always pompous.

The story ranges from Earth to Mars, as ordinary working guy Quaid (Arnold) starts to undergo a recreational memory implant— he'll remember being a secret agent—only to discover he *already* has an artificial memory, that of the life he's now leading. Poor Quaid doesn't know who he is. Unraveling this problem takes him to Mars, and into conflict with the director of Martian operations, cold-eyed Colhaagen (Ronny Cox). He gets caught up in both an insurrection by the mistreated Martian workers and in Colhaagen's attempts to keep the planet oxygen poor. At the climax, ancient alien technology kicks in and, illogically but spectacularly, instantly terraforms Mars.

The screenplay for *Total Recall* is an elaborate expansion of Philip K. Dick's short story "We Can Remember It for You Wholesale." Dan O'Bannon and Ron Shusett (*Alien*) first wrote their script back in 1974 and sold it as a medium-budget Disney project. Though it was considered a very strong script, with a third-act weakness, it didn't get made and passed from studio to studio. It acquired and lost several directors, including David Cronenberg and Bruce Beresford, as well as a series of leading men, including Christopher Reeve, Richard Dreyfuss, and Patrick Swayze. The problem, Hollywood lore has it, was always that third act: how do you wrap up a story like this? The final script is credited to Shusett, O'Bannon, and Gary Goldman, and the screen story to Shusett, O'Bannon, and Jon Povill. By this time, the writers themselves probably don't know just who contributed what, but however it was finally done, the script is rich, intricate, and imaginative.

Despite some story flaws and a needless emphasis on violence, *Total Recall* is the best science fiction movie since *Blade Runner*. Like Ridley Scott, Verhoeven gives us a detailed future without rubbing our noses in the futurosity of it all. Tomorrow is merely where these people happen to live.

The improbable science at the end annoyed many, but the film is emotionally satisfying, and it did very well at the box office. All concerned should be congratulated for making an action-adventure SF movie that required its audience to *think*—and that was also something they enjoyed.

It's really movies like *Total Recall* and *Edward Scissorhands* that hold out the most hope for SF films in the future, not dry, pedantic efforts like *The Handmaid's Tale*. Sure, the adaptation of Atwood's book is admirable, but its goals were muzzy and the results hardly compelling; in fact, *Total Recall* and *Edward Scissorhands* were actually far more daring within their own arenas.

We forget at our peril that movies are a *business* and that they cost a great deal to make—so they have to earn a great deal as well. Many of the most interesting SF ideas are expensive to realize on screen, so the films—for now, anyway—have to be compromises between what we would *like* to see and what people will *pay* to see. Both *Total Recall* and *Edward Scissorhands* took chances, and both paid off financially. They have ensured the likelihood of more big-budget science fiction and fantasy movies in the future.

# Over the Long Haul

### . . .

## *Martha Soukup*

Science fiction, the novitiate soon learns, is not simply a body of literature. It is also a robust and scrappy community—a kind of sentient ant colony in which authors, editors, readers, critics, agents, and publishers come together to argue about everything from the spiral nebulae to the spiraling costs of Nebula banquets.

Communities depend upon benefactors—people such as Martha Soukup, who helps run the Science Fiction Roundtable on GEnie for an amusingly inadequate amount of money and who recently served as SFWA's secretary for no money at all.

Like Ted Chiang, whose "Tower of Babylon" appears in the first half of this volume, Soukup honed her considerable talents at the Clarion Science Fiction Writers Workshop. Upon graduating from that stellar institution, she began selling her fiction with impressive regularity, appearing in *Asimov's, Fantasy and Science Fiction, Amazing, Aborginal,* and such theme anthologies as *Newer York* and *Alternate Presidents*.

"Over the Long Haul" traces to a workshop exercise in which the instructor, A. J. Budrys, tossed out a provocative concept: long-haul rigs controlled by computer operators from their homes. "It seemed immediately obvious to me," Soukup notes, "that the people stuck in those cabs would be teenage mothers. (It then became clear that everyone else in the room thought I was nuts.)

"I liked the opportunity the notion offered to look at issues of personal choice and responsibility in a constrained situation. It also let me do a chase scene, which I think of as wild-eyed experimental writing. A. J. kindly let me use his trucks; all that remained was for me to realize that the story had to be written in Shawana's voice.

"One reason the novelette took a while to sell, I think, is that people thought it dystopian. Having lived two blocks from urban projects, and having read a great deal about welfare hotels, I wish 'Long Haul' were, by comparison, dystopian, or that it could answer the political questions it raises. If I had the answers, I could write novels, instead of short stories that simply question."

Sometimes I think I've been in this truck forever, but of course that's not so. I just have to look at my license card if I want the proof:

"Shawana Mooney," it says, and right next to that the day I got the card, two years ago. Two weeks after little Cilehe was born, which makes it easy to remember her birthday.

That name "Shawana" makes me think sometimes my daddy was a guy named Shawn Parker. My mama sure cried when he got shot dead when I was eight, but she wouldn't say he was my daddy. She just said he was no good and ran drugs and then she cried some more. Mooney, of course, that's my mama's name and her mama's, and it was my great-grandma's too. Also my great-grandpa's. They were married.

Then the card's got my picture, which looks terrible with my eyes all stary the way the camera caught them, but I kind of like the way I had my hair done then, with all those little braids my grandma put in.

I must look awful now. I look at myself in the big side mirror when I fix up my makeup, but I don't really look hard at the whole effect, if you know what I mean. When Tomi gets a little bigger— he's barely four now—maybe I can teach him to fix my hair.

Or maybe we'll get out of this truck.

I think about that a lot, especially when Cilehe gets cranky and yells. Which isn't fair to her of course because what two-year-old wants to grow up in the cab of a truck, six feet wide and six feet deep? Sure, she's got "Sesame Street" like I did—and a lot of other much more boring TV, like it or not—but I could go outside besides, even if my grandma was always warning me about gangs. Cilehe's the kind of baby who needs to move around and tire herself out, which is pretty hard here.

I know exactly how she feels.

But it's none of her doing. I tell myself that. I got her by my own self—well, I had help, but it isn't her fault her daddy isn't in a truck too. They put the welfare parents who actually are raising the kids in the trucks. Now, do you know any guy who's going to take them? Nope. Both their daddies were long gone before that happened.

One truck stop looks a lot like another. I was kind of dozing behind the wheel when it took a big pull right and the truck went off to an exit. I tried to guess where we were—I thought maybe Nebraska. Sure was flat as hell out there.

Cilehe started kicking up a fit. She always acts like the last couple minutes before we stop is a couple of hours, and screaming will make the truck go faster. The only thing that could make the truck go faster is if I hit MANUAL OVERRIDE and drove it myself, and I'd better have a damn good reason for that or it's big trouble. She was screaming for the potty. She just started with that, and she doesn't like the portapotty in the cab. Me neither. I don't care what they say, the thing smells.

Got her in before she messed up her panties, Tomi following quiet as a mouse. He's not quite big enough to send into the boys' room alone yet. Then she didn't want to wash her hands, and when I made her, she got her hands and face and hair and T-shirt and the floor all wet, and glared up at me like I did it. She stomped out of the bathroom with her sneakers going squish, squish, squish.

I looked in to see if I knew any of the drivers. Kimberlea and Avis were both there, still going along the same route I was. I met Avis for the first time in Minneapolis on this run. Kimberlea I met soon after I started. The women on the road tell me you can go forever between seeing someone twice, so that was lucky. As long as we kept going along the same route, taking our full breaks—who wouldn't take her full break?—so they'd be the same length, we'd keep meeting up. Kimberlea is older than my mama, maybe forty, and she used to do keypunching in the very last office that still used it, years and years after everyone else stopped, until the business was sold and they retired the old-time system. Her kids are twelve and eight, and she was even married when she had them.

Avis was having trouble with her boy. Her one-year-old twins were in the big playpen in the middle of the dining room, the boy screaming his head off. I looked at Cilehe, but she just stared at the kid with big round eyes, didn't copy him. The baby wailed, while Avis drank Coke with her face turned away from him, her eyebrows down and her mouth real tight, trying to act like the baby wasn't there.

"But I don't know if I want green or blue," she was saying to Kimberlea.

Kimberlea sighed. "Girl, what do you need with neon fingernails?" I put Cilehe in the pen, away from Avis's boy, and let Tomi sit next to me.

"Just because I'm stuck in a truck all day doesn't mean I can't look good!" Avis is a couple years younger than me, maybe seventeen.

"That sort of thing costs money. You don't get that much to save."

"So what else do I have to spend it on?"

"You can save it," Kimberlea said stubbornly.

"Right, and maybe in twelve years when my babies are teenagers and they let me out, I'll have a couple hundred bucks!" Avis took a long drink of her Coke. Kimberlea and I said hi. "So why not order the implant kit and have something now?"

"Couple hundred dollars is better than nothing. And you could save more than that."

"On what the government gives us?" Avis snorted and peeled open a Snickers.

"I save six dollars a week," Kimberlea said.

"You told us," Avis said.

Last stop, Kimberlea'd laid out her whole plan over breakfast. She's studying for her accounting license. Accounting's just a matter of using spreadsheets and stuff, she said, but they still make you study for it. The course work costs, and then you have to get a license, which is a lot of money even before the bribes. She saves every penny. Doesn't even use up her food vouchers; sells the leftovers back to the government for half value, or sometimes to other truckers for two thirds. Her plate had scraps of meat loaf and carrots. Not even Jell-O for dessert. She stays husky just the same.

"What the fuck you want an accounting license for anyway?" Avis asked. "It's just minimum wage. Your oldest is thirteen next year, so you get out one way or another." Trucking's also a labor option for mothers with just one preteenager, but I've only seen a couple women who chose it when they didn't have to. They'd put her on some other workfare labor. Maybe sidewalk cleaning. That's what I did, five hours a day, before Cilehe. I used to hate it, but it's better than trucking.

Kimberlea took her paper napkin off her lap, folded it neatly, and laid it on her tray. "I don't like being on welfare if I can work," she said. "Not this workfare joke—a real job. I always worked until they took my job away. That's the way I know."

The boy was screaming so loud now even Avis couldn't ignore it any longer. "Shit," she said. She stuffed the rest of the Snickers into her mouth and went to get him.

Kimberlea and I talked for a couple minutes until her watch started beeping. "Back to the road," she said. She gathered up her two kids, who had been reading quietly at another table—don't know how she saves six bucks a week, if she buys them books—and left.

Avis came back. "Damn kid needed a new diaper," she said. "Where's old Kim Burly?"

"Her break was up."

"Stuck-up bitch." She wiggled her fingers in my face. "So do you think green or blue?"

Tomi tugged my arm and pointed. I was set to ignore him, but the room had gone quiet. I looked up.

There was a man in the dining room.

Maybe if you don't truck, you don't know how strange that was. When I was little, I guess most truckers were guys. Then they came up with the remote-driving system, one guy in his living room controlling a dozen trucks. The unions kicked a fuss about that, of course, so everyone yelled at each other until they came up with a couple solutions: early retirement with heaps of compensation for the old truckers—lot of younger guys took that and went into other work— and retraining the truckers that passed the tests to be controllers at a big fat salary. At the same time, they passed a law that there had to be a driver in each truck. For manual override in emergencies, like that was going to happen. But nobody trusts computers and least-ways unions.

Then came the Welfare Labor Act, the workfare act.

Bound to happen, they put us in the trucks. It's boring. It doesn't pay shit—the controllers get the real money. We all know why they put us with two kids in the trucks. It's like, you get yourself one kid, they put you cleaning sidewalks or something and thinking on what happens if you get another one. You get another one anyway, and bam! into a truck. So now you're on the road all the time, only get out at a truck stop and see other drivers and they're all women too. A third kid is too many to live in a truck cab, so you'd get out, but how're you going to get a third one? Locking you in a convent couldn't work any better.

What they say is truck cabs are perfect classrooms, educational TV the kids (and their moms) can't get away from. Getting away from bad influences. Breaking the cycle of poverty.

What it's *about* is punishing us, keeping us away from that nasty stuff that got us here. We all know it. These are the same people who got abortion made illegal, and whittled down sex ed next to nothing. (Though from what my mama told me once before she moved on, people hardly used birth control even when they had teachers telling them about it.) They're punishing us, all right.

I never saw a guy trucking. As far as I ever knew, they didn't even *let* guys choose trucking.

Avis was staring. "Jesus, it's a man!" she whispered.

"Real good," I said. "You remember what they look like."

Maybe I hadn't, though. Oh, he was tall and he was fine. White, like Cilehe's daddy, but dark tan skin. Maybe Latin. His hair came down in a braid over one shoulder, thick and brown and shiny. Cheek-bones cut high like a TV Indian's. He had tight old jeans on. The way they hugged his hips close you could imagine doing yourself.

Man, it had been too long since I'd seen a guy.

He walked over to an empty table across the room and a dozen pairs of eyes followed him. Nobody said a word.

One skinny girl with a baby on her hip went over and stared down at him. "Truckers only in this room," she said in a mean voice.

That broke the silence. Everyone started up with catcalls, hisses, and "Who *cares*?" The girl glared back at all of us. Some of them, when they get put in the trucks, actually buy the crap about our Evil Ways and get worse than any taxpayer.

The guy just smiled up at her so nice your toes curled. "You're right," he said. His voice was like caramel candy. He pulled out his trucker's card.

The girl's lips went white. She grabbed the kid up in her arm, pulled another off her chair, and left the room.

"This is mine," Avis said, to me or maybe just to the universe.

"What are you talking about?" Her eyes looked like a cat's fixing to go after a mouse. Squintier than a cat's, though, in her pasty pimply face. No way a man so fine-looking would go for her.

Not that *I* was after him.

"Seventeen months," Avis said. No need to ask seventeen months since what.

I fluffed my hair up around my forehead. I knew it looked like hell.

Avis was already moving, plowing through a crowd of women all trying to look like they had some casual reason for happening to go

over by that particular table at that particular time. It sure wasn't
worth it to join the mob.

"Look after your sister," I told Tomi. I put him in the pen with
the other kids. "I'll be back in five minutes. Need some fresh air."

"Me too, Mama?" he asked, but he's a good kid. He didn't complain. I didn't want fresh air, I wanted to get out of the room so my
eyes wouldn't be all over that guy. Something got you in this fix, I
told myself. You think you'd learn someday.

Even the place outside for truckers to walk around is separate
from the place car drivers go to let their poodles piddle. Same sky,
though, high and gray, the wind whipping around pretty good. I took
a deep breath of windy air. I told myself I wasn't a kid anymore,
fourteen and stupid like when Tomi's daddy got him on me. When
that didn't work, I tried telling myself he had a whole truck stop full
of girls to pick from. When that didn't work, I looked at my watch
and told myself I only had another ten minutes in my break, and odds
were this guy wasn't going the same way anyway.

I talked to myself until I had me just about convinced.

"Nice day," he said.

I didn't jump. I was great. "Sure, if you hate sun and like smog."

"Somebody must," he said, "or you wouldn't be outside in it."

I turned then. "Oh, I just get tired of girl talk all the time," I
said.

"I wouldn't know," he said. The wind was strong enough to flop
his braid around. Some of his hair was loose and blowing over his
forehead. His eyes were the clearest, lightest brown I'd ever seen.
"The women always seem to stop talking when I come in."

"Yeah, well, they're easily impressed." I couldn't understand why
he was out here with me. Couldn't understand why I was saying bitchy
things to him either.

"But not you, I guess," he said.

"I been around some."

"I can tell you're a woman of experience."

Was he laughing at me? He didn't look like it. I grunted in a
worldly sort of way.

"Cal," he said, sticking his hand out. After a moment I realized
it was his name.

"Shawana," I said. Took his hand. Right when I did, I knew I never should have. Something about man flesh just feels different, and the skin of my hand, I realized, had been starved for the taste of it.

The rest of my skin started up a clamor.

He was still holding on to my hand, so I pulled it back. I tried to think of something regular to say. "Don't see a lot of guys trucking," I said. Oh, smooth. Real smooth.

"Well, you've seen me," he said.

"Don't you have to have kids to get a trucking license?"

"Yes."

I couldn't think of anything to say to that—or too many things: You got kids? How come you have them and not their mamas? Where are they—the mamas and especially the kids? What are you doing out here?

Maybe he read my mind a little. "The baby's in his crib in the truck. I didn't want to wake him."

"Just one baby?"

Cal nodded—the braid went swish, swish.

"How come you're trucking?" Maybe it was rude to ask, but I could have said, Why isn't his mama stuck with him like the usual course of events?—which would've been ruder.

He looked away, which showed off his sharp cheekbones against the gray sky just about perfect. "I needed time to be alone. To think."

"Well, you sure got that," I said. I couldn't not ask any longer. "I didn't think they let guys truck. I thought it was a mother's job."

He rubbed his face in his hands and the air seemed to get even darker. "She—Jess's mother died. When he was born."

Oh, shit. "Jesus, I'm sorry, I didn't mean—"

He looked back at me and tried to smile. "That's okay. You couldn't know."

"I'm sorry."

"Yeah. Well, that's the one exception to the guideline that unwed welfare mothers get all the trucks. If the mother's dead, they let the father do it." His mouth quirked with no smile to it. "After all, their big argument is that the truck's the ideal classroom, so they can't say no. It's for the good of the kid, right?"

I felt bad about my nosiness. The silence stretched out.

"Um, you miss her?"

"Well, it's getting better. I don't think she was going to marry me anyway."

"You were *engaged*?"

He shook his head. "But I thought I could get her to marry me after—" He stopped and looked straight up at the sky, blinking hard.

I grabbed his hand, saying some nonsense like I do when Tomi's crying. Here I'd just been thinking about this guy as a hot body. Then I was holding him and still saying soothing nonsense things.

My watch beeped. He pulled back.

"I gotta be going."

"I'm sorry. Usually I want to be alone, but sometimes it's hard —and in the truck stops there's always such a crowd—"

"It's okay," I said. "I hope things are better."

"Which way are you going?" he asked suddenly.

"How do I know? It's been west on 80, if that's any help. I think I may be going to Salt Lake. I've done that route once or twice."

"Maybe we'll see each other again along the route."

My face got warm. "There's no way to know that."

He smiled an I-know-things-you-don't smile. "I have ways of being more certain."

The watch beeped again. "Well—bye, Cal."

"Until we meet again," he said.

Cilehe was in a real bad mood from being left alone. Tomi was trying to make her laugh, meowing like a cat and rubbing against her feet. Don't know where he ever saw a cat. Maybe on "Sesame Street." My watch was beeping steady now: if I didn't get into the truck in a big hurry, I'd lose all my discretionary money for a week. I helped Tomi out of the pen, yanked Cilehe up by the armpit, and ran to the parking lot.

Cal was leaning against a big black truck like I'd never seen. He looked at us as we scrambled up into the cab. I pushed the button to say we were ready to go. The truck lurched and squealed out of the lot and onto the highway.

It was fractions on the TV—one half, one third, one quarter— over and over and over and over again. Tomi watched for a while. Cilehe just scowled and rocked back and forth. Usually I pick her up when she gets like that. But as long as she wasn't making noise, I had other things to think on.

Out in the walking area, holding Cal, I was just trying to make him feel better. Now it was over, I was noticing all the ways he felt to me. His thick braid of hair squeezed between our chests. His soft flannel shirt and the hard muscles underneath it. The man smell. The little raspy sound when his tight jeans rubbed on mine—

Another twenty minutes and there's no telling what might have happened.

But the road wore on and the fluttery feeling began to die away. The guy had acted like he had reason to think we'd be at the same truck stop down the road, but that was about as likely as running into a whole different guy would be. If only I'd run into him earlier— nearer the beginning of the hour lunch break. Next break would only be twenty minutes, to gas up the truck and grab a quick bite, and he was running more than twenty minutes behind me on the road even if he did go the same direction and stop at the same stop.

Unless he decided to cut his lunch short and get right back on the road—

I began to have another thought I maybe wasn't proud of, a thought about getting us out of the truck.

We stayed on 80 like I'd guessed, which means the long way across Nebraska, not the best scenery for distracting the brain. Corn, wheat—it all just looks green at a distance. About twenty thousand fractions later, the truck pulled itself off.

I looked for the strange black truck, but of course it wasn't there. I'd've seen him pass me on the road. I gassed up, parked, and took the kids into the stop.

Kimberlea wasn't there. Avis was. Didn't really know anyone else, so I sat next to her again.

"That guy left early," she complained.

"Maybe he had to go check on his kid," I said.

"How do you know he has a kid?"

"He's gotta have one or he wouldn't be trucking," I said. "If he didn't bring it in, it must've been in its crib."

"Not much of a parent, if he leaves his kid alone in his truck," Avis said.

I hadn't even thought about that.

"It was probably sleeping, and he didn't want to wake it," I said.

"Why you want to defend him?" she asked.

I shrugged. "No reason. Just seemed to make sense."

"I don't care if he's a lousy parent or Nelly Nurture," she said. (Nelly Nurture is the teenage star of a show on public TV who tells you how to eat when you're pregnant and how to take care of your babies.) "I just care if his parts are all in working order."

Then who should walk in but Cal himself, which Avis saw before I did. "And it looks like a great time to find out!" She jumped up. I couldn't stand to look at the way she embarrassed herself. I wondered at him being right when he said we'd meet again down the road.

"Is this seat taken?" He'd come over to the table, Avis hovering behind him looking mad. More girls were beginning to gather.

"I don't think so."

He sat. "What do you know about teething pain?"

"Well, if you rub his gums it helps. And they sell this stuff in little tubes that numbs them up."

"Could you show me?"

So I took him over to the counter and showed him. He pulled out some vouchers to pay for it. I noticed he had a fat wad of them.

"Will you show me how to use it?"

I told Tomi to look after his baby sister again, and Cal and I went out to the lot, all those female eyes at our backs. There was his truck, black and somehow heavy looking, without the regular Mack or Peterbilt symbols on it.

"Let's stop at your truck first—I have something I'd like to do."

I unlocked it. He opened the door and got in, reaching down his hand to help me up. Cool, firm hand.

First thing he did was fold down the playpen's walls. The pen is big enough to sleep two big kids, and my mattress behind it is big enough to sleep one fat woman. (I'm not fat.) Fold down the walls, and most of the cab is mattress.

"What are you doing?" I asked, though I thought I knew.

"You'll see," he said. On the right wall of the cab, where it had been covered up by the playpen's wall, there was a little panel. You almost couldn't see it even looking straight at it. The place he pushed to make it pop open didn't look any different from the rest of the wall. Inside was a number display, what they call liquid crystal, and a whole lot of tiny little switches. He started messing with them.

"What are you doing?" I asked again.

"Just a second." He messed around some more, closed up the panel, and smiled at me. "Now your central controller's computer thinks you're still on the road and haven't even gotten here yet. Then it'll register you coming here and starting your break in forty minutes. You've got an hour before you have to get going again."

"How can you do that?"

"I've got a few skills."

"If you can do that kind of thing, why are you driving a truck? You could be making real money."

There was a glitter in Cal's eye. He bowed his head down low and said some woman's name—Ellen or something, it was hard to hear. I went over and held his head up against my chest, with his braid snaked over the crook of my arm. Murmured nonsense again. His arms came up around my back and my hands went down behind his jeans.

We used every last inch of that mattress space.

"Oh Christ," I said later, "my babies have been in the stop all this time."

"They'll be okay," he said.

I put the rubber band back on his braid. I'd been playing with it. "They are never alone this long. And what about Jess?" He looked at me. "You said he had teething pain."

"Oh—my God, you're right. I'd better get to him." He started pulling his pants on.

"Do you want me to help show you how to use the medicine?"

"No, that's okay. I'm sure I can figure it out."

"It's no trouble—"

"The instructions are on the tube, right? You go get your kids." He looked at his watch. "You've got ten more minutes."

Ten minutes left! I hadn't been stopped this long in two years.

I left him off at his truck and he kissed me right out in public. "See you next stop," he said.

I hadn't even thought of seeing him again. On the trucking routes, he could have any action he wanted. But if I was his first since Ellen or Helen or whoever, maybe it actually meant something to him.

I felt a little bad about that.

Tomi was sitting in the big pen, holding Cilehe and crying. Not screaming or anything—his face was wet and he was hiccupping.

When I came in, I could see him trying to look brave. He also looked surprised—like he thought I was dead and was amazed to see me.

"C'mon, guys," I said. When we got out, the big black truck was gone.

I had to raise the playpen walls, which took a while since I'd never had them down before. Finally I found the catch that did it. My watch beeped, I pressed the button, and we started off.

Nebraska's a wide state. We probably had another whole stretch of it. At some point I noticed my watch had changed time an hour earlier—Mountain Time Zone. That's one way to measure progress: time travel. Another is to measure the money you save, but unless you're Kimberlea, that's pointless. Just as pointless to measure by the calendar, since Friday's just like Wednesday's just like Sunday, and night is like day but dark and not as many stops.

Another is to measure the seasons go by. But you spend some time driving in the South where it's warmer in winter than North Dakota is some summers. And you spend so little time outside that the weather might as well be television, except for rainstorms crashing against the cab's roof. The babies never get used to that.

Or you can measure the seasons of your own body. Now that means something, because I've always been as regular as clockwork.

For example, I knew it was just about ten days before my next period.

The kids were fussy. Even Tomi. He wanted me to hold him and he wouldn't let me let go. Cilehe screamed. After an hour I blew up.

"If you don't shut up, I'll drive off without you next time!"

Cilehe screamed louder. Tomi's eyes went round and he bit his lips in like he was afraid a word would come out by itself if he didn't hold it back, and tears came down his face like crazy.

"Oh, Jesus, I'm sorry. Mama'd never do that. Mama'd never do that." If he'd been bigger, I'd have told him how much trouble I'd be in at the next checkpoint if I didn't have the kids registered to me. Truck's not much, but jail's worse. Or I might have tried to explain I love my babies and everything I was doing was for them as much as me.

Instead I rocked him until he fell asleep in my lap, while Cilehe cried herself out.

When the truck pulled over, the black truck was there. We parked, I jumped out, and Cal was waiting. "Got something for you," he said to Tomi, and from behind his back he pulled out a big bag of M&Ms. "Can you share those with your little sister?"

I shot him a look. It was an awful lot of candy. But Tomi was so excited I could hardly take it away from him. Cal took Tomi's other hand and we all went into the stop.

"Why don't we grab a couple of burgers and eat in your truck?" Cal said.

"Sure." I explained to Tomi that Mama'd be gone for a while but was coming back. "Be brave for Cilehe," I said.

Cal messed with those switches again while I wolfed down my cheeseburger. You can get really horny again in just a few hours, especially when it's been almost three years since the time before.

He lay with his head on my stomach. "You've really got nice kids," he said.

"Thanks."

"Do they look like their fathers?"

"Actually, I think they favor me more. Too bad for them."

"I don't have any complaints," he said quietly, drawing his hand along the bottom of my jaw.

I felt I was blushing, though I'm a little dark for that. "Go on."

"Your boy's a real little man. What's his name again?"

"Tomi."

"Tomi, right. I hope Jess grows up like that."

"I'm sure he will."

"Do your kids get along well?"

"Sure. Tomi's a great big brother. Kids can get to feel responsible for each other sometimes."

"Do you think so?"

I laughed. "When they aren't trying to kill each other. But I'm glad they have each other. I never had any sisters or brothers. My mama got some kind of infection in her tubes that stopped her from having more babies. I'm sorry about that sometimes."

"But you had friends, other kids you grew up with."

"Yeah."

He looked away. "Jess will never have a sister. He's never spent more than an hour in the company of the same children."

I brushed back the little pieces of hair around his forehead with my fingers. "I'm sorry."

"There's nothing you can do about it." Then he looked straight up at me, his light brown eyes real intense. "Except maybe there is."

"What do you mean?"

"Loan me one of your kids."

"What?"

He pulled himself up out of my lap and took my shoulders. "Let one of your kids ride in my truck for a leg or two. To play with Jess. To get to know him, and be a big brother or sister to him."

I shook his hands off. "That's crazy, Cal! You can't take off with my baby. I might never see you again!"

He patted his hand on the little hidden panel. "I told you we'd see each other again before, and how did it turn out?"

"But how do you know we'll even be staying on the same route?"

"Do you think I could make those changes if I didn't have access to your central controller's data through the remote unit?"

I guessed not. Still— "What if there's a checkpoint, and I have one kid too few and you have one too many? We'd both be arrested, and I don't think they'll accept your asking me so nicely as a good excuse."

"Same source of information," he said. "There's no checkpoint on this route until Utah."

All that from a little panel I hadn't even known was there. "If you can do that sort of stuff," I said, "why aren't you—?"

He put a finger over my lips. "I know I seem complicated," he said. "But just look at me and you'll see how simple I really am. I thought I needed time alone to help me get over—" He stopped and looked away, then he smiled at me. "Now I know I was right." He swapped his own lips for his finger. After a while he leaned back and said, "As a favor to me?"

"I—"

"Or as a favor to Jess. You're a mother. You know what children need. If you help him out, you'll be being the mother he never had."

This was all coming so fast. My first plan began to be pushed away by a whole different Plan B. Which wasn't a bad plan at all, since it could supply everyone's needs and make all of us happy. Another three hours' drive from now, when I saw how things were going, I'd have a pretty good idea how likely Plan B was.

"All right," I said. "For Jess's sake."

I thought the point of M&Ms was not to get chocolate all over your face. Cal took a paper napkin and wiped off Cilehe's mouth, gentle and careful, and rubbed his hand through her hair just like a daddy should.

Tomi stared up at him. I realized for the first time he'd never seen a man that close before.

"Which one?" Cal asked.

I considered. "Tomi looks scared of you. How about Cilehe?"

"That's fine." He picked her up. "You're coming with me, pretty lady."

She started screaming.

"Um—I'm sorry—she's usually not like that." Well, sometimes she'll go a whole day without screaming much. I took her from him and rocked her until she shut it down. I carried her outside to the big black truck.

"I'll take her from here," Cal said, reaching for my baby.

I suddenly didn't much like the looks of that black truck. "Maybe it's not such a good idea," I said.

"Shawana," he said. He leaned forward and kissed me; while kissing me, he took Cilehe from my arms, smooth as silk. "We'll just try it for this leg. If she's unhappy, she goes straight back with you. Maybe your little boy would like to ride in such a big truck next time, huh?" He said that to Tomi, who stared up at him. "Or you might like to have Jess, later," he said to me. "I'd like you to get to know him."

"I'd like that too," I said.

He smiled. He kissed me again, and he ruffled Tomi's hair with the hand that wasn't holding Cilehe. "See you in a few hours," he said, opened his door, and swung the two of them up into the cab so fast I never got more than a glimpse of it, big and dark like the truck's outside, before the door shut. But then he rolled down the window.

"You're a really special lady, did you know?" he said.

The black truck pulled away.

Tomi started to cry.

"Don't," I said to him, "c'mon, don't cry." We went back to the truck, me pulling and pulling on Tomi's arm, him not wanting to move. "Don't cry, it's okay, everything's wonderful, listen to Mama."

After Nebraska is Colorado, which at least isn't flat all the way through. Tomi usually loves hills and mountains, going up and down.

Cilehe hates having her ears pop, hates it when they won't pop. I had to keep reminding myself I didn't have to worry about it.

"Where's Cee, Mama? Where's Cee?"

"Just ahead of us, baby. A couple miles ahead. It's okay, baby."

"Where's Cee?" he insisted. I thought his sister could get on my nerves!

"She's fine, Tomi. Watch the TV."

"Where's Cee?"

Helping us get out of this truck, baby. Up with a man who wants a mother for his son, comfort for his bed, and once he has them won't have any reason to stay in these rolling jail cells. A man who knows enough about computers to get a job that buys stereos and big TVs with channels you can change and nice haircuts that look pretty. A man who's actually wanted to get married, and can want to again.

A man we can all live with just fine, if it means getting out of this truck.

Plan B.

I decided it was some sugar-reaction thing making Tomi so cranky and it would wear down. He did get quiet after a while, after I stopped trying to answer his questions.

It seemed like the longest stretch we'd ever driven. I spent it trying out all the different ways Plan B could work. Ways to become a permanent part of Cal's life. To get out of the truck. I'd never even begun to guess what it's like in it. Some drivers even have told me they'd thought it would be a great way to get away from their mamas nagging on them all the time. Me, I didn't want to risk an illegal abortion. Some nasty nights I've wondered if I did the right thing.

Then I began to worry if I'd done the right thing having Cilehe ride with Cal. She's the cranky one. If she was kicking a shitfit, and if his Jess wasn't the cranky type so he wasn't used to it, he might get a bad impression of me as a mother. It's not my fault she's cranky. Every baby's different. But he might not know that.

When the truck started to pull over, it seemed like three hours. Hell, it seemed like six. I wanted to find out how it had gone, make a little nice with Cal, and let Tomi see his sister so he'd stop pestering me.

It wasn't until we were almost there I saw it wasn't a truck stop.

It was a checkpoint.

There wasn't supposed to be one until Utah! Cal said we were perfectly safe swapping babies until then. Cal was right about everything else—how could he have screwed this up?

There was a knock on the window. "Out of the truck, lady."

"What's this all about?" I called, thinking hard.

"Just come out of the truck, and there won't be any trouble."

There were cops out there, besides the welfare worker who usually just checks your license, makes sure you are who you say you are and your babies are okay. There were cops out there, and they had guns.

"Why do you want to have guns on me?" I called, just to use up some time and think some more.

"Come on out of the truck," the first cop repeated, but another one said, "Child abandonment's a serious charge, lady."

Oh Christ, yes, it is. Worst thing they can catch us at aside from welfare fraud.

"I wouldn't abandon my babies!"

"Maybe so," said the second cop, "but that's not the tip we got from the trucker who just came through."

"She was lying."

"Don't think *he* was." The cop elbowed his friend and said, "Look at her face. She knows who we're talking about."

The other one sniggered. "You can learn a lot about a girl's secrets when you get a piece of her. Maybe we should start an undercover program! I'd volunteer."

I felt like I'd been hit, but I knew I had to stay cool. "Let me get out and I'll explain."

"That's what we're asking you to do, lady—"

They give you a two-week training before they put you on the road. That's hardly enough to begin to know how to drive the truck manually, and it's a couple years since I even had that. But nobody expects us to ever really have to drive, whatever the emergency regs say.

Maybe that's why it caught them flat-footed when a driver made a break for it. It just wasn't possible.

They were just about right, too.

I leaned forward and yanked the handle marked MANUAL OVERRIDE. I hit the gas. I nearly ran over a cop and I did go right through two trees on my way to the highway. A sound of metal crumpling. I couldn't look at the road much because it took all my concentration shifting gears, trying to pick up some speed. It took all my concentration and it still sounded awful. I wondered if I was stripping gears. I wondered if I could do anything wrong that would crash the truck.

He set me up. He stole my baby and he set me up. Why would he steal my baby?

I leaned hard on my horn. A big RV just got out of my way in time.

He must have known the checkpoint was coming up. And you need at least one kid to be a trucker. If there was no little Jess, he needed a baby. If he could alter his trucking card, make it look like Cilehe was his, then his only problem was me telling them at the same checkpoint I didn't have my other baby because he took her from me. I'd still be in trouble, but so would he. And with almost no other guys in the trucks, he'd be easy to track down.

(I was afraid I really gave him Cilehe because I was tired of dealing with her fussing all the time. I never asked to be a mother, but I was one—the worst who ever lived.)

Cars were scattering in front of me. Horns blaring. Out of the corner of my eye I suddenly saw Tomi had climbed up the wall of his playpen to look out at what was going on.

"Get down, Tomi! Get down!" I grabbed out with my right hand and yanked him down hard on the playpen's mattress. The truck lurched. He went spinning across and hit his head on the other pen wall. The walls are light. I could see it give.

I couldn't look to see if he was okay. I had to keep changing lanes while I went faster.

That bastard made sure they wouldn't listen to me. He told them I was a child abandoner, so then anything I said would sound like a lie, to save my ass. He went on the offensive before I had a chance.

I started to hear sirens.

I went faster. I was almost to top gear, driving on the shoulder because it was too hard to keep going around cars.

Thank God we were on a flattish stretch.

All the time I thought Cal was someone I could marry to get me and my babies out of the truck, even feeling guilty because I enjoyed his body but I wasn't likely to love him back—all that time he was setting me up.

I realized I was swearing, fast and steady in a low fierce voice. Tomi whimpered. At least he was awake.

"You damn black truck—you fucker—where are you, you son of a bitch?—you fucker, you stole my baby—you bastard, you lied to me!"

Lights began flashing in my side mirrors. The cops were catching up. I had to catch him before they caught me.

I shifted up. I was almost at top gear.

A couple cars split in front of me, screeching out of the way, and there was the bastard. He was going uphill. Black smoke belched out of a side pipe. I hit the foot of the hill and I remembered I had to downshift, fast. The truck couldn't keep that speed climbing. I made myself do it though I just wanted to go faster and faster until I had him—

The truck made horrible noises. I wasn't in the right gear. I slowed and started to lose ground. He must've seen me by now. I shifted, shifted, shifted until it didn't make those awful noises. I didn't care if my truck was trashed—shit, I'd be in prison anyway, my babies God knows where—but I wasn't going to lose that black monster truck.

He hit the top of the hill and vanished from sight. I got there minutes later—I say minutes, but it must have been five seconds. His truck was picking up speed fast. Mine plunged down while my stomach stayed back up top. Tomi wailed. I shifted up and up and shoved the gas to the floor. I was gaining on him. The lights were close in the side mirrors.

I could make out the face of the nearest cop, he was that close. Could see his little blond moustache, even, and the mean way he looked like he was going to kill me if I didn't do it for him first.

A red sports car was half an inch in front of me, getting closer. I had to hit the brakes, and the engine almost died. Almost. I was hitting on the gearshifter like it was Cal's face, kicking the accelerator like it was his balls.

The black truck ducked ahead of a blue minivan. The van hit its brakes hard and seemed to come right back into me, like Cal had thrown it into my face deliberately.

I swerved. I missed it.

I spent long seconds wrestling with the wheel.

Looked up and saw him cut again in front of some foreign-looking job.

He didn't have it figured right. He was going to plow right into a station wagon in the next lane by the shoulder—

"Cilehe!" I screamed. I hit my horn. I careened onto the shoulder as he careened off it.

There was a steep hill a few yards off the side of the shoulder, and the black truck was about to go straight down it—

I grabbed Tomi, hit the gas hard, and shut my eyes.

The whole world went white.

■ ■ ■

It shouldn't have worked. I couldn't see because the airbags came bursting out and filled my face with canvas.

My truck caught his trailer right on the side, smashed into it, and spun his truck around almost facing us. I went mostly straight, destroying my cab but not quite me or Tomi, cushioned in airbag. I picked up a concussion, though.

The black truck came to a stop angled over the side of the hill. But it didn't roll down.

When the cops helped me out of what was left of my cab, I could hardly see straight. I did see that the black truck's trailer had burst open. I saw broken crates. I saw the ugly black metal shapes inside them. And, thank God, I didn't see Cal. If I'd seen him, I don't know what I would have done to him, concussion and all.

I screamed until they put Cilehe in my arms. She was so quiet and good you'd swear she was her brother.

I had time to think in the hospital. When my head cleared—before then, if you believe the nurses—I demanded they run the tests. It was the biggest relief of my life to learn Plan A hadn't worked. A little bit of Cal growing inside me is the last thing I wanted. I know a baby has nothing to do with his daddy. I'm sure no Shawn Parker. But I wanted no piece of Cal. The plan to have three kids so they'd let me out seems a foolish, childish thing now.

I made them tell me about Cal. They acted like I had no right to know, but they gave in enough to tell me that his real name was

Charles Kavey, he was single and had assets of over a million, and was—surprise—no welfare trucker. He worked with his controller, and they made, said the government-lawyer type, "illicit shipments."

I bet. I don't know anything about high-tech weapons, but I guess I can tell the ugly things when I see them. Interstate 80 could've taken him on to San Francisco, and from there I imagine they could have been smuggled either down to Chile or to the civil war in the Philippines. (News comes on twice a day in the truck, though I always wonder what they're leaving out of it.)

Cal—Charles—and his buddy must have had the system pretty well bamboozled, all the parts that are just computer talking to computer; but when it comes to the checkpoints, human beings make sure your babies match up with what it says on the license. No way around needing a real live kid for that. I guess when he found out about the surprise checkpoint, he was already on the road. He had it down so smooth, he must have used his little trick for getting a kid before. I couldn't even have identified him, if it had ever come to that. He didn't have the braid when he got to the checkpoint—it actually came off somehow, which surprised the hell out of me—and his hair was black and his eyes were dark blue. Contacts and dye. He was real smooth. The bastard enjoyed it too, I bet. Bastard.

He'd had to perform his act on short notice—unless it was a dream when I heard the nurses gossiping. When I did dream after that, the dreams were full of nightmares about a shriveled-up little body jammed in a carton among all the weapons in the black truck's trailer.

Probably the baby's name wasn't even really Jess . . .

My grandma called the hospital. She wanted to know if she could help. She's got so little I hated to ask her, but I did.

After all, I'm back in the truck as soon as the hospital releases me, and I don't want to stay there.

But if I don't eat desserts, don't buy new clothes and makeup for myself, and take what my grandma can give me, I can start studying. Kimberlea manages; so can I. Even with my allowance cut in half in penalty for smashing up the truck. I can read really good. I'm going to take Kimberlea for a role model and order myself some accounting textbooks. Maybe even, years from now, when I'm out and I've gotten used to computers, I can go on studying and get a truck controller's license.

Nobody's going to make me keep doing what they want me to do.

My babies are going to be proud of their mama.

# The Coon Rolled Down and Ruptured His Larinks, A Squeezed Novel by Mr. Skunk

### • • •

## *Dafydd ab Hugh*

Among the more depressing events of 1990 was the re-election to the U.S. Senate of Jesse Helms, the man who convinced Congress to place constraints on grants bestowed by the National Endowment for the Arts. For a brief but frightening interval, the NEA's beneficiaries had to sign the aesthetic equivalent of a loyalty oath, promising not to celebrate sexuality, irreverence, or any other enterprise that makes Jesse Helms nervous—promising, in other words, not to use their arts grants to make art.

One of the many nice things I would like to say about "The Coon Rolled Down and Ruptured His Larinks, A Squeezed Novel by Mr. Skunk"—beyond calling it a wonderfully earthly and demented postapocalypse fable that suggests a collaboration between William S. Burroughs, James Joyce, and Aesop—is that Jesse Helms would never award it an NEA grant. One of the many nice things I would like to say about its politically ardent young author is that, based on my talks with him at SF conventions, I suspect he would never accept any patronage with strings attached.

A visit to the paperback racks reveals that Dafydd ab Hugh is the author of *Heroing*, which concerns, in his words, "quests and schizophrenics," as well as *Warriorwards*, whose theme, he insists, is "the joy of slavery." His newest science-fantasy, *Dux Bellorum*, is "an Arthurian romantic realistic psychedelic conspiracy novel that has been dubbed 'Freemasons in Camelot' by certain more excitable members of polite society." As for "Coon" itself, ab Hugh explains that it is "autobiographical but not literal," thereby putting to rest the rumor that he is a small, furry, black-and-white mammal.

### Chapter one we hear the story

I heard the story from an old Coon at first sitting at my favorite place on the hardground just outside the bowl alley on venture path. Then later he and I played chase and bounce with a ball and bounded it on venture path. But the story kept running around and around inside my ears like it was casting for a scent so I just had to find out more about it.

So I and the Boy Nik Nok and Disha the Dog and Hanki and Yanki the Cats sat in a circle and I told them each and all about the Hidden Den and the Coon who could not talk.

He lived under the jerryfams next to the bowl alley. He told me by whispers that he had ruptured his larinks. That is his throat where he talks, Disha the Dog said (she is very smart, smarter than me and the others especially Hanki and Yanki). Then the Coon acted out the whole story standing on his back legs to mean human being, staggering to tell me he meant stupid and looking back east so I would know he meant stupid like the fourlegs were before Democrazy.

I put what the Coon said in words as best I could and this, was it:

Across the city and too far for a chase there are humans like before Democrazy and they are all sealed up in a den where no air can go in and out, and the Winds of Law have not blown either.

Inside the den the fourlegs are all stupid like before Democrazy too, and they have to work for the humans and cannot think and have no Inalienable Progrets.

Nobody knew what to say after I finished my story. Disha and Nik Nok always ignore me for they see no real difference between a Skunk and a Cat, except for the white stripe and the odie Skunk of course.

But even I knew something had to be done, so I said "if we love Democrazy then something has to be done."

## Chapter two we deleminate the problem

"Well if you love Democrazy and the Winds of Law that made us all Equal then what are we going to do about that den, where there is no Progrets and no Law?"

I was afraid to answer for I knew what the only answer could be and I was only a Skunk!

But I knew I had no choice and neither did Disha and neither even did Nik Nok. He was not of the old Men, the ones who exploded the less fortunate and took advantages. He believed in Democrazy. I had seen him cover his face in the Cord House.

I looked up at Disha and "this is what we will do about that den" said I, "journey all the way across the city and bring Democrazy and the Will of Progrets to this den of unequity."

Disha squatted and made water on the whitestone trail beside my favorite old den.

"Do you really want to take the trip when you might find the Overizon instead?"

Now I thought for a long time before I answered her. Was there even Democrazy and Equality beyond the venture path? I did not know even though I always thought Progrets had spread it everywhere. But after hearing the old Coon's tale I wondered.

"These humans are trying to stop the spread of Democrazy that Progrets started when it loosed the bug that rode the Winds of Law and did us all" I said and I thought I had said a mouthful.

"But will you go" she asked like Friday the teacher coaxing the right answer.


### Chapter three some decide to go

I thought quietly, not looking at her. I do not know what made me ask "who will come with me if I go" but it slipped out.

She waited too long and I knew she was afraid too, then she said "if you go I at least will come with you. You must ask the others for yourself."

We gathered the group again and told them what we were going to do to save Democrazy.

The old Coon had said only one thing more to me, in the whisper again for he could not convoy this by gestures. He whispered that this Hidden Den was across the city of angels at the foot of the other mountains, where the underbuild had fallen in.

As soon as Hanki and Yanki heard this, they said there would be wild things along the way, and then they high tailed it out of there as Cats will, for Cats are hardly smarter than before there was Progrets. Only I and Disha and Nik Nok the Boy stayed.

"Is Disha going to go" asked Nik Nok in a strange voice. "Yes" she said for she had already said she at least would go with me. "Then surely I shall go too" he said.

Disha tilted her head as she looked at him. A gleam in her eyes frightened me, being somehow wrong.

"Then there are three of us" she said, and "when shall we start?"

"Let us wait" said I, "let us wait until the shadows are longer. I bow to the Will of Progrets but I hear there is no Democrazy under a hot sun."

## Chapter four off we go then

All too soon the shadows grew, and the hot Santa's Anus blew from the nightside and we had to set out.

We chased the scents between the fallen walls and square builds sometimes running and sometimes walking when old Disha got tired but all the while making way toward the other mountains.

Nik Nok never seemed to tire as Boys will not, but he stayed very near Disha even when she had to rest.

Soon all the smells were strange to me and I could see nothing I knew, it was not the venture path or anywhere I had been before and I was an easy.

We ran by a fire once. I heard the boom boom boom inside the giant den and I watched until the walls tired and fell in against each other, such is Progrets.

## Chapter five we meet death and Democrazy

All at once as the sun rose in the sky like a big burn, Disha stopped and I almost ran into her.

She perked her ears up and snuffled her nose toward the sun but I could not smell anything yet and there was nothing to see but a hill of metal trash and rotwood. "Come on Nik Nok" she said and started to climb through a notch in the hill.

No one called to me, but I followed anyway for I was not about to get left alone in a strange place.

Then I smelled it too, it was a dead Dog in the bottom of the hill, named Duk Duk. I had played chase and bounce with him not long before.

He was dead and he smelled of junk to me.

Disha and Nik Nok stood together at the top of the hill and I could see the Boy did not really understand death yet, for he called out to Duk Duk. Then I smelled his fear as he began to understand.

Disha must have smelled it too for she moved over to put her head against his thigh.

"Do not be afraid Nik Nok" she said "for I will protect you."

"It is not Junkyard Dogs and falling walls that scare me" he said "but I had a funny feeling in my stomach just now. Something bad is going to come of this extra diction. I have never been away from the bowl alley and venture path before."

Disha muzzled his ear softly and licked it.

"Nik Nok you are still too young to fight wars. You go home and I will be back to play with you very soon."

He put his arms around her neck and "I cannot let you do it alone" he said. "And I am not too young for I became a man a season ago, at night in a dream."

I shivered and looked back at Duk Duk. There were things on him. Every so often his fur would rup and flutter like he itched but it was only the bugs and burrowers who had gotten under his skin. His eyes watched me like they knew something and said "watch us well Skunk, you will come to this in no time yourself!"

Nik Nok and Disha held each other for a little bit, and they ignored me. But I watched them with bright Skunk eyes. I began to know in words what was happening between them. It was not Democrazy, Democrazy was what lay in the ditch with Duk Duk.


### Chapter six the watcher in the dark

About this time I prickled like we were being watched. I looked around but nothing and I decided I was jumpy being so far from the venture path. I said nothing but "please you two let us go."

We walked for a long time until it was full, comfortable dark and cold in the moon.

At last Disha decided we should stop for the night, but it was more for Nik Nok I think than for me. "We are far away from bowl alley and there are marauders here" she said. I saw a hole across the hardground beneath writing words and I told her. "It says exon" she said.

Disha investigated the hole first because she was the leader. It smelled like Rats and burn-juice. She had me ask them if it was alright if we stayed there for a mome, and they said they would ask their king.

### Chapter seven we all eat Cat food

We left them to deleminate and stalked out like mighty hunters in search of food. I still had that same watchy feeling but I was too unsure to tell Disha yet.

I let them in front and stayed behind as quiet as I could. Disha scented the air and cast about for something edible and catchable. We were away from the bowl alley so I knew anyone we caught we could eat (except not a Dog or a Boy or a Skunk of course).

Nik Nok saw something before Disha smelled it, a flash of white on top of a wall on the other side of the hardground and we began to stalk.

We sneaked from build to fall keeping to shadows and picking up our feet so as not to scuff.

Disha slunk forward and Nik Nok clung to the black fur on her back. But he watched her not the prey, even I could see that. He watched her hard muscles flex and stretch beneath her sleek fur and watched her slink lower and lower to the ground invisible in the dark as the Winds of Law.

I listened. Skunks can listen well. I heard Nick Nok's breath catch in his throat as he felt her body beneath his hand. I smelled the same smell I make when the lady Skunks come into season.

When we got across the hardground "split to the left and drive it towards me" Disha snuffled to Nik Nok. I crept away from them both and poked my head around the corner.

It was a Cat fat and lazy licking himself, full and stuffed and paying no tensions to Progrets and the bitter world.

Clever Nik Nok reached into his bag and found our best ball, took aim and beaned the Cat right where it counts.

At first he flew into the air and screamed out "oh shit" then he began to run for his life with Nik Nok pounding after and me behind them as fast as four Skunk legs could carry me.

"Help! Do not eat me!" the Cat added for good measure but he did not turn around to see if we were agreeable to this suggestion.

We chased him along the wall jumping over the stones and falls for he was fleeing for his very life. He tried to jump up a telephone tree but Nik Nok jumped up after him and he could climbor as well as the Cat and he jumped down again and ran down an alley for he was fleeing for his very life. Nik Nok disappeared after him and at once I heard a snarl and a Cat scream. When I poked an eye around the corner I saw Disha had the Cat cornered against the whitestone at the other end.

"Oh please please do not eat me!" the Cat cried in terror as Disha padded closer. I smelled the water of his fear and saw his eyes wide and wet and almost I asked Disha to seize and desist, for Cats are nearly Skunks. But then I reminated I was hungry.

"Why not eat you" she asked "you are an inferior being, to wit a Cat. Cats are made to be eaten."

"But I have a wife" argued the Cat "and she will have no one to provide for her if I am dead and eaten."

"Oh that is no problem just bring her here, and I shall solve her problem too!" retorted Disha.

The Cat perked up at this suggestion which I would not have thought he would and suggested "very well, just let me go and I shall get her." It seemed a reasonable request except of course I doubted his sincerity in returning, for you can never trust a Cat.

"Not so fast Mr. Dinner" said Disha. "I would not have you tire yourself by walking all that way and all the way back. I think it is best if we avoid inconveniencing your wife and just eat you now."

Nik Nok and I had said nothing so far, for Disha was doing well on her own.

"But surely you do not want to deplete the food supply" said the Cat, thinking furiously which is very out of character for a Cat "you should eat the aged and the sick not Cats like me in their prime who can still sire kittens."

"But if we do not eat you then *we* will die and I too can still whelp pups and Nik Nok can now sire children, so he tells me."

"But you must further the cause of Progrets and kill only the Cats who have not become smart."

"That would mean all of you" retorted Disha, thinking no doubt of Hanki and Yanki.

"But surely you are not against Democrazy are you?"

I worried because I reminated the looks that Disha and Nik Nok had given each other lately. But Disha just laughed all the time edging closer to the Cat. The Cat saw this and arched his back and hissed. He was fighting for his very life now.

"If you were stupid enough to get caught" debated Disha "then killing you *is* Progrets!"

"Yes it is eat or be eaten" said Nik Nok.

The Cat could see his situation was now desperate and he tried one last gambol.

"But you should not eat me for we are brothers, we fourlegs must all stick together in the city of the angels."

"So" said Disha with sudden anger "I shall eat you anyway because I am hungry, and that after all is the only real argument." Then she rushed forward and caught the Cat who in the end did not even try to escape for he knew he was a goner.

"Disha"asked Nik Nok, "why *should* we not eat our brothers?"


### Chapter eight Democrazy is violented

"Good kill" I said, but nobody heard me. Nik Nok gave Disha a hug that was not entirely innocent I think.

Nik Nok ran his hand gently over Disha's soft fur, and watched with Raccoon eyes as her hard muscles underneath flexed and stretched as she tore and tugged at the Cat, getting him open.

She chewed off a warm hindquarter, hesitated a moment and then laid it in Nik Nok's lap. "Here beautiful" she said "you take the first Cat cut."

He picked it up slowly, pulled the fur off and sunk his teeth in and tore off a juicy hunk.

I slunk back into the shadows for I realized I was not wanted at this particle mome. But I watched for we Skunks have very good eyes.

He chewed and held his hunk out to Disha, and she ate from the same piece. They looked into each other's eyes and Disha put her paw on Nik Nok's forearm and I heard the Boy panting like he was chasing something invisible.

I was frightened. I knew this was not Democrazy and that the Winds of Law would blow across us for this.

Fresh Cat has an effect, the meat is tangy without dipping it in the black specks and the blood sends a wild hair through the back of your jaw and makes you squint. This time it was dubbly so for the frightened Cat had pushed excitement through his whole body, I could smell it even from where I was. But they hungered for more than food even so.

The Cat blood dripped down Nik Nok's chin and he wiped it with his hand and held it out for Disha to lick. The kill smell was making even me excited, but I stayed in the shadows again for I love Progrets and Democrazy.

He ripped a piece of catsmeat off the leg and offered the next bite to Disha, and moved closer and closer to her. He dipped his finger in the blood and drew a line with it along Disha's head and down her nose.

She licked his finger as he let it trail over her lips and all at once they did not even care about the Cat. They moved a little away and I darted forward and caught a piece. But I watched as I ate and I shivered wondering what the Winds of Law would feel like.

### Chapter nine for the strong of heart

Disha began licking Nik Nok's throat and then his chest and his ling began to swell. I smelled the lady Dog smell. Nik Nok was shaking and gasping like he had run a race and Disha turned herself around and knelt her front legs down. "Gently" she said, "slowly do not rush it or you will hurt me."

"I do not know how" said Nik Nok and his voice was thick and white.

"Hold my tail up out of the way. I will tell you if you are doing something wrong." She suddenly caught her breath and held it.

"Does it feel good" she asked him.

"Like nothing I have ever felt and better even than when I used my hand before!" he told her.

"Wait wait" Disha said "it is too tight yet." But then she whined and snuffled and sounded very excited herself, and Nik Nok found the going easier. I hoped that they had forgotten I was watching them

for I did not want to foul soot—either like the Cat, or even like Disha!
For if you start out violenting Democrazy one time why not do anything you want then?

He held the fur on her side with one hand and the going was easier. His other hand kept stroking her tail and rubbing it against his bare belly.

"Does this feel like this always" he asked.

She sighed only "will of Democrazy."

I closed my eyes at the Blast Femmy and listened only. I was reminating when I had last had a lady, and it was long ago and usually I cannot reminate it, but the scent remimbered me. I lay quiet and listened to Disha and Nik Nok.

The Boy cried out suddenly, not even afraid of a Junkyard Dog hearing him but when afterward he started to pull out she said "do not dare stop! Keep going even if you are finished for I am not."

"But how" he asked "I am not hard anymore." I opened my eyes again because maybe the horror was almost over, and I wanted to see what it looked like when you violented Democrazy.

"Damn you just keep going I am almost there, you are hard enough." So of course he did. At last it happened to Disha too, but she did not cry out as he had. She went stiff all over and her tail stood straight up against his stomach.

He bent over to lay his body against her back and his head on hers and still stayed in her. He licked Disha's ears very gently.

"I have been with many other Dogs before" she said "and you are so much better for you took much more care with me than they do. They are all only interested in pleasuring themselves and something happens and they get big and lumpy and cannot pull out. But that never stops them from trying. They cannot do it slow and gentle like you do." Nik Nok said nothing but he did not look as happy as he might, for perhaps he saw to the future then.


### Chapter ten love and Democrazy

"And there is more about you" she added "but I cannot say what it is, the thought of you is like gas that has floated up to my heart and is pushing everything else aside and nearly bursting out my chest."

They held each other as mates. I think they had forgotten all about me and Progrets and the Hidden Den.

"Let us stay here forever Disha" said Nik Nok, "we can do it again as soon as—"

But Disha got a junk look on her face, and she looked at me and I almost turned and ran even though she is my friend. She is still a Dog and I only a Skunk, and she is more equal.

I tried to talk but I was too afraid.

"I know that you saw but you cannot talk about what you have just seen" snarled Disha, and all I could do was shake my head. They had violented Democrazy and I was afraid.

Now Nik Nok looked frightened, for he had not thought about the Winds of Law before he foolishly fell in love.

"But why not? Do we not love each the other?"

"Love" sneered Disha, "what does love have to do with the Will of Democrazy? We are cranimals now, for all of our friends on venture path cannot stand the thought of what we have done and it is eat or be eaten. So if this Skunk talks we shall be goners you and I."

I curled up in a ball shaking, meaning I would not say anything and betray my friends to Democrazy and thus I too became victim to the Winds of Law, as you will see at the novel ending.

"Let us stay" said Nik Nok, "and never return to face the bath of Democrazy."

"No beautiful" said Disha to Nik Nok, "for we must eat and go back to today's den. We set out again when the sun sinks. Have you forgotten our quest?"

With a wasteful look he looked down at himself. He had fallen out of her. His ling was still wet from inside Disha and he wiped it with his hand and rubbed some on his nose so he could smell her all the way back.

That is how I found out about love in the streets.


### Chapter eleven a junk waffle

When we got back King Rat said it was all right to stay if we gave him some Cat, which we did and then he let us stay the day inside the exon.

It was hot but even so all three of us huddled next to each other. We needed each other's solstice.

So it was that I jumped in fear when I suddenly heard a junk howl from outside, across the hardground and the paths and the metal autobiles that we were going to cross the next day, even towards the other mountains.

The scream scraped like a falling wall and rumbled like a thunderbum "damn all of you die horrible!" it said, and then "it is not the Junkyard Dogs what we learned to mean to me!"

It was junk, through' and through and I wondered if he would try to break into the exon and get us. It was death and dismembrane. It was howls and horrors, junk city, junk waffle, Junkyard Dog!

Soon his howls came closer, and he said things that did not mean anything but fear and death except maybe to another junk: "anyone we caught we could eat once—kill them! Do not let them—I *tore* all living creatures in *piece!*"

In between these cries I heard him run around and around the exon moaning like a cub with stomach rot and coughing like a redstone mountain falling down in an earthshake, and even that made me afraid and by the way they shivered I knew Disha and Nik Nok were too. You never know what these Junkyard Dogs will do for they are mad and do not drink water and if they bite you you become junk yourself.

We heard each curly nailed paw tickity-tickity scrabbing the hardground, round and round and round until it was as if brats were throwing stones, bounding chinks of redstone in a circle to pen us inside.

Then "I held onto the fur on hunks of metal!" he suddenly hissed from right beneath our windrow!

We got up as quiet as we could and crouched by the door because he might smell us and try to get in at us. I had even heard of a Junkyard Dog leaping straight through a glass windrow! for after all they cannot feel pain, being junk anyway and outside Democrazy.

Something tugged at my mind about some of the things he said. Then, when he sang like a jay from just underneath the windrow "not so fast, Mr. Dinner!" I knew what I reminated.

The junk things he said were our own words turned, like a poison snake into something other, frightful.

The junk had been stalking us and listening the whole time. My watchy feeling had been true.

We listened hard and tried to track him as he trotted around and around crazily, but the Winds of Law and the Santa's Anus kept howling too and knocking things over so it was hard to tell which was which.

There was too much to see in the exon. There were tables and broken windrows and spilled blackoil, and three very frightened Dogs Boys and Skunks slunking around trying to watch and listen at each and every windrow.

We strained and looked but he never stepped out and showed himself. Of course we imagined he was everywhere and sometimes it even seemed he was here in the exon with us, but it always turned out to be just one of the three of us knocking something over.

Then a thump on the roof and "my favorite place, the hardgrover moon!" he croaked from above.

We all fell to silence and held our collectivist breaths.

I for one could hear the junk panting and wheezing on the roof. Slowly he walked to one side, tickity-tickity. Slowly he walked back, scritchity-scritchity, tickity—and *stopped*.

"I know you" he whispered, so clear we could hear the hair stand on our backs. "Anyone we caught we could eat *once*" he added, so quiet we could hear pieces and drips of junk spatter on the metal roof.

Then with a terrible creak like the roof caving in and dropping him there among us, he leaped and was gone. There was a frightful bulge, left there in the roof right in the middle of the den.

I do not know how long we stayed up and shivered but we never heard anything more from him that day.

## Chapter twelve Law and Custom

That night we made good time towards the other mountains and climbored over many crickley hills of autobiles and metals. We were so tired that after we found a dead Rat and ate lunch we were too beat to even play chase and bounce with our other ball, and we plodded again as soon as we had swallowed our food.

I kept listening hard for the Junkyard Dog but either he had decided to let us alone which I doubted or he was very, very good at stalking.

I was afraid it was the latter. None of us heard anything we could say was surely him but many a scrape and click that could have been his flank against a wall, and could have been his claws on top an unbroken piece of hardground but could have been anything else either.

My feeling was stronger than ever. We were all an easy but could not sit around worrying about a Junkyard Dog so we tried to ignore him and run on.

I knew that Disha and Nik Nok wanted to be alone so I kept my distance. I listened though, for a Skunk has good ears. Mostly I listened for the Junkyard Dog but I heard every word that Disha said to Nik Nok, or vice verses.

Disha said that even though everybody is all for Democrazy nobody agrees what it is, so we hide what we think for fear we will be too different and become company dinner, and this is Custom. Even back before there was Law to enforce the will of Democrazy there was Custom, and Custom is stronger even than Law.

I kept hoping they would both see the light and allow Custom and Progrets to get in the way of cranimal love.

Custom says we can eat only what we can eat and that we cannot love anybody who is too different. If you break Custom, it is company dinner for you, boy, just like happened to Taggo. But his violentation provided us with a lovely feast, so you see what goes around comes around and Progrets is always satisfied. This is some of what the two of them said, Disha and Nik Nok:

"What love can this be" he said "when we can never be together with friends, and cannot make children?"

But she said "I have made many pups already and the last thing I need now is more when I cannot always feed what I have."

He said "but does this love violent Democrazy? What will happen to us?"

She said "sometimes two people that can touch each other are more important then the Custom of Democrazy, for love itself *is* Progrets and even Democrazy must obey."

She said "before the plague that did us all there was hardly any love. Love can only live between equals. Back then everyone was either lesser or greater than everyone else so how could there be true love? Now there is perfect equality and Democrazy and we can finally love."

But as Disha said this last I thought I heard the ghost of a sour chasm, for she knew as well as did I what Democrazy would think of her love for Nik Nok.

He said "what is love really?" I thought Disha would answer because she is wise and a Dog but she just walked on, thinking.

At last I could not keep my silence, and I answered for her what my mother had heard from a Zoocamel long ago:

I said "love is knowing each other like worms know the dead."

Disha stopped. "That is pretty good for a Skunk" she admitted and said "this cannot happen when one is more than the other, because how can the lesser know the greater? And how can the greater respect one who is less than she?"

Nik Nok asked "is this how it was before the plague that did us all?"


### Chapter thirteen Disha has a tail

"In the days before the plague" she said "the Dogs could not talk or even think, and neither could the other animals. This I know, this I know. Men were all that were intelly and they were even more intelly than the Dogs and Men are now. They set about to make some of the fourlegs intelly too."

"Some say" she said "they only wanted servants and they could not use each other as they always had because of Servile Rights, but I have always admired the early Men and I prefer to think they truly believed we should all be crated equally. This I know, this I know."

"In any case" she said "they did it, and they did it by crating an unnatural plague that would do us, Dogs and Cats and other mamuals. This I know, this I know."

"I am not sure what a plague is" asked Nik Nok, and I listened hard for I had never understood that explanation either as often as Disha had shown this tail.

"A plague is a little bug that crawls into every bump and hole in your body" she admitted. "Whenever you get sick that is caused by these bugs, and that is a plague.

"Anyway, they deliberately fected some of us Dogs with this

plague and then sat back on their haunches to see what would develop. This I know, this I know."

"And this is where Progrets and Democrazy came from" whispered the Boy out of rivulance.

"What developed" she smugged "is that one of these plague Dogs escaped. The men were not as smart as they thought and Fang the Savor got away with the plague bug still fecting him."

"This I know, this I know" said both I and Nik Nok at once.

"The Dogs were first and then next the plague fected the Rats and the Skunks and the Coons and the Zoomals and everything else. The Cats were last for they were always so full of themselves licking their body that they kept licking the bugs right off until they wised up! And that is why Dogs are first and Cats are last and all others fall in between."

"This I know, this I know" we supplied for her.

I had forgotten all about the Junkyard Dog, so intent was I on Disha's tail.

"Ah but Men are a different story" she continued finally. "For the rest of us it was a climb up the hill for more intelly, but the Men had the easy route and came down the hill backwards. We met Democrazically in the middle, for the plague has finally made us *all* equal . . . the furries and birds and scales and frogs and even some of the fish are getting more intelly all of the time.

"Until at last today" she whispered "when I can love you truly as my grandmother could never love your grandfather. This I know, Nik Nok. This I know."

"What is the use of more intelly" asked Nik Nok angrily "if the Old Men did not have love? I am *glad* for this plague even if I *am* stupider than men were before! I am glad for our love, Disha."

She stopped and bit at a flea on her hind leg for a mome.

"Even" she snuffled "if you can no longer understand the things of Men?"

"Things?"

"The autobiles and the glass mountains, the redstone dens, the hardground, telephone trees, walls and builds and all? If you can no longer understand them?"

"Then" he said "they are not the things of men anymore" and there he had her.

### Chapter fourteen our junk fears are real eyes

"These things of men are not any of them as warm and pretty and furry as you" said Nik Nok and I began to get an easy because here again was love against Democrazy.

"You will not always have me" Disha warned. "Dogs do not live as long as men do for that is something the plague did not change."

"I am here now" he said "and you too and what is tomorrow? Maybe I will die first if that Junkyard Dog is still shuddowing us."

I wondered which was worth more, love or Progrets and I could feel my tail raise in horror. Is wonder a crime against Democrazy?

Then all at once I heard a sound I must have been listening for all day and dreading, a rumbling cough like a redstone mountain falling down in an earthshake, a moaning like a cub with stomach rot and out of the shuddows of a heap of dead autobiles staggered the Junkyard Dog in the flesh, what was left of it!

All three of us froze in terror and I felt urine trickle down my leg. I also raised my tail and sprayed my wad but I doubted the Junkyard Dog would care about how he smelled as long as he got to bite us, all three!

He staggered forward stiff-legged and I thought, maybe he is already dead but does not know it yet.

In little sharp words he said "you might think my sex will eat me . . . and the part of her I was in squeezed Democrazy."

"Go away" Disha said with tried authority, but "I am who I have been and can eat once anybody I have caught" answered the Junkyard Dog.

"Go away!" I whimpered for I cold not find my voice. I felt like the silent Coon.

"If you were stupid enough you *is* Progrets" said he.

And with that he lunged at us and we three broke in all four directions and I ran up a wall of dead autobiles before I even knew it was blocking. Then I looked back and saw Disha. She had frozen in fear and could not move and she stood nose to nose with the Junkyard Dog who was dripping white at the mouth. I do not know why she did not run or why he had not bitten her yet. I shivered in fear.

But then I heard a cranky squeak and Nik Nok rose from the

build he had hidden behind. He found his voice and charged the Junkyard Dog screaming like a Commonest.

It broke the spell. Disha unfroze and bolted away but oddly the Junkyard Dog did not charge the Boy and tear him to shreds like I thought, he turned instead and with a deaf move slashed Disha as she ran by. She screamed and skittered away but I could see the blood flowing from her hind leg. The junk ran in circles three times laughing like a falling pile of autobiles.

Disha shook, tail between her legs. Nik Nok only stared, his face the color of my stripe. We all knew what would happen to her now.

"Well if I am already bit" said she sounding strange and quiet and queerly calm "then you can no longer frighten me, Junk. This I know, this I know." And she leapt upon him as if she were junk herself and they fought tearing and biting and the Junkyard Dog had the worst of it for Disha tore off his ear and opened up his throat.

He fell to his knees and still had mind enough to submit but he was a goner anyway. My throat lumped, because I knew Disha was a goner too. Worse, she would finally be like him and might even bite me then too or Nik Nok. I knew she would never allow that to happen, but there was only one thing that could stop it and that was the Duk Duk path.

The Junk fell over on his side and now blood was flowing out of his throat in spurts so I knew Disha had struck paydirt. But just for a moment his eyes seemed to clear a little and he raised his head with a big strain and said "that hurt. You are bigger than I suggested. Knelt—knelt her front legs into the pocket of my clothes."

Then "the truck is the key. Hold my tail up out of conveniencing my wife and putting it in. If machines make the wall only machines can onetwothree-one. Against the will of Del so wet."

His voice became weaker and he whispered "keep going even if you are finished, then we will, die. At first, even I could, at first, both our hearts, need meat. Even I, the rules must roll, even I, could hear my life, with me, pounding after.

"Cats" he croaked "are made just outside the bowl. But the truck is the key, you must understand. I smell onions."

Then all at once he pulled himself up as if he had not even been mauled, he looked at us and shrugged and explained "*anyone* we caught we could eat once." Then he settled back with a sigh and moved no more, for he was gone.

## Chapter fifteen where Democrazy
## gets it in the end

We watched him for a long time to make sure he would not pop back up again and say something or maybe bite someone else but he was permanently dead. We moved on without spirit.

We found a den-hole among the dead autobiles that was empty after we chased out a scrawny Cat. Nik Nok made a halfheart grab and missed but we did not miss it, none of us was hungry anyway. I was still full from the night before, and the way Disha looked I did not even ask her if she wanted the Cat so he got lucky that night. After we settled in I shrunked farther back in the pile so Disha and her love could be alone together.

She was quiet as though submitting but the way she held her head seemed more like quiet domination. She knew she was horribly dead because the Junkyard Dog drew blood.

"Nik Nok" she said "you know we have only a little time left together now. Let us not waste it."

Skunks have very good eyes.

They violented Democrazy again in the day-heat, but this time it was gentle and slow like the black river instead of laughing and plunging like a waterfoul. She licked his belly very lightly and he breathed into her ear and stroked the underside of her tail and when he went inside her she coughed in surprise that it was so smooth and easy. Once he forgot and grabbed her wounded and stiffening leg to pull himself in deeper and she jerked away, but she never made a sound except right at the very end when she moaned just a little. This time she finished before he did but she was true to her word and kept on until he was done.

Afterward they lay together and talked without words while Nik Nok picked fleas out of her fur. They slept face to face even though she being a Dog was not exactly built for it.

Now that I knew what Nik Nok would soon lose I found I no longer cared about Custom and let Democrazy be hanged. Love *is* Progrets. Strange creatures fluttered in my stomach.

As the sun set we rose. When the air became stullen, and we resumed our journey I began to wish Nik Nok had nabbed the cat afterall. The stullen air was even browner than yestereve and blood red with the setting sun so it would be hard to main train a course for the other mountains across the city of angels. Disha said we would be there by the dawn's oily light, and could the underbuild be far away then?

### Chapter sixteen we explore Disha's tunnel of love

Well we were not at the mountains by sun-up but we kept at our quest even through the daylight for we were tired, and wanted it all over. We saw no more Junkyard Dogs but my funny-watchy feeling continued, and I felt like everyone we saw was Junk in some way or another.

Finally through the cracked and fallen builds, Disha spied the arch with the folded arms that reprehented an underbuild. "We shall enter sex the line here" said she "and follow it along towards the sea that swallows the sun. Soon we shall find the fallen underbuild and thence the hidden den."

So down we went and into the stingy in blackness.

It swallowed us both and three but I felt no comfort, for this was not a den nor a hidey-hole but a build—a build of men and it reeked of them and their Undemocrazy. In some places I found a cold metal road and ran along it for a way, but the ticking of my claws against the hardmetal sent shivers through us all and Disha asked me to walk on the grabble to the side. I was happy to oblige for to tell the truth, I did not like the sound either and even Nik Nok cast his eyes down and grew silent at the echoes. We walked for a passing in silence but I cannot say how long for there are no momes in the dark.

### Chapter seventeen we find the hidden den at last!

The journey through the wendless tunnel passed an easily, for even the Santa's Anus and the Winds of Law could not brush us down there. At last we began to see cracks of light in the overhead, and then whole pocks of hardground and finally we discovered the Great Buildfall that the Coon had reminated. We climbored out of the underbuild into bright and treacherous sunlight, and saw stretched down below us the last defense against Democrazy.

It was a build squat like a stone spider and it was all gleaming, while the other builds around it were broken and dulled. There were men in strange clothing outside: they wore thick brown clothes that covered them completely and round hats that surrounded their heads and they looked out of glass windrows in their hats. I did not need for Disha to tell me that the clothes were meant to keep out Progrets but she did anyway. When I objected she said that she had only been telling Nik Nok.

We watched them for a long time. When they went inside two big doors opened for them, but they opened into a little room that did not seem worth the efforts.

"So how do we get Progrets beyond those doors" Disha asked.

"Maybe we can knock a hole through them" asked Nik Nok, but Disha injected. "We might be able to dig our way through one door if we were quick enough, but long before we got through the other door those men would do us. But maybe there is only one wall, perhaps we should consecrate on that."

We crept forward and studied the build some more.

"Nik Nok" said Disha "if these humans have never been fected by Progrets, that means these walls have stood for many seasons. They must be very strong walls indeed for there have been earthshakes and many storms."

I tried watching the men (or were they women? I could not tell inside their clothing). I began to have a glimmering in my mind like moonlight on the water.

Something the Junkyard Dog said kept buzzing to be reminated, but I could not pull it out and look at it.

The den was in a deep canyon from our vintage point with a long path of mostly straight unbroken hardground leading down towards it. It was to this path that my eyes looked. It had something to do with the important thing the Junkyard Dog said that I could not reminate. Oh how I wished I were a Dog or a Man, that could reminate everything!

"Let us explore the path" I asked "and see if we can find anything." Since neither Disha nor Nik Nok had a better suggestion we turned about and began walking back along the hardground away from the hidden den.

I looked at everything we passed trying to reminate what I knew was in my mind. I reminated, that the Junkyard Dog in between all his gibbers had said something that would help us now.

### Chapter eighteen we discover the
### key to the mysteries

I looked at an arco and a hydrant and a lot of square builds and a store but none of them joggled my memory.

And then I saw the autobile truck and at once the thought leapt back into my mind.

"I reminate!" I cried "the truck is the key said the Junkyard Dog!"

Disha looked at the truck and then at me, saying "that is what *I* am now, a Junkyard Dog." At once I regretted my hasty words but "you are right, I reminate him saying that too" she added.

"But what could he know about today" I asked "for you killed him yesterday."

"To the junk" she said "there is no yesterday or tomorrow, it sees backward and forward in days the way we see left and right along venture path. But what does that mean, the truck is the key?"

It was the biggest autobile truck I had ever seen. Even Nik Nok could not reach its top and it had more wheels than there are numbers in the city of angels. It was stopped along the edge of the hardground and was covered with foul-smelling rust.

For a long time we all three stared at the truck trying to figure out how it was the key. Then Nik Nok whispered "if machines make the wall then maybe machines can . . ."

"Can what" I asked.

"That was something else he said" said the Boy. "Only machines can what, break the wall?"

"If we could get the truck rolling down the hardground" Disha said thinking loud "maybe it would roll fast enough that it could smash through the wall and into the Den."

Nik Nok looked at the autobile for a long time.

"It is a very big truck" he said at last.

"But how do we get it rolling" I asked.

"And more important" asked Nik Nok "once we do how do we make sure it stays on the hardground and does not hit a tree and stop?"

"That wheel in front of the chair makes it go left and right" answered Disha like a know-all "for I have spoken with Hanaka Tag the eldest and she told me of these autobiles."

"Well I think these men make the machine come alive" retorted Nik Nok "do you know how to bring it to life also?"

"We do not need to" Disha declammed though she did not sound too sure and I could tell she was only guessing "for if we can get it rolling then the hill will make it go fast enough."

I kept my mouth shut during this ax change, for I am only a Skunk. I listened well though for we Skunks have very good ears.

Nik Nok fumbled with the latch until he could get the metal open and we looked inside.

"What we must do" said Disha "is get it rolling and then one of us stays inside to turn the hoop-wheel and make the truck go left and right to stay on the hardground."

"But then what" asked Nik Nok, full of frights and astonishments "what will happen when it hits the Den? Will I be killed?"

Disha smiled. "Whichever one of us it is in the truck must jump clear before the crash my love." She touched his side gently with her graying muzzle, for she was not as young as she had been the season before.

The truck was not rolling so we decided something was blocking it. After we ran around for a few momes looking, Disha saw some pieces of wood under the wheels. We tried to pull them out, but even Nik Nok could not so he knocked them out finally with a rock. The truck ground and groaned but still did not roll. We climbored up to look, and there were lots of metal pulls.

"One of these must be what makes the truck stop and go" announced Disha, but I think she put on more show of know-all than she really had. Nik Nok began pulling and pushing on the pulls, and Disha was vindulated because when he pulled a partically hard one the truck screamed and began to roll slowly. It rolled down the hill warbling like a broken thunderbum.

Nik Nok was afraid even when it went so slow. Then it picked up speed and we all shivered.

I was so frightened I could not move and I feared I would not be able to jump out, when the time came being so frightened.

Disha had Nik Nok turn the hoop-wheel, for she did not have the strength in her jaws and it was almost too hard for him!

"Reminate my love" she cautioned "keep the door from latching for we must be ready to fly out at the very last mome."

Nik Nok touched her paw and looked into her eyes, "oh I love you so *much*" he said with a tear in his eye. I could not figure out why his eyes were wet. Was there dust in them?

The autobile truck got faster and faster and soon Nik Nok was barely able to keep it on the hardground and away from trees and builds. I began to be afraid and sick as if I had eaten wormroot when I looked to the side and saw the world whizzing past me faster than a sparrow flies, and almost would have jumped out right then except that I knew Disha would not let us be killed, especially not Nik Nok. She rested her muzzle against his ear, and I could barely hear her snuffle "you are precious to me too. Life is precious."

Then we roared around the last turn with Nik Nok straining to make the hoop-wheel turn so that the autobile truck would stay where it was supposed. We were heading right for the Den.

Some of the Men saw us coming and ran out waiving their hands and then tried to ride their own autobile into our path. They must have known what we were doing and were ready to give their lives to thwart the will of Democrazy, such was their fear of Progrets. But their autobile could not run fast enough and it only hit the back of the truck and did not even turn us. Just before we hit Disha snuffled "junk bonds, but love is stronger." Then "NOW!" she barked "JUMP NOW!"

Nik Nok pushed open the door and just before he jumped he grabbed me by the scruff and saved my life!

We were lucky we were on grass and not on hardground for we hit and hit hard. I rolled over and over the Boy and ended up on my back watching the truck plow into the Den.

I do not know if Disha ever had a chance. Just before the crash I saw her still in the truck, gripping the hoop with her mouth and keeping the truck aimed true.

Then I heard a thunderbum like I had never imagined and the whole wall of the Last Old Den caved in like a buildfall in an earthshake. We had opened the last remnant of yesterday to the clouds of Progrets and the plague.

### Chapter nineteen

But Disha was dead.

### Chapter twenty triumph of Democrazy

I was still shaking from the fall I thought. I looked about unable to move, but I could not see Nik Nok and I was alone.

I saw the truck went much deeper into the Den than I imagined, it went right through three rooms.

Dust and smoke puffed on the Winds of Law around inside and in and out of the hole we had made and I knew that the bugs of Democrazy were drifting in too and would bear fruit.

Now all of us would be truly equal and the fourlegs would be liberated.

Then I saw Disha.

She had been thrown from the truck. She lay on the ground covered in blood.

Nik Nok held her broken lifeless body in his arms and tried to kiss her back to life, and the tears were streaming down his cheeks. "What is this? What is this" he asked touching the salty water.

"I think that means you are a Man again" I said "for Democrazy has triumphed. Our brethren and sistern are free and equal now."

But a junk voice in my head, maybe Disha's ghost whispered "you cannot be both."

Disha pulled me into the Hidden Den, deeper and deeper than we had been even in the underbuild for it was a darkness of the heart not of the air and her ghost glowed like the moon.

I saw a Rat shivering and shaking and looking at me with wide eyes. "We have come to liberate you" I said to resure him, but he only made a scrittering sound and ran away.

I stopped in panic. What was that sound? What did he say?

Then a Dog came out and I called to him, for he was a brother of Disha and I wanted to tell him of her sacrifice and how he was free now.

"You are free Mr. Dog" I said, and "the free live free, you must go out into the city of angels now and learn the Will of Democrazy."

At first he snarled, but I knew he was only reacting to a strange Skunk. But when he heard my words he settled down and began to moan in pleasure at his newfound equality.

But then the moans turned into a whimper and he crawled on his belly to me. I backed up in consarnation for what was he, to wit a Dog doing playing subservant to a mere Skunk? Where was his equality before the Winds of Law?

Then I smelled his fear.

It ran unchecked down his leg and I could hear his heart racing like the truck that brought him Democrazy in the first place. He was terrified and did not understand.

"You would do well to buck up and be a Dog" I chastised "for this is Progrets and the Will of Democrazy!" I boldly approached to lead him out into the real world, but instead he barked . . . and it was not words he barked. It was a cough, a grunt and held no more meaning than fear and confusion.

He may have been a Dog, but he was still only an animal. He was no brother of Disha.

We turned and ran at the same time in opposite directions. Terror gripped me too, for I suddenly realized that I was in another land.

There was no Democrazy here today, no matter what the bugs may say tomorrow and I was more afraid than I had been of the Junkyard Dog.

A Man stood in my path. "Do not stop me" I announced "for I am Progrets!"

He screamed and staggered back against the wall of the Den covering his face. Another man heard me and tried to bean me with a stick crying "another one, kill him! Break his throat like the other!" and I did not need to ask to know that they meant the Coon. Now I knew how he had come to rupture his larinks. I ran like a Commonest.

At once the whole Den came alive against me, Men and Fourlegs and it was I who was fleeing for my very life. I found the hole, I do not know how. And then I was through. I did not stop running until I found the fallen underbuild again, and there was Nik Nok. But Disha's body was not with him and he would not tell me where it was.

## Chapter twenty-one to the winners
## go the spoiled

I will not tell you of the journey back across the waste, to the venture
path with Nik Nok carrying me under one arm. All I reminate is that
the Dogs snarled fiercely and the builds rumbled and shook, but none
of them could touch us for Disha trotted right beside us still, and her
laugh echoed around us as we slept the day away.

By the night we returned the color finally crept back into Nik
Nok's face, and he could smile though he vanished the next day and
I never saw him again.

When I knew he had gone Overizon I felt a tear in my eye. I,
the last of our extra diction, learned to cry.

## Chapter twenty-two Mr. Skunk lowers his tale

I have nothing left to say. I am getting old and soon I will be a feast
myself if you can stand the smell.

I, a Skunk am the very last of us who is able to cry since Nik
Nok left and Disha died. I see you do not even understand what it
is, except perhaps dust in my eye or a thorn in my paw.

In the high build at the end of venture path is a tower with a
bell at the top, but it is silent now for there are none with the will
to ring it. Pigeons roost under the metal and I hear them call to each
other through the long, hot days: "home! Fly home! Come home!"

They know nothing else to say, but it is a miracle that they can
say even that, and I think that the plague is finally doing them as
well. I think this means that soon we shall be equal to the pigeons
too and only able to call each other home without even knowing
where our home lies.

That is true Democrazy after all, and there is an end to love.

I will not be there to see, thank Democrazy.

Long reign Progrets! I bow to the Will, the Winds, and Inalienable
Progrets!

I confess that sometimes I wonder: have we lost something urgent? But I do not think wondering should be a crime against
Democrazy.

# The Hemingway Hoax

### ...

## *Joe Haldeman*

Joe Haldeman's vision of a corrupted and cuckolded Hemingway
scholar could easily have appeared twice on the 1990 final Nebula
ballot, for the longer, novel version clearly had its partisans. As it
happens, only the novella became a nominee.

Born in Oklahoma City in 1943, Haldeman attended the University of Maryland, taking a B.S. in physics and astronomy in 1967.
Upon his graduation, the U.S. Army sent him to Vietnam, where
he was severely wounded, subsequently receiving a Purple Heart
and, as he modestly puts it, "other standard medals."

In 1976, Haldeman won both the Hugo Award and the Nebula
Award for *The Forever War*, a novel that, beyond its genre elements,
clearly owes much to his combat experiences. He garnered a second
Hugo in 1977 for his story "Tricentennial," and in 1983 his poetry
brought him a Rhysling Award. Haldeman's other novels include
*All My Sins Remembered, Mindbridge, Tool of the Trade*, and *Buying Time*, and his stories are collected in *Infinite Dreams* and *Dealing
in Futures*. He currently divides his time between Gainesville, Florida, where he produces fiction and bicycles, and Cambridge, Massachusetts, where he produces fiction and teaches in the writing
department at MIT.

"That this work exists at all in novella form," Haldeman explains, "is a tribute to the editing skill of Gardner Dozois. I sent
him the novel, *The Hemingway Hoax*, to consider for serialization
in *Asimov's*, and he liked it, but he couldn't schedule it in time. If
I could cut it by half, or even a third, though, he thought he could
squeeze it in as a one-shot novella.

"Hardly seemed possible. The novel was already under sixty
thousand words, and (I thought) an admirably trim and tight little
structure. There was no way you could cut twenty thousand words
out of it and have it still make sense. Gardner offered to try."

To make a long story short, Dozois made a short novel shorter.
He excised sentences, paragraphs, and five entire chapters—cuts
that, Haldeman feels, "did simplify and concentrate the narrative."
So here it is, "The Hemingway Hoax," not a *Reader's Digest* bas-
tardization, not Haldeman Lite, but a plenary work of science fiction
art, bringing *Nebula Awards 26* to a mind-bending finish.

## 1. The Torrents of Spring

Our story begins in a run-down bar in Key West, not so many years from now. The bar is not the one Hemingway drank at, nor yet the one that claims to be the one he drank at, because they are both too expensive and full of tourists. This bar, in a more interesting part of town, is a Cuban place. It is neither clean nor well-lighted, but has cold beer and good strong Cuban coffee. Its cheap prices and rascally charm are what bring together the scholar and the rogue.

Their first meeting would be of little significance to either at the time, though the scholar, John Baird, would never forget it. John Baird was not capable of forgetting anything.

Key West is lousy with writers, mostly poor writers, in one sense of that word or the other. Poor people did not interest our rogue, Sylvester Castlemaine, so at first he didn't take any special note of the man sitting in the corner scribbling on a yellow pad. Just another would-be writer, come down to see whether some of Papa's magic would rub off. Not worth the energy of a con.

But Castle's professional powers of observation caught at a detail or two and focused his attention. The man was wearing jeans and a faded flannel shirt, but his shoes were expensive Italian loafers. His beard had been trimmed by a barber. He was drinking Heineken. The pen he was scribbling with was a fat Mont Blanc Diplomat, two hundred bucks on the hoof, discounted. Castle got his cup of coffee and sat at a table two away from the writer.

He waited until the man paused, set the pen down, took a drink. "Writing a story?" Castle said.

The man blinked at him. "No . . . just an article." He put the cap on the pen with a crisp snap. "An article about stories. I'm a college professor."

"Publish or perish," Castle said.

The man relaxed a bit. "Too true." He riffled through the yellow pad. "This won't help much. It's not going anywhere."

"Tell you what . . . bet you a beer it's Hemingway or Tennessee Williams."

"Too easy." He signaled the bartender. "*Dos cervezas.* Hemingway, the early stories. You know his work?"

"Just a little. We had to read him in school—*The Old Man and the Fish*? And then I read a couple after I got down here." He moved over to the man's table. "Name's Castle."

"John Baird." Open, honest expression; not too promising. You can't con somebody unless he thinks he's conning you. "Teach up at Boston."

"I'm mostly fishing. Shrimp nowadays." Of course Castle didn't normally fish, not for things in the sea, but the shrimp part was true. He'd been reduced to heading shrimp on the Catalina for five dollars a bucket. "So what about these early stories?"

The bartender set down the two beers and gave Castle a weary look.

"Well . . . they don't exist." John Baird carefully poured the beer down the side of his glass. "They were stolen. Never published."

"So what can you write about them?"

"Indeed. That's what I've been asking myself." He took a sip of the beer and settled back. "Seventy-four years ago they were stolen. December 1922. That's really what got me working on them; thought I would do a paper, a monograph, for the seventy-fifth anniversary of the occasion."

It sounded less and less promising, but this was the first imported beer Castle had had in months. He slowly savored the bite of it.

"He and his first wife, Hadley, were living in Paris. You know about Hemingway's early life?"

"Huh uh. Paris?"

"He grew up in Oak Park, Illinois. That was kind of a prissy, self-satisfied suburb of Chicago."

"Yeah, I been there."

"He didn't like it. In his teens he sort of ran away from home, went down to Kansas City to work on a newspaper.

"World War I started, and like a lot of kids, Hemingway couldn't get into the army because of bad eyesight, so he joined the Red Cross and went off to drive ambulances in Italy. Take cigarettes and chocolate to the troops.

"That almost killed him. He was just doing his cigarettes-and-chocolate routine and an artillery round came in, killed the guy next to him, tore up another, riddled Hemingway with shrapnel. He claims then that he picked up the wounded guy and carried him back to the trench, in spite of being hit in the knee by a machine-gun bullet."

"What do you mean, 'claims'?"

"You're too young to have been in Vietnam."

"Yeah."

"Good for you. I was hit in the knee by a machine-gun bullet myself, and went down on my ass and didn't get up for five weeks. He didn't carry anybody one step."

"That's interesting."

"Well, he was always rewriting his life. We all do it. But it seemed to be a compulsion with him. That's one thing that makes Hemingway scholarship challenging."

Baird poured the rest of the beer into his glass. "Anyhow, he actually was the first American wounded in Italy, and they made a big deal over him. He went back to Oak Park a war hero. He had a certain amount of success with women."

"Or so he says?"

"Right, God knows. Anyhow, he met Hadley Richardson, an older woman but quite a number, and they had a steamy courtship and got married and said the hell with it, moved to Paris to live a sort of Bohemian life while Hemingway worked on perfecting his art. That part isn't bullshit. He worked diligently and he did become one of the best writers of his era. Which brings us to the lost manuscripts."

"Do tell."

"Hemingway was picking up a little extra money doing journalism. He'd gone to Switzerland to cover a peace conference for a news service. When it was over, he wired Hadley to come join him for some skiing.

"This is where it gets odd. On her own initiative, Hadley packed up all of Ernest's work. All of it. Not just the typescripts, but the handwritten first drafts and the carbons."

"That's like a Xerox?"

"Right. She packed them in an overnight bag, then packed her own suitcase. A porter at the train station, the Gare de Lyon, put them aboard for her. She left the train for a minute to find something to read—and when she came back, they were gone."

"Suitcase and all?"

"No, just the manuscripts. She and the porter searched up and down the train. But that was it. Somebody had seen the overnight bag sitting there and snatched it. Lost forever."

That did hold a glimmer of professional interest. "That's funny. You'd think they'd get a note then, like 'If you ever want to see your stories again, bring a million bucks to the Eiffel Tower' sort of thing."

"A few years later, that might have happened. It didn't take long for Hemingway to become famous. But at the time, only a few of the literary intelligentsia knew about him."

Castle shook his head in commiseration with the long-dead thief. "Guy who stole 'em probably didn't even read English. Dumped 'em in the river."

John Baird shivered visibly. "Undoubtedly. But people have never stopped looking for them. Maybe they'll show up in some attic someday."

"Could happen." Wheels turning.

"It's happened before in literature. Some of Boswell's diaries were recovered because a scholar recognized his handwriting on an old piece of paper a merchant used to wrap a fish. Hemingway's own last book, he put together from notes that had been lost for thirty years. They were in a couple of trunks in the basement of the Ritz, in Paris." He leaned forward, excited. "Then after he died, they found another batch of papers down here, in a back room in Sloppy Joe's. It could still happen."

Castle took a deep breath. "It could be made to happen, too."

"Made to happen?"

"Just speakin', you know, in theory. Like some guy who really knows Hemingway, suppose he makes up some stories that're like those old ones, finds some seventy-five-year-old paper and an old, what do you call them, not a word processor—"

"Typewriter."

"Whatever. Think he could pass 'em off for the real thing?"

"I don't know if he could fool me," Baird said, and tapped the side of his head. "I have a freak memory: eidetic, photographic. I have just about every word Hemingway ever wrote committed to memory." He looked slightly embarrassed. "Of course that doesn't make me an expert in the sense of being able to spot a phony. I just wouldn't have to refer to any texts."

"So take yourself, you know, or somebody else who spent all his life studyin' Hemingway. He puts all he's got into writin' these stories—he knows the people who are gonna be readin' 'em; knows what they're gonna look for. And he hires like an expert forger to make the pages look like they came out of Hemingway's machine. So could it work?"

Baird pursed his lips and for a moment looked professorial. Then he sort of laughed, one syllable through his nose. "Maybe it could. A man did a similar thing when I was a boy, counterfeiting the memoirs of Howard Hughes. He made millions."

"Millions?"

"Back when that was real money. Went to jail when they found out, of course."

"And the money was still there when he got out."

"Never read anything about it. I guess so."

"So the next question is, how much stuff are we talkin' about? How much was in that old overnight bag?"

"That depends on who you believe. There was half a novel and some poetry. The short stories, there might have been as few as eleven or as many as thirty."

"That'd take a long time to write."

"It would take forever. You couldn't just 'do' Hemingway; you'd have to figure out what the stories were about, then reconstruct his early style—do you know how many Hemingway scholars there are in the world?"

"Huh uh. Quite a few."

"Thousands. Maybe ten thousand academics who know enough to spot a careless fake."

Castle nodded, cogitating. "You'd have to be real careful. But then you wouldn't have to do all the short stories and poems, would you? You could say all you found was the part of the novel. Hell, you could sell that as a book."

The odd laugh again. "Sure you could. Be a fortune in it."

"How much? A million bucks?"

"A million . . . maybe. Well, sure. The last new Hemingway made at least that much, allowing for inflation. And he's more popular now."

Castle took a big gulp of beer and set his glass down decisively. "So what the hell are we waiting for?"

Baird's bland smile faded. "You're serious?"

### 2. in our time

Got a ripple in the Hemingway channel.
> Twenties again?
> No, funny, this one's in the 1990s. See if you can track it down?
> Sure. Go down to the armory first and—
> Look—no bloodbaths this time. You solve one problem and start ten
more.
> Couldn't be helped. It's no tea party, twentieth century America.
> Just use good judgment. That Ransom guy . . .
> Manson. Right. That was a mistake.

### 3. A Way You'll Never Be

You can't cheat an honest man, as Sylvester Castlemaine well knew, but then again, it never hurts to find out just how honest a man is. John Baird refused his scheme, with good humor at first, but when Castle persisted, his refusal took on a sarcastic edge; maybe a tinge of outrage. He backed off and changed the subject, talking for a half hour about commercial fishing around Key West, and then said he had to run. He slipped his business card into John's shirt pocket on the way out. ("Sylvester Castlemaine, Consultant," it claimed.)

John left the place soon, walking slowly through the afternoon heat. He was glad he hadn't brought the bicycle; it was pleasant to walk in the shade of the big aromatic trees, a slight breeze on his face from the Gulf side.

One could do it. One could. The problem divided itself into three parts; writing the novel fragment, forging the manuscript, and devising a suitable story about how one had uncovered the manuscript.

The writing part would be the hardest. Hemingway is easy enough to parody—one fourth of the take-home final he gave in English 733 was to write a page of Hemingway pastiche, and some of his graduate students did a credible job—but parody was exactly what one would not want to do.

It had been a crucial period in Hemingway's development, those three years of apprenticeship the lost manuscripts represented. Two stories survived, and they were maddeningly dissimilar. "My Old Man," which had slipped down behind a drawer, was itself a pastiche, reading like pretty good Sherwood Anderson, but with an O. Henry twist at the end—very unlike the bleak understated quality that would distinguish the stories that were to make Hemingway's reputation. The other, "Up in Michigan," had been out in the mail at the time of the loss. It was a lot closer to Hemingway's ultimate style, a spare and, by the standards of the time, pornographic description of a woman's first sexual experience.

John riffled through the notes on the yellow pad, a talismanic gesture, since he could have remembered any page with little effort. But the sight of the words and the feel of the paper sometimes helped him think.

One would not do it, of course. Except perhaps as a mental exercise. Not to show to anybody. Certainly not to profit from.

You wouldn't want to use "My Old Man" as the model, certainly; no one would care to publish a pastiche of a pastiche of Anderson, now undeservedly obscure. So "Up in Michigan." And the first story he wrote after the loss, "Out of Season," would also be handy. That had a lot of the true Hemingway strength.

You wouldn't want to tackle the novel fragment, of course, not just as an exercise, over a hundred pages . . .

Without thinking about it, John dropped into a familiar fugue state as he walked through the run-down neighborhood, his freak memory taking over while his body ambled along on autopilot. This is the way he usually remembered pages. He transported himself back to the Hemingway collection at the JFK Library in Boston, last November, snow swirling outside the big picture windows overlooking the harbor, the room so cold he was wearing coat and gloves and could see his breath. They didn't normally let you wear a coat up there, afraid you might squirrel away a page out of the manuscript collection, but they had to make an exception because the heat pump was down.

He was flipping through the much-thumbed Xerox of Carlos Baker's interview with Hadley, page 52: "Stolen suitcase," Baker asked; "lost novel?"

The typescript of her reply appeared in front of him, more clear than the cracked sidewalk his feet negotiated: "This novel was a knockout, about Nick, up north in Michigan—hunting, fishing, all sorts of experiences—stuff on the order of "Big Two-Hearted River," with more action. Girl experiences well done, too." With an enigmatic addition, evidently in Hadley's handwriting, "Girl experiences too well done."

That was interesting. John hadn't thought about that, since he'd been concentrating on the short stories. Too well done? There had been a lot of talk in the eighties about Hemingway's sexual ambiguity—*gender* ambiguity, actually—could Hadley have been upset, sixty years after the fact, remembering some confidence that Hemingway had revealed to the world in that novel, something girls knew that boys were not supposed to know? Playful pillow talk that was filed away for eventual literary exploitation?

He used his life that way. A good writer remembered everything and then forgot it when he sat down to write, and reinvented it so the writing would be more real than the memory. Experience was important, but imagination was more important.

Maybe I would be a better writer, John thought, if I could learn how to forget. For about the tenth time today, like any day, he regretted not having tried to succeed as a writer, while he still had the independent income. Teaching and research had fascinated him when he was younger, a rich boy's all-consuming hobbies, but the end of this fiscal year would be the end of the monthly checks from the trust fund. So the salary from Boston University wouldn't be mad money any more, but rent and groceries in a city suddenly expensive.

Yes, the writing would be the hard part. Then forging the manuscript, that wouldn't be easy. Any scholar would have access to copies of thousands of pages that Hemingway typed before and after the loss. Could one find the typewriter Hemingway had used? Then duplicate his idiosyncratic typing style—a moment's reflection put a sample in front of him, spaces before and after periods and commas . . .

He snapped out of the reverie as his right foot hit the first step on the back staircase up to their rented flat. He automatically stepped over the fifth step, the rotted one, and was thinking about a nice tall glass of iced tea as he opened the screen door.

"Scorpions!" his wife screamed, two feet from his face.

"What?"

"We have scorpions!" Lena grabbed his arm and hauled him to the kitchen.

"Look!" She pointed at the opaque plastic skylight. Three scorpions, each about six inches long, cast sharp silhouettes on the milky plastic. One was moving.

"My word."

"Your *word!*" She struck a familiar pose, hands on hips, and glared up at the creatures. "What are we going to do about it?"

"We could name them."

"John."

"I don't know." He opened the refrigerator. "Call the bug man."

"The bug man was just here yesterday. He probably flushed them out."

He poured a glass of cold tea and dumped two envelopes of artificial sweetener into it. "I'll talk to Julio about it. But you know they've been there all along. They're not bothering anybody."

"They're bothering the hell out of me!"

He smiled. "Okay. I'll talk to Julio." He looked into the oven. "Thought about dinner?"

"Anything you want to cook, sweetheart. I'll be damned if I'm going to stand there with three . . . poisonous . . . arthropods staring down at me."

"Poised to jump," John said, and looked up again. There were only two visible now, which made his skin crawl.

"Julio wasn't home when I first saw them. About an hour ago."

"I'll go check." John went downstairs and Julio, the landlord, was indeed home but was not impressed by the problem. He agreed that it was probably the bug man, and they would probably go back to where they came from in a while, and gave John a flyswatter.

John left the flyswatter with Lena, admonishing her to take no prisoners, and walked a couple of blocks to a Chinese restaurant. He brought back a few boxes of take-out, and they sat in the living room and wielded chopsticks in silence, listening for the pitter-patter of tiny feet.

"Met a real live con man today." He put the business card on the coffee table between them.

" 'Consultant'?" she read.

"He had a loony scheme about counterfeiting the missing stories." Lena knew more about the missing stories than 98 percent of the people who Hemingway-ed for a living. John liked to think out loud.

"Ah, the stories," she said, preparing herself.

"Not a bad idea, actually, if one had a larcenous nature." He concentrated for a moment on the slippery moo goo gai pan. "Be millions of bucks in it."

He was bent over the box. She stared hard at his bald spot. "What exactly did he have in mind?"

"We didn't bother to think it through in any detail, actually. You go and find . . ." He got the slightly wall-eyed look that she knew meant he was reading a page of a book a thousand miles away. "Yes. A 1921 Corona portable, like the one Hadley gave him before they were married. Find some old paper. Type up the stories. Take them to Sotheby's. Spend money for the rest of your life. That's all there is to it."

"You left out jail."

"A mere detail. Also the writing of the stories. That could take weeks. Maybe you could get arrested first, write the stories in jail, and then sell them when you got out."

"You're weird, John."

"Well. I didn't give him any encouragement."

"Maybe you should've. A few million would come in handy next year."

"We'll get by."

" 'We'll get by.' You keep saying that. How do you know? You've never had to 'get by.' "

"Okay, then. We won't get by." He scraped up the last of the fried rice. "We won't be able to make the rent and they'll throw us out on the street. We'll live in a cardboard box over a heating grate. You'll have to sell your body to keep me in cheap wine. But we'll be happy, dear." He looked up at her, mooning. "Poor but happy."

"Slap-happy." She looked at the card again. "How do you know he's a con man?"

"I don't know. Salesman type. Says he's in commercial fishing now, but he doesn't seem to like it much."

"He didn't say anything about any, you know, criminal stuff he'd done in the past?"

"Huh uh. I just got the impression that he didn't waste a lot of time mulling over ethics and morals." John held up the Mont Blanc pen. "He was staring at this, before he came over and introduced himself. I think he smelled money."

Lena stuck both chopsticks into the half-finished carton of boiled rice and set it down decisively. "Let's ask him over."

"He's a sleaze, Lena. You wouldn't like him."

"I've never met a real con man. It would be fun."

He looked into the darkened kitchen. "Will you cook something?"

She followed his gaze, expecting monsters. "If you stand guard."

### 4. Romance is Dead
### (*subtitle The Hell it is*)

"Be a job an' a half," Castle said, mopping up residual spaghetti sauce with a piece of garlic bread. "It's not like your Howard Hughes guy, or Hitler's notebooks."

"You've been doing some research." John's voice was a little slurred. He'd bought a half gallon of Portuguese wine, the bottle wrapped in straw like cheap Chianti, the wine not quite that good. If you could get past the first couple of glasses, it was okay. It had been okay to John for some time now.

"Yeah, down to the library. The guys who did the Hitler notebooks, hell, nobody'd ever seen a real Hitler notebook; they just studied his handwriting in letters and such, then read up on what he did day after day. Same with the Howard Hughes, but that was even easier, because most of the time nobody knew what the hell Howard Hughes was doing anyhow. Just stayed locked up in that room."

"The Hughes forgery nearly worked, as I recall," John said. "If Hughes himself hadn't broken silence . . ."

"Ya gotta know that took balls. 'Scuse me, Lena." She waved a hand and laughed. "Try to get away with that while Hughes was still alive."

"How did the Hitler people screw up?" she asked.

"Funny thing about that one was how many people they fooled. Afterwards everybody said it was a really lousy fake. But you can bet that before the newspapers bid millions of dollars on it, they showed it to the best Hitler-ologists they could find, and they all said it was real."

"Because they wanted it to be real," Lena said.

"Yeah. But one of the pages had some chemical in it that wouldn't be in paper before 1945. That was kinda dumb."

"People would want the Hemingway stories to be real," Lena said quietly, to John.

John's gaze stayed fixed on the center of the table, where a few strands of spaghetti lay cold and drying in a plastic bowl. "Wouldn't be honest."

"That's for sure," Castle said cheerily. "But it ain't exactly armed robbery, either."

"A gross misuse of intellectual . . . intellectual . . ."

"It's past your bedtime, John," Lena said. "We'll clean up." John nodded and pushed himself away from the table and walked heavily into the bedroom.

Lena didn't say anything until she heard the bedsprings creak. "He isn't always like this," she said quietly.

"Yeah. He don't act like no alky."

"It's been a hard year for him." She refilled her glass. "Me, too. Money."

"That's bad."

"Well, we knew it was coming. He tell you about the inheritance?" Castle leaned forward. "Huh uh."

"He was born pretty well off. Family had textile mills up in New Hampshire. John's grandparents died in an auto accident in the forties and the family sold off the mills—good timing, too. They wouldn't be worth much today.

"Then John's father and mother died in the sixties, while he was in college. The executors set up a trust fund that looked like it would keep him in pretty good shape forever. But he wasn't interested in money. He even joined the army, to see what it was like."

"Jesus."

"Afterwards, he carried a picket sign and marched against the war—you know, Vietnam.

"Then he finished his Ph.D. and started teaching. The trust fund must have been fifty times as much as his salary, when he started out. It was still ten times as much, a couple of years ago."

"Boy . . . howdy." Castle was doing mental arithmetic and algebra with variables like Porsches and fast boats.

"But he let his sisters take care of it. He let them reinvest the capital."

"They weren't too swift?"

"They were idiots! They took good solid blue-chip stocks and tax-free municipals, too 'boring' for them, and threw it all away gambling on commodities." She grimaced. "*Pork* bellies? I finally had John go to Chicago and come back with what was left of his money. There wasn't much."

"You ain't broke, though."

"Damned near. There's enough income to pay for insurance and eventually we'll be able to draw on an IRA. But the cash payments stop in two months. We'll have to live on John's salary. I suppose I'll get a job, too."

"What you ought to get is a typewriter."

Lena laughed and slouched back in her chair. "That would be something."

"You think he could do it? I mean if he would, do you think he could?"

"He's a good writer." She looked thoughtful. "He's had some stories published, you know, in the literary magazines. The ones that pay four or five free copies."

"Big deal."

She shrugged. "Pays off in the long run. Tenure. But I don't know whether being able to write a good literary story means that John could write a good Hemingway imitation."

"He knows enough, right?"

"Maybe he knows too much. He might be paralyzed by his own standards." She shook her head. "In some ways he's an absolute nut about Hemingway. Obsessed, I mean. It's not good for him."

"Maybe writing this stuff would get it out of his system."

She smiled at him. "You've got more angles than a protractor."

"Sorry; I didn't mean to—"

"No." She raised both hands. "Don't be sorry; I like it. I like you, Castle. John's a good man but sometimes he's too good."

He poured them both more wine. "Nobody ever accused me of that."

"I suspect not." She paused. "Have you ever been in trouble with the police? Just curious."

"Why?"

"Just curious."

He laughed. "Nickel-and-dime stuff, when I was a kid. You know, jus' to see what you can get away with." He turned serious. "Then I pulled two months' hard time for somethin' I didn't do. Wasn't even in town when it happened."

"What was it?"

"Armed robbery. Then the guy came back an' hit the same goddamn store! I mean, he was one sharp cookie. He confessed to the first one and they let me go."

"Why did they accuse you in the first place?"

"Used to think it was somebody had it in for me. Like the clerk who fingered me." He took a sip of wine. "But hell. It was just dumb luck. And dumb cops. The guy was about my height, same color hair, we both lived in the neighborhood. Cops didn't want to waste a lot of time on it. Jus' chuck me in jail."

"So you do have a police record?"

"Huh uh. Girl from the ACLU made sure they wiped it clean. She wanted me to go after 'em for what, false arrest an' wrongful imprisonment. I just wanted to get out of town."

"It wasn't here?"

"Nah. Dayton, Ohio. Been here eight, nine years."

"That's good."

"Why the third degree?"

She leaned forward and patted the back of his hand. "Call it a job interview, Castle. I have a feeling we may be working together."

"Okay." He gave her a slow smile. "Anything else you want to know?"

## 5. The Doctor and the Doctor's Wife

John trudged into the kitchen the next morning, ignored the coffeepot, and pulled a green bottle of beer out of the fridge. He looked up at the skylight. Four scorpions, none of them moving. Have to call the bug man today.

Red-wine hangover, the worst kind. He was too old for this. Cheap-red-wine hangover. He eased himself into a soft chair and carefully poured the beer down the side of the glass. Not too much noise, please.

When you drink too much, you ought to take a couple of aspirin, and some vitamins, and all the water you can hold, before retiring.

If you drink too much, of course, you don't remember to do that.

The shower turned off with a bass clunk of plumbing. John winced and took a long drink, which helped a little. When he heard the bathroom door open he called for Lena to bring the aspirin when she came out.

After a few minutes she brought it out and handed it to him. "And how is Dr. Baird today?"

"Dr. Baird needs a doctor. Or an undertaker." He shook out two aspirin and washed them down with the last of the beer. "Like your outfit."

She was wearing only a towel around her head. She simpered and struck a dancer's pose and spun daintily around. "Think it'll catch on?"

"Oh my yes." At thirty-five, she still had the trim model's figure that had caught his eye in the classroom, fifteen years before. A safe, light tan was uniform all over her body, thanks to liberal sunblock and the private sunbathing area on top of the house—private except for the helicopter that came low overhead every weekday at 1:15. She always tried to be there in time to wave at it. The pilot had such white teeth. She wondered how many sunbathers were on his route.

She undid the towel and rubbed her long blond hair vigorously. "Thought I'd cool off for a few minutes before I got dressed. Too much wine, eh?"

"Couldn't you tell from my sparkling repartee last night?" He leaned back, eyes closed, and rolled the cool glass back and forth on his forehead.

"Want another beer?"

"Yeah. Coffee'd be smarter, though."

"It's been sitting all night."

"Pay for my sins." He watched her swivel lightly into the kitchen and, more than ever before, felt the difference in their ages. Seventeen years; he was half again as old as she. A young man would say the hell with the hangover, go grab that luscious thing and carry her back to bed. The organ that responded to this meditation was his stomach, though, and it responded very audibly.

"Some toast, too. Or do you want something fancier?"

"Toast would be fine." Why was she being so nice? Usually if he drank too much, he reaped the whirlwind in the morning.

"Ugh." She saw the scorpions. "Five of them now."

"I wonder how many it will hold before it comes crashing down. Scorpions everywhere, stunned. Then angry."

"I'm sure the bug man knows how to get rid of them."

"In Africa they claim that if you light a ring of fire around them with gasoline or lighter fluid, they go crazy, run amok, stinging themselves to death in their frenzies. Maybe the bug man could do that."

"Castle and I came up with a plan last night. It's kinda screwy but it might just work."

"Read that in a book called *Jungle Ways*. I was eight years old and believed every word of it."

"We figured out a way that it would be legal. Are you listening?"

"Uh huh. Let me have real sugar and some milk."

She poured some milk in a cup and put it in the microwave to warm. "Maybe we should talk about it later."

"Oh no. Hemingway forgery. You figured out a way to make it legal. Go ahead. I'm all ears."

"See, you tell the publisher first off what it is, that you wrote it and then had it typed to look authentic."

"Sure, be a big market for that."

"In fact, there could be. You'd have to generate it, but it could happen." The toast sprang up and she brought it and two cups of coffee into the living room on a tray. "See, the bogus manuscript is only one part of a book."

"I don't get it." He tore the toast into strips, to dunk in the strong Cuban coffee.

"The rest of the book is in the nature of an exegesis of your own text."

"If that con man knows what exegesis is, then I can crack a safe."

"That part's my idea. You're really writing a book *about* Hemingway. You use your own text to illustrate various points—'I wrote it this way instead of that way because . . .'"

"It would be different," he conceded. "Perhaps the second most egotistical piece of Hemingway scholarship in history. A dubious distinction."

"You could write it tongue-in-cheek, though. It could be really amusing, as well as scholarly."

"God, we'd have to get an unlisted number, publishers calling us

night and day. Movie producers. Might sell ten copies, if I bought
nine."

"You really aren't getting it, John. You don't have a particle of
larceny in your heart."

He put a hand on his heart and looked down. "Ventricles, auricles.
My undying love for you, a little heartburn. No particles."

"See, you tell the publisher the truth . . . but the publisher doesn't
have to tell the truth. Not until publication day."

"Okay. I still don't get it."

She took a delicate nibble of toast. "It goes like this. They print
the bogus Hemingway up into a few copies of bogus bound galleys.
Top secret."

"My exegesis carefully left off."

"That's the ticket. They send it out to a few selected scholars,
along with Xeroxes of a few sample manuscript pages. All they say,
in effect, is 'Does this seem authentic to you? Please keep it under
your hat, for obvious reasons.' Then they sit back and collect blurbs."

"I can see the kind of blurbs they'd get from Scott or Mike or
Jack, for instance. Some variation of 'What kind of idiot do you think
I am?' "

"Those aren't the kind of people you send it to, dope! You send
it to people who think they're experts but aren't. Castle says this is
how the Hitler thing almost worked—they knew better than to show
it to historians in general. They showed it to a few people and didn't
quote the ones who thought it was a fake. Surely you can come up
with a list of people who would be easy to fool."

"Any scholar could. Be a different list for each one; I'd be on
some of them."

"So they bring it out on April Fool's Day. You get the front page
of the *New York Times Book Review*. *Publishers Weekly* does a story.
Everybody wants to be in on the joke. Best-seller list, here we come."

"Yeah, sure, but you haven't thought it through." He leaned back,
balancing the coffee cup on his slight pot belly. "What about the guys
who give us the blurbs, those second-rate scholars? They're going to
look pretty bad."

"We did think of that. No way they could sue, not if the letter accompanying the galleys is carefully written. It doesn't have to
say—"

"I don't mean getting sued. I mean I don't want to be responsible for hurting other people's careers—maybe wrecking a career, if the person was too extravagant in his endorsement, and had people looking for things to use against him. You know departmental politics. People go down the chute for less serious crimes than making an ass of yourself and your institution in print."

She put her cup down with a clatter. "You're always thinking about other people. Why don't you think about yourself for a change?" She was on the verge of tears. "Think about *us*."

"All right, let's do that. What do you think would happen to my career at BU if I pissed off the wrong people with this exercise? How long do you think it would take me to make full professor? Do you think BU would make a full professor out of a man who uses his specialty to pull vicious practical jokes?"

"Just do me the favor of thinking about it. Cool down and weigh the pluses and minuses. If you did it with the right touch, your department would love it—and God, Harry wants to get rid of the chairmanship so bad he'd give it to an ax murderer. You know you'll make full professor about thirty seconds before Harry hands you the keys to the office and runs."

"True enough." He finished the coffee and stood up in a slow creak. "I'll give it some thought. Horizontally." He turned toward the bedroom.

"Want some company?"

He looked at her for a moment. "Indeed I do."

### 6. in our time

Back already?

Need to find a meta-causal. One guy seems to be generating the danger flag in various timelines. John Baird, who's a scholar in some of them, a soldier in some, and a rich playboy in a few. He's always a Hemingway nut, though. He does something that starts off the ripples in '95, '96, '97; depending on which timeline you're in—but I can't seem to get close to it. There's something odd about him, and it doesn't have to do with Hemingway specifically.

But he's definitely causing the eddy?

Has to be him.

All right. Find a meta-causal that all the doom lines have in common, and forget about the others. Then go talk to him.

There'll be resonance—

But who cares? Moot after A.D. 2006.

That's true. I'll hit all the doom lines at once, then: neutralize the meta-causal, then jump ahead and do some spot checks.

Good. And no killing this time.

I understand. But—

You're too close to 2006. Kill the wrong person and the whole thing could unravel.

Well, there are differences of opinion. We would certainly feel it if the world failed to come to an end in those lines.

As you say, differences of opinion. My opinion is that you better not kill anybody or I'll send you back to patrol the fourteenth century again.

Understood. But I can't guarantee that I can neutralize the meta-causal without eliminating John Baird.

Fourteenth century. Some people love it. Others think it was nasty, brutish, and long.


## 7. A Clean, Well-Lighted Place

Most of the sleuthing that makes up literary scholarship takes place in settings either neutral or unpleasant. Libraries' old stacks, attics metaphorical and actual; dust and silverfish, yellowed paper and fading ink. Books and letters that appear in card files but not on shelves.

Hemingway researchers have a haven outside of Boston, the Hemingway Collection at the University of Massachusetts's John F. Kennedy Library. It's a triangular room with one wall dominated by a picture window that looks over Boston Harbor to the sea. Comfortable easy chairs surround a coffee table, but John had never seen them in use; worktables under the picture window provided realistic room for computer and clutter. Skins from animals the Hemingways had dispatched in Africa snarled up from the floor, and one wall was dominated by Hemingway memorabilia and photographs. What made the room Nirvana, though, was row upon row of boxes containing tens of thousands of Xerox pages of Hemingway correspondence, manuscripts, clippings—everything from a boyhood shopping list to all extant versions of every short story and poem and novel.

John liked to get there early so he could claim one of the three computers. He snapped it on, inserted a CD, and typed in his code number. Then he keyed in the database index and started searching.

The more commonly requested items would appear onscreen if you asked for them—whenever someone requested a physical copy of an item, an electronic copy automatically was sent into the database—but most of the things John needed were obscure, and he had to haul down the letterboxes and physically flip through them, just like some poor scholar inhabiting the first nine tenths of the twentieth century.

Time disappeared for him as he abandoned his notes and followed lines of instinct, leaping from letter to manuscript to note to interview, doing what was in essence the opposite of the scholar's job: a scholar would normally be trying to find out what these stories had been about. John instead was trying to track down every reference that might restrict what he himself could write about, simulating the stories.

The most confining restriction was the one he'd first remembered, walking away from the bar where he'd met Castle. The one-paragraph answer that Hadley had given to Carlos Baker about the unfinished novel, that it was a Nick Adams story about hunting and fishing up in Michigan. John didn't know anything about hunting and most of his fishing experience was limited to watching a bobber and hoping it wouldn't go down and break his train of thought.

There was the one story that Hemingway had left unpublished, "Boys and Girls Together," mostly clumsy self-parody. It covered the right period and the right activities, but using it as a source would be sensitive business, tiptoeing through a minefield. Anyone looking for a fake would go straight there. Of course John could go up to the Michigan woods and camp out, see things for himself and try to re-create them in the Hemingway style. Later, though. First order of business was to make sure there was nothing in this huge collection that would torpedo the whole project—some postcard where Hemingway said, "You're going to like this novel because it has a big scene about cleaning fish."

The short stories would be less restricted in subject matter. According to Hemingway, they'd been about growing up in Oak Park and Michigan and the battlefields of Italy.

That made him stop and think. The one dramatic experience he shared with Hemingway was combat—fifty years later, to be sure, in Vietnam, but the basic situations couldn't have changed that much. Terror, heroism, cowardice. The guns and grenades were a little more streamlined, but they did the same things to people. Maybe do a World War I story as a finger exercise, see whether it would be realistic to try a longer growing-up-in-Michigan pastiche.

He made a note to himself about that on the computer, oblique enough not to be damning, and continued the eyestraining job of searching through Hadley's correspondence, trying to find some further reference to the lost novel—damn!

Writing to Ernest's mother, Hadley noted that "the taxi driver broke his typewriter" on the way to the Constantinople conference —did he get it fixed, or just chuck it? A quick check showed that the typeface of his manuscripts did indeed change after July 1924. So they'd never be able to find it. There were typewriters in Hemingway shrines in Key West, Billings, Schruns; the initial plan had been to find which was the old Corona, then locate an identical one and have Castle arrange a swap.

So they would fall back on Plan B. Castle had claimed to be good with mechanical things, and thought if they could find a 1921 Corona, he could tweak the keys around so they would produce a convincing manuscript—lowercase "s" a hair low, "e" a hair high, and so forth.

How he could be so sure of success without ever having seen the inside of a manual typewriter, John did not know. Nor did he have much confidence.

But it wouldn't have to be a perfect simulation, since they weren't out to fool the whole world, but just a few reviewers who would only see two or three Xeroxed pages. He could probably do a close enough job. John put it out of his mind and moved on to the next letter.

But it was an odd coincidence for him to think about Castle at that instant, since Castle was thinking about him. Or at least asking.

## 8. The Coming Man

"How was he when he was younger?"

"He never was younger." She laughed and rolled around inside the compass of his arms to face him. "Than you, I mean. He was in his mid-thirties when we met. You can't be much over twenty-five."

He kissed the end of her nose. "Thirty this year. But I still get carded sometimes."

"I'm a year older than you are. So you have to do anything I say."

"So far so good." He'd checked her wallet when she'd gone into the bathroom to insert the diaphragm, and knew she was thirty-five. "Break out the whips and chains now?"

"Not till next week. Work up to it slowly." She pulled away from him and mopped her front with the sheet. "You're good at being slow."

"I like being asked to come back."

"How 'bout tonight and tomorrow morning?"

"If you feed me lots of vitamins. How long you think he'll be up in Boston?"

"He's got a train ticket for Wednesday. But he said he might stay longer if he got onto something."

Castle laughed. "Or into something. Think he might have a girl up there? Some student like you used to be?"

"That would be funny. I guess it's not impossible." She covered her eyes with the back of her hand. "The wife is always the last to know."

They both laughed. "But I don't think so. He's a sweet guy but he's just not real sexy. I think his students see him as kind of a favorite uncle."

"You fell for him once."

"Uh huh. He had all of his current virtues plus a full head of hair, no pot belly—and, hm, what am I forgetting?"

"He was hung like an elephant?"

"No, I guess it was the millions of dollars. That can be pretty sexy."

## 9. Wanderings

It was a good thing John liked to nose around obscure neighborhoods shopping; you couldn't walk into any old K Mart and pick up a 1921 Corona portable. In fact, you couldn't walk into any typewriter shop in Boston and find one, not any. Nowadays they all sold self-contained word processors, with a few dusty electrics in the back room. A few had fancy manual typewriters from Italy or Switzerland; it had been almost thirty years since the American manufacturers had made a machine that wrote without electronic help.

He had a little better luck with pawnshops. Lots of Smith-Coronas, a few L.C. Smiths, and two actual Coronas that might have been old enough. One had too large a typeface and the other, although the typeface was the same as Hemingway's, was missing a couple of letters: Th quick b own fox jump d ov   th  lazy dog. The challenge of writing a convincing Hemingway novel without using the letters "e" and "r" seemed daunting. He bought the machine anyhow, thinking they might ultimately have two or several broken ones that could be concatenated into one reliable machine.

The old pawnbroker rang up his purchase and made change and slammed the cash drawer shut. "Now you don't look to me like the kind of man who would hold it against a man who . . ." He shrugged. "Well, who sold you something and then suddenly remembered that there was a place with lots of those somethings?"

"Of course not. Business is business."

"I don't know the name of the guy or his shop; I think he calls it a museum. Up in Brunswick, Maine. He's got a thousand old type-writers. He buys, sells, trades. That's the only place I know of you might find one with the missing whatever-you-call-ems."

"Fonts." He put the antique typewriter under his arm—the handle was missing—and shook the old man's hand. "Thanks a lot. This might save me weeks."

With some difficulty John got together packing materials and shipped the machine to Key West, along with Xeroxes of a few dozen pages of Hemingway's typed copy and a note suggesting Castle see what he could do. Then he went to the library and found a Brunswick telephone directory. Under "Office Machines & Supplies" was listed Crazy Tom's Typewriter Museum and Sales Emporium. John rented a car and headed north.

The small town had rolled up its sidewalks by the time he got there. He drove past Crazy Tom's and pulled into the first motel. It had a neon VACANCY sign but the innkeeper had to be roused from a deep sleep. He took John's credit card number and directed him to Room 14 and pointedly turned on the NO sign. There were only two other cars in the motel lot.

John slept late and treated himself to a full "trucker's" breakfast at the local diner: two pork chops and eggs and hash browns. Then he worked off ten calories by walking to the shop.

Crazy Tom was younger than John expected, thirtyish with an unruly shock of black hair. A manual typewriter lay upside down on an immaculate worktable, but most of the place was definitely maculate. Thousands of peanut shells littered the floor. Crazy Tom was eating them compulsively from a large wooden bowl. When he saw John standing in the doorway, he offered some. "Unsalted," he said. "Good for you."

John crunched his way over the peanut-shell carpet. The only light in the place was the bare bulb suspended over the worktable, though two unlit high-intensity lamps were clamped on either side of it. The walls were floor-to-ceiling gloomy shelves holding hundreds of typewriters, mostly black.

"Let me guess," the man said as John scooped up a handful of peanuts. "You're here about a typewriter."

"A specific one. A 1921 Corona portable."

"Ah." He closed his eyes in thought. "Hemingway. His first. Or I guess the first after he started writing. A '27 Corona, now, that'd be Faulkner."

"You get a lot of calls for them?"

"Couple times a year. People hear about this place and see if they can find one like the master used, whoever the master is to them. Sympathetic magic and all that. But you aren't a writer."

"I've had some stories published."

"Yeah, but you look too comfortable. You do something else. Teach school." He looked around in the gloom. "Corona Corona." Then he sang the six syllables to the tune of "Corina, Corina." He walked a few steps into the darkness and returned with a small machine and set it on the table. "Newer than 1920 because of the way it says 'Corona' here. Older than 1927 because of the tab setup." He found a piece of paper and a chair. "Go on, try it."

John typed out a few quick foxes and aids to one's party. The typeface was identical to the one on the machine Hadley had given Hemingway before they'd been married. The up-and-down displacements of the letters were different, of course, but Castle should be able to fix that once he'd practiced with the backup machine.

John cracked a peanut. "How much?"

"What you need it for?"

"Why is that important?"

"It's the only one I got. Rather rent it than sell it." He didn't look like he was lying, trying to push the price up. "A thousand to buy, a hundred a month to rent."

"Tell you what, then. I buy it, and if it doesn't bring me luck, you agree to buy it back at a pro ratum. My one thousand dollars minus ten percent per month."

Crazy Tom stuck out his hand. "Let's have a beer on it."

"Isn't it a little early for that?"

"Not if you eat peanuts all morning." He took two long-necked Budweisers from a cooler and set them on paper towels on the table. "So what kind of stuff you write?"

"Short stories and some poetry." The beer was good after the heavy greasy breakfast. "Nothing you would've seen unless you read magazines like *Iowa Review* and *Triquarterly*."

"Oh yeah. Foldouts of Gertrude Stein and H.D. I might've read your stuff."

"John Baird."

He shook his head. "Maybe. I'm no good with names."

"If you recognized my name from *The Iowa Review* you'd be the first person who ever had."

"I was right about the Hemingway connection?"

"Of course."

"But you don't write like Hemingway for no *Iowa Review*. Short declarative sentences, truly this truly that."

"No, you were right about the teaching, too. I teach Hemingway up at Boston University."

"So that's why the typewriter? Play show and tell with your students?"

"That, too. Mainly I want to write some on it and see how it feels."

From the back of the shop, a third person listened to the conversation with great interest. He, it, wasn't really a "person," though he could look like one: he had never been born and he would never die. But then he didn't really exist, not in the down-home pinch-yourself-ouch! way that you and I do.

In another way, he did *more* than exist, since he could slip back and forth between places you and I don't even have words for.

He was carrying a wand that could be calibrated for heart attack, stroke, or metastasized cancer on one end; the other end induced a kind of aphasia. He couldn't use it unless he materialized. He walked toward the two men, making no crunching sounds on the peanut shells because he weighed less than a thought. He studied John Baird's face from about a foot away.

"I guess it's a mystical thing, though I'm uncomfortable with that word. See whether I can get into his frame of mind."

"Funny thing," Crazy Tom said, "I never thought of him typing out his stories. He was always sitting in some café writing in notebooks, piling up saucers."

"You've read a lot about him?" That would be another reason not to try the forgery. This guy comes out of the woodwork and says, "I sold John Baird a 1921 Corona portable."

"Hell, all I do is read. If I get two customers a day, one of 'em's a mistake and the other just wants directions. I've read all of Hemingway's fiction and most of the journalism and I think all of the poetry. Not just the *Querschnitt* period; the more interesting stuff."

The invisible man was puzzled. Quite obviously John Baird planned some sort of Hemingway forgery. But then he should be growing worried over this man's dangerous expertise. Instead, he was radiating relief.

What course of action, inaction? He could go back a few hours in time and steal this typewriter, though he would have to materialize for that, and it would cause suspicions. And Baird could find another. He could kill one or both of them, now or last week or next, but that would mean duty in the fourteenth century for more than forever—when you exist out of time, a century of unpleasantness is long enough for planets to form and die.

He wouldn't have been drawn to this meeting if it were not a strong causal nexus. There must be earlier ones, since John Baird did not just stroll down a back street in this little town and decide to change history by buying a typewriter. But the earlier ones must be too weak, or something was masking them.

Maybe it was a good timeplace to get John Baird alone and explain things to him. Then use the wand on him. But no, not until he knew exactly what he was preventing. With considerable effort of will and expenditure of something like energy, he froze time at this instant and traveled to a couple of hundred adjacent realities that were all in this same bundle of doomed timelines.

In most of them, Baird was here in Crazy Tom's Typewriter Museum and Sales Emporium. In some, he was in a similar place in New York. In two, he was back in the Hemingway collection. In one, John Baird didn't exist: the whole planet was a lifeless blasted cinder. He'd known about that timeline; it had been sort of a dry run.

"He did both," John then said in most of the timelines. "Sometimes typing, sometimes fountain pen or pencil. I've seen the rough draft of his first novel. Written out in a stack of seven French schoolkids' copybooks." He looked around, memory working. A red herring wouldn't hurt. He'd never come across a reference to any other specific Hemingway typewriter, but maybe this guy had. "You know what kind of machine he used in Key West or Havana?"

Crazy Tom pulled on his chin. "Nope. Bring me a sample of the typing and I might be able to pin it down, though. And I'll keep an eye out—got a card?"

John took out a business card and his checkbook. "Take a check on a Boston bank?"

"Sure. I'd take one on a Tierra del Fuego bank. Who'd stiff you on a seventy-year-old typewriter?" Sylvester Castlemaine might, John thought. "I've had this business almost twenty years," Tom continued. "Not a single bounced check or bent plastic."

"Yeah," John said. "Why would a crook want an old typewriter?" The invisible man laughed and went away.

## 10. Banal Story

```
Dear Lena & Castle,

    Typing this on the new/old machine to give you an idea

about what has to be modified to mimic EH's:

abcdefghijklmnopqrstuvwxyz    ABCDEFGHIJKLMNOPQRSTUVWXYZ

234567890../    "#$%_&'()*?

    Other mechanical things to think about --
```

1.  Paper -- One thing that made people suspicious about
the Hitler forgery is that experts know that old paper smells
old. And of course there was that fatal chemical-composition
error that clinched it.

As we discussed, my first thought was that one of us
would have to go to Paris and nose around  in old attics and
so forth, trying to find either a stack of 75-year-old paper or
an old blank book we could cut pages out of. But in the JFK
Library collection I found out that EH actually did bring some
American-made paper along with him. A lot of the rough draft
of in our time -- written in Paris a year or two after our
"discovery" -- was typed on the back of 6x7" stationery from
his parents' vacation place in Windemere, Xerox enclosed. It
should be pretty easy to duplicate on a hand press, and of
course it will be a lot easier to find 75-year-old American
paper. One complication, unfortunately, is that I haven't
really seen the paper; only a Xerox of the pages. Have to
come up with some pretext to either visit the vault or have
a page brought up, so I can check the color of the ink, mem-
orize the weight and deckle of the paper, check to see how the
edges are cut . . .

I'm starting to sound like a real forger. 'n for a penny,
though, in for a pound. One of the critics who's sent the
fragment might want to see the actual document, and compare it
with the existing Windemere pages.

2.  Inks. This should not be a problem. Here's a recipe

for typewriter ribbon ink from a 1918 book of commercial formulas:

8 oz. lampblack

4 oz. gum arabic

1 quart methylated spirits

That last one is wood alcohol. The others ought to be available in Miami if you can't find them on the Rock.

Aging the ink on the paper gets a little tricky. I haven't been able to find anything about it in the libraries around here; no FORGERY FOR FUN & PROFIT. May check in New York before coming back.

(If we don't find anything, I'd suggest baking it for a few days at a temperature low enough not to greatly affect the paper, and then interleaving it with blank sheets of the old paper and pressing them together for a few days, to restore the old smell, and further absorb the residual ink solvents.)

Toyed with the idea of actually allowing the manuscript to mildew somewhat, but that might get out of hand and actually destroy some of it -- or for all I know we'd be employing a species of mildew that doesn't speak French. Again, thinking like a true forger, which may be a waste of time and effort, but I have to admit is kind of fun. Playing cops and robbers at my age.

Well, I'll call tonight. Miss you, Lena.

Your partner in crime,

John.

## 11. A Divine Gesture

When John returned to his place in Boston, there was a message on his answering machine: "John, this is Nelson Van Nuys. Harry told me you were in town. I left something in your box at the office and I strongly suggest you take it before somebody else does. I'll be out of town for a week, but give me a call if you're here next Friday. You can take me and Doris out to dinner at Panache."

Panache was the most expensive restaurant in Cambridge. Interesting. John checked his watch. He hadn't planned to go to the office, but there was plenty of time to swing by on his way to returning the rental car. The train didn't leave for another four hours.

Van Nuys was a fellow Hemingway scholar and sometime drinking buddy who taught at Brown. What had he brought ninety miles to deliver in person, rather than mail? He was probably just in town and dropped by. But it was worth checking.

No one but the secretary was in the office, noontime, for which John was obscurely relieved. In his box were three interdepartmental memos, a textbook catalog, and a brown cardboard box that sloshed when he picked it up. He took it all back to his office and closed the door.

The office made him feel a little weary, as usual. He wondered whether they would be shuffling people around again this year. The department liked to keep its professors in shape by having them haul tons of books and files up and down the corridor every couple of years.

He glanced at the memos and pitched them, irrelevant since he wasn't teaching in the summer, and put the catalog in his briefcase. Then he carefully opened the cardboard box.

It was a half-pint Jack Daniel's bottle, but it didn't have bourbon in it. A cloudy greenish liquid. John unscrewed the top and with the sharp Pernod tang the memory came back: he and Van Nuys had wasted half an afternoon in Paris years ago, trying to track down a source of true absinthe. So he had finally found some.

Absinthe. Nectar of the gods, ruination of several generations of French artists, students, workingmen—outlawed in 1915 for its addictive and hallucinogenic qualities. Where had Van Nuys found it?

He screwed the top back on tightly and put it back in the box and put the box in his briefcase. If its effect really was all that powerful, you probably wouldn't want to drive under its influence. In Boston traffic, of course, a little lane weaving and a few mild collisions would go unnoticed.

Once he was safely on the train, he'd try a shot or two of it. It couldn't be all that potent. Child of the sixties, John had taken LSD, psilocybin, ecstasy, and peyote, and remembered with complete accuracy the quality of each drug's hallucinations. The effects of absinthe wouldn't be nearly as extreme as its modern successors. But it was probably just as well to try it first in a place where unconsciousness or Steve Allen imitations or speaking in tongues would go unremarked.

He turned in the rental car and took a cab to South Station rather than juggle suitcase, briefcase, and typewriter through the subway system. Once there, he nursed a beer through an hour of the Yankees murdering the Red Sox, and then rented a cart to roll his burden down to Track 3, where a smiling porter installed him aboard the *Silver Meteor*, its range newly extended from Boston to Miami.

He had loved the train since his boyhood in Washington. His mother hated flying and so they often clickety-clacked from place to place in the snug comfort of first-class compartments. Eidetic memory blunted his enjoyment of the modern Amtrak version. This compartment was as large as the ones he had read and done puzzles in, forty years before—amazing and delighting his mother with his proficiency in word games—but the smell of good old leather was gone, replaced by plastic, and the fittings that had been polished brass were chromed steel now. On the middle of the red plastic seat was a Hospitality Pak, a plastic box encased in plastic wrap that contained a wedge of indestructible "cheese food," as if cheese had to eat, a small plastic bottle of cheap California wine, a plastic glass to contain it, and an apple, possibly not plastic.

John hung up his coat and tie in the small closet provided beside where the bed would fold down, and for a few minutes he watched with interest as his fellow passengers and their accompaniment hurried or ambled to their cars. Mostly old people, of course. Enough young ones, John hoped, to keep the trains alive a few decades more.

"Mr. Baird?" John turned to face a black porter, who bowed slightly and favored him with a blinding smile of white and gold. "My name is George, and I will be at your service as far as Atlanta. Is everything satisfactory?"

"Doing fine. But if you could find me a glass made of glass and a couple of ice cubes, I might mention you in my will."

"One minute, sir." In fact, it took less than a minute. That was one aspect, John had to admit, that had improved in recent years: the service on Amtrak in the sixties and seventies had been right up there with Alcatraz and the Hanoi Hilton.

He closed and locked the compartment door and carefully poured about two ounces of the absinthe into the glass. Like Pernod, it turned milky on contact with the ice.

He swirled it around and breathed deeply. It did smell much like Pernod, but with an acrid tang that was probably oil of wormwood. An experimental sip: the wormwood didn't dominate the licorice flavor, but it was there.

"Thanks, Nelson," he whispered, and drank the whole thing in one cold fiery gulp. He set down the glass and the train began to move. For a weird moment that seemed hallucinatory, but it always did, the train starting off so smoothly and silently.

For about ten minutes he felt nothing unusual, as the train did its slow tour of Boston's least attractive backyards. The conductor who checked his ticket seemed like a normal human being, which could have been a hallucination.

John knew that some drugs, like amyl nitrite, hit with a swift slap, while others creep into your mind like careful infiltrators. This was the way of absinthe; all he felt was a slight alcohol buzz, and he was about to take another shot, when it subtly began.

There were *things* just at the periphery of his vision, odd things with substance, but somehow without shape, that of course moved away when he turned his head to look at them. At the same time a whispering began in his ears, just audible over the train noise, but not intelligible, as if in a language he had heard before but not understood. For some reason the effects were pleasant, though of course they could be frightening if a person were not expecting weirdness. He enjoyed the illusions for a few minutes, while the scenery outside mellowed into woodsy suburbs, and the visions and voices stopped rather suddenly.

He poured another ounce and this time diluted it with water. He remembered the sad woman in "Hills Like White Elephants" lamenting that everything new tasted like licorice, and allowed himself to wonder what Hemingway had been drinking when he wrote that curious story.

Chuckling at his own—what? effrontery?—John took out the 1921 Corona and slipped a sheet of paper into it and balanced it on his knees. He had earlier thought of the first two lines of the WWI pastiche; he typed them down and kept going:

```
The dirt on the sides of the trenches was never completely
dry in the morning.  If Nick could find an old newspaper he
would put it between his chest and the dirt when he went out to
lean on the side of the trench and wait for the light.  First
light was the best time.  You might have luck and see a muzzle
flash.  But patience was batter than luck.  Wait to see a hel-
met or a head without a helmet.

     Nick looked at the enemy line through a rectangular box of
wood that went through the trench at about ground level.  The
other end of the box was covered by a square of gauze the color
of dirt.  A person looking directly at it might see the muzzle
flash when Nick fired through the box.  But with luck, the
flash would be the last thing he saw.

     Nick had fired through the gauze six times, perhaps
killing three enemy, and the gauze now had a ragged hole in
the center.
```

Okay, John thought, he'd be able to see slightly better through the hole in the center, but staring that way would reduce the effective field of view, so he would deliberately try to look to one side or the other. How to type that down in a simple way? Someone cleared his throat.

John looked up from the typewriter. Sitting across from him was

Ernest Hemingway, the weathered, wise Hemingway of the famous Karsh photograph.

"I'm afraid you must not do that," Hemingway said.

John looked at the half-full glass of absinthe and looked back. Hemingway was still there. "Jesus Christ," he said.

"It isn't absinthe." Hemingway's image rippled and he became the handsome teenager who had gone to war, the war John was writing about. "I am quite real. In a way, I am more real than you are." As it spoke it aged: the mustachioed leading-man-handsome Hemingway of the twenties; the slightly corpulent, still-magnetic media hero of the thirties and forties; the beard turning white, the features hard and sad and then twisting with impotence and madness, and then a sudden loud report and the cranial vault exploding, the mahogany veneer of the wall splashed with blood and brains and imbedded chips of skull. There was a strong smell of cordite and blood. The almost headless corpse shrugged, spreading its hands. "I can look like anyone I want." The mess disappeared and it became the young Hemingway again.

John slumped and stared.

"This thing you just started must never be finished. This Hemingway pastiche. It will ruin something very important."

"What would it ruin? I'm not even planning to—"

"Your plans are immaterial. If you continue with this project it will profoundly affect the future."

"You're from the future?"

"I'm from the future and the past and other temporalities that you can't comprehend. But all you need to know is that you must not write this Hemingway story. If you do, I or someone like me will have to kill you."

It gestured and a wand the size of a walking stick, half black and half white, appeared in its hand. It tapped John's knee with the white end. There was a slight tingle.

"Now you won't be able to tell anybody about me, or write anything about me down. If you try to talk about me, the memory will disappear—and reappear moments later, along with the knowledge that I will kill you if you don't cooperate." It turned into the bloody corpse again. "Understood?"

"Of course."

"If you behave, you will never have to see me again." It started to fade.

"Wait. What do you really look like?"

"This . . ." For a few seconds John stared at an ebony presence deeper than black, at once points and edges and surfaces and volume and hints of further dimensions. "You can't really see or know," a voice whispered inside his head. He reached into the blackness and jerked his hand back, rimmed with frost and numb. The thing disappeared.

He stuck his hand under his armpit and feeling returned. That last apparition was the unsettling one. He had Hemingway's appearance at every age memorized, and had seen the corpse in the mind's eye often enough. A drug could conceivably have brought them all together and made up this fantastic demand—which might actually be nothing more than a reasonable side of his nature trying to make him stop wasting time on this silly project.

But that thing. His hand was back to normal. Maybe a drug could do that, too, make your hand feel freezing. LSD did more profound things than that. But not while arguing about a manuscript.

He considered the remaining absinthe. Maybe take another big blast of it and see whether ol' Ernie comes back again. Or no—there was a simpler way to check.

The bar was four rocking and rolling cars away, and bouncing his way from wall to window helped sober John up. When he got there, he had another twinge for the memories of the past. Stained Formica tables. No service; you had to go to a bar at the other end. Acrid with cigarette fumes. He remembered linen tablecloths and endless bottles of Coke with the names of cities from everywhere stamped on the bottom and, when his father came along with them, the rich sultry smoke of his Havanas. The fat Churchills from *Punch* that emphysema stopped just before Castro could. "A Coke, please." He wondered which depressed him more, the red can or the plastic cup with miniature ice cubes.

The test. It was not in his nature to talk to strangers on public conveyances. But this was necessary. There was a man sitting alone who looked about John's age, a Social Security–bound hippie with wire-rimmed John Lennon glasses, white hair down to his shoulders, bushy gray beard. He nodded when John sat down across from him, but didn't say anything. He sipped beer and looked blankly out at the gathering darkness.

"Excuse me," John said, "but I have a strange thing to ask you."

The man looked at him. "I don't mind strange things. But please don't try to sell me anything illegal."

"I wouldn't. It may have something to do with a drug, but it would be one I took."

"You do look odd. You tripping?"

"Doesn't feel like it. But I may have been . . . slipped something." He leaned back and rubbed his eyes. "I just talked to Ernest Hemingway."

"The writer?"

"In my roomette, yeah."

"Wow. He must be pretty old."

"He's dead! More than thirty years."

"Oh wow. Now that is something weird. What he say?"

"You know what a pastiche is?"

"French pastry?"

"No, it's when you copy . . . when you create an imitation of another person's writing. Hemingway's, in this case."

"Is that legal? I mean, with him dead and all."

"Sure it is, as long as you don't try to foist it off as Hemingway's real stuff."

"So what happened? He wanted to help you with it?"

"Actually, no . . . he said I'd better stop."

"Then you better stop. You don't fuck around with ghosts." He pointed at the old brass bracelet on John's wrist. "You in the 'Nam."

" 'Sixty-eight," John said. "Hue."

"Then you oughta know about ghosts. You don't fuck with ghosts."

"Yeah." What he'd thought was aloofness in the man's eyes, the set of his mouth, was aloneness, something slightly different. "You okay?"

"Oh yeah. Wasn't for a while, then I got my shit together." He looked out the window again, and said something weirdly like Hemingway: "I learned to take it a day at a time. The day you're in's the only day that's real. The past is shit and the future, hell, some day your future's gonna be that you got no future. So fuck it, you know? One day at a time."

John nodded. "What outfit were you in?"

"Like I say, man, the past is shit. No offense?"

"No, that's okay." He poured the rest of his Coke over the ice and stood up to go.

"You better talk to somebody about those ghosts. Some kinda shrink, you know? It's not that they're not real. But just you got to deal with 'em."

"Thanks. I will." John got a little more ice from the barman and negotiated his way down the lurching corridor back to his compartment, trying not to spill his drink while also juggling fantasy, reality, past, present, memory . . .

He opened the door and Hemingway was there, drinking his absinthe. He looked up with weary malice. "Am I going to have to kill you?"

What John did next would have surprised Castlemaine, who thought he was a nebbish. He closed the compartment door and sat down across from the apparition. "Maybe you can kill me and maybe you can't."

"Don't worry. I can."

"You said I wouldn't be able to talk to anyone about you. But I just walked down to the bar car and did."

"I know. That's why I came back."

"So if one of your powers doesn't work, maybe another doesn't. At any rate, if you kill me you'll never find out what went wrong."

"That's very cute, but it doesn't work." It finished off the absinthe and then ran a finger around the rim of the glass, which refilled out of nowhere. "You're making assumptions about causality that are necessarily naïve, because you can't perceive even half of the dimensions that you inhabit."

"Nevertheless, you haven't killed me yet."

"And assumptions about my 'psychology' that are absurd. I am no more a human being than you are a paramecium."

"I'll accept that. But I would make a deal with a paramecium if I thought I could gain an advantage from it."

"What could you possibly have to deal with, though?"

"I know something about myself that you evidently don't, that enables me to overcome your don't-talk restriction. Knowing that might be worth a great deal to you."

"Maybe something."

"What I would like in exchange is, of course, my life, and an explanation of why I must not do the Hemingway pastiche. Then I wouldn't do it."

"You wouldn't do it if I killed you, either."

John sipped his Coke and waited.

"All right. It goes something like this. There is not just one universe, but actually uncountable zillions of them. They're all roughly the same size and complexity as this one, and they're all going off in a zillion different directions, and it is one hell of a job to keep things straight."

"You do this by yourself? You're God?"

"There's not just one of me. In fact, it would be meaningless to assign a number to us, but I guess you could say that altogether, we are God . . . and the Devil, and the Cosmic Puppet Master, and the Grand Unification Theory, the Great Pumpkin, and everything else. When we consider ourselves as a group, let me see, I guess a human translation of our name would be the Spacio-Temporal Adjustment Board."

"STAB?"

"I guess that is unfortunate. Anyhow, what STAB does is more the work of a scalpel than a knife." The Hemingway scratched its nose, leaving the absinthe suspended in midair. "Events are supposed to happen in certain ways, in certain sequences. You look at things happening and say cause-and-effect, or coincidence, or golly, that couldn't have happened in a million years—but you don't even have a clue. Don't even try to think about it. It's like an ant trying to figure out general relativity."

"It wouldn't have a clue. Wouldn't know where to start."

The apparition gave him a sharp look and continued. "These universes come in bundles. Hundreds of them, thousands, that are pretty much the same. And they affect each other. Resonate with each other. When something goes wrong in one, it resonates and screws up all of them."

"You mean to say that if I write a Hemingway pastiche, hundreds of universes are going to go straight to hell?"

The apparition spread its hands and looked to the ceiling. "Nothing is simple. The only thing that's simple is that nothing is simple.

"I'm a sort of literature specialist. American literature of the nineteenth and twentieth centuries. Usually. Most of my timespace is taken up with guys like Hemingway, Teddy Roosevelt, Heinlein, Bierce. Crane, Spillane, Twain."

"Not William Dean Howells?"

"Not him or James or Carver or Coover or Cheever or any of those guys. If everybody gave me as little trouble as William Dean Howells I could spend most of my timespace on a planet where the fishing was good."

"Masculine writers?" John said. "But not all hairy-chested macho types."

"I'll give you an A-minus on that one. They're writers who have an accumulating effect on the masculine side of the American national character. There's no one word for it, though it is a specific thing: individualistic, competence-worshiping, short-term optimism and long-term existentialism. 'There may be nothing after I die but I sure as hell will do the job right while I'm here, even though I'm surrounded by idiots.' You see the pattern?"

"Okay. And I see how Hemingway fits in. But how could writing a pastiche interfere with it?"

"That's a limitation I have. I don't know specifically. I do know that the accelerating revival of interest in Hemingway from the seventies through the nineties is vitally important. In the Soviet Union as well as the United States. For some reason, I can feel your pastiche interfering with it." He stretched out the absinthe glass into a yard-long amber crystal, and it changed into the black-and-white cane. The glass reappeared in the drink holder by the window. "Your turn."

"You won't kill me after you hear what I have to say?"

"No. Go ahead."

"Well . . . I have an absolutely eidetic memory. Everything I've ever seen—or smelled or tasted or heard or touched, or even dreamed—I can instantly recall.

"Every other memory freak I've read about was limited—numbers, dates, calendar tricks, historical details—and most of them were idiot savants. I have at least normal intelligence. But from the age of about three, I have never forgotten anything."

The Hemingway smiled congenially. "Thank you. That's exactly it." It fingered the black end of the cane, clicking something. "If you had the choice, would you rather die of a heart attack, stroke, or cancer?"

"That's it?" John said. The Hemingway nodded. "Well, you're human enough to cheat. To lie."

"It's not something you could understand. Stroke?"

"It might not work."

"We're going to find out right now." The Hemingway lowered the cane.

"Wait! What's death? Is there . . . anything I should do, anything you know?"

The rod stopped, poised an inch over John's knee. "I guess you just end. Is that so bad?"

"Compared to not ending, it's bad."

"That shows how little you know. I and the ones like me can never die. If you want something to occupy your last moment, your last thought, you might pity me."

John stared straight into its eyes. "Fuck you."

The cane dropped. A fireball exploded in his head.

### 12. Marriage is a Dangerous Game

"We'll blackmail him." Castle and Lena were together in the big antique bathtub, in a sea of pink foam, her back against his chest.

"Sure," she said. " 'If you don't let us pass this manuscript off as the real thing, we'll tell everybody you faked it.' Something wrong with that, but I can't quite put my finger on it."

"Here, I'll put mine on it."

She giggled. "Later. What do you mean, blackmail?"

"Got it all figured out. I've got this friend Pansy, she used to be a call girl. Been out of the game seven, eight years; still looks like a million bucks."

"Sure. We fix John up with this hooker—"

"Call girl isn't a hooker. We're talkin' class."

"In the first place, John wouldn't pay for sex. He did that in Vietnam and it still bothers him."

"Not talkin' about pay. Talkin' about fallin' in love. While she meanwhile fucks his eyeballs out."

"You have such a turn of phrase, Sylvester. Then while his eyeballs are out, you come in with a camera."

"Yeah, but you're about six steps ahead."

"Okay, step two; how do we get them together? Church social?"

"She moves in next door." There was another upstairs apartment, unoccupied. "You and me and Julio are conveniently somewhere else when she shows up with all these boxes and that big flight of stairs."

"Sure, John would help her. But that's his nature; he'd help her if she were an ugly old crone with leprosy. Carry a few boxes, sit down for a cup of coffee, maybe. But not jump into the sack."

"Okay, you know John." His voice dropped to a husky whisper and he cupped her breasts. "But I know men, and I know Pansy . . . and Pansy could give a hard-on to a corpse."

"Sure, and then fuck his eyeballs out. They'd come out easier."

"What?"

"Never mind. Go ahead."

"Well . . . look. Do you know what a call girl does?"

"I suppose you call her up and say you've got this eyeball problem."

"Enough with the eyeballs. What she does, she works for an escort service. That part of it's legal. Guy comes into town, business or maybe on vacation, he calls up the service and they ask what kind of companion he'd like. If he says, like, give me some broad with a tight ass, can suck the chrome off a bumper hitch, they say, like, 'I'm sorry, sir, but this is not that kind of service.' But mostly the customers are pretty hip to it, they say, oh, a pretty young blonde who likes to go dancing."

"Meanwhile they're thinking about bumper hitches and eyeballs."

"You got it. So it starts out just like a date, just the guy pays the escort service like twenty bucks for getting them together. Still no law broken."

"Now about one out of three, four times, that's it. The guy knows what's going on, but he don't get up the nerve to ask, or he really doesn't know the score, and it's like a real dull date. I don't think that happened much with Pansy."

"In the normal course of things, though, the subject of bumper hitches comes up."

"Uh huh, but not from Pansy. The guy has to pop the question. That way if he's a cop it's, what, entrapment."

"Do you know whether Pansy ever got busted?"

"Naw. Mainly the cops just shake down the hookers, just want a blow job anyhow. This town, half of 'em want a blow job from guys.

"So they pop the question and Pansy blushes and says, for you, I guess I could. Then, on the way to the motel or wherever she says, you know, I wouldn't ask this if we weren't such good friends, but I got to make a car payment by tomorrow, and I need like two hundred bucks before noon tomorrow."

"And she takes MasterCard and Visa."

"No, but she sure as hell knows where every bank machine in town is. She even writes up an IOU." Castle laughed. "Told me a guy from Toledo's holdin' five grand of IOUs from her."

"All right, but that's not John. She could suck the chrome off his eyeballs and he still wouldn't be interested in her if she didn't know Hemingway from hummingbirds."

Castle licked behind her ear, a weird gesture that made her shiver. "That's the trump card. Pansy reads like a son of a bitch. She's got like a thousand books. So this morning I called her up and asked about Hemingway."

"And?"

"She's read them all."

She nodded slowly. "Not bad, Sylvester. So we promote this love affair and sooner or later you catch them in the act. Threaten to tell me unless John accedes to a life of crime."

"Think it could work? He wouldn't say, hell, go ahead and tell her?"

"Not if I do my part . . . starting tomorrow. I'm the best, sweetest, lovingest wife in this sexy town. Then in a couple of weeks Pansy comes into his life, and there he is, luckiest man alive. Best of both worlds. Until you accidentally catch them *in flagrante delicioso.*"

"So to keep both of you, he goes along with me."

"It might just do it. It might just." She slowly levered herself out of the water and smoothed the suds off her various assets.

"Nice."

"Bring me that bumper hitch, Sylvester. Hold on to your eyeballs."

## 13. In Another Country

John woke up with a hangover of considerable dimension. The diluted glass of absinthe was still in the drink holder by the window. It was just past dawn, and a verdant forest rushed by outside. The rails made a steady hum; the car had a slight rocking that would have been pleasant to a person who felt well.

A porter knocked twice and inquired after Mr. Baird. "Come in," John said. A short white man, smiling, brought in coffee and Danish.

"What happened to George?"

"Pardon me, sir? George who?"

John rubbed his eyes. "Oh, of course. We must be past Atlanta."

"No, sir." The man's smile froze as his brain went into nutty-passenger mode. "We're at least two hours from Atlanta."

"George . . . is a tall black guy with gold teeth who—"

"Oh, you mean George Mason, sir. He does do this car, but he picks up the train in Atlanta, and works it to Miami and back. He hasn't had the northern leg since last year."

John nodded slowly and didn't ask what year it was. "I understand." He smiled up and read the man's name tag. "I'm sorry, Leonard. Not at my best in the morning." The man withdrew with polite haste.

Suppose that weird dream had not been a dream. The Hemingway creature had killed him—the memory of the stroke was awesomely strong and immediate—but all that death amounted to was slipping into another universe where George Mason was on a different shift. Or perhaps John had gone completely insane.

The second explanation seemed much more reasonable.

On the tray underneath the coffee, juice, and Danish was a copy of *USA Today*, a paper John normally avoided because, although it had its comic aspects, it didn't have any funnies. He checked the date, and it was correct. The news stories were plausible—wars and rumors of war—so at least he hadn't slipped into a dimension where Martians ruled an enslaved Earth or Barry Manilow was president. He turned to the weather map and stopped dead.

Yesterday the country was in the middle of a heat wave that had lasted weeks. It apparently had ended overnight. The entry for Boston, yesterday, was "72/58/sh." But it hadn't rained and the temperature had been in the nineties.

He went back to the front page and began checking news stories. He didn't normally pay much attention to the news, though, and hadn't seen a paper in several days. They'd canceled their *Globe* delivery for the six weeks in Key West, and he hadn't been interested enough to go seek out a newsstand.

There was no mention of the garbage collectors' strike in New York; he'd overheard a conversation about that yesterday. A long obituary for a rock star he was sure had died the year before.

An ad for DeSoto automobiles. That company had gone out of business when he was a teenager.

Bundles of universes, different from each other in small ways. Instead of dying, or maybe because of dying, he had slipped into another one. What would be waiting for him in Key West?

Maybe John Baird.

He set the tray down and hugged himself, trembling. Who or what was he in this universe? All of his memories, all of his personality, were from the one he had been born in. What happened to the John Baird that was born in this one? Was he an associate professor in American Literature at Boston University? Was he down in Key West wrestling with a paper to give at Nairobi—or working on a forgery? Or was he a Fitzgerald specialist snooping around the literary attics of St. Paul, Minnesota?

The truth came suddenly. Both John Bairds were in this compartment, in this body. And the body was slightly different.

He opened the door to the small washroom and looked in the mirror. His hair was a little shorter, less gray, beard better trimmed.

He was less paunchy and . . . something felt odd. There was feeling in his thigh. He lowered his pants and there was no scar where the sniper bullet had opened his leg and torn up the nerves there.

That was the touchstone. As he raised his shirt, the parallel memory flooded in. Puckered round scar on the abdomen; in this universe the sniper had hit a foot higher—and instead of the convalescent center in Cam Ranh Bay, the months of physical therapy and then back into the war, it had been peritonitis raging; surgery in Saigon and Tokyo and Walter Reed, and no more army.

But slowly they converged again. Amherst and U. Mass—perversely using the G.I. Bill in spite of his access to millions—the doctorate on *The Sun Also Rises* and the instructorship at BU, meeting Lena and virtuously waiting until after the semester to ask her out. Sex on the second date, and the third . . . but there they verged again. This John Baird hadn't gone back into combat to have his midsection sprayed with shrapnel from an American grenade that bounced off a tree; never had dozens of bits of metal cut out of his dick—and in the ensuing twenty-five years had made more use of it. Girlfriends and even one disastrous homosexual encounter with a stranger. As far as he knew, Lena was in the dark about this side of him; thought that he had remained faithful other than one incident seven years after they married. He knew of one affair she had had with a colleague, and suspected more.

The two Johns' personalities and histories merged, separate but one, like two vines from a common root, climbing a single support.

Schizophrenic but not insane.

John looked into the mirror and tried to address his new or his old self—John A, John B. There were no such people. There was suddenly a man who had existed in two separate universes, and, in a way, it was no more profound than having lived in two separate houses.

The difference being that nobody else knows there is more than one house.

He moved over to the window and set his coffee in the holder; picked up the absinthe glass and sniffed it, considered pouring it down the drain, but then put it in the other holder, for possible future reference.

Posit this: is it more likely that there are bundles of parallel universes prevailed over by a Hemingway lookalike with a magic cane, or that John Baird was exposed to a drug that he had never experienced before and it had had an unusually disorienting effect?

He looked at the paper. He had not hallucinated two weeks of drought. The rock star had been dead for some time. He had not seen a DeSoto in twenty years, and that was a hard car to miss. Tailfins that had to be registered as lethal weapons.

But maybe if you take a person who remembers every trivial thing, and zap his brain with oil of wormwood, that is exactly the effect: perfectly recalled things that never actually happened.

The coffee tasted repulsive. John put on a fresh shirt and decided not to shave and headed for the bar car. He bought the last imported beer in the cooler and sat down across from the long-haired white-bearded man, who had an earring that had either escaped his notice before or not existed in the other universe.

The man was staring out at the forest greening by. "Morning," John said.

"How do." The man looked at him with no sign of recognition.

"Did we talk last night?"

He leaned forward. "What?"

"I mean did we sit in this car last night and talk about Hemingway and Vietnam and ghosts?"

He laughed. "You're on somethin', man. I been on this train since two in the mornin' and ain't said boo to nobody but the bartender."

"You were in Vietnam?"

"Yeah, but that's over; that's shit." He pointed at John's bracelet. "What, you got ghosts from over there?"

"I think maybe I have."

He was suddenly intense. "Take my advice, man; I been there. You got to go talk to somebody. Some shrink. Those ghosts ain't gonna go 'way by themself."

"It's not that bad."

"It ain't the ones you killed." He wasn't listening. "Fuckin' dinks, they come back but they don't, you know, they just stand around." He looked at John and tears came so hard they actually spurted from his eyes. "It's your fuckin' friends, man, they all died and they come back now . . ." He took a deep breath and wiped his face. "They used to come back every night. That like you?" John shook his head, helpless, trapped by the man's grief. "Every fuckin' night, my old lady, finally she said, you go to a shrink or go to hell." He fumbled with the button on his shirt pocket and took out a brown plastic prescription bottle and stared at the label. He shook out a capsule. "Take a swig?" John pushed the beer over to him. He washed the pill down without touching the bottle to his lips.

He sagged back against the window. "I musta not took the pill last night, sometimes I do that. Sorry." He smiled weakly. "One day at a time, you know? You get through the one day. Fuck the rest. Sorry." He leaned forward again suddenly and put his hand on John's wrist. "You come outta nowhere and I lay my fuckin' trip on you. You don' need it."

John covered the hand with his own. "Maybe I do need it. And maybe I didn't come out of nowhere." He stood up. "I will see somebody about the ghosts. Promise."

"You'll feel better. It's no fuckin' cure-all but you'll feel better."

"Want the beer?"

He shook his head. "Not supposed to."

"Okay." John took the beer and they waved at each other and he started back.

He stopped in the vestibule between cars and stood in the rattling roar of it, looking out the window at the flashing green blur. He put his forehead against the cool glass and hid the blur behind the dark red of his eyelids.

Were there actually a zillion of those guys each going through a slightly different private hell? Something he rarely asked himself was, "What would Ernest Hemingway have done in this situation?"

He'd probably have had the sense to leave it to Milton.

## 14. The Dangerous Summer

Castle and Lena met him at the station in Miami and they drove back to Key West in Castle's old pickup. The drone of the air conditioner held conversation to a minimum, but it kept them cool, at least from the knees down.

John didn't say anything about his encounter with the infinite, or transfinite, not wishing to bring back that fellow with the cane just yet. He did note that the two aspects of his personality hadn't quite become equal partners yet, and small details of this world kept surprising him. There was a monorail being built down to Pigeon Key, where Disney was digging an underwater park. Gasoline stations still sold Regular. Castle's car radio picked up TV as well as AM/FM, but sound only.

Lena sat between the two men and rubbed up against John affectionately. That would have been remarkable for John-one and somewhat unusual for John-two. It was a different Lena here, of course; one who had had more of a sex life with John, but there was something more than that, too. She was probably sleeping with Castle, he thought, and the extra attention was a conscious or unconscious compensation, or defense.

Castle seemed a little harder and more serious in this world than the last, not only from his terse moodiness in the pickup, but from recollections of parallel conversations. John wondered how shady he actually was; whether he'd been honest about his police record.

(He hadn't been. In this universe, when Lena had asked him whether he had ever been in trouble with the police, he'd answered a terse "no." In fact, he'd done eight hard years in Ohio for an armed robbery he hadn't committed—the real robber hadn't been so stupid, here—and he'd come out of prison bitter, angry, an actual criminal. Figuring the world owed him one, a week after getting out he stopped for a hitchhiker on a lonely country road, pulled a gun, walked him a few yards off the road into a field of high corn, and shot him point-blank at the base of the skull. It didn't look anything like the movies.)

(He drove off without touching the body, which a farmer's child found two days later. The victim turned out to be a college student who was on probation for dealing—all he'd really done was buy a kilo of green and make his money back by selling bags to his friends, and one enemy—so the papers said DRUG DEALER FOUND SLAIN IN GANGLAND-STYLE KILLING and the police pursued the matter with no enthusiasm. Castle was in Key West well before the farmer's child smelled the body, anyhow.)

As they rode along, whatever Lena had or hadn't done with Castle was less interesting to John than what *he* was planning to do with her. Half of his self had never experienced sex, as an adult, without the sensory handicaps engendered by scar tissue and severed nerves in the genitals, and he was looking forward to the experience with a relish that was obvious, at least to Lena. She encouraged him in not-so-subtle ways, and by the time they crossed the last bridge into Key West, he was ready to tell Castle to pull over at the first bush.

He left the typewriter in Castle's care and declined help with the luggage. By this time Lena was smiling at his obvious impatience; she was giggling by the time they were momentarily stalled by a truculent door key; laughed her delight as he carried her charging across the room to the couch, then clawing off a minimum of clothing and taking her with fierce haste, wordless, and keeping her on a breathless edge he drifted the rest of the clothes off her and carried her into the bedroom, where they made so much noise Julio banged on the ceiling with a broomstick.

They did quiet down eventually, and lay together in a puddle of mingled sweat, panting, watching the fan push the humid air around. "Guess we both get to sleep in the wet spot," John said.

"No complaints." She raised up on one elbow and traced a figure eight on his chest. "You're full of surprises tonight, Dr. Baird."

"Life is full of surprises."

"You should go away more often—or at least come back more often."

"It's all that Hemingway research. Makes a man out of you."

"You didn't learn this in a book," she said, gently taking his penis and pantomiming a certain motion.

"I did, though; an anthropology book." In another universe. "It's what they do in the Solomon Islands."

"Wisdom of Solomon," she said, lying back. After a pause: "They have anthropology books at JFK?"

"Uh, no." He remembered he didn't own that book in this universe. "Browsing at Wordsworth's."

"Hope you bought the book."

"Didn't have to." He gave her a long slow caress. "Memorized the good parts."

■ ■ ■

On the other side of town, six days later, she was in about the same position on Castle's bed, and even more exhausted.

"Aren't you overdoing the loving little wifey bit? It's been a week."

She exhaled audibly. "What a week."

"Missed you." He nuzzled her and made an unsubtle preparatory gesture.

"No, you don't." She rolled out of bed. "Once is plenty." She went to the mirror and ran a brush through her damp hair. "Besides, it's not me you missed. You missed *it*." She sat at the open window, improving the neighborhood's scenery. "*It*'s gonna need a Teflon lining installed."

"Old boy's feelin' his oats?"

"Not feeling *his* anything. God, I don't know what's gotten into him. Four, five times a day; six."

"Screwed, blewed, and tattooed. You asked for it."

"As a matter of fact, I didn't. I haven't had a chance to start my little act. He got off that train with an erection, and he still has it. No woman would be safe around him. Nothing wet and concave would be safe."

"So does that mean it's a good time to bring in Pansy? Or is he so stuck on you he wouldn't even notice her?"

She scowled at the brush, picking hair out of it. "Actually, Castle, I was just about to ask you the same thing. Relying on your well-known expertise in animal behavior."

"Okay." He sat up. "I say we oughta go for it. If he's a walkin' talkin' hard-on like you say . . . Pansy'd pull him like a magnet. You'd have to be a fuckin' monk not to want Pansy."

"Like Rasputin."

"Like who?"

"Never mind." She went back to the brush. "I guess, I guess one problem is that I really am enjoying the attention. I guess I'm not too anxious to hand him over to this champion sexpot."

"Aw, Lena—"

"Really. I do love him in my way, Castle. I don't want to lose him over this scheme."

"You're not gonna lose him. Trust me. You catch him dickin' Pansy, get mad, forgive him. Hell, you'll have him wrapped around your finger."

"I guess. You make the competition sound pretty formidable."

"Don't worry. She's outta there the next day."

"Unless she winds up in love with him. That would be cute."

"He's almost twice her age. Besides, she's a whore. Whores don't fall in love."

"They're women, Castle. Women fall in love."

"Yeah, sure. Just like on TV."

She turned away from him; looked out the window. "You really know how to make a woman feel great, you know?"

"Come on." He crossed over and smoothed her hair. She turned around but didn't look up. "Don't run yourself down, Lena. You're still one hell of a piece of ass."

"Thanks." She smiled into his leer and grabbed him. "If you weren't such a poet I'd trade you in for a vibrator."

## 15. In Praise of His Mistress

Pansy was indeed beautiful, even under normal conditions: delicate features, wasp waist combined with generous secondary sexual characteristics. The conditions under which John first saw her were calculated to maximize sexiness and vulnerability. Red nylon running shorts, tight and very short, and a white sleeveless T-shirt from a local bar that was stamped LAST HETEROSEXUAL IN KEY WEST—all clinging to her golden skin with a healthy sweat, the cloth made translucent enough to reveal no possibility of underwear.

John looked out the screen door and saw her at the other door, struggling with a heavy box while trying to make the key work. "Let me help you," he said through the screen, and stepped across the short landing to hold the box while she got the door open.

"You're too kind." John tried not to stare as he handed the box back. Pansy, of course, was relieved at his riveted attention. It had taken days to set up this operation, and would take more days to bring it to its climax, so to speak, and more days to get back to normal. But she did owe Castle a big favor and this guy seemed nice enough. Maybe she'd learn something about Hemingway in the process.

"More to come up?" John asked.

"Oh, I couldn't ask you to help. I can manage."

"It's okay. I was just goofing off for the rest of the day."

It turned out to be quite a job, even though there was only one load from a small rented truck. Most of the load was uniform and heavy boxes of books, carefully labeled LIT A-B, GEN REF, ENCY 1-12, and so forth. Most of her furniture, accordingly, was cinder blocks and boards, the standard student bookshelf arrangement.

John found out that despite a couple of dozen boxes marked LIT, Pansy hadn't majored in literature, but rather Special Education; during the school year, she taught third grade at a school for the retarded in Key Largo. She didn't tell him about the several years she'd spent as a call girl, but if she had, John might have seen a connection that Castle would never have made—that the driving force behind both of the jobs was the same, charity. The more-or-less easy forty dollars an hour for going on a date and then having sex was a factor, too, but she really did like making lonely men feel special, and had herself felt more like a social worker than a woman of easy virtue.

And the hundreds of men who had fallen for her, for love or money, weren't responding only to her cheerleader's body. She had a sunny disposition and a natural, artless way of concentrating on a man that made him for a while the only man in the world.

John would not normally be an easy conquest. Twenty years of facing classrooms full of coeds had given him a certain wariness around attractive young women. He also had an impulse toward faithfulness, Lena having suddenly left town, her father ill. But he was still in the grip of the weird overweening horniness that had animated him since inheriting this new body and double-image personality. If Pansy had said, "Let's do it," they would be doing it so soon that she would be wise to unwrap the condom before speaking. But she was being as indirect as her nature and mode of dress would allow.

"Do you and your wife always come down here for the summer?"

"We usually go somewhere. Boston's no fun in the heat."

"It must be wonderful in the fall."

And so forth. It felt odd for Pansy, probably the last time she would ever seduce a man for reasons other than personal interest. She wanted it to be perfect. She wanted John to have enough pleasure in her to compensate for the embarrassment of their "accidental" exposure, and whatever hassle his wife would put him through afterwards.

She was dying to know why Castle wanted him set up, but he refused to tell. How Castle ever met a quiet, kindly gentleman like John was a mystery, too—she had met some of Castle's friends, and they had other virtues.

Quiet and kindly, but horny. Whenever she contrived, in the course of their working together, to expose a nipple or a little beaver, he would turn around to adjust himself, and blush. More like a teenager, discovering his sexuality, than a middle-aged married man.

He was a pushover, but she didn't want to make it too easy. After they had finished putting the books up on shelves, she said thanks a million; I gotta go now, spending the night house-sitting up in Islamorada. You and your wife come over for dinner tomorrow? Oh, then come on over yourself. No, that's all right, I'm a big girl. Roast beef okay? See ya.

Driving away in the rented truck, Pansy didn't feel especially proud of herself. She was amused at John's sexiness and looking forward to trying it out. But she could read people pretty well, and sensed a core of deep sadness in John. Maybe it was from Vietnam; he hadn't mentioned it, but she knew what the bracelet meant.

Whatever the problem, maybe she'd have time to help him with it—before she had to turn around and add to it.

Maybe it would work out for the best. Maybe the problem was with his wife, and she'd leave, and he could start over . . .

Stop kidding yourself. Just lay the trap, catch him, deliver him. Castle was not the kind of man you want to disappoint.

## 16. Fiesta

She had baked the roast slowly with wine and fruit juice, along with dried apricots and apples plumped in port wine, seasoned with cinnamon and nutmeg and cardamom. Onions and large cubes of acorn squash simmered in the broth. She served new potatoes steamed with parsley and dressed Italian style, with garlicky olive oil and a splash of vinegar. Small Caesar salad and air-light *pan de agua*, the Cuban bread that made you forget every other kind of bread.

The way to a man's heart, her mother had contended, was through his stomach, and although she was accustomed to aiming rather lower, she thought it was probably a good approach for a longtime married man suddenly forced to fend for himself. That was exactly right for John. He was not much of a cook but he was an accomplished eater.

He pushed the plate away after three helpings. "God, I'm such a pig. But that was irresistible."

"Thank you." She cleared the table slowly, accepting John's offer to help. "My mother's 'company' recipe. So you think Hadley might have just thrown the stories away, and made up the business about the train?"

"People have raised the possibility. There she was, eight years older than this handsome hubby—with half the women on the Left Bank after him, at least in her mind—and he's starting to get published, starting to build a reputation . . ."

"She was afraid he was going to 'grow away' from her? Or did they have that expression back then?"

"I think she was afraid he would start making money from his writing. She had an inheritance, a trust fund from her grandfather,

that paid over two thousand a year. That was plenty to keep the two
of them comfortable in Paris. Hemingway talked poor in those days,
starving artist, but he lived pretty well."

"He probably resented it, too. Not making the money himself."

"That would be like him. Anyhow, if she chucked the stories to
ensure his dependency, it backfired. He was still furious thirty years
later—three wives later. He said the stuff had been 'fresh from the
mint,' even if the writing wasn't so great, and he was never able to
reclaim it."

She opened a cabinet and slid a bottle out of its burlap bag, and
selected two small glasses."Sherry?" He said why not? and they moved
into the living room.

The living room was mysteriously devoid of chairs, so they had
to sit together on the small couch. "You don't actually think she did
it."

"No." John watched her pour the sherry. "From what I've read
about her, she doesn't seem at all calculating. Just a sweet gal from
St. Louis who fell in love with a cad."

"Cad. Funny old-fashioned word."

John shrugged. "Actually, he wasn't really a cad. I think he sincerely loved every one of his wives . . . at least until he married them."

They both laughed. "Of course it could have been something in
between," Pansy said. "I mean, she didn't actually throw away the
manuscripts, but she did leave them sitting out, begging to be stolen.
Why did she leave the compartment?"

"That's one screwy aspect of it. Hadley herself never said, not on
paper. Every biographer seems to come up with a different reason:
she went to get a newspaper, she saw some people she recognized
and stepped out to talk with them, wanted some exercise before the
long trip . . . even Hemingway had two different versions—she went
out to get a bottle of Evian water or to buy something to read. That
one pissed him off, because she did have an overnight bag full of the
best American writing since Mark Twain."

"How would you have felt?"

"Felt?"

"I mean, you say you've written stories, too. What if somebody,
your wife, made a mistake and you lost everything?"

He looked thoughtful. "It's not the same. In the first place, it's just a hobby with me. And I don't have that much that hasn't been published—when Hemingway lost it, he lost it for good. I could just go to a university library and make new copies of everything."

"So you haven't written much lately?"

"Not stories. Academic stuff."

"I'd love to read some of your stories."

"And I'd love to have you read them. But I don't have any here. I'll mail you some from Boston."

She nodded, staring at him with a curious intensity. "Oh hell," she said, and turned her back to him. "Would you help me with this?"

"What?"

"The zipper." She was wearing a clingy white summer dress. "Undo the zipper a little bit."

He slowly unzipped it a few inches. She did it the rest of the way, stood up and hooked her thumbs under the shoulder straps and shrugged. The dress slithered to the floor. She wasn't wearing anything else.

"You're blushing." Actually, he was doing a good imitation of a beached fish. She straddled him, sitting back lightly on his knees, legs wide, and started unbuttoning his shirt.

"Uh," he said.

"I just get impatient. You don't mind?"

"Uh . . . no?"

## 17. On Being Shot Again

John woke up happy but didn't open his eyes for nearly a minute, holding on to the erotic dream of the century. Then he opened one eye and saw it hadn't been a dream: the tousled bed in the strange room, unguents and sex toys on the nightstand, the smell of her hair on the other pillow. A noise from the kitchen; coffee and bacon smells.

He put on pants and went into the living room to pick up the shirt where it had dropped. "Good morning, Pansy."

"Morning, stranger." She was wearing a floppy terry-cloth bathrobe with the sleeves rolled up to her elbows. She turned the bacon carefully with a fork. "Scrambled eggs okay?"

"Marvelous." He sat down at the small table and poured himself a cup of coffee. "I don't know what to say."

She smiled at him. "Don't say anything. It was nice."

"More than nice." He watched her precise motions behind the counter. She broke the eggs one-handed, two at a time, added a splash of water to the bowl, plucked some chives from a windowbox and chopped them with a small Chinese cleaver, rocking it in a staccato chatter; scraped them into the bowl, and followed them with a couple of grinds of pepper. She set the bacon out on a paper towel, with another towel to cover. Then she stirred the eggs briskly with the fork and set them aside. She picked up the big cast-iron frying pan and poured off a judicious amount of grease. Then she poured the egg mixture into the pan and studied it with alertness.

"Know what I think?" John said.

"Something profound?"

"Huh-uh. I think I'm in a rubber room someplace, hallucinating the whole thing. And I hope they never cure me."

"I think you're a butterfly who's dreaming he's a man. I'm glad I'm in your dream." She slowly stirred and scraped the eggs with a spatula.

"You like older men?"

"One of them." She looked up, serious. "I like men who are considerate . . . and playful." She returned to the scraping. "Last couple of boyfriends I had were all dick and no heart. Kept to myself the last few months."

"Glad to be of service."

"You could rent yourself out as a service." She laughed. "You must have been impossible when you were younger."

"Different." Literally.

She ran hot water into a serving bowl, then returned to her egg stewardship. "I've been thinking."

"Yes?"

"The lost-manuscript stuff we were talking about last night, all the different explanations." She divided the egg into four masses and turned each one. "Did you ever read any science fiction?"

"No. Vonnegut."

"The toast." She hurriedly put four pieces of bread in the toaster. "They write about alternate universes. Pretty much like our own, but different in one way or another. Important or trivial."

"What, uh, what silliness."

She laughed and poured the hot water out of the serving bowl, and dried it with a towel. "I guess maybe. But what if . . . what if all of those versions were equally true? In different universes. And for some reason they all came together here." She started to put the eggs into the bowl when there was a knock on the door.

It opened and Ernest Hemingway walked in. Dapper, just twenty, wearing the Italian army cape he'd brought back from the war. He pointed the black-and-white cane at Pansy. "Bingo."

She looked at John and then back at the Hemingway. She dropped the serving bowl; it clattered on the floor without breaking. Her knees buckled and she fainted dead away, executing a half turn as she fell so that the back of her head struck the wooden floor with a loud thump and the bathrobe drifted open from the waist down.

The Hemingway stared down at her frontal aspect. "Sometimes I wish I were human," it said. "Your pleasures are intense. Simple, but intense." It moved toward her with the cane.

John stood up. "If you kill her—"

"Oh?" It cocked an eyebrow at him. "What will you do?"

John took one step toward it and it waved the cane. A waist-high brick wall surmounted by needle-sharp spikes appeared between them. It gestured again and an impossible moat appeared, deep enough to reach down well into Julio's living room. It filled with water and a large crocodile surfaced and rested its chin on the parquet floor, staring at John. It yawned teeth.

The Hemingway held up its cane. "The white end. It doesn't kill, remember?" The wall and moat disappeared and the cane touched Pansy lightly below the navel. She twitched minutely but continued to sleep. "She'll have a headache," it said. "And she'll be somewhat confused by the uncommunicatable memory of having seen me. But that will all fade, compared to the sudden tragedy of having her new lover die here, just sitting waiting for his breakfast."

"Do you enjoy this?"

"I love my work. It's all I have." It walked toward him, footfalls splashing as it crossed where the moat had been. "You have not personally helped, though. Not at all."

It sat down across from him and poured coffee into a mug that said ON THE SIXTH DAY GOD CREATED MAN—SHE MUST HAVE HAD PMS.

"When you kill me this time, do you think it will 'take'?"

"I don't know. It's never failed before." The toaster made a noise. "Toast?"

"Sure." Two pieces appeared on his plate; two on the Hemingway's. "Usually when you kill people, they stay dead?"

"I don't kill that many people." It spread margarine on its toast; gestured, and marmalade appeared. "But when I do, yeah. They die all up and down the Omniverse, every timespace. All except you." He pointed toast at John's toast. "Go ahead. It's not poison."

"Not my idea of a last meal."

The Hemingway shrugged. "What would you like?"

"Forget it." He buttered the toast and piled marmalade on it, determined out of some odd impulse to act as if nothing unusual were happening. Breakfast with Hemingway, big deal.

He studied the apparition and noticed that it was somewhat translucent, almost like a traditional TV ghost. He could barely see a line that was the back of the chair, bisecting its chest below shoulderblade level. Was this something new? There hadn't been too much light in the train; maybe he had just failed to notice it before.

"A penny for your thoughts."

He didn't say anything about seeing through it. "Has it occurred to you that maybe you're not *supposed* to kill me? That's why I came back?"

The Hemingway chuckled and admired its nails. "That's a nearly content-free assertion."

"Oh really." He bit into the toast. The marmalade was strong, pleasantly bitter.

"It presupposes a higher authority, unknown to me, that's watching over my behavior, and correcting me when I do wrong. Doesn't exist, sorry."

"That's the oldest one in the theologian's book." John set down the toast and kneaded his stomach; shouldn't eat something so strong first thing in the morning. "You can only *assert* the nonexistence of something; you can't prove it."

"What you mean is *you* can't." The Hemingway held up the cane and looked at it. "The simplest explanation is that there's something wrong with the cane. There's no way I can test it; if I kill the wrong person there's hell to pay up and down the Omniverse. But what I can do is kill you without the cane. See whether you come back again, some timespace."

Sharp, stabbing pains in his stomach now. "Bastard." Heart pounding slow and hard: shirt rustled in time to its spasms.

"Cyanide in the marmalade. Gives it a certain *frisson*, don't you think?"

He couldn't breathe. His heart pounded once, and stopped. Vicious pain in his left arm, then paralysis. From an inch away, he could just see the weave of the white tablecloth. It turned red and then black.

## 18. The Sun Also Rises

From blackness to brilliance: the morning sun pouring through the window at a flat angle. He screwed up his face and blinked.

Suddenly smothered in terry cloth, between soft breasts. "John, John."

He put his elbow down to support himself, uncomfortable on the parquet floor, and looked up at Pansy. Her face was wet with tears. He cleared his throat. "What happened?"

"You, you started putting on your foot and . . . you just fell over. I thought . . ."

John looked down over his body, hard ropy muscle and deep tan under white body hair, the puckered bullet wound a little higher on the abdomen. Left leg ended in a stump just above the ankle.

Trying not to faint. His third past flooding back. Walking down a dirt road near Kontum, the sudden loud bang of the mine and he pitched forward, unbelievable pain, rolled over and saw his bloody boot yards away; gray, jagged shinbone sticking through the bloody smoking rag of his pants leg, bright crimson splashing on the dry dust, loud in the shocked silence; another bloodstain spreading between his legs, the deep mortal pain there—and he started to buck and scream and two men held him while the medic took off his belt and made a tourniquet and popped morphine through the cloth and unbuttoned his fly and slowly worked his pants down: penis torn by shrapnel, scrotum ripped open in a bright red flap of skin, bloody gray-blue egg of a testicle separating, rolling out. He fainted, then and now.

And woke up with her lips against his, her breath sweet in his lungs, his nostrils pinched painfully tight. He made a strangled noise and clutched her breast.

She cradled his head, panting, smiling through tears, and kissed him lightly on the forehead. "Will you stop fainting now?"

"Yeah. Don't worry." Her lips were trembling. He put a finger on them. "Just a longer night than I'm accustomed to. An overdose of happiness."

The happiest night of his life, maybe of three lives. Like coming back from the dead.

"Should I call a doctor?"

"No. I faint every now and then." Usually at the gym, from pushing too hard. He slipped his hand inside the terry cloth and covered her breast. "It's been . . . do you know how long it's been since I . . . did it? I mean . . . three times in one night?"

"About six hours." She smiled. "And you can say 'fuck.' I'm no schoolgirl."

"I'll say." The night had been an escalating progression of intimacies, gymnastics, accessories. "Had to wonder where a sweet girl like you learned all that."

She looked away, lips pursed, thoughtful. With a light fingertip she stroked the length of his penis and smiled when it started to uncurl. "At work."

"What?"

"I was a prostitute. That's where I learned the tricks. Practice makes perfect."

"Prostitute. Wow."

"Are you shocked? Outraged?"

"Just surprised." That was true. He respected the sorority and was grateful to it for having made Vietnam almost tolerable, an hour or so at a time. "But now you've got to do something really mean. I could never love a prostitute with a heart of gold."

"I'll give it some thought." She shifted. "Think you can stand up?"

"Sure." She stood and gave him her hand. He touched it but didn't pull; rose in a smooth practiced motion, then took one hop and sat down at the small table. He started strapping on his foot.

"I've read about those new ones," she said, "the permanent kind."

"Yeah; I've read about them, too. Computer interface, graft your nerves onto sensors." He shuddered. "No, thanks. No more surgery."

"Not worth it for the convenience?"

"Being able to wiggle my toes, have my foot itch? No. Besides, the VA won't pay for it." That startled John as he said it: here, he hadn't grown up rich. His father had spent all the mill money on a photocopy firm six months before Xerox came on the market. "You say you 'were' a prostitute. Not anymore?"

"No, that was the truth about teaching. Let's start this egg thing over." She picked up the bowl she had dropped in the other universe. "I gave up whoring about seven years ago." She picked up an egg, looked at it, set it down. She half turned and stared out the kitchen window. "I can't do this to you."

"You . . . can't do what?"

"Oh, lie. Keep lying." She went to the refrigerator. "Want a beer?"

"Lying? No, no thanks. What lying?"

She opened a beer, still not looking at him. "I like you, John. I really like you. But I didn't just . . . spontaneously fall into your arms." She took a healthy swig and started pouring some of the bottle into a glass.

"I don't understand."

She walked back, concentrating on pouring the beer, then sat down gracelessly. She took a deep breath and let it out, staring at his chest. "Castle put me up to it."

"*Castle?*"

She nodded. "Sylvester Castlemaine, boy wonder."

John sat back stunned. "But you said you don't do that anymore," he said without too much logic. "Do it for money."

"Not for money," she said in a flat, hurt voice.

"I should've known. A woman like you wouldn't want . . ." He made a gesture that dismissed his body from the waist down.

"You do all right. Don't feel sorry for yourself." Her face showed a pinch of regret for that, but she plowed on. "If it were just the obligation, once would have been enough. I wouldn't have had to fuck and suck all night long to win you over."

"No," he said, "that's true. Just the first moment, when you undressed. That was enough."

"I owe Castle a big favor. A friend of mine was going to be

prosecuted for involving a minor in prostitution. It was a setup, pure and simple."

"She worked for the same outfit you did?"

"Yeah, but this was freelance. I think it was the escort service that set her up, sort of delivered her and the man in return for this or that."

She sipped at the beer. "Guy wanted a three-way. My friend had met this girl a couple of days before at the bar where she worked part-time . . . she looked old enough; said she was in the biz."

"She was neither?"

"God knows. Maybe she got caught as a juvie and made a deal. Anyhow, he'd just slipped it to her and suddenly cops are comin' in the windows. Threw the book at him. 'Two inches, twenty years,' my friend said. He was a county commissioner somewhere, with enemies. Almost dragged my friend down with him. I'm *sorry*." Her voice was angry.

"Don't be," John said, almost a whisper. "It's understandable. Whatever happens, I've got last night."

She nodded. "So two of the cops who were going to testify got busted for possession, cocaine. The word came down and everybody remembered the woman was somebody else."

"So what did Castle want you to do? With me?"

"Oh, whatever comes natural—or *un*natural, if that's what you wanted. And later be doing it at a certain time and place, where we'd be caught in the act."

"By Castle?"

"And his trusty little VCR. Then I guess he'd threaten to show it to your wife, or the university."

"I wonder. Lena . . . she knows I've had other women."

"But not lately."

"No. Not for years."

"It might be different now. She might be starting to feel, well, insecure."

"Any woman who looked at you would feel insecure."

She shrugged. "That could be part of it. Could it cost you your job, too?"

"I don't see how. It would be awkward, but it's not as if you were one of my students—and even that happens, without costing the guy his job." He laughed. "Poor old Larry. He had a student kiss and tell, and had to run the Speakers' Committee for four or five years. Got allergic to wine and cheese. But he made tenure."

"So what is it?" She leaned forward. "Are you an addict or something?"

"Addict?"

"I mean how come you even *know* Castle? He didn't pick your name out of a phone book and have me come seduce you, just to see what would happen."

"No, of course not."

"So? I confess, you confess."

John passed a hand over his face and pressed the other hand against his knee, bearing down to keep the foot from tapping. "You don't want to be involved."

"What do you call last night, Spin the Bottle? I'm in*volved*!"

"Not the way I mean. It's illegal."

"Oh golly. Not really."

"Let me think." John picked up their dishes and limped back to the sink. He set them down there and fiddled with the straps and pad that connected the foot to his stump, then poured himself a cup of coffee and came back, not limping.

He sat down slowly and blew across the coffee. "What it is, is that *Castle* thinks there's a scam going on. He's wrong. I've taken steps to ensure that it couldn't work." His foot tapped twice.

"You think. You hope."

"No, I'm sure. Anyhow, I'm stringing Castle along because I need his expertise in a certain matter."

" 'A certain matter,' yeah. Sounds wholesome."

"Actually, that part's not illegal."

"So tell me about it."

"Nope. Still might backfire."

She snorted. "You know what might *back*fire. Fucking with Castle."

"I can take care of him."

"You don't know. He may be more dangerous than you think he is."

"He talks a lot."

"You men." She took a drink and poured the rest of the bottle into the glass. "Look, I was at a party with him, couple of years ago. He was drunk, got into a little coke, started babbling."

"*In vino veritas?*"

"Yeah, and Coke is It. But he said he'd killed three people, strangers, just to see what it felt like. He liked it. I more than halfway believe him."

John looked at her silently for a moment, sorting out his new memories of Castle. "Well . . . he's got a mean streak. I don't know about murder. Certainly not over this thing."

"Which is?"

"You'll have to trust me. It's not because of Castle that I can't tell you." He remembered her one universe ago, lying helpless while the Hemingway lowered its cane onto her nakedness. "Trust me?"

She studied the top of the glass, running her finger around it. "Suppose I do. Then what?"

"Business as usual. You didn't tell me anything. Deliver me to Castle and his video camera; I'll try to put on a good show."

"And when he confronts you with it?"

"Depends on what he wants. He knows I don't have much money." John shrugged. "If it's unreasonable, he can go ahead and show the tape to Lena. She can live with it."

"And your department head?"

"He'd give me a medal."

### 19. in our time

So it wasn't the cane. He ate enough cyanide to kill a horse, but evidently only in one universe.

You checked the next day in all the others?

All 119. He's still dead in the one where I killed him on the train—

That's encouraging.

—but there's no causal resonance in the others.

Oh, but there is some resonance. He remembered you in the universe where you poisoned him. Maybe in all of them.

That's impossible.

Once is impossible. Twice is a trend. A hundred and twenty means something is going on that we don't understand.

What I suggest—

No. You can't go back and kill them all one by one.

If the wand had worked the first time, they'd all be dead anyhow. There's no reason to think we'd cause more of an eddy by doing them one at a time.

It's not something to experiment with. As you well know.

I don't know how we're going to solve it otherwise.

Simple. Don't kill him. Talk to him again. He may be getting frightened, if he remembers both times he died.

Here's an idea. What if someone else killed him?

I don't know. If you just hired someone—made him a direct agent of your will—it wouldn't be any different from the cyanide. Maybe as a last resort. Talk to him again first.

All right. I'll try.

## 20. Of Wounds and Other Causes

Although John found it difficult to concentrate, trying not to think about Pansy, this was the best time he would have for the foreseeable future to summon the Hemingway demon and try to do something about exorcising it. He didn't want either of the women around if the damned thing went on a killing spree again. They might just do as he did, and slip over into another reality—as unpleasant as that was, it was at least living—but the Hemingway had said otherwise. There was no reason to suspect it was not the truth.

Probably the best way to get the thing's attention was to resume work on the Hemingway pastiche. He decided to rewrite the first page to warm up, typing it out in Hemingway's style:

### ALONG WITH YOUTH

#### 1. Mitraigliatrice

The dirt on the side of the trench was never dry in the morning . If Fever could find a dry newspaper he could put it between his chest and the dirt when he went out to lean on the side of the trench and wait for the light .First light was

the best time . You might have luck and see a muzzle flash to
aim at . But patience was better than luck . Wait to see a
helmet or a head without a helmet .

Fever looked at the enemy trench line through a
rectangular box of wood that pushed through the trench wall at
about ground level . The other end of the box was covered with
a square of gauze the color of dirt . A man looking directly
at it might see the muzzle flash when Fever fired through the
box . But with luck , the flash would be the last thing he
saw .

Fever had fired through the gauze six times . He' d
potted at least three Austrians . Now the gauze had a ragged
hole in the center . One bullet had come in the other way , an
accident , and chiseled a deep gouge in the floor of the wooden
box .Fever knew that he would be able to see the splinters
sticking up before he could see any detail at the enemy trench
line.

That would be maybe twenty minutes . Fever wanted a
cigarette . There was plenty of time to go down in the bunker
and light one . But it would fox his night vision . Better to
wait .

Fever heard movement before he heard the voice . He
picked up one of the grenades on the plank shelf to his left
and his thumb felt the ring on the cotter pin . Someone was
crawling in front of his position . Slow crawling but not too
quiet . He slid his left forefinger through the ring and
waited .

-----Help me, came a strained whisper .

Fever felt his shoulders tense . Of course many Austrians could speak Italian .

-----I am wounded . Help me . I can go no farther .

-----What is your name and unit , ~~Fever~~ Fever whispered through the box .

-----Jean-Franco Dante . Four forty-seventh.

That was the unit that had taken such a beating at the evening show . -----At first light they will kill me .

-----All right. But I 'm coming over with a grenade in my hand . If you kill me , you die as well .

-----I will commend this logic to your superior officer . Please hurry .

Fever slid his rifle into the wooden box and eased himself to the top of the trench . He took the grenade out of his pocket and carefully worked the pin out, the arming lever held secure . He kept the pin around his finger so he could replace it .

He inched his way down the slope , guided by the man's whispers . After a few minutes his probing hand found the man's shoulder . -----Thank God . Make haste , now .

The soldier's feet were both shattered by a mine . He would have to be carried .

-----Don't cry out, Fever said . This will hurt .

-----No sound , the soldier said . And when Fever raised him up onto his back there was only a breath . But his

canteen was loose . It fell on a rock and made a loud hollow
sound .

Firecracker pop above them and the night was all glare
and bobbing shadow . A big machine-gun opened up rong, cararong,
rong , rong . Fever headed for the parapet above as fast as he
could but knew it was hopeless . He saw dirt spray twice to his
right and then felt the thud of the bullet into ~~a~~ the Italian , who
said " Jesus " as if only annoyed , and they almost made it then
but on the lip of the trench a hard snowball hit Fever behind
the kneecap and they both went down in a tumble . They fell two
yards to safety but the Italian was already dead .

Fever had sprained his wrist and hurt his nose falling and they hurt worse than the bullet . But he couldn't move
his toes and he knew that must be bad . Then it started to
hurt .

A rifleman closed the Italian's eyes and with the
help of another clumsy one dragged Fever down the trench to the
medical bunker . It hurt awfully and his shoe filled up with
blood and he puked . They stopped to watch him puke and then
dragged him the rest of the way .

The surgeon placed him between two keresene lanterns .
He removed the puttee and shoe and cut the bloody pants leg with
a straight razor . He rolled Fever onto his stomach and had four
men hold him down while he probed for the bullet . The pain was
great but Fever was insulted enough by  the four men not to cry
out . He heard the bullet clink into a metal dish . It sounded
like the canteen .

"That's a little too pat, don't you think?" John turned around and there was the Hemingway, reading over his shoulder. " 'It sounded like the canteen,' indeed." Khaki army uniform covered with mud and splattered with bright blood. Blood dripped and pooled at its feet.

"So shoot me. Or whatever it's going to be this time. Maybe I'll rewrite the line in the next universe."

"You're going to run out soon. You only exist in eight more universes."

"Sure. And you've never lied to me." John turned back around and stared at the typewriter, tensed.

The Hemingway sighed. "Suppose we talk, instead."

"I'm listening."

The Hemingway walked past him toward the kitchen. "Want a beer?"

"Not while I'm working."

"Suit yourself." It limped into the kitchen, out of sight, and John heard it open the refrigerator and pry the top off of a beer. It came back out as the five-year-old Hemingway, dressed up in girl's clothing, both hands clutching an incongruous beer bottle. It set the bottle on the end table and crawled up onto the couch with childish clumsiness.

"Where's the cane?"

"I knew it wouldn't be necessary this time," it piped. "It occurs to me that there are better ways to deal with a man like you."

"Do tell." John smiled. "What is 'a man like me'? One on whom your cane for some reason doesn't work?"

"Actually, what I was thinking of was curiosity. That is supposedly what motivates scholars. You *are* a real scholar, not just a rich man seeking legitimacy?"

John looked away from the ancient eyes in the boy's face. "I've sometimes wondered myself. Why don't you cut to the chase, as we used to say. A few universes ago."

"I've done spot checks on your life through various universes," the child said. "You're always a Hemingway buff, though you don't always do it for a living."

"What else do I do?"

"It's probably not healthy for you to know. But all of you are drawn to the missing manuscripts at about this time, the seventy-fifth anniversary."

"I wonder why that would be."

The Hemingway waved the beer bottle in a disarmingly mature gesture. "The Omniverse is full of threads of coincidence like that. They have causal meaning in a dimension you can't deal with."

"Try me."

"In a way, that's what I want to propose. You will drop this dangerous project at once, and never resume it. In return, I will take you back in time, back to the Gare de Lyon on December 14, 1921."

"Where I will see what happens to the manuscripts."

Another shrug. "I will put you on Hadley's train, well before she said the manuscripts were stolen. You will be able to observe for an hour or so, without being seen. As you know, some people have theorized that there never was a thief; never was an overnight bag; that Hadley simply threw the writings away. If that's the case, you won't see anything dramatic. But the absence of the overnight bag would be powerful indirect proof."

John looked skeptical. "You've never gone to check it out for yourself?"

"If I had, I wouldn't be able to take you back. I can't exist twice in the same timespace, of course."

"How foolish of me. Of course."

"Is it a deal?"

John studied the apparition. The couch's plaid upholstery showed through its arms and legs. It did appear to become less substantial each time. "I don't know. Let me think about it a couple of days."

The child pulled on the beer bottle and it stretched into a long amber stick. It turned into the black-and-white cane. "We haven't tried cancer yet. That might be the one that works." The child slipped off the couch and sidled toward John. "It does take longer and it hurts. It hurts 'awfully.' "

John got out of the chair. "You come near me with that and I'll drop-kick you into next Tuesday."

The child shimmered and became Hemingway in his mid-forties, a big-gutted barroom brawler. "Sure you will, Champ." It held out the cane so that the tip was inches from John's chest. "See you around." It disappeared with a barely audible pop, and a slight breeze as air moved to fill its space.

John thought about that as he went to make a fresh cup of coffee.

He wished he knew more about science. The thing obviously took up space, since its disappearance caused a vacuum, but there was no denying that it was fading away.

Well, not fading. Just becoming more transparent. That might not affect its abilities. A glass door is as much of a door as an opaque one, if you try to walk through it.

He sat down on the couch, away from the manuscript so he could think without distraction. On the face of it, this offer by the Hemingway was an admission of defeat. An admission, at least, that it couldn't solve its problem by killing him over and over. That was comforting. He would just as soon not die again, except for the one time.

But maybe he should. That was a chilling thought. If he made the Hemingway kill him another dozen times, another hundred . . . what kind of strange creature would he become? A hundred overlapping autobiographies, all perfectly remembered? Surely the brain has a finite capacity for storing information; he'd "fill up," as Pansy said. Or maybe it wasn't finite, at least in his case—but that was logically absurd. There are only so many cells in a brain. Of course he might be "wired" in some way to the John Bairds in all the other universes he had inhabited.

And what would happen if he died in some natural way, not dispatched by an interdimensional assassin? Would he still slide into another identity? That was a lovely prospect: sooner or later he would be 130 years old, on his deathbed, dying every fraction of a second for the rest of eternity.

Or maybe the Hemingway wasn't lying, this time, and he had only eight lives left. In context, the possibility was reassuring.

The phone rang; for a change, John was grateful for the interruption. It was Lena, saying her father had come home from the hospital, much better, and she thought she could come on home day after tomorrow. Fine, John said, feeling a little wicked; I'll borrow a car and pick you up at the airport. Don't bother, Lena said; besides, she didn't have a flight number yet.

John didn't press it. If, as he assumed, Lena was in on the plot with Castle, she was probably here in Key West, or somewhere nearby. If she had to buy a ticket to and from Omaha to keep up her end of the ruse, the money would come out of John's pocket.

He hung up and, on impulse, dialed her parents' number. Her father answered. Putting on his professorial tone, he said he was Maxwell Perkins, Blue Cross claims adjuster, and he needed to know the exact date when Mr. Monaghan entered the hospital for this recent confinement. He said you must have the wrong guy; I haven't been inside a hospital in twenty years, knock on wood. Am I not speaking to John Franklin Monaghan? No, this is John *Frederick* Monaghan. Terribly sorry, natural mistake. That's okay; hope the other guy's okay, good-bye, good night, sir.

So tomorrow was going to be the big day with Pansy. To his knowledge, John hadn't been watched during sex for more than twenty years, and never by a disinterested, or at least dispassionate, observer. He hoped that knowing they were being spied upon wouldn't affect his performance. Or knowing that it would be the last time.

A profound helpless sadness settled over him. He knew that the last thing you should do, in a mood like this, was go out and get drunk. It was barely noon, anyhow. He took enough money out of his wallet for five martinis, hid the wallet under a couch cushion, and headed for Duval Street.

## 21. Dying, Well or Badly

John had just about decided it was too early in the day to get drunk. He had polished off two martinis in Sloppy Joe's and then wandered uptown because the tourists were getting to him and a band was setting up, depressingly young and cheerful. He found a grubby bar he'd never noticed before, dark and smoky and hot. In the other universes it was a yuppie boutique. Three Social Security drunks were arguing politics almost loudly enough to drown out the game show on the television. It seemed to go well with the headache and sour stomach he'd reaped from the martinis and the walk in the sun. He got a beer and some peanuts and a couple of aspirin from the bartender, and sat in the farthest booth with a copy of the local classified-ad newspaper. Somebody had obscurely carved FUCK ANARCHY in the tabletop.

Nobody else in this world knows what anarchy *is*, John thought, and the helpless anomie came back, intensified somewhat by drunken sentimentality. What he would give to go back to the first universe and undo this all by just not . . .

Would that be possible? The Hemingway was willing to take him back to 1921; why not back a few weeks? Where the hell was that son of a bitch when you needed him, it, whatever.

The Hemingway appeared in the booth opposite him, an Oak Park teenager smoking a cigarette. "I felt a kind of vibration from you. Ready to make your decision?"

"Can the people at the bar see you?"

"No. And don't worry about appearing to be talking to yourself. A lot of that goes on around here."

"Look. Why can't you just take me back to a couple of weeks before we met on the train, back in the first universe? I'll just . . ."
The Hemingway was shaking its head slowly. "You can't."

"No. As I explained, you already exist there—"

"You said that *you* couldn't be in the same place twice. How do you know I can't?"

"How do you know you can't swallow that piano? You just can't."

"You thought I couldn't talk about you, either; you thought your stick would kill me. I'm not like normal people."

"Except in that alcohol does nothing for your judgment."

John ate a peanut thoughtfully. "Try this on for size. At 11:46 on June 3, a man named Sylvester Castlemaine sat down in Dos Hermosas and started talking with me about the lost manuscripts. The forgery would never have occurred to me if I hadn't talked to him. Why don't you go back and keep him from going into that café? Or just go back to 11:30 and kill him."

The Hemingway smiled maliciously. "You don't like him much."

"It's more fear than like or dislike." He rubbed his face hard, remembering. "Funny how things shift around. He was kind of likable the first time I met him. Then you killed me on the train, and in the subsequent universe he became colder, more serious. Then you killed me in Pansy's apartment, and in this universe he has turned mean. Dangerously mean, like a couple of men I knew in Vietnam. The ones who really love the killing. Like you, evidently."

It blew a chain of smoke rings before answering. "I don't 'love' killing, or anything else. I have a complex function and I fulfill it, because that is what I do. That sounds circular because of the limitations of human language.

"I can't go killing people right and left just to see what happens. When a person dies at the wrong time it takes forever to clean things up. Not that it wouldn't be worth it in your case. But I can tell you with certainty that killing Castlemaine would not affect the final outcome."

"How can you say that? He's responsible for the whole thing." John finished off most of his beer and the Hemingway touched the mug and it refilled. "Not poison."

"Wouldn't work," it said morosely. "I'd gladly kill Castlemaine any way you want—cancer of the penis is a possibility—if there was even a fighting chance that it would clear things up. The reason I know it wouldn't is that I am not in the least attracted to that meeting. There's no probability nexus associated with it, the way there was with your buying the Corona or starting the story on the train, or writing it down here. You may think that you would never have come up with the idea for the forgery on your own, but you're wrong."

"That's preposterous."

"Nope. There are universes in this bundle where Castle isn't involved. You may find that hard to believe, but your beliefs aren't important."

John nodded noncommittally and got his faraway remembering look. "You know . . . reviewing in my mind all the conversations we've had, all five of them, the only substantive reason you've given me not to write this pastiche, and I quote, is that 'I or someone like me will have to kill you.' Since that doesn't seem to be possible, why don't we try some other line of attack?"

It put out the cigarette by squeezing it between thumb and forefinger. There was a smell of burning flesh. "All right, try this: give it up or I'll kill Pansy. Then Lena."

"I've thought of that, and I'm gambling that you won't, or can't. You had a perfect opportunity a few days ago—maximum dramatic effect—and you didn't do it. Now you say it's an awfully complicated matter."

"You're willing to gamble with the lives of the people you love?"

"I'm gambling with a lot. Including them." He leaned forward. "Take me into the future instead of the past. Show me what will happen if I succeed with the Hemingway hoax. If I agree that it's terrible, I'll give it all up and become a plumber."

The old, wise Hemingway shook a shaggy head at him. "You're asking me to please fix it so you can swallow a piano. I can't. Even I can't go straight to the future and look around; I'm pretty much tied to your present and past until this matter is cleared up."

"One of the first things you said to me was that you were from the future. And the past. And 'other temporalities,' whatever the hell that means. You were lying then?"

"Not really." It sighed. "Let me force the analogy. Look at the piano."

John twisted half around. "Okay."

"You can't eat it—but after a fashion, I can." The piano suddenly transformed itself into a piano-shaped mountain of cold capsules, which immediately collapsed and rolled all over the floor. "Each capsule contains a pinch of sawdust or powdered ivory or metal, the whole piano in about a hundred thousand capsules. If I take one with each meal, I will indeed eat the piano, over the course of the next three hundred-some years. That's not a long time for me."

"That doesn't prove anything."

"It's not a *proof*; it's a demonstration." It reached down and picked up a capsule that was rolling by and popped it into its mouth. "One down, 99,999 to go. So how many ways could I eat this piano?"

"Ways?"

"I mean I could have swallowed any of the hundred thousand first. Next I can choose any of the remaining 99,999. How many ways can—"

"That's easy. One hundred thousand factorial. A huge number."

"Go to the head of the class. It's ten to the godzillionth power. That represents the number of possible paths—the number of futures—leading to this one guaranteed, preordained event: my eating the piano. They are all different, but in terms of whether the piano gets eaten, their differences are trivial.

"On a larger scale, every possible trivial action that you or anybody else in this universe takes puts us into a slightly different future than would have otherwise existed. An overwhelming majority of actions, even seemingly significant ones, make no difference in the long run. All of the futures bend back to one central, unifying event—except for the ones that you're screwing up!"

"So what is this big event?"

"It's impossible for you to know. It's not important, anyhow."

Actually, it would take a rather cosmic viewpoint to consider the event unimportant: the end of the world.

Or at least the end of life on Earth. Right now there were two earnest young politicians, in the United States and Russia, who on 11 August 2006 would be president and premier of their countries. On that day, one would insult the other beyond forgiveness, and a button would be pushed, and then another button, and by the time the sun set on Moscow, or rose on Washington, there would be nothing left alive on the planet at all—from the bottom of the ocean to the top of the atmosphere; not a cockroach, not a paramecium, not a virus, and all because there are some things a man just doesn't have to take, not if he's a real man.

Hemingway wasn't the only writer who felt that way, but he was the one with the most influence on this generation. The apparition who wanted John dead, or at least not typing, didn't know exactly what effect his pastiche was going to have on Hemingway's influence, but it was going to be decisive and ultimately negative. It would prevent or at least delay the end of the world in a whole bundle of universes, which would put a zillion adjacent realities out of kilter, and there would be hell to pay all up and down the Omniverse. Many more people than six billion would die—and it's even possible that all of Reality would unravel, and collapse back to the Primordial Hiccup from whence it came.

"If it's not important, then why are you so hell-bent on keeping me from preventing it? I don't believe you."

"*Don't* believe me, then!" At an imperious gesture, all the capsules rolled back into the corner and reassembled into a piano, with a huge crashing chord. None of the barflies heard it. "I should think you'd cooperate with me just to prevent the unpleasantness of dying over and over."

John had the expression of a poker player whose opponent has inadvertently exposed his hole card. "You get used to it," he said. "And it occurs to me that sooner or later I'll wind up in a universe that I really like. This one doesn't have a hell of a lot to recommend it." His foot tapped twice and then twice again.

"No," the Hemingway said. "It will get worse each time."

"You can't know that. This has never happened before."

"True so far, isn't it?"

John considered it for a moment. "Some ways. Some ways not."

The Hemingway shrugged and stood up. "Well. Think about my offer." The cane appeared. "Happy cancer." It tapped him on the chest and disappeared.

The first sensation was utter tiredness, immobility. When he strained to move, pain slithered through his muscles and viscera, and stayed. He could hardly breathe, partly because his lungs weren't working and partly because there was something in the way. In the mirror beside the booth he looked down his throat and saw a large white mass, veined, pulsing. He sank back into the cushion and waited. He remembered the young wounded Hemingway writing his parents from the hospital with ghastly cheerfulness: "If I should have died it would have been very easy for me. Quite the easiest thing I ever did." I don't know, Ernie; maybe it gets harder with practice. He felt something tear open inside and hot stinging fluid trickled through his abdominal cavity. He wiped his face, and a patch of necrotic skin came off with a terrible smell. His clothes tightened as his body swelled.

"Hey buddy, you okay?" The bartender came around in front of him and jumped. "Christ, Harry, punch nine-one-one!"

John gave a slight ineffectual wave. "No rush," he croaked.

The bartender cast his eyes to the ceiling. "Always on my shift?"

## 22. Death in the Afternoon

John woke up behind a dumpster in an alley. It was high noon and the smell of fermenting garbage was revolting. He didn't feel too well in any case; as if he'd drunk far too much and passed out behind a dumpster, which was exactly what had happened in this universe.

In this universe. He stood slowly to a quiet chorus of creaks and pops, brushed himself off, and staggered away from the malefic odor. Staggered, but not limping—he had both feet again, in this present. There was a hand-sized numb spot at the top of his left leg where a .51 caliber machine-gun bullet had missed his balls by an inch and ended his career as a soldier.

And started it as a writer. He got to the sidewalk and stopped dead. This was the first universe where he wasn't a college professor. He taught occasionally—sometimes creative writing; sometimes

Hemingway—but it was only a hobby now, and a nod toward respectability.

He rubbed his fringe of salt-and-pepper beard. It covered the bullet scar there on his chin. He ran his tongue along the metal teeth the army had installed thirty years ago. Jesus. Maybe it does get worse every time. Which was worse, losing a foot or getting your dick sprayed with shrapnel, numb from several nerves, plus bullets in the leg and face and arm? If you knew there was a Pansy in your future, you would probably trade a foot for a whole dick. Though she had done wonders with what was left.

Remembering furiously, not watching where he was going, he let his feet guide him back to the oldsters' bar where the Hemingway had showed him how to swallow a piano. He pushed through the door and the shock of air-conditioning brought him back to the present.

Ferns. Perfume. Lacy underthings. An epicene sales clerk sashayed toward him, managing to look worried and determined at the same time. His nose was pierced, decorated with a single diamond button. "Si-i-ir," he said in a surprisingly deep voice, "may I *help* you?"

Crotchless panties. Marital aids. The bar had become a store called The French Connection. "Guess I took a wrong turn. Sorry." He started to back out.

The clerk smiled. "Don't be shy. Everybody needs *some*thing here."

The heat was almost pleasant in its heavy familiarity. John stopped at a convenience store for a sixpack of greenies and walked back home.

An interesting universe; much more of a divergence than the other had been. Reagan had survived the Hinckley assassination and actually went on to a second term. Bush was elected rather than succeeding to the presidency, and the country had not gone to war in Nicaragua. The Iran/Contra scandal nipped it in the bud.

The United States was actually cooperating with the Soviet Union in a flight to Mars. There were no DeSotos. Could there be a connection?

And in this universe he had actually met Ernest Hemingway.

Havana, 1952. John was eight years old. His father, a doctor in this universe, had taken a break from the New England winter to treat his family to a week in the tropics. John got a nice sunburn the first day, playing on the beach while his parents tried the casinos. The next day they made him stay indoors, which meant tagging along with his parents, looking at things that didn't fascinate eight-year-olds.

For lunch they went to La Florida, on the off chance that they might meet the famous Ernest Hemingway, who supposedly held court there when he was in Havana.

To John it was a huge dark cavern of a place, full of adult smells. Cigar smoke, rum, beer, stale urine. But Hemingway was indeed there, at the end of the long dark wood bar, laughing heartily with a table full of Cubans.

John was vaguely aware that his mother resembled some movie actress, but he couldn't have guessed that that would change his life. Hemingway glimpsed her and then stood up and was suddenly silent, mouth open. Then he laughed and waved a huge arm. "Come on over here, daughter."

The three of them rather timidly approached the table, John acutely aware of the careful inspection his mother was receiving from the silent Cubans. "Take a look, Mary," Hemingway said to the small blond woman knitting at the table. "The Kraut."

The woman nodded, smiling, and agreed that John's mother looked just like Marlene Dietrich ten years before. Hemingway invited them to sit down and have a drink, and they accepted with an air of genuine astonishment. He gravely shook John's hand, and spoke to him as he would to an adult. Then he shouted to the bartender in fast Spanish, and in a couple of minutes John's parents had huge daiquiris and he had a Coke with a wedge of lime in it, tropical and grown-up. The waiter also brought a tray of boiled shrimp. Hemingway even ate the heads and tails, crunching loudly, which impressed John more than any Nobel Prize. Hemingway might have agreed, since he hadn't yet received one, and Faulkner had.

For more than an hour, two Cokes, John watched as his parents sat hypnotized in the aura of Hemingway's famous charm. He put them at ease with jokes and stories and questions—for the rest of his life John's father would relate how impressed he was with the so-phistication of Hemingway's queries about cardiac medicine—but it was obvious even to a child that they were in awe, electrified by the man's presence.

Later that night John's father asked him what he thought of Mr.

Hemingway. Forty-four years later, John of course remembered his exact reply: "He has fun all the time. I never saw a grown-up who plays like that."

Interesting. That meeting was where his eidetic memory started. He could remember a couple of days before it pretty well, because they had still been close to the surface. In other universes, he could remember back well before grade school. It gave him a strange feeling. All of the universes were different, but this was the first one where the differentness was so tightly connected to Hemingway.

He was flabby in this universe, fat over old tired muscle, like Hemingway at his age, perhaps, and he felt a curious anxiety that he realized was a real *need* to have a drink. Not just desire, not thirst. If he didn't have a drink, something very very bad would happen. He knew that was irrational. Knowing didn't help.

John carefully mounted the stairs up to their apartment, stepping over the fifth one, also rotted in this universe. He put the beer in the refrigerator and took from the freezer a bottle of icy vodka—that was different—and poured himself a double shot and knocked it back, medicine drinking.

That would spike the hangover pretty well. He pried the top off a beer and carried it into the living room, thoughtful as the alcoholic glow radiated through his body. He sat down at the typewriter and picked up the air pistol, a fancy Belgian target model. He cocked it and with a practiced two-handed grip aimed at a paper target across the room. The pellet struck less than half an inch low.

All around the room the walls were pocked from where he'd fired at roaches and, once, a scorpion. Very Hemingway-ish, he thought; in fact, most of the ways he was different from the earlier incarnations of himself were in Hemingway's direction.

He spun a piece of paper into the typewriter and made a list:

```
            EH & me --

-- both had doctor fathers

-- both forced into music lessons

-- in high school wrote derivative stuff that didn't show promise
```

-- Our war wounds were evidently similar in severity and
location. Maybe my groin one was worse; army doctor there
said that in Korea (and presumably W/I), without helicopter
dustoff, I would have been dead on the battlefield. (Having
been wounded in the kneecap and foot myself, I know that H's
story about carrying the wounded guy on his back is unlikely.
It was a month before I could put any stress on the knee.) He
mentioned genital wounds, possibly similar to mine, in a letter
to Bernard Baruch, but there's nothing in the Red Cross report
about them.

But in both cases, being wounded and surviving was the
central experience of our youth. Touching death.

-- We each wrote the first draft of our first novel in six weeks
(but his was better and more ambitious).

-- Both had unusual critical success from the beginning.

-- Both shy as youngsters and gregarious as adults.

-- Always loved fishing and hiking and guns; I loved the bullfight
from my first corrida, but may have been influenced by H's books.

-- Spain in general

--have better women than we deserve

-- drink too much

-- hypochondria

-- accident proneness

-- a tendency toward morbidity

-- One difference. I will never stick a shotgun in my mouth
and pull the trigger. Leaves too much of a mess.

He looked up at the sound of the cane tapping. The Hemingway
was in the Karsh wise-old-man mode, but was nearly transparent in
the bright light that streamed from the open door. "What do I have
to do to get your attention?" it said. "Give you cancer again?"

"That was pretty unpleasant."

"Maybe it will be the last." It half sat on the arm of the couch
and spun the cane around twice. "Today is a big day. Are we going
to Paris?"

"What do you mean?"

"Something big happens today. In every universe where you're alive, this day glows with importance. I assume that means you've decided to go along with me. Stop writing this thing in exchange for the truth about the manuscripts."

As a matter of fact, he had been thinking just that. Life was confusing enough already, torn between his erotic love for Pansy and the more domestic, but still deep, feeling for Lena . . . writing the pastiche was kind of fun, but he did have his own fish to fry. Besides, he'd come to truly dislike Castle, even before Pansy had told him about the setup. It would be fun to disappoint him.

"You're right. Let's go."

"First destroy the novel." In this universe, he'd completed seventy pages of the Up-in-Michigan novel.

"Sure." John picked up the stack of paper and threw it into the tiny fireplace. He lit it several places with a long barbecue match, and watched a month's work go up in smoke. It was only a symbolic gesture, anyhow; he could retype the thing from memory if he wanted to.

"So what do I do? Click my heels together three times and say 'There's no place like the Gare de Lyon'?"

"Just come closer."

John took three steps toward the Hemingway and suddenly fell up down sideways—

It was worse than dying. He was torn apart and scattered throughout space and time, being nowhere and everywhere, everywhen, being a screaming vacuum forever—

Grit crunched underfoot and coal smoke was choking-thick in the air. It was cold. Gray Paris skies glowered through the long skylights, through the complicated geometry of the black steel trusses that held up the high roof. Bustling crowds chattering French. A woman walked through John from behind. He pressed himself with his hands and felt real.

"They can't see us," the Hemingway said. "Not unless I will it."

"That was awful."

"I hoped you would hate it. That's how I spend most of my timespace. Come on." They walked past vendors selling paper packets of roasted chestnuts, bottles of wine, stacks of baguettes and cheeses. There were strange resonances as John remembered the various times he'd been here more than a half century in the future. It hadn't changed much.

"There she is." The Hemingway pointed. Hadley looked worn, tired, dowdy. She stumbled, trying to keep up with the porter who strode along with her two bags. John recalled that she was just recovering from a bad case of the grippe. She'd probably still be home in bed if Hemingway hadn't sent the telegram urging her to come to Lausanne because the skiing was so good, at Chamby.

"Are there universes where Hadley doesn't lose the manuscripts?"

"Plenty of them," the Hemingway said. "In some of them he doesn't sell 'My Old Man' next year, or anything else, and he throws all the stories away himself. He gives up fiction and becomes a staff writer for the *Toronto Star*. Until the Spanish Civil War; then he joins the Abraham Lincoln Battalion and is killed driving an ambulance. His only effect on American literature is one paragraph in *The Autobiography of Alice B. Toklas*."

"But in some, the stories actually do see print?"

"Sure, including the novel, which is usually called *Along with Youth*. There." Hadley was mounting the steps up into a passenger car. There was a microsecond of agonizing emptiness, and they materialized in the passageway in front of Hadley's compartment. She and the porter walked through them.

"*Merci*," she said, and handed the man a few *sous*. He made a face behind her back.

"*Along with Youth*?" John said.

"It's a pretty good book, sort of prefiguring *A Farewell to Arms*, but he does a lot better in universes where it's not published. *The Sun Also Rises* gets more attention."

Hadley stowed both the suitcase and the overnight bag under the seat. Then she frowned slightly, checked her wristwatch, and left the compartment, closing the door behind her.

"Interesting," the Hemingway said. "So she didn't leave it out in plain sight, begging to be stolen."

"Makes you wonder," John said. "This novel. Was it about World War One?"

"The trenches in Italy," the Hemingway said.

A young man stepped out of the shadows of the vestibule, looking in the direction Hadley took. Then he turned around and faced the two travelers from the future.

It was Ernest Hemingway. He smiled. "Close your mouth, John.

You'll catch flies." He opened the door to the compartment, picked up the overnight bag, and carried it into the next car.

John recovered enough to chase after him. He had disappeared.

The Hemingway followed. "What *is* this?" John said. "I thought you couldn't be in two timespaces at once."

"That wasn't me."

"It sure as hell wasn't the real Hemingway. He's in Lausanne with Lincoln Steffens."

"Maybe he is and maybe he isn't."

"He knew my *name!*"

"That he did." The Hemingway was getting fainter as John watched.

"Was he another one of you? Another STAB agent?"

"No. Not possible." It peered at John. "What's happening to you?" Its features went slack with a look of disbelief. "Oh, no. It was *you.*"

"What was me?"

"Just now." It gestured toward the other car. "The bag, the manuscripts. Of *course!*"

Hadley burst into the car and ran right through them, shouting in French for the conductor. She was carrying a bottle of Evian water.

"Well," John said, "that's what—"

The Hemingway was gone. John just had time to think *Marooned in 1922?* when the railroad car and the Gare de Lyon dissolved in an in-bursting cascade of black sparks, and it was no easier to handle the second time, spread impossibly thin across all those light-years and millennia, wondering whether it was going to last forever this time, realizing that it did anyhow, and coalescing with an impossibly painful *snap:*

Looking at the list in the typewriter. He reached for the Heineken; it was still cold. He set it back down. "God," he whispered. "I hope that's that."

The situation called for higher octane. He went to the freezer and took out the vodka. He sipped the gelid syrup straight from the bottle, and almost dropped it when out of the corner of his eye he saw the overnight bag.

He sat the open bottle on the counter and sleepwalked over to the dining room table. It was the same bag, slightly beat-up, monogrammed EHR, Elizabeth Hadley Richardson. He opened it and inside was a thick stack of manila envelopes.

He took the top one and carried it and the vodka bottle back to his chair. His hands were shaking. He opened the folder and stared at the familiar typing.

ERNEST M. HEMINGWAY


ONE - EYE  FOR  MINE

*Fever stood up . In the moon light he could ~~xx~~ see blood starting on his hands . His pants were torn at the knee and he knew it would be bleeding ~~there~~ too . He watched the lights of the caboose disappear in the trees where the track curved .

That lousy crut of a brakeman . He would get him ~~someday~~ some day .
                    scuffed
Fever ~~kicked~~ off the end of a tie and sat down to pick the cinders out of his hands and knee . He could use some water . The brakeman had his canteen .

He could smell a campfire . He wondered if it would be smart to go find it . He knew about the wolves ·, the human kind that lived along the rails and the disgusting things they liked He wasn 't afraid of them but you didn 't look for trouble .

You don 't have to look for trouble , his father would say . Trouble will find you . His father didn' t tell him about wolves , though , ~~or about women~~ .

There was a noise in the brush . Fever stood up and slipped his hand around the horn grip of the fat Buck clasp knife in his pocket .

The screen door creaked open and he looked up to see Pansy walk in with a strange expression on her face. Lena followed, looking even stranger. Her left eye was swollen shut and most of that side of her face was bruised blue and brown.

He stood up, shaking with the sudden collision of emotions. "What the hell—"

"Castle," Pansy said. "He got outta hand."

"Real talent for understatement." Lena's voice was tightly controlled but distorted.

"He went nuts. Slappin' Lena around. Then he started to rummage around in a closet, rave about a shotgun, and we split."

"I'll call the police."

"We've already been there," Lena said. "It's all over."

"Of course. We can't work with—"

"No, I mean he's a *criminal*. He's wanted in Mississippi for second-degree murder. They went to arrest him, hold him for extradition. So no more Hemingway hoax."

"What Hemingway hoax?" Pansy said.

"We'll tell you all about it," Lena said, and pointed at the bottle. "A little early, don't you think? You could at least get us a couple of glasses."

John went into the kitchen, almost floating with vodka buzz and anxious confusion. "What do you want with it?" Pansy said oh-jay and Lena said ice. Then Lena screamed.

He turned around and there was Castle standing in the door, grinning. He had a pistol in his right hand and a sawed-off shotgun in his left.

"You cunts," he said. "You fuckin' cunts. Go to the fuckin' cops."

There was a butcher knife in the drawer next to the refrigerator, but he didn't think Castle would stand idly by and let him rummage for it. Nothing else that might serve as a weapon, except the air pistol. Castle knew that it wouldn't do much damage.

He looked at John. "You three're gonna be my hostages. We're gettin' outta here, lose 'em up in the Everglades. They'll have a make on my pickup, though."

"We don't have a car," John said.

"I *know* that, asshole! There's a Hertz right down on One. You go rent one and don't try nothin' cute. I so much as *smell* a cop, I blow these two cunts away."

He turned back to the women and grinned crookedly, talking hard-guy through his teeth. "Like I did those two they sent, the spic and the nigger. They said somethin' about comin' back with a warrant to look for the shotgun and I was just bein' as nice as could be, I said hell, come on in, don't need no warrant. I got nothin' to hide, and when they come in I take the pistol from the nigger and kill the spic with it and shoot the nigger in the balls. You shoulda heard him. Some nigger. Took four more rounds to shut him up."

Wonder if that means the pistol is empty, John thought. He had Pansy's orange juice in his hand. It was an old-fashioned Smith & Wesson .357 Magnum six-shot, but from this angle he couldn't tell whether it had been reloaded. He could try to blind Castle with the orange juice.

He stepped toward him. "What kind of car do you want?"

"Just a *car*, damn it. Big enough." A siren whooped about a block away. Castle looked wary. "Bitch. You told 'em where you'd be."

"No," Lena pleaded. "We didn't tell them anything."

"Don't do anything stupid," John said.

Two more sirens, closer. "I'll show you *stupid!*" He raised the pistol toward Lena. John dashed the orange juice in his face.

It wasn't really like slow motion. It was just that John didn't miss any of it. Castle growled and swung around and in the cylinder's chambers John saw five copper-jacketed slugs. He reached for the gun and the first shot shattered his hand, blowing off two fingers, and struck the right side of his chest. The explosion was deafening and the shock of the bullet was like being hit simultaneously in the hand and chest with baseball bats. He rocked, still on his feet, and coughed blood-spatter on Castle's face. Castle fired again, and the second slug hit him on the other side of the chest, this time spinning him half around. Was somebody screaming? Hemingway said it felt like an icy snowball, and that was pretty close, except for the inside part, your body saying, well, time to close up shop. There was a terrible familiar radiating pain in the center of his chest, and John realized that he was having a totally superfluous heart attack. He pushed off from the dinette and staggered toward Castle again. He made a grab for the shotgun and Castle emptied both barrels into his abdomen. He dropped to his knees and then fell over on his side. He couldn't feel anything. Things started to go dim and red. Was this going to be the last time?

Castle cracked the shotgun and the two spent shells flew up in an arc over his shoulder. He took two more out of his shirt pocket and dropped one. When he bent over to pick it up, Pansy leaped past him. In a swift motion that was almost graceful—it came to John that he had probably practiced it over and over, acting out fantasies—he slipped both shells into their chambers and closed the gun with a flip of the wrist. The screen door was stuck. Pansy was straining at the knob with both hands. Castle put the muzzles up to the base of her skull and pulled one trigger. Most of her head covered the screen or went through the hole the blast made. The crown of her skull, a bloody bowl, bounced off two walls and went spinning into the kitchen. Her body did a spastic little dance and folded, streaming life.

Lena was suddenly on his back, clawing at his face. He spun and slammed her against the wall. She wilted like a rag doll and he hit her hard with the pistol on the way down. She unrolled at his feet, out cold, and with his mouth wide open laughing silently he lowered the shotgun and blasted her pointblank in the crotch. Her body jack-knifed and John tried with all his will not to die but blackness crowded in and the last thing he saw was that evil grin as Castle reloaded again, peering out the window, presumably at the police.

It wasn't the terrible sense of being spread infinitesimally thin over an infinity of pain and darkness; things had just gone black, like closing your eyes. If this is death, John thought, there's not much to it.

But it changed. There was a little bit of pale light, some vague figures, and then colors bled into the scene, and after a moment of disorientation he realized he was still in the apartment, but apparently floating up by the ceiling. Lena was conscious again, barely, twitching, staring at the river of blood that pumped from between her legs. Pansy looked unreal, headless but untouched from the neck down, lying in a relaxed, improbable posture like a knocked-over department store dummy, blood still spurting from a neck artery out through the screen door.

His own body was a mess, the abdomen completely excavated by buckshot. Inside the huge wound, behind the torn coils of intestine, the shreds of fat and gristle, the blood, the shit, he could see sharp splintered knuckles of backbone. Maybe it hadn't hurt so much because the spinal cord had been severed in the blast.

He had time to be a little shocked at himself for not feeling more. Of course most of the people he'd known who had died did die this way, in loud spatters of blood and brains. Even after thirty years of the occasional polite heart attack or stroke carrying off friend or acquaintance, most of the dead people he knew had died in the jungle.

He had been a hero there, in this universe. That would have surprised his sergeants in the original one. Congressional Medal of Honor, so-called, which hadn't hurt the sales of his first book. Knocked out the NVA machine-gun emplacement with their own satchel charge, then hauled the machine gun around and wiped out their mortar and command squads. He managed it all with bullet wounds in the face and triceps. Of course without the bullet wounds he wouldn't have lost his cool and charged the machine-gun emplacement, but that wasn't noted in the citation.

A pity there was no way to trade the medals in—melt them down into one big fat bullet and use it to waste that crazy motherfucker who was ignoring the three people he'd just killed, laughing like a hyena while he shouted obscenities at the police gathering down below.

Castle fires a shot through the lower window and then ducks and a spray of automatic-weapon fire shatters the upper window, filling the air with a spray of glass; bullets and glass fly painlessly through John where he's floating and he hears them spatter into the ceiling and suddenly everything is white with plaster dust—it starts to clear and he is much closer to his body, drawing down closer and closer; he merges with it and there's an instant of blackness and he's looking out through human eyes again.

A dull noise and he looked up to see hundreds of shards of glass leap up from the floor and fly to the window; plaster dust in billows sucked up into bullet holes in the ceiling, which then disappeared.

The top windowpane reformed as Castle *un*crouched, pointed the shotgun, then jerked forward as a blossom of yellow flame and white smoke rolled back into the barrel.

His hand was whole, the fingers restored. He looked down and saw rivulets of blood running back into the hole in his abdomen, then individual drops; then it closed and the clothing restored itself; then one of the holes in his chest closed up and then the other.

The clothing was unfamiliar. A tweed jacket in this weather? His hands had turned old, liver spots forming as he watched. Slow like a plant growing, slow like the moon turning, thinking slowly too, he reached up and felt the beard, and could see out of the corner of his eye that it was white and long. He was too fat, and a belt buckle bit painfully into his belly. He sucked in and pried out and looked at the buckle, yes, it was old brass and said GOTT MIT UNS, the buckle he'd taken from a dead German so long ago. The buckle Hemingway had taken.

John got to one knee. He watched fascinated as the stream of blood gushed back into Lena's womb, disappearing as Castle, grinning, jammed the barrels in between her legs, flinched, and did a complicated dance in reverse (while Pansy's decapitated body writhed around and jerked upright); Lena, sliding up off the floor, leaped up between the man's back and the wall, then fell off and ran backwards as he flipped the shotgun up to the back of Pansy's neck and seeming gallons of blood and tissue came flying from every direction to assemble themselves into the lovely head and face, distorted in terror as she jerked awkwardly at the door and then ran backwards, past Castle as he did a graceful pirouette, unloading the gun and placing one shell on the floor, which flipped up to his pocket as he stood and put the other one there.

John stood up and walked through some thick resistance toward Castle. Was it *time* resisting him? Everything else was still moving in reverse: two empty shotgun shells sailed across the room to snick into the weapon's chambers; Castle snapped it shut and wheeled to face John—

But John wasn't where he was supposed to be. As the shotgun swung around, John grabbed the barrels—hot!—and pulled the pistol out of Castle's waistband. He lost his grip on the shotgun barrels just as he jammed the pistol against Castle's heart and fired. A spray of blood from all over the other side of the room converged on Castle's back and John felt the recoil sting of the Magnum just as the shotgun muzzle cracked hard against his teeth, mouthful of searing heat then blackness forever, back in the featureless infinite timespace hell that the Hemingway had taken him to, forever, but in the next instant, a new kind of twitch, a twist . . .

## 23. The Time Exchanged

What does that mean, you "lost" him?

We were in the railroad car in the Gare de Lyon, in the normal observation mode. This entity that looked like Hemingway walked up, greeted us, took the manuscripts, and disappeared.

Just like that.

No. He went into the next car. John Baird ran after him. Maybe that was my mistake. I translated instead of running.

That's when you lost him.

Both of them. Baird disappeared, too. Then Hadley came running in—

Don't confuse me with Hadleys. You checked the adjacent universes.

All of them, yes. I think they're all right.

Think?

Well . . . I can't quite get to that moment. When I disappeared, it's as if I were still there for several more seconds, so I'm excluded.

And John Baird is still there?

Not by the time I can insert myself. Just Hadley running around—

No Hadleys. No Hadleys. So naturally you went back to 1996.

Of course. But there is a period of several minutes there from which I'm excluded as well. When I can finally insert myself, John Baird is dead.

Ah.

In every doomline, he and Castlemaine have killed each other. John is lying there with his head blown off, Castle next to him with his heart torn out from a pointblank pistol shot, with two very distraught women screaming while police pile in through the door. And this.

The overnight bag with the stories.

I don't think anybody noticed it. With Baird dead, I could spot-check the women's futures; neither of them mentions the bag. So perhaps the mission is accomplished.

Well, Reality is still here. So far. But the connection between Baird and this Hemingway entity is disturbing. That Baird is able to return to 1996 without your help is *very* disturbing. He has obviously taken on some of your characteristics, your abilities, which is why you're excluded from the last several minutes of his life.

I've never heard of that happening before.

It never has. I think that John Baird is no more human than you and I.

Is?

I suspect he's still around somewhen.

## 24. Islands in the Stream

and the unending lightless desert of pain becomes suddenly one small bright spark and then everything is dark red and a taste, a bitter taste, Hoppe's No. 9 gun oil and the twin barrels of the fine Boss pigeon gun cold and oily on his tongue and biting hard against the roof of his mouth; the dark red is light on the other side of his eyelids, sting of pain before he bumps a tooth and opens his eyes and mouth and lowers the gun and with shaking hands unloads—no, *dis*loads—both barrels and walks backwards, shuffling in the slippers, slumping, stopping to stare out into the Idaho morning dark, helpless tears coursing up from the snarled white beard, walking backwards down the stairs with the shotgun heavily cradled in his elbow, backing into the storeroom and replacing it in the rack, then back up the stairs and slowly put the keys there in plain sight on the kitchen windowsill, a bit of mercy from Miss Mary, then sit and stare at the cold bad coffee as it warms back to one acid sip—

A tiny part of the mind saying *wait! I am John Baird it is 1996*

and back to a spiritless shower, numb to the needle spray, and cramped constipation and a sleep of no ease; an evening with Mary and George Brown tiptoeing around the blackest of black-ass worse and worse each day, only one thing to look forward to

*got to throw out an anchor*

faster now, walking through the Ketchum woods like a jerky cartoon in reverse, fucking FBI and IRS behind every tree, because you sent Ezra that money, felt sorry for him because he was crazy, what a fucking joke, should have finished the *Cantos* and shot himself.

*effect preceding cause but I can read or hear scraps of thought somehow*

speeding to a blur now, driving in reverse hundreds of miles per hour back from Ketchum to Minnesota, the Mayo Clinic, holding the madness in while you talk to the shrink, promise not to hurt myself have to go home and write if I'm going to beat this, figuring what he wants to hear, then the rubber mouthpiece and smell of your own hair and flesh slightly burnt by the electrodes then deep total blackness

*sharp stabs of thought sometimes stretching*

hospital days blur by in reverse, cold chrome and starch white, a couple of mouthfuls of claret a day to wash down the pills that seem to make it worse and worse

*what will happen to me when he's born?*

When they came back from Spain was when he agreed to the Mayo Clinic, still all beat-up from the plane crashes six years before in Africa, liver and spleen shot to hell, brain too, nerves, can't write or can't stop: all day on one damned sentence for the Kennedy book but a hundred thousand fast words, pure shit, for the bullfight article. Paris book okay but stuck. Great to find the trunks in the Ritz but none of the stuff Hadley lost.

*Here it stops.* A frozen tableau:

Afternoon light slanting in through the tall cloudy windows of the Cambon bar, where he had liberated, would liberate, the hotel in August 1944. A good large American-style martini gulped too fast in the excitement. The two small trunks unpacked and laid out item by item. Hundreds of pages of notes that would become the Paris book. But nothing before '23, of course. *the manuscripts* The novel and the stories and the poems still gone. One moment nailed down with the juniper sting of the martini and then time crawling rolling flying backwards again—

*no control?*

Months blurring by, Madrid Riviera Venice feeling sick and busted up, the plane wrecks like a quick one-two punch brain and body, blurry sick even before them at the Finca Vigia, can't get a fucking thing done after the Nobel Prize, journalists day and night, the prize bad luck and bullshit anyhow but need the $35,000

damn, had to shoot Willie, cat since the boat-time before the war, but winged a burglar too, same gun, just after the Pulitzer, now that was all right

*slowing down again—Havana—the Floridita—*

Even Mary having a good time, and the Basque jai alai players too, though they don't know much English, most of them, interesting couple of civilians, the doctor and the Kraut lookalike, but there's something about the boy that makes it hard to take my eyes off him, looks like someone I guess, another round of Papa Dobles, that boy, what is it about him? and then the first round, with lunch, and things speeding up to a blur again

out on the Gulf a lot, enjoying the triumph of *The Old Man and the Sea*, the easy good-paying work of providing fishing footage for the movie, and then back into 1951, the worst year of his life that far, weeks of grudging conciliation, uncontrollable anger, and black-ass depression from the poisonous critical slime that followed *Across the River*, bastards gunning for him, Harold Ross dead, mother Grace dead, son Gregory a dope addict hip-deep into the dianetics horseshit, Charlie Scribner dead but first declaring undying love for that asshole Jones

most of the forties an anxious blur, Cuba Italy Cuba France Cuba China, found Mary kicked Martha out, thousand pages on the fucking *Eden* book wouldn't come together Bronze Star better than Pulitzer

Martha a chromeplated bitch in Europe but war is swell otherwise, liberating the Ritz, grenades rifles pistols and bomb runs with the RAF, China boring compared to it and the Q-ship runs off Cuba, hell, maybe the bitch was right for once, just kid stuff and booze

marrying the bitch was the end of my belle epoch, easy to see from here, the thirties all sunshine Key West Spain Key West Africa Key West, good hard writing with Pauline holding down the store, good woman but sorry I had to

sorry I had to divorce

*stopping*

Walking Paris streets after midnight:

I was never going to throw back at her losing the manuscripts. Told Steffens that would be like blaming a human for the weather, or death. These things happen. Nor say anything about what I did the night after I found out she really had lost them. But this one time we got to shouting and I think I hurt her. Why the hell did she have to bring the carbons what the hell did she think carbons were for stupid stupid stupid and she crying and she giving me hell about Pauline Jesus any woman who could fuck up Paris for you could fuck up a royal flush

*it slows down around the manuscripts or me—*

golden years the mid-twenties everything clicks Paris Vorarlburg Paris Schruns Paris Pamplona Paris Madrid Paris Lausanne

couldn't believe she actually

most of a novel dozens of poems stories sketches—*contes*, Kitty called them by God woman you show me your *conte* and I'll show you mine so drunk that night I know better than to drink that much absinthe so drunk I was half crawling going up the stairs to the apartment I saw weird I saw God I saw *I saw myself standing there on the fourth landing with Hadley's goddamn bag*

I waited almost an hour, that seemed like no time or all time, and when he, when I, when he came crashing up the stairs he blinked twice, then I walked through me groping, shook my head without looking back and managed to get the door unlocked

*flying back through the dead winter French countryside, standing in the bar car fighting hopelessness to Hadley crying so hard she can't get out what was wrong with Steffens standing gaping like a fish in a bowl*

twisting again, painlessly inside out, I suppose through various dimensions, seeing the man's life as one complex chord of beauty and purpose and ugliness and chaos, my life on one side of the Möbius strip, consistent through its fading forty-year span, starting, *starting*, here:

the handsome young man sits on the floor of the apartment holding himself, rocking racked with sobs, one short manuscript crumpled in front of him, the room a mess with drawers pulled out, their contents scattered on the floor, it's like losing an arm a leg (a foot a testicle), it's like losing your youth and along with youth

with a roar he stands up, eyes closed fists clenched, wipes his face dry and stomps over to the window

breathes deeply until he's breathing normally

strides across the room, kicking a brassiere out of his way

stands with his hand on the knob and thinks this:

*life can break you but you can grow back strong at the broken places*

and goes out slamming the door behind him, somewhat conscious of having been present at his own birth.

With no effort I find myself standing earlier that day in the vestibule of a train. Hadley is walking away, tired, looking for a vendor. I turn and confront two aspects of myself.

"Close your mouth, John. You'll catch flies."

They both stand paralyzed while I slide open the door and pull the overnight bag from under the seat. I walk away and the universe begins to tingle and sparkle.

I spend forever in the black void between timespaces. I am growing to enjoy it.

I appear in John Baird's apartment and set down the bag. I look at the empty chair in front of the old typewriter, the green beer bottle sweating cold next to it, and John Baird appears, looking dazed, and I have business elsewhere, elsewhen. A train to catch. I'll come back for the bag in twelve minutes or a few millennia, after the bloodbath that gives birth to us all.

### 25. A Moveable Feast

He wrote the last line and set down the pencil and read over the last page sitting on his hands for warmth. He could see his breath. Celebrate the end with a little heat.

He unwrapped the bundle of twigs and banked them around the pile of coals in the brazier. Crazy way to heat a room but it's France. He cupped both hands behind the stack and blew gently. The coals glowed red and then orange and with the third breath the twigs smoldered and a small yellow flame popped up. He held his hands over the fire, rubbing the stiffness out of his fingers, enjoying the smell of the birch as it cracked and spit.

He put a fresh sheet and carbon into the typewriter and looked at his penciled notes. Final draft? Worth a try:

```
Ernest M. Hemingway,
74 rue du Cardinal Lemoine,
Paris, France


        ++  U P   I N   M I C H I G A N  ++


        Jim Gilmore came to Horton's Bay from Canada.

    He bought the blacksmith shop from old man Hortom
```

Shit, a typo. He flinched suddenly, as if struck, and shook his head to clear it. What a strange sensation to come out of nowhere. A sudden cold stab of grief. But larger somehow than grief for a person.

Grief for everybody, maybe. For being human.

From a typo?

He went to the window and opened it in spite of the cold. He filled his lungs with the cold damp air and looked around the familiar orange and gray mosaic of chimney pots and tiled roofs under the dirty winter Paris sky.

He shuddered and eased the window back down and returned to the heat of the brazier. He had felt it before, exactly that huge and terrible feeling. But where?

For the life of him he couldn't remember.

# Appendixes
· · ·
## *About the Nebula Awards*

Throughout the year, the members of the Science Fiction Writers of America read and recommend novels and stories for the annual Nebula Awards. The editor of the *Nebula Awards Report* collects the recommendations and publishes them in a newsletter. Near the end of the year, the editor tallies the endorsements, draws up a preliminary ballot, and sends it to all active members. The five most popular novels, novellas, novelettes, and short stories are listed on the final ballot, which subsequently goes out to SWFA's eligible voters.

For purposes of the Nebula Award, a novel is 40,000 words or more; a novella is 17,500 to 39,999 words; a novelette is 7,500 to 17,499 words; and a short story is 7,499 words or fewer.

Founded in 1965 by Damon Knight, the Science Fiction Writers of America began with a charter membership of seventy-eight writers. Today it boasts nearly a thousand members. Early in his tenure, Lloyd Biggle, Jr., SFWA's first secretary-treasurer, proposed that the organization periodically select and publish the year's best stories. This notion quickly evolved into the elaborate balloting process, an annual awards banquet, and a series of Nebula anthologies.

Judith Ann Lawrence designed the trophy from a sketch by Kate Wilhelm. It is a block of Lucite containing a rock crystal and a spiral nebula made of metallic glitter. The prize is handmade, and no two are exactly alike.

The Grand Master Nebula Award goes to a living author for a lifetime of achievement. The membership bestows it no more than six times in a decade. In accordance with SFWA's bylaws, the president nominates a candidate, normally after consulting with past presidents and the board of directors. This nomination then goes before the officers. If a majority approves, that candidate becomes a Grand Master. Past recipients include Robert A. Heinlein (1974), Jack Williamson (1975), Clifford D. Simak (1976), L. Sprague de Camp (1978), Fritz Leiber (1981), Andre Norton (1983), Arthur C. Clarke (1985), Isaac Asimov (1986), Alfred Bester (1987), and Ray Bradbury (1988). As of this writing, all but Heinlein, Simak, and Bester are still alive.

The twenty-sixth annual Nebula Awards banquet was held at the Roosevelt Hotel in New York City on April 27, 1991. Beyond the awards for novel, novella, novelette, and short story, a Grand Master Nebula went to Lester del Rey, the eleventh SF professional to be so honored.

# Selected Titles from the 1990 Preliminary Nebula Ballot

The following four lists serve a dual purpose. They enable interested readers to track down the particular pieces of fiction discussed by Kathryn Cramer in her opening essay, " 'Democrazy,' the Marketplace, and the American Way," and they provide an overview of those works, authors, ideas, and periodicals that attracted SFWA's notice during 1990. Finalists are excluded from this catalog, as these are documented in the introduction.

## Novels

*Queen of Angels* by Greg Bear (Warner Books)
*Voyage to the Red Planet* by Terry Bisson (William Morrow)
*Earth* by David Brin (Bantam)
*The Vor Game* by Lois McMaster Bujold (Baen)
*Silent Dances* by A. C. Crispin and Kathleen O'Malley (Ace)
*Carmen Dog* by Carol Emshwiller (Mercury House)
*Brain Rose* by Nancy Kress (William Morrow)
*The Quiet Pools* by Michael P. Kube-McDowell (Ace)
*Thomas the Rhymer* by Ellen Kushner (William Morrow)
*Arachne* by Lisa Mason (William Morrow)
*Dragondoom* by Dennis McKiernan (Bantam)
*Fire on the Border* by Kevin O'Donnell Jr. (Penguin)
*Vineland* by Thomas Pynchon (Little, Brown)
*Paradise* by Mike Resnick (Tor)
*Venus of Shadows* by Pamela Sargent (Doubleday Foundation)
*Golden Fleece* by Robert Sawyer (Warner)

## Novellas

"The King" by Donald Barthelme (Harper and Row)

"The Rose and the Scalpel" by Gregory Benford (*Amazing Stories*, January 1990)

"The First Since Ancient Persia" by John Brunner (*Amazing Stories*, July 1990)

"Lord of Fishes" by Bernard Deitchman (*Analog*, August 1990)

"Stout Hearts" by J. R. Dunn (*Amazing Stories*, March 1990)

"Mammy Morgan Played the Organ, Her Daddy Beat the Drum" by Michael F. Flynn (*Analog*, November 1990)

"Funnel Hawk" by Tom Ligon (*Analog*, August 1990)

"The Ragged Rock" by Judith Moffett (*Isaac Asimov's Science Fiction Magazine*, October 1990)

"Bwana" by Mile Resnick (*Isaac Asimov's Science Fiction Magazine*, January 1990)

"A Short, Sharp Shock" by Kim Stanley Robinson (*Isaac Asimov's Science Fiction Magazine*, November 1990)

"Skull City" by Lucius Shepard (*Isaac Asimov's Science Fiction Magazine*, July 1990)

"Naught for Hire" by John Stith (*Analog*, July 1990)

"Backlash" by W. R. Thompson (*Analog*, March 1990)

"Elegy for Angels and Dogs" by Walter Jon Williams (*Isaac Asimov's Science Fiction Magazine*, May 1990)

"Solip System" by Walter Jon Williams (*Isaac Asimov's Science Fiction Magazine*, September 1990)

## Novelettes

"Hyena Eyes" by Ray Aldridge (*Fantasy and Science Fiction*, June 1990)

"Bestseller" by Michael Blumlein (*Fantasy and Science Fiction*, February 1990)

"After Magic" by Bruce Boston (EOTU Group Press)

"Sea Change" by Alan Brennert (*Fantasy and Science Fiction*, February 1990)

"Dr. Pak's Preschool" by David Brin (*Fantasy and Science Fiction*, July 1990)

"The Icarus Epidemic" by Jayge Carr (*Analog*, April 1990)

"Gerda and the Wizard" by Rob Chilson (*Isaac Asimov's Science Fiction Magazine*, March 1990)

"Every Trembling Blossom, Every Singing Bird" by Ronald Anthony Cross (*Fantasy and Science Fiction*, March 1990)

"Limekiller at Large" by Avram Davidson (*Isaac Asimov's Science Fiction Magazine*, June 1990)

"The Caress" by Greg Egan (*Isaac Asimov's Science Fiction Magazine*, January 1990)

"Cyberella" by Sheila Finch (*Fantasy and Science Fiction*, July 1990)

"Giant, Giant Steps" by Robert Frazier (*Amazing Stories*, May 1990)

"Angel Alone" by Carolyn Ives Gilman (*Fantasy and Science Fiction*, April 1990)

"Personal Silence" by Molly Gloss (*Isaac Asimov's Science Fiction Magazine*, January 1990)

"Simulation Six" by Stephen Gould (*Isaac Asimov's Science Fiction Magazine*, March 1990)

"Passages" by Joe Haldeman (*Analog*, March 1990)

"Buddha Nostril Bird" by John Kessel (*Isaac Asimov's Science Fiction Magazine*, March 1990)

"Invaders" by John Kessel (*Fantasy and Science Fiction*, October 1990)

"Travellers" by Damian Kilby (*Isaac Asimov's Science Fiction Magazine*, February 1990)

"Inertia" by Nancy Kress (*Analog*, January 1990)

"The Last Feast of Harlequin" by Thomas Ligotti (*Fantasy and Science Fiction*, April 1990)

"Timekeeper" by John Morressy (*Fantasy and Science Fiction*, January 1990)

"Mrs. Byers and the Dragon" by Keith Roberts (*Isaac Asimov's Science Fiction Magazine*, August 1990)

"A Braver Thing" by Charles Sheffield (*Isaac Asimov's Science Fiction Magazine*, February 1990)

"The Shores of Bohemia" by Bruce Sterling (*Universe 1*, Doubleday Foundation)

"UFO" by Michael Swanwick (*Aboriginal Science Fiction*, September–October 1990)

"Gaudi's Dragon" by Ian Watson (*Isaac Asimov's Science Fiction Magazine*, October 1990)

"In the Upper Cretaceous with the Summerfire Brigade" by Ian Watson (*Fantasy and Science Fiction*, August 1990)

"Eternity, Baby" by Andrew Weiner (*Isaac Asimov's Science Fiction Magazine*, November 1990)

"The King of the Neanderthals" by Wayne Wightman (*Fantasy and Science Fiction*, November 1990)

"Memories that Dance like Dust in Summer Heat" by N. Lee Wood (*Amazing Stories*, January 1990)

### Short Stories

"The Cold Cage" by Ray Aldridge (*Fantasy and Science Fiction*, February 1990)

"We Were Butterflies" by Ray Aldridge (*Fantasy and Science Fiction*, August 1990)

"Side Effect" by Roger MacBride Allen (*Analog*, March 1990)

"For No Reason" by Patricia Anthony (*Isaac Asimov's Science Fiction Magazine*, September 1990)

"My Advice to the Civilized" by John Barnes (*Isaac Asimov's Science Fiction Magazine*, April 1990)

"Dry Niger" by M. Shayne Bell (*Isaac Asimov's Science Fiction Magazine*, August 1990)

"Snapshots from the Butterfly Plague" by Michael Bishop (*Omni*, December 1990)

"Over Flat Mountain" by Terry Bisson (*Omni*, June 1990)

"The Secret of Life" by David Brin (*Amazing Stories*, July 1990)

"Where Are You Now, Guy de Maupassant, Now That We Need You?" by F. M. Busby (*Isaac Asimov's Science Fiction Magazine*, May 1990)

"The Sadness of Detail" by Jonathan Carroll (*Omni*, February 1990)

"Curious Elation" by Michael Cassutt (*Fantasy and Science Fiction*, September 1990)

"Wolfrunner" by Mary E. Choo (*Sword and Sorceress VI*)

"Missolonghi 1824" by John Crowley (*Isaac Asimov's Science Fiction Magazine*, March 1990)

"Captain Coyote's Last Hunt" by Brad Denton (*Isaac Asimov's Science Fiction Magazine*, March 1990)

"What the EPA Don't Know Won't Hurt Them" by Suzette Elgin (*Fantasy and Science Fiction*, March 1990)

"Shore Leave Blacks" by Nancy Etchemendy (*Fantasy and Science Fiction*, March 1990)

"One Night in Television City" by Paul di Fillipo (*Universe 1*, Doubleday Foundation)

"Sweet, Savage Sorcerer" by Esther Friesner (*Amazing Stories*, January 1990)

"The Blue Love Potion" by Lisa Goldstein (*Isaac Asimov's Science Fiction Magazine*, June 1990)

"Midnight News" by Lisa Goldstein (*Isaac Asimov's Science Fiction Magazine*, March 1990)

"Reflected Light" by Nina Kiriki Hoffman (*Amazing Stories*, July 1990)

"The First Time" by K. W. Jeter (*Alien Sex*, Dutton)

"Touchdown" by Nancy Kress (*Isaac Asimov's Science Fiction Magazine*, October 1990)

"Projects" by Geoffrey Landis (*Isaac Asimov's Science Fiction Magazine*, June 1990)

"A Tale of the Brahmin's Wife" by Geoffrey Landis (*Analog*, April 1990)

"Another Goddamned Showboat" by Barry Malzberg (*What Might Have Been, Volume 2*, Bantam Spectra)

"Playback" by Barry Malzberg (*Universe 1*, Doubleday Foundation)

"Angels" by Bruce McAllister (*Isaac Asimov's Science Fiction Magazine*, May 1990)

"I, Said the Cow" by Judith Moffett (*Fantasy and Science Fiction*, January 1990)

"The Utility Man" by Robert Reed (*Isaac Asimov's Science Fiction Magazine*, November 1990)

"Ride 'Em, Cyboy" by Jennifer Roberson (*Aboriginal Science Fiction*, March–April 1990)

"Mules" by Madeleine E. Robins (*Fantasy and Science Fiction*, April 1990)

"Zurich" by Kim Stanley Robinson (*Fantasy and Science Fiction*, March 1990)

"White City" by Lew Shiner (*Isaac Asimov's Science Fiction Magazine*, June 1990)

"Three Boston Artists" by Sarah Smith (*Aboriginal Science Fiction*, July–August 1990)

"The Final Gift" by Michael Stackpole (*Amazing Stories*, March 1990)

"The Sword of Damocles" by Bruce Sterling (*Isaac Asimov's Science Fiction Magazine*, February 1990)

"Voice in the Desert" by Judith Tarr (*Amazing Stories*, March 1990)

"VRM-547" by W. R. Thompson (*Analog*, February 1990)

"Designated Hitter" by Harry Turtledove (*Fantasy and Science Fiction*, June 1990)

"Jewelly Erased" by Mary Turzillo (*Space and Time 77*)

"Unnatural Strangers" by Wayne Wightman (*Fantasy and Science Fiction*, April 1990)

"War Bride" by Rick Wilber (*Alien Sex*, Dutton)

"Cibola" by Connie Willis (*Isaac Asimov's Science Fiction Magazine*, December 1990)

"Lenin in Odessa" by George Zebrowski (*Amazing Stories*, March 1990)

## *Past Nebula Award Winners*

### 1965

Best Novel: *Dune* by Frank Herbert
Best Novella: "The Saliva Tree" by Brian W. Aldiss
"He Who Shapes" by Roger Zelazny (tie)
Best Novelette: "The Doors of His Face, the Lamps of His Mouth" by Roger Zelazny
Best Short Story: " 'Repent, Harlequin!' Said the Ticktockman" by Harlan Ellison

### 1966

Best Novel: *Flowers for Algernon* by Daniel Keyes
*Babel-17* by Samuel R. Delany (tie)
Best Novella: "The Last Castle" by Jack Vance

Best Novelette: "Call Him Lord" by Gordon R. Dickson
Best Short Story: "The Secret Place" by Richard McKenna

## 1967

Best Novel: *The Einstein Intersection* by Samuel R. Delany
Best Novella: "Behold the Man" by Michael Moorcock
Best Novelette: "Gonna Roll the Bones" by Fritz Leiber
Best Short Story: "Aye, and Gomorrah" by Samuel R. Delany

## 1968

Best Novel: *Rite of Passage* by Alexei Panshin
Best Novella: "Dragonrider" by Anne McCaffrey
Best Novelette: "Mother to the World" by Richard Wilson
Best Short Story: "The Planners" by Kate Wilhelm

## 1969

Best Novel: *The Left Hand of Darkness* by Ursula K. Le Guin
Best Novella: "A Boy and His Dog" by Harlan Ellison
Best Novelette: "Time Considered as a Helix of Semi-Precious Stones" by Samuel R. Delany
Best Short Story: "Passengers" by Robert Silverberg

## 1970

Best Novel: *Ringworld* by Larry Niven
Best Novella: "Ill Met in Lankhmar" by Fritz Leiber
Best Novelette: "Slow Sculpture" by Theodore Sturgeon
Best Short Story: No award

## 1971

Best Novel: *A Time of Changes* by Robert Silverberg
Best Novella: "The Missing Man" by Katherine MacLean
Best Novelette: "The Queen of Air and Darkness" by Poul Anderson
Best Short Story: "Good News from the Vatican" by Robert Silverberg

## 1972

Best Novel: *The Gods Themselves* by Isaac Asimov
Best Novella: "A Meeting with Medusa" by Arthur C. Clarke
Best Novelette: "Goat Song" by Poul Anderson
Best Short Story: "When It Changed" by Joanna Russ

## 1973

Best Novel: *Rendezvous with Rama* by Arthur C. Clarke
Best Novella: "The Death of Doctor Island" by Gene Wolfe
Best Novelette: "Of Mist, and Grass, and Sand" by Vonda N. McIntyre
Best Short Story: "Love Is the Plan, the Plan Is Death" by James
    Tiptree, Jr.
Best Dramatic Presentation: *Soylent Green*

## 1974

Best Novel: *The Dispossessed* by Ursula K. Le Guin
Best Novella: "Born with the Dead" by Robert Silverberg
Best Novelette: "If the Stars Are Gods" by Gordon Eklund and Greg-
    ory Benford
Best Short Story: "The Day Before the Revolution" by Ursula K.
    Le Guin
Best Dramatic Presentation: *Sleeper*
Grand Master: Robert A. Heinlein

## 1975

Best Novel: *The Forever War* by Joe Haldeman
Best Novella: "Home Is the Hangman" by Roger Zelazny
Best Novelette: "San Diego Lightfoot Sue" by Tom Reamy
Best Short Story: "Catch That Zeppelin!" by Fritz Leiber
Best Dramatic Presentation: *Young Frankenstein*
Grand Master: Jack Williamson

## 1976

Best Novel: *Man Plus* by Frederik Pohl
Best Novella: "Houston, Houston, Do You Read?" by James Tip-
    tree, Jr.
Best Novelette: "The Bicentennial Man" by Isaac Asimov
Best Short Story: "A Crowd of Shadows" by Charles L. Grant
Grand Master: Clifford D. Simak

## 1977

Best Novel: *Gateway* by Frederik Pohl
Best Novella: "Stardance" by Spider and Jeanne Robinson
Best Novelette: "The Screwfly Solution" by Raccoona Sheldon

Best Short Story: "Jeffty Is Five" by Harlan Ellison
Special Award: *Star Wars*

**1978**

Best Novel: *Dreamsnake* by Vonda N. McIntyre
Best Novella: "The Persistence of Vision" by John Varley
Best Novelette: "A Glow of Candles, A Unicorn's Eye" by Charles L. Grant
Best Short Story: "Stone" by Edward Bryant
Grand Master: L. Sprague de Camp

**1979**

Best Novel: *The Fountains of Paradise* by Arthur C. Clarke
Best Novella: "Enemy Mine" by Barry Longyear
Best Novelette: "Sandkings" by George R. R. Martin
Best Short Story: "giANTS" by Edward Bryant

**1980**

Best Novel: *Timescape* by Gregory Benford
Best Novella: "The Unicorn Tapestry" by Suzy McKee Charnas
Best Novelette: "The Ugly Chickens" by Howard Waldrop
Best Short Story: "Grotto of the Dancing Deer" by Clifford D. Simak

**1981**

Best Novel: *The Claw of the Conciliator* by Gene Wolfe
Best Novella: "The Saturn Game" by Poul Anderson
Best Novelette: "The Quickening" by Michael Bishop
Best Short Story: "The Bone Flute" by Lisa Tuttle°
Grand Master: Fritz Leiber

**1982**

Best Novel: *No Enemy But Time* by Michael Bishop
Best Novella: "Another Orphan" by John Kessel
Best Novelette: "Fire Watch" by Connie Willis
Best Short Story: "A Letter from the Clearys" by Connie Willis

° This Nebula Award was declined by the author.

## 1983

Best Novel: *Startide Rising* by David Brin
Best Novella: "Hardfought" by Greg Bear
Best Novelette: "Blood Music" by Greg Bear
Best Short Story: "The Peacemaker" by Gardner Dozois
Grand Master: Andre Norton

## 1984

Best Novel: *Neuromancer* by William Gibson
Best Novella: "PRESS ENTER ■" by John Varley
Best Novelette: "Bloodchild" by Octavia E. Butler
Best Short Story: "Morning Child" by Gardner Dozois

## 1985

Best Novel: *Ender's Game* by Orson Scott Card
Best Novella: "Sailing to Byzantium" by Robert Silverberg
Best Novelette: "Portraits of His Children" by George R. R. Martin
Best Short Story: "Out of All Them Bright Stars" by Nancy Kress
Grand Master: Arthur C. Clarke

## 1986

Best Novel: *Speaker for the Dead* by Orson Scott Card
Best Novella: "R & R" by Lucius Shepard
Best Novelette: "The Girl Who Fell Into the Sky" by Kate Wilhelm
Best Short Story: "Tangents" by Greg Bear
Grand Master: Isaac Asimov

## 1987

Best Novel: *The Falling Woman* by Pat Murphy
Best Novella: "The Blind Geometer" by Kim Stanley Robinson
Best Novelette: "Rachel in Love" by Pat Murphy
Best Short Story: "Forever Yours, Anna" by Kate Wilhelm
Grand Master: Alfred Bester

## 1988

Best Novel: *Falling Free* by Lois McMaster Bujold
Best Novella: "The Last of the Winnebagos" by Connie Willis

Best Novelette: "Schrödinger's Kitten" by George Alec Effinger
Best Short Story: "Bible Stories for Adults, No. 17: The Deluge" by
    James Morrow
Grand Master: Ray Bradbury

**1989**

Best Novel: *The Healer's War* by Elizabeth Ann Scarborough
Best Novella: "The Mountains of Mourning" by Lois McMaster
    Bujold
Best Novelette: "At the Rialto" by Connie Willis
Best Short Story: "Ripples in the Dirac Sea" by Geoffrey Landis

Those who are interested in category-related awards should also
consult *A History of the Hugo, Nebula, and International Fantasy
Awards* by Donald Franson and Howard DeVore, Misfit Press, 1987.
Periodically updated, the book is available from Howard DeVore,
4705 Weddel, Dearborn, Michigan 48125. According to George Zebrowski, "The book's special value is in its listings of recommended
works for the preliminary Nebula ballot and the number of votes
received."

# Permissions Acknowledgments